NOWHERE MAN

Niles picked up the paper and admired it as if it were an Old Master. " 'Nowhere Man'. Beautiful. In a day or two, at most, everyone in town'll be calling him that—even the police. What *are* the police calling him, your pals at Homicide? And how's your movie coming?"

"I haven't shot a foot of film. They're interested in the idea of a movie, but they're reluctant to have cameras following them around. Any anyway, they're consumed by Dimanche."

Niles lifted an eight-by-ten glossy of Dimanche off his desk and held it out as he had held the paper. "Interesting, don't you think? Two people murdered in the same city on the same day—one so anonymous, so solitary, he doesn't seem to be missing from anyone's life; the other so famous, so celebrated, that to hear people talk you'd think everyone in world had been her closest friend."

Also featuring Detective Jake Neuman
SWEET JUSTICE

NOWHERE MAN

Jerry Oster

Mysterious Press books (UK) are published
in association with Arrow Books Limited
62-65 Chandos Place, London WC2N 4NW

An imprint of Century Hutchinson Limited

London Melbourne Sydney Auckland
Johannesburg and agencies throughout
the world

First published in Great Britain 1988
by Mysterious Press

Printed and bound in Great Britain by
Anchor Brendon Limited, Tiptree, Essex

ISBN 0 09 959410 2

For Diane Cleaver

NOWHERE MAN

1
_____

Swaddled in an unseasonable great gray coat, the shape could have been man or woman.

He or she—or it—came from between two of the delivery vans parked in a row along the west side of Crosby between Prince and Houston—vans that by day ferried the wares of chic gourmet foodshops and boutiques and art galleries.

The runner faltered, unaccustomed to seeing anyone on his early-morning run. Anyone, that is, who approached him, hand outstretched, as did the shape.

This morning, the runner had gone out even earlier than usual—by accident. It was a while before he realized how much earlier. He'd noticed, while running past Washington Square Park, that there were no other runners out, which was odd because at this time of year serious runners were upping their distance in anticipation of next month's marathon, running twice a day, some of them, at all hours in all weathers. Odd, too, that there were so many people in the park. Yes, it was Indian summer, and the park was still frequented round the clock; but what was odd was that the hangers-out were awake, were running on the energy of the night before, not run down and hung over in the grip of the morning after. One of them, a black teenager, ran beside him for a few strides along Washington Square West, turning down his blaster to make conversation. "Hey, bro. Got a match?" He stopped and laughed at his own joke and turned the Commodores back up loud: "Night Shift."

On MacDougal Street, between Third and Bleecker, he noticed that the steel shutters were drawn on the falafel stand that was always just opening up as he ran by a little after six. (Morning after morning he wondered why: Who ate that kind of food at that hour? Or was it a front for something?) Across Houston, just north of Prince, he saw from the clock in the window of the storefront day-care center that it was just after four.

He'd waked himself, he concluded, though he'd imagined the alarm had gone off and grappled with the clock as if turning it off; without looking at the clock, he'd gotten out of bed and gone into the bathroom and dressed in his running clothes, hung from the shower rod to dry from yesterday's run. So as not to wake her, he hadn't gone into the kitchen to put water on a low flame to be ready for coffee when he got back, hadn't put on the radio to hear the temperature. He would put water on while he showered when he got back; he could tell from a hand out the bathroom window that he didn't need a sweatshirt or sweat pants, though he had the week before, when autumn sent a scouting party. It must have been quarter to four when he'd awakened: No wonder she hadn't stirred; no wonder the doorman had slept on his stool.

MacDougal ended at Prince and he turned east to Sullivan and ran south on it until it ended at Broome, then down Sixth Avenue to Grand, then east again, across Thompson, West Broadway, Wooster, Greene, Mercer, Broadway. He turned north on Crosby and ran past Spring, past Prince.

She might not wake when he got back. He might shower and shave and dress and be gone without rousing her. That might be better: He could call her later and say that he was sorry, and having missed him and wondered about him and perhaps even worried about him, she would have forgotten how angry she was. She hadn't, after all, been so angry that she'd walked out, gone home, saying it wasn't going to work and she was going to stop trying because he just wouldn't try, not hard enough.

*   *   *

2

The runner faltered, for he was accustomed to seeing only a few other runners (all of whom circumnavigated Washington Square Park, a route he found tedious, hence his foray into SoHo); the bodies draped on the benches in the park, run down and hung over in the grip of the morning after; the counterman in the falafel stand; sometimes a middle-aged man—a different one each time—walking a dog—a different dog—on MacDougal or Sullivan; the counterman at a deli that opened early at the corner of Sixth and Broome (though not so early that it had been open this morning); the attendants at the all-night garage; some feral men who slept on a brightly lighted loading dock on Crosby just north of Houston; an NYU guard, maybe, stepping outside the security office on Washington Place for some air; the runners-around-the-park again, for he swung back for a quarter lap around the park before ending his run under the arch at Fifth Avenue; and, of course, his doorman, Teddy—and, on weekends, Pat. No one, that is, who approached him, hand outstretched, as did the shape.

He faltered and had three thoughts:

The first, that he or she—or it—was offering him something: a talisman or a treasure to be cached away. A romantic, ridiculous notion.

The second, which stepped on the heels of the first, that he was being challenged, that the shape was the street's guardian, its . . . What was the name? Cerberus? No, Cerberus was a dog, a three-headed dog. Charon—that was it; Charon the ferryman. More apt because more sinister, but no less silly. For one thing, did Charon ever turn anyone back from Hell?

The third, which ought to have been his first (this was New York City, after all, the Capital of the World, home to thousands—often, it seemed, millions—of homeless), that he was having the touch put on him for a handout. That made sense, although it made no sense at all that a panhandler would think someone dressed in a singlet, shorts and running shoes had any spare change.

The runner's third thought was his last, for what the shape held out was not a trinket, not a prohibitive hand, but a gun. The bullet blew a hole in his forehead and put an end to thinking.

* * *

"You hear that?"

"What?"

"That noise. Like a backfire."

"All I can hear, Jer, is the surf on the beach at Waikiki, which is where we're gonna be, we're gonna kiss this crummy garage, these crummy cars goodbye, soon's we figure a way to beat the Lotto."

"There's no way to beat the Lotto, Artie."

"There's action, there's a way to beat it."

"Tell that to Jackie Sharps."

"Whattaya mean?"

"I mean he's doing points in Rahway, that's what I mean. Tell him, 'Jackie, there's action, there's a way to beat it. Fact you're doing points in Rahway, Jackie, breaks a the game.'"

"He found the *way*, Jerry. He was *in* the bank when they nailed him."

"And now he's in Rahway, getting some *shvartzer's shmeckle* up his ass. You bring down the blue Marquis?"

Like all good comedy teams, they were mismatched—Jerry short and stout, Artie tall and lank. Like all good comedy teams, they were asynchronous. "What about the Ping-Pong balls?" Artie said.

"The blue Marquis's for six. You should a brought it down. What Ping-Pong balls?"

"Guy wants it at six, I'll bring it down at five a six. They pump air into those big jars full a Ping-Pong balls, right? The balls fly around, they open the little trapdoor, one a the balls flies up and the number on it's one a the numbers that wins, right?"

"What about the gray Fleetwood?"

"The gray Fleetwood's for seven, for chrissake. Bring it down now, where you gonna put it, in the street? The street's full a vans. We could fix the balls, Jerry, is what I'm saying. I mean, somebody makes the balls, right, somebody puts 'em in the big jars. Maybe there's a way to fix 'em so they're too heavy to fly up when they open the little trapdoor or too big to fit through it, like, all but the ones we bet on, the ones we get the guy who makes 'em or the guy who puts 'em in the big jars to make sure they're, you know, not like the other balls."

"Hey, who's that?"

4

"You listening to me, Jer? Or what?"

"There. 'Cross the street. One a them bag ladies, looks like."

"Looks like a guy."

"Looks like a bag lady, wearing a lot a coats."

"The fuck can they wear all them coats in the middle a summer?"

"It was cold last week. I wore long johns."

" 'Cause you're a scumbag, Jerry. . . . What about the broad takes the Ping-Pong balls out a the jars? For a piece a fifty-two million you think she'd, like, pick the balls we bet on?"

Jerry laughed. "Sure, Artie. Call her up, why don't you?"

"What if I told you I got a date with her?"

"Bullshit."

"I knew if I told you that's what you'd say. Face it, you're jealous."

"Hah."

"No shit. You're jealous, babe. You're jealous 'cause you know she's got nice tits—you said so yourself, last time we watched the Lotto on TV."

"What's her name?"

"You think I'm gonna tell you?"

"What's her name, Artie?"

"Angela."

"Angela what?"

"Muldoon."

"Bullshit."

"What can I tell you? She's half guinea, half mick."

"What half's her box?"

"Hey, watch your mouth."

"When're you going out with her, Artie?"

Artie bent to tie his shoe.

"Yeah? Yeah?"

"I'm not going *out* with her, but I like, you know, met her, like. Her sister's a nurse, like my sister. I could definitely get a date with her, I axed her. First I wanna work out a plan."

"Know what somebody told me once, Artie?"

"That you're a scumbag?"

"Somebody told me once don't mix business and broads. Know who told me that?"

"Your mother?"

5

"Keep my mother out a it. You don't want me axing what half's Angela's box, you keep my mother out a it. Who told me don't mix business and broads was Jackie Sharps."

"Jackie Sharps, Jackie Sharps, Jackie Sharps."

"Who's doing points in Rahway on account a he mixed 'em, business and broads. Before he hit that bank, he went out with a teller worked there. She told him the layout, the days they made the Purpleator Courier drops, the setup. Jackie thinks she sang."

"Hey, look."

"What?"

"Look, Jer. A guy. Let's go see."

"I ought a bring down the blue Marquis."

"Come *on.*"

They moved sideways, on the balls of their feet, arms outstretched. Urban crabs.

"Holy shit."

"Jesus."

"Don't touch him, Artie."

"I gotta touch him to see if he's dead, don't I?"

"He's *dead?*"

"Oh, fuck. Look. Right between the eyes."

"I'm gonna be sick, man."

"What's this?"

"Come on, man. We should call the cops, or something."

"Look. Jerry, look."

"I don't wanna look."

"Jerry, look. Sticking out a his shorts."

"I don't wanna look."

"It's a Lotto ticket."

"Who the fuck cares, man?"

"What if it's the winning ticket, Jer?"

"Who the fuck *cares,* man?"

"I'm keeping it."

"*Art*ie."

"Don't say nothing, Jer. When the cops come. Okay?"

"Okay."

"Don't say *noth*ing, Jer. Swear to God?"

"Yeah."

6

"Swear to *God?*"
"I said yeah."
"Do it."
"I . . . I swear to God."

2

Charly Johnstone wedged herself between the arms of a seat in the center of the third row orchestra of the Kean Theater just as the curtain went up. "Another opening, another show," Charly hummed.

The curtain went right down again, for this was a rehearsal, not a performance, and a technical rehearsal for the stage crew, as well. The director, Jay Dillen, wanted a rise that—as he put it to the stage manager—"has some tension in it."

"Tension," Charly whispered to her companion, a reporter from a suburban New Jersey newspaper (the *East Underpass Gazette*, Charly'd been calling it around the Mayfair Public Relations office), "is something this production has a plethora of. Don't write that, love. Write that the rehearsals and previews have been a soufflé of unprecedented smoothness. That's s-o-u—"

"Charly!" Dillen said, for Charly's whisper could command a taxi from a block away. He added sweetly, "Thank you, darling."

They watched the curtain go up and down a few more times.

"That last one felt plenty tense to me." Charly leaned away to look the reporter over. "I'm sure I'm not the first to remark on your uncanny resemblance to Woody Allen. Is the, uh, rialto your regular beat? I think not, for Charly knows every scrivener and freeloader on Broadway, not to mention every whore and cutpurse."

"I cover local politics, mostly," the reporter said. "Town council, the school board. But I also do neighborhood theater and opera. On my own time."

"Right." Charly slid down in her seat. There was no such thing, ran the motto of the publicity racket, as bad publicity, and no newspaper too inconsequential to place an item in; but there were also opportunities, not to be squandered, for catnaps.

The reporter got out a minute spiral notebook with a yellow cover. "Uh, what's the play about?"

"A good question. A question that in my time—we're talking geological time here: eons, not just a few decades—I've heard not a few critics ask their wives at intermission of not a few plays, lest their reviews betray that they were snoozing when they ought to've been paying heed to the poetry being proclaimed above their pin-sized heads. The play is a play within a play within a play within a play within a play and so on, back —or is it forward?—to infinity. It's a play—this is so terribly clever—about an actress who is murdered on the eve of her Broadway debut in a play about an actress who is murdered on the eve of her Broadway debut in a play about an actress who is murdered et cetera, et cetera, et cetera. A play that makes *Noises Off* look like *Godot*, a Chinese box of a play, which reminds me of a delightfully filthy joke I just heard. Two, uh, Oriental gentlemen were walking down the—"

*"Char*ly!"

Charly clasped her hands in front of her, like an attentive schoolgirl. When nothing happened, she twisted around in her seat. "Well, what's holding things up, then? Ah. I see. This is a banner occasion, a red-letter day. This is in the nature of a command performance, love. The gentleman in the gray suit— the eight-hundred-dollar gray suit? Martin Klein, the last of the great Broadway moguls, a man who eats David Merrick for lunch, with Jimmy Nederlander for an appetizer and Joe Papp for dessert. The old bag—make that dowager—on his arm? Vivian Thibault Wyndham, heiress, benefactress, and any other -esses you care to throw in. A rich old broad, in a word, who's underwriting this here endeavor to the tune of— Well, never mind. That's not for your ears, love, I'm afraid. Sitting down at the end of the row here, just so you'll have all the players' names and numbers, looking like a bad copy of Keith Richards, is Kevin Last, Dimanche's main squeeze and, in the play, her antagonist, making, like Dimanche, his first appearance on the stage of legitimate theater, although, like her, he's brought down the house at many a rock-and-roll emporium with his 'eavy-met'l antics. Kevin doesn't make his entrance till Scene Two. The chap in the leather *shmatte,* you must know, is Jay Dillen, the director, the man without whom the play would be just words on a page, the actors just so many lumps of—"

"Quiet please, ladies and gentlemen. And Charly. Curtain, please."

"Funny. Very funny. . . . Ah, there she is, the fabulous Dimanche. Would you look at her. Isn't she lovely? God, what a face! A Modigliani face, *People* magazine once called it, inaccurately. A face by Giacometti, *Newsweek* said, ditto. The face of an alien priestess, *Rolling Stone* hazarded, scoring, I think, a near miss, but then smudging the image by calling her a white Grace Jones. Grace Jones, puh-leez.

"You'll want to make a note of what she's wearing. Women readers love it, and your editors, well, they'll be so impressed. As you can see, this scene takes place in a dressing room backstage at a theater not unlike this theater, a theater at which there is to be a performance of a play about an actress who is murdered on the eve of her debut in a play about an actress, and so on. She's wearing the sort of thing the playwright, at any rate, imagines actresses wear in respose, and apparently the costume designer concurs—a white quilted polyester robe with black velvet lapels by Fernando Sanchez from Bergdorf Goodman. Underneath it—you'll glimpse them if God is your co-pilot; they're *all* she has on underneath—black silk tap pants by Argenti, the name on every smart woman's hips. Her hair . . . you'll want to write about her hair . . . natural blond—trust me—cut short and blunt not at some salon where all they know are the styles they see in magazines but at Astor Place haircutters, where the customers and the barbers conspire daily—

10

hourly—to set new styles. A dream, ain't she? A walking, talking, living, breathing—"

"All right, could we hold it a minute, please." Jay Dillen strode down the aisle from the temporary desk at which he'd been sitting halfway back in the orchestra, a pair of horn-rimmed glasses flapping from his neck on a cord. He ran a hand through his wavy pepper-and-salt hair. "Dimanche, honey, the line is—"

"I know the line," Dimanche said, demurely belting the robe, which she'd worn brazenly open, albeit with her back to the footlights, during the scene, a scene in which she occupied the stage alone, soliloquizing at her reflection in a mirror.

Dillen spread his arms. "Well, then?"

"You see, love," Charly whispered, "we're witnessing yet another in a series of what folks in show biz call creative differences. Dimanche knows the line, she avers, and I believe her, but it's her considered opinion that the line is deficient in . . . whatever. It rings falsely to her, not only in the context of the play but in that of what actors call *sub*text, which, if I had to define it, and I can see by the furrows in your brow that I must—"

"Goddamn it, Charly!" Dillen was at the end of their row and glowered down it.

"Jay?" Dimanche had come to the front of the stage and sat cross-legged. That singular face—narrow, angular, austere, alien—could, when she wanted it to, become the face of a waif, a persona her posture contributed to. "I'm not being difficult. You feel one way, I feel another. I've been acting according to your feeling for a while now. All I'm asking is that you give me a chance to act according to mine. Just to see how it plays. Cass wins every exchange she has. If she's to be sympathetic, she has to lose a few; she has to be at a loss for words now and then. I like the idea that the time she'd most be at a loss for words was when she was talking to herself, which is why I tried stammering just now, which you took to mean I hadn't learned my lines. I know my lines. I've known my lines since a few days after I got the part. You're a professional. I'm new at this. But I'm not new at living. If Cass doesn't seem real, if she doesn't seem alive, then no one's going to care that she gets killed."

"Hear, hear," Charly whispered. "You'll notice, by the way, that a figure who would seem to be pivotal to such an exchange —i.e., the playwright, B.G. Harris—is not present. The reason for her absence is that she's at this very moment tap, tap, tapping at her typewriter in a room backstage, trying to reshape another scene whose, uh, viability Dimanche called into question."

Dillen puckered his lips repeatedly, looking like a fish out of water. It wasn't his idea of collaboration to allow himself to be contradicted openly—and so gently—and he searched for a way to rejoin. Then he saw the gun peeking from the pocket of Dimanche's robe. "What the *hell* is that?"

Dimanche knew without looking what he was talking about. "Jay—"

"Goddamn it, Dimanche, first you had it sticking out of your pants in Scene Four, now you want the audience to wonder about it from the minute the curtain goes up?"

"Wonder about it, yes." Dimanche raised a finger as if at a precocious pupil. "But that's all. Not know what it means, not know that it's a prop from the play within the play. Just wonder."

Dillen lifted his arms and let them fall. "What *I* wonder is where's the motivation?"

Dimanche smiled. "By Scene Four, Jay, when they see Cass has the gun in the hip pocket of her jeans, they'll understand what the motivation's been from the start. It's simple enough: Cass wants to die. She'll kill herself, if that's what it takes; she'll kill someone else, and take death as the consequence; she'll struggle with someone—her mother, Buddy, Todd, Diana, it doesn't matter—in the hope the gun'll go off and kill her. You're a professional. I'm new at this. But you don't have to be a professional to understand the motivation. You only have to've lived a little life."

Dillen struck the pose of a man who had lived a great deal of it. "Which brings us to something I hadn't proposed to bring up right now, but since it's come up, Freddy tells me you've been taking that gun home with you, that you've been taking it out in the *street*. That's crazy, babe. You'll get arrested. You'll get killed. What if it falls out of your pocket? What if you get hit by a bus?"

12

"Freddy," Charly whispered, "is the stage manager. Keeps track of props, that sort of thing."

Dimanche's smile was sadder. "Jay, if I don't know what it feels like to carry a gun around, I won't know what it *feels* like. If I get hit by a bus, people will know what they've always wondered about"—she lifted a panel of her robe, not provocatively but like a child showing off a new garment—"that I wear black tap pants. Cass needs the gun, Jay, the way she needs oxygen—*more* than she needs oxygen. Without oxygen, she'd just be dead; without the gun, she'd be nothing."

"God, what an insight," Charly said. "Too bad she's not reviewing this production, instead of laboring in it. You're not to write a word of this, love. If so much as a comma of this exchange appears in your quaint little publication, I'll beat you to death with a *Playbill* and hang your carcass from the half-price-ticket booth in Times Square."

The threat was unnecessary; the reporter was still transfixed by the glimpse of Dimanche's underwear, a secret that, since God was not only not his copilot but not even in the same squadron, he'd never dreamed he'd share.

Dillen, a six-footer, seemed to be getting shorter. "All right, maybe. But a *real* gun? I mean, carry a prop gun. We'll get you a prop gun, Dimanche, with a shoulder holster and everything."

"Jay, we've been through this. I stood at the back of the orchestra while Freddy walked through Scene Four with a prop gun in his pocket and it *looked* like a prop gun, a *cheap* prop gun. He said that was the best props could come up with, and if that's the best, I don't want it." She took the gun from her pocket and held it out in both hands. "Do you know how heavy a real gun is? Feel it. It's astonishingly heavy."

"All right, Dimanche. On stage—maybe. But on the street?"

Dimanche waved a hand in exasperation. "It's not as if I'm—" she began, but was interrupted, or let herself be, by a mild ruckus at the rear of the theater.

Dillen turned, too, to see what it was, and so did Charly.

"Oh, Christ. *Exeunt omnes*—or the lady who signs the checks, at any rate. Now you're not to write, love, that Mrs. Wyndham left the rehearsal prematurely, in high dudgeon and her Silver Cloud. Come to think of it, why don't you come back another day, closer to opening night, when all the wrinkles've been ironed out, all the snags unsnagged, all the—"

"Charly, I want to see you in my office." Dillen headed back up the aisle. "We're going to take a half-hour break, everybody. Be back here at three-thirty sharp."

Charly tapped a fingernail on the reporter's notebook. "Soufflé. S-o-u-f-f-l-e, *accent aigu.*"

Hands on her hips, holding open her Fernando Sanchez robe, facing the mirrored wall of her dressing room, Dimanche studied with as much disinterest as she could summon up the woman it gave back to her: blond hair cut short and blunt; yellow-green eyes in that singular face; an eminent collarbone; small breasts with strikingly dark areolae given that she was a natural blonde; a high waist made higher by her black silk tap pants; dancer's legs and feet. With as much disinterest as she could summon up because Dimanche rarely met a mirror she didn't like. This one was generous enough to subdue the bruises.

She startled at a knock, and closed her robe. "What?"

"It's me."

"Go away."

Kevin Last opened the door and came in. "You okay?"

"No, I'm not okay. And no, I don't want company."

He sat on her couch. "You want me to help you with your lines?"

Dimanche picked the script up off her dressing table and threw it in a corner—near him, but not at him. "You're as bad as the rest of them. I *know* my lines. The *lines* don't make sense."

Kevin breathed in through his nose. "Maybe we should *do* a couple of lines." He put a hand in the pocket of his Kenzo jacket.

"I told you—no drugs. This isn't rock-and-roll, Kevin; it's Broadway."

"Shit, babe. You're number one with a bullet. You don't need this gig."

She crossed her arms. "You know what our problem is, Kevin? I speak English; you speak musician." She cocked her

14

head thoughtfully. And their problem was the play's: She topped Kevin every time.

"Bad Brains're at CB's," Kevin said, which followed from what she'd said but not from its implication. "You want to catch them?"

She turned back to her dressing table. "I have to make a phone call, Kevin. Would you please excuse me?"

He was up and at the door faster than she'd anticipated. "Our *prob*lem, bitch, is you forgot who you used to be." He slammed the door after him.

Dimanche sat for a moment, her hand on the receiver. Crossing her legs, she felt the heaviness in the pocket of her robe. She took out the .38 caliber revolver and put it on the table.

On the street. *It's not as if I'm on the* street, *out with the people.* That was what she'd started to say back in the theater. She wasn't on the street at all, except to get from the stage door to her limo, from her limo to her front door. She never went shopping anymore; the designers came to her, staged private fashion shows in her living room, displaying endless variations on black leather miniskirts, black camisoles, blue denim jackets, purple lace fingerless gloves, purple stiletto heels (while she sat there smiling secretly at the .38 Special in the waistband of her black leather miniskirt). She never went to restaurants (except for private parties), museums and galleries (except for openings), movies (except for screenings), concerts or clubs (except when the public was excluded). She never went, without exception, for walks, bus rides, subway trips, to parks, to the beach, bicycling, roller-skating, ice-skating, to a pizza parlor, to toss a Frisbee—all the things she'd done before she got so famous that to do any of them would be to start a riot, one that in her mind would end with the streets littered with the bodies of hundreds of teenage girls, all with blond hair cut short and blunt, black leather miniskirts, black camisoles, blue denim jackets, purple lace fingerless gloves, purple stiletto heels, one bracelet of elephant hair, one of copper, rhinestone chokers around their necks. She'd tried doing a few of those things for a while after getting that famous, doing them in disguise. It didn't take much—off with the bracelets and the choker, a bandanna on her head, a pair of unfashionable dark glasses, a baggy sweatshirt, a pair of old jeans, sneakers; she

15

still had such things around, on high shelves and in the backs of closets. And it had worked: Once, she'd walked from Fifty-ninth and Fifth to Thirty-fourth and Seventh, then taken the subway to the Village, without getting a second look from any-one who noticed her; another time, she'd walked over to Wash-ington Square Park, sat on the edge of the fountain, read *Rolling Stone,* had a hot dog, watched Tony the fireman do his shtick, gone home, without even an attempted pickup, without a solicitation from the Home Boys selling drugs. But both times she'd wanted to blow her cover, to tear off the rag on her head and hurl away the glasses and strip off the sweatshirt to reveal the camisole she'd worn underneath—to stay in touch with who she really was, or had become—and stand with her trade-mark spread-leg pose, arms akimbo, and whisper, as she did into a microphone when she came onstage, as she was sure she would be able to do unamplified and be heard as well as if she'd screamed, "Who wants to party?" For it sustained her now, her fame; she needed it as she needed oxygen, as Cass needed her gun.

So Kevin was right, or partly. She hadn't forgotten who she used to be; she just couldn't risk remembering.

She dialed the phone and brightened when it was answered. "Hi. Can you come see me for a little while? I need a friend."

3

"He knows."

"Who?"

"The cop. McIvan."

"The fuck could he know, Jerry?"

"Lookit the way he's watching us."

"No, Jerry, *don't* lookit the way he's watching us. You keep on looking it the way he's watching us, he's gonna start wondering what you're looking it, what're you so nervous about."

"What if he axes us about it?"

"Relax, Jerry."

"About the Lotto ticket, I mean."

"Hey, Jerry. If you say it one more time, maybe he'll hear you, then he *will* ax you about it. Right now, he don't know from no Lotto ticket, so don't keep saying Lotto ticket."

"You're saying it."

" 'Cause I know how to say it quiet, like, without moving my mouth a lot."

"He knows. Lookit him."

"All right, lookit him, Jerry. Lookit him. He doesn't know shit. Does he look like he knows shit? Lookit, he's patting all his pockets, like he forgot something, like he forgot who he is."

*　　　*　　　*

17

Detective Lieutenant Timothy McIver was only taking inventory: In one hip pocket, he had a handkerchief with his initials on it, and in the other, a comb with the name of the pharmacy that had given it away as a promotion.

In his left pant pocket, along with a grocery list (tuna fish, bread, chicken noodle soup, chicken breasts, Stove Top stuffing, Pepsi, Bud Light), he had a ticket from a Chinese laundry and a stub from the RKO Proctor's Sevenplex in New Rochelle, where the night before he and his wife had seen *Hollywood Vice Squad II*. In his right pant pocket, along with two dimes, a nickel, two pennies and two subway tokens, he had two tens, a five and two singles in a silver-plated money clip with his initials on it (a present from his daughter for his fiftieth birthday).

In his left sport coat pocket he had a flier announcing a meeting of the Detectives Endowment Association, in his right a pack of Merits and a gold-plated lighter engraved *To Tim, With love, Margaret,* a twentieth wedding anniversary present from his wife. In his left inside pocket he had a wallet with his driver's license, membership cards from the DEA, the Automobile Club of New York, the Silver Screen Video Club and the New Rochelle Y, an A & P check-cashing card, a Social Security card, a Blue Cross Blue Shield group identification card, a Westchester County Board of Elections identification card, a blood donor's card and a card that came with the wallet, with his name, address and telephone number filled in—by Margaret, who'd known he wouldn't.

In his right inside pocket he had his shield and his Police Department ID card. His shoulder holster had his name embossed on the strap; his service revolver had a registration number. On his left ring finger was a St. John's University class ring, class of '58, with his name on the inside of the band. His shirt had a laundry mark, his sport coat still had a dry-cleaning tag stapled to the lining. The keys on the ring on his belt were stamped with the names of locksmiths.

Why couldn't the two carhops from the E-Z-Park Garage have found *his* body in the middle of Crosby Street? He'd've known in a few seconds who the DOA was and all he'd have to do was find who killed him.

The DOA in the middle of Crosby Street wasn't as forthcoming. Except that he was six two or three, weighed one sixty to one seventy, had wavy brown hair and no identifying marks, McIver knew nothing about him.

For one thing, the dead man's face wasn't what you could call a face anymore, not after serving as the target, at pretty close range, for a .45 caliber bullet. For another, the dead man wore a red Hind singlet, blue-and-white-striped Brooks running shorts with a built-in supporter, white footlet socks, gray-and-red New Balance running shoes—and that was all. He had no watch, no bracelet, no rings, no chains around his neck; he carried no wallet, no keys, no money, no nothing. The pocket of his shorts—if you could call it a pocket; it was an inch wide and two inches deep—was empty.

McIver stepped over the chalk outline of the dead man in the middle of Crosby Street and walked the thirty yards to the E-Z-Park Garage, where the carhops who had called 911 were sitting on folding chairs, telling their story for the several dozenth time to other garage employees, customers, passersby, people who worked in the other loft buildings along the street doing jobs that if McIver spent all afternoon and night and all the next day he wouldn't know any more about than he did now, which was nothing.

He kept on going past the carhops—for he'd heard their story three or four times and knew that they didn't know the dead man, that they hadn't seen or heard anything or anybody, that they weren't witnesses, they just happened to be in the neighborhood—to where his partner, Detective Sergeant Nate Bloomfield, was leaning against a wall writing in his notebook.

"I got hold of the shoe company, Tim," Bloomfield said. "They're up in Mass. Guy I talked to said he thought if they looked at the shoes they could tell when they were made, maybe narrow down when they were shipped, maybe to where. He gave me the number of their New York sales rep, to save us a trip to Mass. He can look the shoes over if we want him to."

McIver grunted.

"He didn't know for sure, the guy at the shoe company, but

19

he said maybe the same thing's true of the shirt and the shorts and the socks—if the manufacturer looked at them they could tell when they were made, maybe narrow down when they were shipped, maybe to where."

McIver nodded.

"You got any other ideas, Tim?"

McIver shook his head.

"It's a bitch."

McIver tucked in his shirt.

"Remember the time we had a DOA with no clothes on over by Roosevelt Hospital? Or was it St. Luke's? Anyway, the guy was spread all over the sidewalk. Turned out to be a piece of cake, didn't it? The guy had a hospital ID bracelet on his wrist and the glass was broken in the window he jumped through. It was St. Luke's."

McIver sniffed.

"Or the DOA—a broad—with just a bra and panties and half her guts leaking out in the lobby of the Chrysler Building? Another piece of cake—except we had to climb about twenty flights. We just followed the bloodstains up to where she worked—what was it, a travel agency? no, a, uh, you know, place where they change foreign currency—and there was her boss with his brains all over the desk."

McIver scratched his ear.

"This one's tougher."

"Umm," McIver said.

Bloomfield laughed. "You know, Tim, I was just thinking about all the stuff I got in my pockets—a wallet, a shield, all kinds of ID, a driver's license, cards, a dry-cleaning ticket, all kinds of stuff. Why couldn't they have found *my* body? We'd know who the DOA was and all we'd have to do is find who shot him. Speaking of shooting, Tim, the girl's here, the woman, the filmmaker, the director, the one who's making a movie about us, about cops, Nell Ward. She's got a cameraman with her, she wants to know if she can shoot the DOA—" Bloomfield laughed. "I said, '*Shoot* him? Somebody already did.' She said she meant *film* him with, you know, a camera."

"Film him just lying there?"

"I guess so, yeah."

McIver shrugged. "I guess so, yeah."

20

"Thank you, Lieutenant." Nell Ward was at McIver's elbow.

He looked at her, then looked away, for he couldn't just look at her, he had to stare. She was beautiful and strange, not like other women he came across, who even when they were beautiful were never strange—unless they were hookers or dopers or losers, in which case their strangeness was just sadness. Nell Ward was strange because she dressed in men's clothes—not just slacks and blouses and low-heeled shoes, but *men's* clothes: a double-breasted navy blazer, today, over a white cable-knit tennis sweater, baggy white slacks, saddle shoes, a pinstripe shirt, a bow tie; no hat, today, but her long blond hair was pinned up and from the front her hairdo looked like a man's— and strange because when he did look at her, looked into her eyes, he saw a sign that said *No Trespassing*. "It's not, uh, pretty, Miss Ward. You should keep the blanket over him."

"Of course. I'm not trying to shock people. I'm trying to show what it's like."

" 'It'?"

"Police work. Who do you think killed him, Lieutenant? Not what individual—I know it's too soon for that—but what sort of person?"

McIver shrugged. "A killer sort of person."

Nell Ward smiled. "Okay, it was a dumb question. I asked only because I've been playing cop and figured I already knew the answer."

"Yeah? What's the answer?"

"I'd just be playing cop."

"Play. There's no charge."

"Don't people often get killed by people they know?"

"Sometimes, yeah."

"Often."

"Okay, often."

"I think he was killed by someone he knew, not knew personally necessarily but who'd seen him before and whom he'd seen, someone who knew his route, who knew how vulnerable he'd be, dressed in as little as he was. Clothes do more than conceal, they protect."

"Umm."

"Someone he recognized, maybe—would slow down for. His speed—one assumes he was fast—was his only defense."

21

"Hunh. Interesting. Killed him why? For his wallet, his watch, his jewelry? He doesn't have any of those things on him, but maybe he never did. I don't know anything about running and I've never mugged anybody, but if I was going to I don't think I'd mug a runner . . . dressed in as little as they are."

Nell Ward touched his elbow. "Just playing cop, Lieutenant. Excuse me while I go play director. Thanks for letting me shoot —uh, film."

"Yeah," McIver said. He went over to Bloomfield. "Have another go at the carhops, Nate. They're acting funny; they keep looking at me like they think I know something they don't want me to."

The killer was looking at Tim McIver too, wondering what he knew, wondering if it passed through his mind that the killer might be standing there watching.

Somewhere, sometime, the killer had read something about pyromaniacs, about how they often watched the fires they'd set, about how an arson investigator could sometimes look over the crowd gathered at a fire and pick out the individual who'd lighted it. Could a cop look over the crowd gathered at the scene of a murder and know that the killer was present?

Astonishing, how cool the killer felt, how relaxed. A flushed face, sweat under the arms—that would be normal; but there was no fever, no perspiration, testimony that everything had gone perfectly.

Perfectly, though not as planned. He'd gotten up earlier than usual, but that had perfectly suited the killer's plan, for it had been that much darker and the streets had been that much emptier. Perfectly dark, perfectly empty.

His regularity had been his undoing, the unvarying routine he'd lived by—the asshole. He'd bragged about it, as if it were a virtue—that he ran from A to B to C to A again, at so many miles per hour, so many feet per minute, so many inches per second: he'd worked it all out, calculated, measured, figured— the asshole.

What a high it had been, seeing him stagger, seeing him fall, seeing his calculated, measured, regular life come crumbling down around him; seeing his mouth moving, as if he were trying to formulate what was happening to him, seeing the

22

pain in his eyes that wasn't just physical pain but distress at his inability to do what he did to everything else in his life—reduce it to safe, manageable numbers.

The asshole.

4

Martin Klein wept real tears. "I'll be a laughingstock."

"Mamet who?" Charly Johnstone tucked the phone into the folds of her chin and lighted a Sherman's cigarette with an Ohio Blue Tip match from the box she carried in her pocketbook—a yellow drawstring net bag labeled URGENT NEWSFILM. "I don't care if there's an O'Neill opening the same night. I want Tavern on the Green. . . . Yes, O'Neill's dead, Mickey, and yes, I don't want Elaine's, it's too far uptown, and yes, I don't want Sardi's, it's too small."

"Forget the opening night party," Klein said. "I'm going to kill myself—tomorrow, maybe."

Charly raised her voice from a shout to a yell. "Mickey? We definitely need Tavern on the Green. Martin's going to kill himself. Call Liz Smith, will you? I'll call Suzy." She hung up.

Jay Dillen laughed.

"The fuck's so funny, hard-on?" Klein felt in his pockets, came up with a napkin from the Carnegie Deli and blew his nose.

"Life." Dillen filled a coffee mug from a bottle of Peters Val mineral water. "Every waking minute."

"Tell it to Vivian Thibault Wyndham. Call Vivian Thibault Wyndham—when was the last time you saw a principal backer

24

walk out of a rehearsal?—and tell her how funny life is. What kind of water is that? It's not Perrier." Klein pronounced it to rhyme with *derriere*.

"It's German," Dillen said.

"You drink German water in my office? Water made by the scum gods of the earth. What do they charge for that?"

"This is my office, Marty. It's two for ninety-nine at Gristede's."

Klein snorted. "You better start shopping for bargains and forget about your kids' orthodontia and maybe stop in a pawnshop and get an estimate on that watch—what is it, a Rolex? —because this play doesn't start looking like a Broadway play pretty soon and not a Hadassah fund-raiser, you're going to be up the creek without a pot to piss in."

Dillen took a sip of water. "I don't have any kids, Marty. And we've got three weeks of previews left."

"Yesterday I want this play looking like a Broadway play, not in three weeks, not in three days, not in three hours."

Dillen looked at his watch—an Omega. "In three hours, B.G.'ll be finished with the new scene."

Klein picked up the mug and sniffed at the water. "That was my first mistake, backing a play by a woman writer."

Charly wagged a finger. "Careful, Martin. Tread lightly, my love."

"A woman who doesn't even use her real name—"

"History is replete, Martin, with unkind mothers who give their daughters names that hang about their necks like albatrosses—albatri?—all of their natural lives."

"B.G. What is she, a rock group? What is it, this albatross of a name? And Di*manche*"—he made it rhyme with *the ranch*— "what kind of name is Di*manche*, anyway? She's not French. Is she? That was my second mistake, hiring an actress who's not an actress, she's a pop star, according to what I read in the papers today in a little item about how this play's in trouble. What is a pop star, anyway? Is that pop like in popular? How many people does it take to be popular, enough to pay the nut?"

Dillen, whose real name was Davidovich, said, "The play just needs some fine tuning, Marty."

"No play is writ in stone, Martin," Charly said. "A play is a living thing—a living, breathing organism."

25

"Fine tuning. I should get a mechanic, not a writer. I should get a mechanic, not a press agent—Char*lene*. I don't understand why I have to read in the papers day after day how this living, breathing organism's in trouble. I know it's in trouble; what do I have to read it in the papers for? It's your job to keep things out of the papers as well as get things in. I should get a mechanic instead of Di*manche,* a mechanic instead of a director, 'cause you know what occurred to me, Jay, while you were standing there listening to her saying she knew her lines, she just doesn't like her lines? It occurred to me that you might've said it's not her job to like them, it's her job to say them. Was I wrong to think that? Am I old-fashioned? It's not like I sit around talking about the Lunts all the time, the way some people do. Helen Hayes, the Barrymores. I'm a pretty hip guy. I went to see the Living Theatre once. I hired a pop star to play the lead in a goddamn Broadway play, I should've had my head examined, I should be doing the crying."

"You're a prince, Martin," Charly said. "A traditionalist, but not so freighted with nostalgia that you cross the street without looking out for the cars, dreaming of hansom cabs and one-horse open sleighs; a perfectionist but with a mind open to the possibilities of improvisation. A prince, in short. A legend, a—"

"Stop jerking me off, will you, and give me a good reason why I shouldn't get a new publicist, a new director, a new leading lady, and send the Bee Gees back to Australia."

"Indiana," Dillen said.

"It's *très* simple, Martin," Charly said. "What's the old saw? 'First the page, then the stage.' Not to mention first the casting, the blocking, the rehearsing, the flacking—"

"Tell it to Vivian Thibault Wyndham," Klein said. "Call Vivian Thibault—Where're you going?"

"To the ladies'." In a black broad-brimmed hat, purple caftan, gray shawl and red-white-and-blue Etonic running shoes, Charly looked like a ship under full sail without any rigging.

"That's why there'll never be a woman President," Klein said. "The Russians'll be landing off Coney Island and she'll be in the ladies'. What do you want?"

Dillen's assistant, who had put her head about an inch in the doorway, retreated half that distance. "Mr. Dillen, I'm having trouble getting through to the coast. They asked me to try again in about half an hour."

"Thank you, Mindy," Dillen said.

Klein picked up the cup again and took a sip. "Now Mindy's a nice name. The *coast?* What call to the coast? Hey, Jay—what're you, lining up a gig directing a picture so when this play goes down the tubes you'll be sitting pretty? Or what?"

"Amanda's in L.A."

"You're not still pissed off about that, are you? About Di*manche* getting the part instead of Amanda?"

Dillen shook his head.

"Don't lie to me, Jay. You are."

Dillen shrugged. "I was disappointed, yes. Was. I was looking forward to a chance to work with Amanda. Now it looks as though she'll get the Roeg film, so everything's worked out for the best."

"Amanda Becker. Good name. A real name—like Meryl Streep, not like Di*manche*. I should've listened to you, Jay."

"I think, Marty, that I was the one who said Amanda wasn't right—that the part was too much against type."

"Type, schmype. I want a hit, not a bomb. You want a hit, you go with the heavy hitters, not the pop stars. Was it, you know, sticky, you and Amanda being, you know, involved, and having to tell her she wasn't right for the part?"

"A little sticky. But it worked out all right."

"All right for her, maybe. A Roeg film. But not all right for me." He took another sip. "This isn't bad, for water from the scum gods of the earth. You should keep on being frugal like this, 'cause you're going to be up the creek without a pot to piss in."

"Maybe I'll win the lottery," Dillen said.

"You bought a ticket?"

"Of course. It's wonderful to be part of such collective excitement. The whole city's alive with expectation. It's like a subway series, the Jets and the Giants in the Super Bowl."

"You know what the odds are? The odds're six million to one."

"Someone's got to win."

"Not so. Not true. Not at all. It's not a horse race, one horse wins even if he goes over the finish line backwards, even if they have to kick him across. It's a guessing game, only you guess a number that doesn't even exist yet when you guess it. The number comes up, nobody guessed it, nobody wins, the money goes back in the kitty. Why do you think the kitty's fifty-two million? 'Cause nobody guessed the number all those other weeks."

Dillen stood. "It costs a dollar, Marty. As much as two bottles of sparkling water. It's a kick to think that a dollar can buy fifty-two million dollars."

"Tell it to some poor slob in the South Bronx with six kids and his mother-in-law in a two-room apartment, car payments, TV payments, washing machine payments. He doesn't think it's a kick; he thinks he's got a chance. He's got no chance, Jay. And it's no kick except a kick in the ass. The lottery is a plot —a plot to keep the poor slobs in the South Bronx from sharpening broomsticks and waving tire irons and marching on City Hall, the White House, Congress, whatever, asking for their piece of the great American dream. . . . What numbers did you bet?"

Dillen laughed and went to the door.

"Where're you going?"

"To the men's."

"Terrific. And I'll just sit here and kill myself."

"Where to, Mrs. Wyndham?"

"I believe I'll walk home, Eugene. I've just had a rather trying experience and I need to walk off my discontent."

"Yes, ma'am. This is a rough neighborhood, ma'am."

"Don't be silly, Eugene. It's broad daylight."

"Yes, ma'am, but—"

"I'll be going to the club at six, Eugene. You may take what's left of the afternoon off until then."

"Thank you, Mrs. Wyndham": you dippy old dame, walking through Times Square in a hundred large Perry Ellis Russian sable coat—and it's still summer, practically; a Black, Starr & Frost gold necklace with nine rubies and a hundred and five diamonds; a Paloma Picasso gold signet-ring watch; twenty or thirty large worth of dress and shoes and shit. You want to walk through Times Square looking like that in broad daylight? Be my guest. See you at six—what's left of you.

B.G. Harris stared at the sheet of white twenty-pound bond in the IBM Selectric III typewriter. It said nothing.

Of course it said nothing. It was Sphinx paper. To get a sphinx to talk, you first had to answer its riddle.

What's the question, Sphinx?

. . . .

You can hardly expect me to answer if you don't ask me the question.

. . . .

Shit.

She pushed the typewriter away from her, lifted her Jansport backpack onto the desk and took a bottle of Valium from one of its pockets. She opened the cap and dumped out the capsules. One, two, three, four, five, six, seven, eight, nine, ten, eleven, twelve, thirteen . . .

"Hey, don't I know you?"

Amanda Becker moved on the back seat to where the cab-driver couldn't see her in the rearview mirror. "I don't believe so."

"Yeah. I've seen you on TV."

"I don't believe so."

"I don't mean on a sitcom, like, or anything. On a talk show. Carson, Letterman, one of them."

"Is there any way to get around this traffic?"

"You mean, get off the expressway, go on the back streets?"

"Yes."

"Yeah, sure. I mean, I can give it a shot. The thing of it is, with the lights and all, it could take just as long."

"I don't mind, as long as we're moving."

"I know you. I know I know you. By the time we get to Manhattan, I'll've figured out who you are. I don't forget a face. I had Elliott Gould last week."

Amanda Becker drew the collar of her trench coat closer around her face. Elliott Gould, indeed.

"Uh, gentlemen?" Charly said.

"What?" Klein said.

"There is one little thing that we've managed for several days now not to discuss."

"Yeah? What?"

"The, uh, mugging."

"Don't remind me," Klein said.

"I thought you handled it well, Charly," Dillen said. "All the pieces I read were straightforward and, well, sympathetic."

"Indeed . . ." Charly lighted a new Sherman's with an Ohio Blue Tip. "Indeed, well, that's Charly's job, isn't it? And who wouldn't seem sympathetic in this case? After all, uh, mugged in broad daylight, practically, just a few doors from her elegant town house in historic Greenwich Village, because everyone knows that notwithstanding Martin's attempts to characterize her otherwise, Dimanche is no debutante, no tyro, no neopostmodernist bohemian hustler from the East Village come uptown *pour épater les bourgeoisie.* Dimanche is a star of the first magnitude, a diamond of the first water, a Bendel bonnet, a Shakes—"

"What, Charly?" Klein drummed his fingertips on the desktop. "What're you saying?"

Charly blew a perfect smoke ring and watched it disintegrate. "We got off easy, gentlemen. The scandal-devouring, gossip-spewing New York press corps behaved like kittens before bowls of milk the other afternoon when we assembled them at Dimanche's elegant town house in historic Greenwich Village, served them coffee and croissants from Patisserie Lanciani and told them that the reason Dimanche would be looking like Rocky for a few days was that just the evening before, in broad daylight, practically, just a few doors from that elegant town house in historic Greenwich Village, Dimanche was, uh, mugged. By an unknown male Hispanic perpetrator, as the police put it, in his early to mid twenties, five foot six to five foot eight, one hundred thirty to one hundred forty pounds, wearing blue jeans, a black windbreaker, hatless, and in running shoes —dark blue with white stripes across the instep—three of them. Stripes, that is, not insteps."

"I wish you wouldn't do that," Klein said.

"Merely aspiring toward precision, Martin."

"I wish you wouldn't say, 'Uh, mugged.' "

"Ah. Yes. There's the rub, isn't there? How did we use to disparage people when we were younger? We were younger, Martin—remember? Even Charly was younger. How did we use to disparage people when we were younger—twosomes whose veracity we had reason to doubt? 'One lies, and the other swears to it.' Remember ever saying that, Martin? I'm sure there's a Yiddish variation that would have come more trippingly off your tongue, being a child of the shtetl as you are, not having been raised, as Charly was, in Larchmont. But nonetheless, I'm sure you must've said it, or something like it. 'One lies, and the other swears to it.' Dimanche lied, and Charly swore to it—as did we all—when confronted by the scandal-devouring, gossip-spewing New York press corps. Dimanche lied, as well, to the police, but Charly wasn't there for that, nor were any of us, Dimanche having elected to undergo that ordeal on her own, having summoned the police without informing her producer, her director, her publicist, beforehand of the necessity that she do so, did so even though she knew that had we been apprised of that necessity we would have dropped everything, hailed taxis, generally come running pell-mell."

"Charly?" Dillen said.

Charly dropped her cigarette in the cup of Peters Val. "Yes, love?"

Dillen sat and swished the cigarette around with a fingertip. "If Dimanche lied—"

"Oh, Dimanche lied."

"—if Dimanche lied, it seems to me that the worst that will happen is the police won't catch the mugger—"

"Apprehend the perpetrator, Jay. Apprehend the perpetrator. When in Rome—"

"—which is hardly rare in New York City in the nineteen eighties."

"The late eighties. We're in the late eighties now, Jay—do you realize that? God."

Dillen spread a hand. "So that'll be that. Dimanche will be just another victim of just another crime carried out by just another criminal who continues to roam the streets."

31

"Horrible, isn't it?" Charly lighted another Sherman's. "Ghastly."

"So you're not saying that in the absence of an apprehended perpetrator, the newspapers are going to start speculating about whether the crime actually occurred. You're not saying that until they find—or the police do—the smoking gun, the newspapers are going to be skeptical about the means by which the wounds were actually incurred."

"For a man whose forte is action, Jay, you have a way with words. That is precisely what I'm saying."

"No," Klein said.

"No?"

"No. What you're saying, isn't it," Klein said, "is who smacked her the fuck around?"

Charly laughed. "For a mogul, Martin, you, too, have a way with words. More precisely, what I'm saying is, is it important to *know* who smacked her the fuck around or is the mere fact of knowing that she *was* smacked the fuck around sufficient? We don't know it, of course; we've intuited it, inferred it, deduced it; no one has said it in so many words—that is to say, Dimanche hasn't. And is it likely that the police, speaking of deduction, will come to a similar conclusion, will intuit, infer and deduce that Dimanche was not, uh, mugged, and that the bruises on her face are indicative of someone's having smacked her the fuck around?"

"Someone she knew," Dillen said.

"A boyfriend," Klein said. "Kevin Last."

"Mindy?" Dillen bent over the intercom. "Ask Kevin to come in here, please."

Charly spoke through a cloud of smoke. "Do you think that's wise, Jay?"

Klein held his head. "I knew I made a mistake. Never hire a leading lady whose boyfriend's in a supporting role. I'm going to tell Mrs. Wyndham this—that the leading lady of the play of which she is the principal backer is getting slapped the fuck around by one of the supporting actors?"

"I don't think it's wise, Jay. I think our effort has to be not roiling the waters but smoothing them. If Dimanche wants to extend the run, as it were, of her farce, well, who are we to put up a closing notice? The point, I think, is simply that we must do what we can to make sure that the police, if they do intuit, infer and deduce what we have intuited, inferred and deduced —or is it deducted? no, that's something else—that they see that Dimanche's lie was a white one, that it was not intended to delude the police but to salvage a reputation, ensure against consternating her public—that it was, well, a trouper's gesture: The show must go on. And secondly, though hardly secondarily, we must do what we can to make sure that the scandal-devouring, gossip-spewing New York press corps does not learn that the police, if they do intuit, infer and deduce what we have intuited—"

"I think we get the point, Charly," Dillen said.

"Good," Charly said.

"What?" Klein said.

Mindy stood in the office door, her fingers in her mouth, her eyes wide.

"What is it, Mindy?" Dillen said.

"Oh, God."

"What, child? Tell Charly."

"Dimanche . . ."

"Yes?"

"I asked you to find Kevin, Mindy."

"I—"

"Did you find him?"

"Let her talk, Jay. Honestly."

"I . . . I thought he might be . . . I went to her . . . I knocked. . . . The door was . . . Oh, Mr. Dillen." She ran into his arms.

"What, Mindy?"

"She's dead. Dimanche is dead."

5

Retired Detective Lieutenant Jacob Neuman stared at the television set as if the ball game he was watching were the seventh game of the World Series and he'd bet his life's savings on it. Mookie Wilson took a pitch too close to take, but the umpire called it ball four. Goose Gossage called the umpire a name everyone in the television audience from adolescence on up could lip-read. Neuman chuckled.

"You can get them at any discount drugstore," Maria Aguayo Neuman said.

"Get what, babe? Sorry, I was watching the game."

"A vibrator."

She had said vibrator; he hadn't dozed and dreamed.

"Duane Reade has them, I am sure," Maria said.

Neuman read the functions on the wireless remote of the brand-new videocassette recorder: *Play. Record. Stop. Pause/Still. Fast Forward. Rewind.* How many functions did a vibrator have? "Yeah, well, uh. So couldn't you, uh, sort of, you know, go in yourself, when you're, you know, shopping? You could go this afternoon, 'cause we've got to buy a Lotto ticket, don't forget. There's a Duane Reade on Queens Boulevard right next to that candy store that sells Lotto tickets. I'll go with you even, 'cause there's sure to be a line to buy Lotto tickets and you hate standing on lines. Me, I don't mind it so much. I can read the *Post* or that new book I got. By that umpire? Ron Luciano? Did I tell you what it's called? *The Fall of the Roman Umpire.* Hah. And you can go into Duane Reade." Wally Backman sacrificed Wilson to second. "The hell is he bunting for? They're three runs behind. Three runs behind, ninth inning, you hit-and-run."

"I am asking you to do this for me, Jacob. I would be embarrassed to buy one for myself."

"Yeah, well. But what I mean is. Who's to know who you're buying it for? I mean, people buy them 'cause they have stiff necks and stuff, right? They don't just buy them to . . ."

"To masturbate?" Maria said.

How could she be embarrassed to buy something with which to masturbate but not embarrassed to say that that was what she was buying it for? "I don't get it, Maria. I thought everything was, you know, pretty okay in that department. I know it's not like it was when we were kids, but, well, we're not kids." Hernandez foul-popped to Garvey near the first-base dugout. "Come on, Keith, wait for your pitch."

"We were never kids, Jacob," Maria said. "You were forty when we married; I was thirty-seven. We were both quite inexperienced."

"Yeah, well. Still. That didn't mean we didn't know what went where or anything. I mean, you know, it didn't mean you didn't . . . you know. Did it? I mean, you do, don't you?"

"Do what, Jacob?"

"Maria. Jesus."

"Have orgasms? Come?"

Neuman let go of the breath he'd been holding. "Yeah. You know."

"Yes, I have a kind of orgasm. But Morton says—"

"Shit."

"I beg your pardon."

Carter hit a seed at Nettles, who picked it and tagged Mookie, who had run willy-nilly, ending the inning and the game: Padres 6, Mets 3. "Morton. I knew you'd been seeing him again."

"I see Morton every week, Jacob," Maria said.

"*Every* week? I thought it was like, you know, once a month."

"It was twice a month until I decided that that was not often enough, that I needed the continuity of seeing him every week. But you know this. I told you this. Perhaps you were not listening. Perhaps you were too wrapped up in the fortunes of your beloved Mets."

"Are we going to go into that again? I told you, baseball relaxes me. I need relaxing. Doctor Hanley says so. How come I have to call my doctor Doctor Hanley and you get to call your doctor *Mor*ton?"

"Morton is not a doctor."

"Your shrink, then."

"He is not a shrink, either. He has a Ph.D. in psychology."

Neuman used the remote to shut off the VCR and the television. "Shit."

"I should have told you the Mets lost," Maria said. "I do not think it is relaxing for you to watch them lose. If you insist on taping these games—"

"They're playing on the west coast, for Christ's sake. You want me to stay up till three in the morning? You think that'd be relaxing? So I tape the game, I watch it the next day, so what? That's what I got it for." He pointed the remote at her. "And don't you go telling me the score tomorrow. They play the Dodgers tonight. Gooden against Valenzuela. I don't want to know the score when I watch it tomorrow."

"We have to talk, Jacob."

"We *are* talking." Neuman got up and went into the kitchen. "Talk. I can hear you."

What he heard was the front door slam.

"Shit."

The phone rang. Her sister, probably; she had fifteen or twenty. Or her cousin; there were millions of cousins, at home in San Juan, in Miami, in Jersey City, in the Bronx, in the attic, probably. Or one of her friends—her girlfriends, her pals, her chums, her buddyettes. Or Morton. Calling to remind her to stay grounded, stay present, not to block her energy, to breathe, to keep her anus relaxed. She wasn't embarrassed to tell him that Morton had told her not to clench her anus. The asshole.

The phone stopped ringing. Neuman made a peanut butter and jelly sandwich. He took a bite. The phone rang and he grabbed the receiver off the wall.

"What?"

"Jake, it's Miles."

Neuman heard it as *it smiles,* and drew a vivid picture for himself of Maria, naked on her back on the bed, bucking rhythmically with the vibrator between her legs, a vibrator with one of those smiling faces painted on it: *Have A Nice Day.* "Who?"

"Miles Easterly, Jake. I just called you, but there was no answer. Maybe I forgot to dial seven-one-eight. I still forget to do that a lot. Habits're hard to change, aren't they, Jake? Jesus. I quit smoking, Jake, finally. I thought it'd be easy. Hell, I'd done it hundreds of times before. Hah. But it's hard, Jake. Jesus, it's hard. I gained about twenty pounds. I spend about a hundred dollars a day on gum. Sugarless, not that that means anything when you're eating a pizza for lunch two, three times a week. A whole pie, Jake, not a couple of slices."

"Miles, what do you want?"

"Jesus, Jake. I haven't talked to you in—what?—two years. I thought I'd see how you're doing."

"I'm doing good."

"You, uh, still like it—retirement?"

"It's okay, yeah. Yeah, I like it."

"You play a lot of golf, I bet, hunh, Jake?"

"No. I hate golf."

"I must've been thinking of someone else. Teddy Quinn—that's it. Teddy Quinn plays golf, now that he's retired. He moved way the hell out on the island, to where they have, you know, those golf courses, so he could play golf. So what do you do, Jake—to, you know, pass the time?"

"I don't know. Sometimes I think about the guys in the Department who haven't called me in two years. Sometimes I make a list of them. Sometimes if I see their pictures in the paper 'cause they, you know, made a good collar or something, got a promotion—you're a DCI now, Miles: who'd've thought it? —I cut out the picture and stick it up on the wall in the den and throw darts at it—"

"Jake."

"I haven't done it, but I've been thinking about maybe getting the pictures blown up, at one of those stores, you know, where they blow up pictures for you, and taking it out to the range—I still got privileges at Rodman's Neck, I think—or to that shooting gallery on—what it is?—West Two-oh—and having them hang the pictures up for me and maybe emptying a couple of clips at them, just for old time's sake. I haven't done it, but I've been thinking about maybe doing it."

"Jesus, Jake. I'm sorry."

"Yeah."

"It's just that, you know, time flies."

"Yeah, well, let me tell you something, Miles. For me it doesn't fly. For me it crawls. For me it kind of lays there and maybe twitches once in a while so I know it's not dead and maybe moves an inch or two to kind of tease me but then the next time I look it's back where it started. Digital clocks. That's part of the problem. A regular clock, you look at it, unless it's right on the button of noon or midnight or three or six or nine or something, you don't really register what time it is, only about what time it is. A digital clock, you look at it, it tells you exactly what time it is, no two ways about it.

"It's eleven thirty-three right now, Miles. Did you know that? If you asked me what time it was and I said eleven thirty-three, you'd think I'd maybe gone off the deep end, wouldn't you, gone around the bend, was a good candidate to be eating my gun, needed a rest, should maybe think about retiring. Wouldn't you? 'Cause eleven-thirty would've been good enough for you, or twenty-five of twelve. So when you retire, Miles, make sure you don't have any digital clocks around the house, or I guess you'll probably have a condo in Florida, won't you, with all the money you're saving not buying cigarettes, except you said you spend a lot on food. Well, that's too bad. Anyway, listen—good luck with the quitting smoking, Miles. Nice talking to you."

"Jesus Christ, Jake."

"Yeah," Neuman said, and hung up.

Neuman watched the whole game again, fast-forwarding through the commercials. The Mets still lost. Then he watched *As the World Turns*. It hadn't turned much since the last time he'd watched it, six months before. Maria came back at two thirty-six with a Duane Reade bag. She went upstairs with it and shut the bedroom door. Neuman went up after her and started to go in but knocked instead. "Babe?"

"There are some men outside," Maria said. *"Tus panas."*

She hadn't gotten a vibrator; she'd hired some gigolos. No: *panas* meant pals. Didn't it? What did he know? He didn't know any Spanish, just had a Hispanic wife. He went to the hallway window and looked out. Miles Easterly and Lou Klinger and Steve Federici leaned on an unmarked squad car painted a utilitarian brown that was like no other color in the world and might as well have been Day-Glo orange for all it disguised the car's purpose—Day-Glo orange with the word COPS in bright blue on the sides. A fourth man was at the wheel, wearing a brown fedora, reading the *News:* PADRES NIP METS, the back-page headline said. At least his eyes were still good, even if his wife needed a vibrator. Nip, hell; they'd won by three; he'd seen it twice.

Neuman went into the bathroom and splashed water on his face. While he dried it, he looked at it in the mirror, which he did about twice a year—really looked at it: on his birthday, maybe, though not always, and on a day in the depths of winter, a February day when it seemed that winter would never end, that daylight would be forever rationed. He didn't always look older on his birthday; he always looked older on that day in February (sometimes it was in March, sometimes in April, sometimes even in May, for spring was the tardiest season), older than the year before, older than the day before, for that moment in the depth of winter (even when the calendar said it was spring) was the moment when he was most aware of how little he had accomplished—over the winter and over his life.

Looking in the mirror now, really looking at his face, then turning to look at himself in the full-length mirror on the bathroom door, he didn't see a retired New York City Police Department detective lieutenant, former commander of the Uptown West Special Homicide Investigations Unit, winner of a breastful of medals and a special mayoral commendation. He didn't see a veteran of thirty-three years in the Department and fourteen years of marriage. He didn't see a fifty-four-year-old fat man with exiguous hair, dressed in a white Fruit of the Loom T-shirt, khaki Dee Cee work pants, dark brown nylon ankle socks with beige figuring, black low-cut Converse All-

Star basketball shoes. He didn't see Jacob Neuman at all; he saw Bobby Redfield, his ex-partner, his dead ex-partner. He saw Bobby Redfield, trim and dark and mercurial, because that's whom the men downstairs—Chief Inspector Lou Klinger, Manhattan borough commander; Deputy Chief Inspector Miles Easterly, Klinger's executive officer; Detective Second Grade Steve Federici; and the fourth man, the man in the brown fedora reading that the Padres had nipped the Mets when *noshed on* would have been a better verb—whom they would see when they greeted him, whom they saw when they thought of him, why they hadn't called him—not one of them, nor anyone else from the Department, either—in more than two years.

"So where're the cameras?" Neuman said.

Klinger took his hands out of his pockets and smoothed back his hair, as if there were cameras. "Hello, Jake."

Easterly spread his arms. He looked as if he'd gained forty pounds. "Jake. Hey, listen—about the business on the phone—"

"No, really—where are they?"

"Hello, Lieutenant." Federici said it, then ducked his head, then made himself look right at Neuman. "How you been?"

Neuman looked away and then looked back. "Okay, Steve. How're you?"

Klinger looked up and down the street of identical attached two-story brick houses with nominal front yards and driveways slanting down to one-car basement garages. Most of the windows were curtained or had their blinds drawn, for there was nothing to see but across the street an identical row of identical attached two-story brick houses with nominal front yards and driveways slanting down to one-car basement garages, most of their windows curtained or with their blinds drawn, for there was nothing to see but . . . "Any chance we could step inside, Jake? Just for a few minutes."

"I don't think so," Neuman said. "I don't want the cameras in the house."

Klinger looked at Easterly. "Did you tell him?"

"No, Lou. Honest. I didn't—"

"Tell me what? Tell me what, Lou? Tell me what, Miles? What were you supposed to tell me? And who the fuck is that?"

He ducked to see the man in the brown fedora, but couldn't bend low enough. "Some asshole from Inspectional Services? You going to stir this up one more time, drag Bobby's reputation through the mud one more time? Give it a rest, will you?"

"Hi." The man in the brown fedora had opened the door and come around to the front of the car—except that it wasn't a man, it was a woman, a woman in a man's brown double-breasted suit, blue tab-collar shirt, brown-and-yellow hand-painted necktie, brown wing-tip shoes. She had fine blond hair tucked up under the hat, pale skin, gray-green eyes, wide, thin lips, large teeth, a nice smile. "I'm Nell Ward."

Neuman didn't smile back, or shake the hand she offered him. He felt her difference from the rest of them, her—despite the getup—femaleness.

"I'm a filmmaker," Nell Ward said. "I'm making a movie about cops—a documentary. That's what they're talking about: When you asked about cameras, they thought you knew."

She stopped where someone else might've gone on, might've explained it to death. He liked that.

"There're no cameras around now," Nell Ward said. "I'm just doing what we call preproduction—interviewing people, scouting locations. Preparation's ninety percent of it."

He liked people who were prepared. Maria was always prepared: whenever they went anywhere, she mapped the route, even mapped alternates, checked the gas, the oil, packed a lunch or a snack, listened to the weather forecast; now she'd probably bring her vibrator, and a converter to plug it into the dashboard cigarette lighter.

Federici took a step forward; the others had retreated. "Can we take a walk, maybe, Jake? Just us. Around the block or something?"

Klinger made a move, the move of a book commander about to squelch an attempt at improvisation. But something about the set of Federici's shoulders and about the way Neuman looked right into the younger man's eyes made him hold back.

They turned the corner before they spoke. A Long Island Rail Road train click-clacked through a cut up ahead of them. A plane out of Kennedy rose up and up overhead, its jets laboring. Cars swished on Queens Boulevard, out of sight a few blocks away. Everyone was going somewhere—everyone but them, for they stopped and faced each other.

"You look good, Lieutenant," Federici said.

"I'm retired, Steve, so it's just Jake. You look good too."

Federici plucked at the button of his lightweight navy blazer. "I put on a little weight. Not from eating, from working out. I've been running a lot, pumping a little iron. I'm going to run in the marathon this year."

"Yeah, well. You look good. You were kind of skinny. What did Matty McGovern use to call you—the Italian Scallion? You still working with Matty?"

"Yeah. Yeah, I still work with Matty. He's been out sick for a while, though. Maybe you heard. Something wrong with his gut."

"I didn't hear, no. You married or anything, Steve?"

"Nah. You know."

"Yeah."

"Lieutenant. Jake. They want you to take a case."

"I'm retired, Steve. It's only in the movies, on TV, a cop comes out of retirement to take a case. That's why I asked where the cameras were."

Federici laughed. "I thought you'd gone off the deep end, Lieutenant. I thought you were a twenty-story building with an elevator that only went to eighteen."

Neuman laughed. "You thought I was a candidate to maybe eat my gun or something."

"Yeah."

"You get your Lotto ticket, Steve?" Neuman said.

Federici's look said he thought Neuman *was* a candidate to maybe eat his gun or something, then patted his breast pocket. "Right here."

"What numbers did you play? If you don't mind my asking."

"My birthday—1, 22, 53—except the numbers on the tickets only go up to 48, so I switched 53 around to 35. One, 22, 35 for my birthday, and 12, 5, 6 for my address: 12 Perry Street—Perry has five letters—sixth floor. So in order they're 1, 5, 6, 12, 22, 35."

Neuman nodded. "Sound like good numbers, except, I don't know, 1, 5 and 6 are kind of close together. It could happen, no question it could happen, but I think I'll spread my numbers out a little bit."

"You don't have your ticket yet, hunh, Jake?"

"I was going to go today, 'cause I had to go to the Duane Reade on Queens Boulevard and there's a candy store right next door that sells Lotto tickets. But I didn't go. Maria went out. Maybe she got one." They had turned back and were nearly at the corner. Neuman leaned forward to look down the block at the unmarked car. Nell Ward had her hat off and was tossing it in the air and catching it with stiff fingers, like a child. Her hair fell nearly to her waist. Klinger and Easterly were laughing at something she'd said.

Federici took a deep breath. "Jake, a woman was killed—"

"Bobby didn't do it. Bobby's dead."

"You probably read about it, right? Dimanche? You know who she is, right? The singer? The punk rock star? That's not her real name; her real name's Juliet Marko. You've heard her sing, right? 'Miss Me Tomorrow,' 'Every Woman in LA,' 'Breathless'? Eight number-one singles on her first album, sold out Radio City, Madison Square Garden, the Nassau Coliseum, everyplace." He was getting a little frantic, for Neuman's was the face of a man altogether ignorant of Dimanche, her repertoire, her venues. "She was in a movie—*After the Deluge;* she was going to be in this Broadway play, it was going to open in a couple of weeks, a play about an actress who gets murdered with a thirty-eight Special. Dimanche was killed in her dressing room yesterday afternoon, Jake. Shot in the chest with a thirty-eight Special—not the one that's a prop; one with a silencer—"

"Bobby didn't do it. Bobby's dead."

Federici moved to where Neuman had to look at him. "Remember that desk Bobby had, Jake?"

Neuman wondered if Federici had gone off the deep end, was a twenty-story building with an elevator that only went to eighteen, a candidate to maybe eat his gun or something. *"Desk?"*

"The big wooden job. Everybody else had a metal desk, Bobby had that big wooden job. They were going to throw it out; it was taking up half the squad room. I asked if I could have it, and they said if I moved it I could have it, so I got a buddy of mine with a van and we moved it to my place. We had to take the drawers out to lift it and when I put them back in at my place I found this list. It'd kind of worked its way down inside the back of the desk. It was a list of women Bobby'd gone out with. I mean, I'm not saying Bobby was going to kill every woman on the list, but it was . . . Well, it was scary, is what it was, 'cause that's what it looked like—a hit list. . . . Where're you going, Jake?"

Neuman was nearly to the corner. "Home, Steve. I got things to do." Better things than be reminded any more than he already had been that Detective Sergeant Robert Redfield, one-half of one of the most famous partnerships in the recent history of the New York City Police Department (they'd been known as Newman and Redford—that's how famous they'd been), had been in his free time a misogynistic killer, a murderer of beautiful, talented, successful women he courted and bedded and then bumped off. Better things than be reminded any more than he already had been that as well as he'd known his partner—his moves, his style, the way his mind worked—he hadn't known him well at all, certainly not well enough. Better things than be reminded any more than he already had been that as many criminals as he had collared in thirty-three years in the Department and murderers in seventeen years in the Homicide Division, he hadn't collared the one whose moves, whose style, the workings of whose mind ought to have made him the easiest collar. Better things than be reminded any more than he already had been that he'd fucked up and that his retirement wasn't a retirement at all but a penance—one for which there would never be absolution. "Good seeing you, Steve."

Federici didn't raise his voice, for he knew Neuman knew without hearing what he was saying. "Dimanche knew Bobby, Jake. He went out with her. She was on his list."

Neuman stood just outside the kitchen door, out of range. "I'm going to take a drive with the fellows."

Maria laid a veal cutlet on the floured cutting board. "I have always known you would go back to work."

"It's not what you think, Maria. It's got nothing to do with what we were talking about. It's about Bobby."

44

She took another cutlet from the butcher paper and laid it alongside the first, more perfunctorily. His cutlet. "Bobby is dead."

"Yeah, well."

She turned to face him, wiping her floured hands on her apron. "You look awful."

Neuman looked down at the clothes he'd changed into: a pair of black brogues from his days on the street, white socks, black chinos, a lime green Jack Nicklaus golf shirt (he hated golf, but liked Jack Nicklaus), a navy windbreaker with a broken zipper and frayed cuffs, a brown felt snap-brim hat with the brim turned up all around. "Yeah, well. I'm just taking a drive with the fellows."

"Are you taking the car?"

"Uh, no. I mean, are you going to?"

She nodded. "I called Morton and he had a cancellation, so he can see me today even though it is not my regular day."

"Jesus, Maria."

She turned back to the counter. "I'm going to fix these cutlets now. You can have a cold dinner. There's some leftover potato salad in the refrigerator and some bread in the breadbox. The butter is in the refrigerator. You will need to get some beer. I will plug in the coffeepot when I leave, so it will be ready when you come back. . . . You are coming back?"

"Come on, babe. Jesus."

"Bobby is dead, Jacob. He is free; he has no more problems. It is only the living who have problems."

6

"I had a dream yesterday—about Jackie Sharps."

"Yeah, so?"

"I dreamed we was in the same cell with him at Rahway, doing points."

"You're a scumbag, Jerry."

"We should a told the cops about the bag lady."

"What bag lady?"

"The one we saw—'cross the street."

"You *were* dreaming, Jer. You dreamed we saw a bag lady."

"We *saw* her—'cross the street. I said who's that and you said who and I said 'cross the street, looks like one a them bag ladies and you said looks like a guy and I said looks like a bag lady, wearing a lot a coats and you said the fuck can they wear all them coats in the middle a summer and I said it was cold last week, I wore long johns."

"The fuck do you have, Jer, one a them pornographic memories?"

"So maybe she offed him. The guy with the *Lotto* ticket."

Artie laughed. "There ain't no guy with a Lotto ticket, Jer. There's just us."

"Where you going, Artie?"

"To get the blue Marquis. It's almost six, almost quitting time."

"Shit. I go home, go to sleep, I'll probably have another dream."

"Two more days, babe. Two more days. Then we kiss this place goodbye, take the fifty-two mil, fly to Waikiki."

"What if it ain't the winning ticket? It ain't the winning ticket, two more days, one a us'll be getting the blue Marquis."

"It's the winning ticket, Jerry. Trust me."

"Yeah, well, what if it *is* the winning ticket? The fuck do we do then?"

"I *tol*ja, Jer. We kiss this place goodbye, say *aloha* to Waikiki."

"First we gotta cash in the ticket."

"So?"

"So on TV they always show the guy who sold the winning ticket, the, you know, the newsstand guy or the guy in the candy store. The fuck're we gonna do they talk to the guy who sold the winning ticket, he says he never sold us no ticket?"

"You know how many tickets they sold last time, Jerry? The time the prize was forty-one mil?"

"How many?"

"Thirty-six million, one hunnert twelve thousand, six twenty-six. It was in the paper. So how the fuck's the guy who sold the winning ticket gonna remember who he sold it to?" Artie laughed. "Unless he's like you, got a pornographic memory."

"Well, what if he does?"

"Jerry, relax. He's not gonna remember."

"Yeah, well, what if somebody else has the same number?"

"Hey, Jer, we're talking fifty-two mil here, not a couple a hunnert bucks, like from a World Series pool or something— two, three guys split it 'cause they all got the same amount a runs in a inning. So we split it with somebody, big fucking deal. Somebody else has the same number, it's twenty-six mil for him, twenty-six mil for us; thirteen mil for you, thirteen mil for me. You think you can live on thirteen mil, Jer? *Two* other guys have the same number, it's seventeen million, three hunnert thirty-three thousand, three thirty-three for them, seventeen million, three hunnert thirty-three thousand, three thirty-three for us; eight million, six hunnert sixty-six thousand, six sixty-six for you, eight million, six hunnert sixty-six thousand, six sixty-six for me. See? I figured this all out on my sister's calculator. I got a pornographic memory too. You think you can live on eight million, six hunnert sixty-six thousand, six sixty-six, Jer? I think you'll manage. I mean, you might have to cut back on bagels a little, maybe only have five or six Benzes. You might have to forget about the house in Miami Beach, get by with the ones in Hawaii, Vegas and Atlantic City. You can kiss the airplane, the yacht, the pony goodbye, Jer, you have to manage on eight million, six hunnert sixty-six thousand, six sixty-six." Artie laughed again, slapping his thigh. "I mean, shit, you might have to work here weekends, to, you know, pick up a little spare cash."

"We should a told the cops about the bag lady."

"You are a scumbag, Jerry."

"We should a told the cops about the bag lady, Artie, 'cause when the guy who sold the winning ticket, the newsstand guy or the guy in the candy store, when he remembers he sold the winning ticket to the guy in the jogging shorts, remembers because he *was* in jogging shorts— I mean, how many guys in jogging shorts stop to buy a Lotto ticket at four in the morning, which was what he must a done 'cause otherwise why carry it around on him? Thirty-six million, or whatever you said? No. One— Remembers because he *was* in jogging shorts, recognizes from seeing his picture in the paper that he's the guy got offed, tells the cops that's the guy he sold the ticket to, not us, the cops figure we must a offed the guy, took his ticket, which we did—"

"We didn't off him, Jerry."

"But we took his *tick*et, Artie. We took his *tick*et. So the cops come around, say you took his *tick*et, didn't you, you *offed* him, didn't you? We say we took his *tick*et, but we didn't *off* him, maybe the *bag* lady offed him, they say what *bag* lady, we say the *bag* lady we saw 'cross the street, they say you didn't tell us about no *bag* lady, we say there was one, they say, yeah, sure, what you mean, you murderers, is you're telling us there was one *now,* but you didn't tell us *yes*terday, you're just trying to get off the hook. *That's* why we should a told them about the *bag* lady, Artie. *That's* why. And not only that—"

"Yeah, what? I can't wait to hear this."

"Not only that, the guy in the jogging shorts who got offed is the guy we seen running by here every day, just about."

"Bullshit."

"What're you, telling me you don't remember we seen the guy? Every day for, I don't know, a year, just about. Around six, six-thirty, usually, 'cause I remember once I almost backed into him with the blue Marquis."

"So?"

"So we should a told the cops that."

Artie laughed. "You are a scumbag, Jerry. You know that? First: Did you see the picture in the paper a the guy who got offed?"

"Yeah. I mean, I didn't *look* at it, but I saw it."

"Right. And what did you see when you didn't look at it? I'll tell you what you saw, you saw a guy lying on the floor with his feet sticking out from under a blanket, that's what you saw—"

"The drawing. They had a drawing. I saw the drawing. A picture, like—one a them composition pictures."

"Com*pos*ites, scumbag. Com*pos*ites. They had a com*pos*ite picture a what they think the guy looked like. You know why they had a com*pos*ite picture a what they think the guy looked like? 'Cause the guy didn't have any face left, he was shot with a forty-five. You know why else they had a com*pos*ite picture a what they think the guy looked like? 'Cause all they *know* about the guy is what they think he looked like. He didn't have a wallet. He didn't have a ID. He didn't even have keys."

"He had a Lotto ticket," Jerry said.

"No, Jer. We got the Lotto ticket. The winning ticket—2, 5, 8, 9, 42, 44. Trust me. We got the winning ticket and he's got shit. Nobody's even missed him. Nobody's said hey, maybe that's my husband, he went out jogging, I haven't seen him since . . . my boyfriend, my brother, my son, my cousin, my next-door neighbor, guy who works for me, whatever. He's no-body. Nowhere. Who got killed that's on the front page a the papers, Jer? Dimanche, that's who. You see what the papers're calling the guy in the jogging shorts, Jer? Did you? Did you? Nowhere Man. They're calling him Nowhere Man."

" 'Nowhere Man.' You mean like the Beatles?" Nell Ward held a copy of the New York *Dispatch* as far out in front of her as she could, as if to deny that she was actually reading it. "Sitting in a nowhere land, something something something to nobody?"

Terry Niles, in whose column the appellation had been given birth, smiled. "It's nice to know people your age are conversant with the Beatles."

Nell tossed the paper on Niles's desk. "It's catchy. You always were catchy, Terry—like a lot of people your age."

"So catchy," Niles said, "that every other paper in town picked it up, or will. And if they don't, it'll just be out of spite."

"I must be suffering under a delusion," Nell said. "Isn't the *Dispatch* the paper nobody reads, the paper the head of some department store said he wouldn't advertise in because its readers were his shoplifters?"

"A hundred-forty-four-point headline in search of a story," Niles prompted her. He walked back and forth as he spoke, a pitchman, a vaudevillian. "A contest masquerading as a newspaper. Have you heard the joke about our latest contest? Find a fact inside the *Dispatch* and win a million dollars. But what you fail to understand, Nell, darling, being not only a child but a child of the electronic media, is the special place occupied by the *Dispatch* in the hierarchy of New York City print journalism. The *Times*, the good, gray *Times*, is, was, and always will be the paper of record, as interested—more interested, its detractors would say—in the Talk of Burkina Faso as in the talk of the city in which it's published. The *News*, which once upon a time styled itself the Tiger Paper, taking up the cudgels for John Q. Public, speaking in a cynical populist voice that was nothing if not colorful—'How Now, Kremlin Kruds?' was a famous editorial page headline hailing the United States for surpassing the Russians in some heat of the space race—is now a schizophrenic pussycat, its redundant gossip columns the last vestige of the tabloidism it abandoned in its desire, its unrequited desire, to be taken seriously. Each has its readers, to be sure—as, of course, does *Newsday*, which aspires to be 'New

York's *Newsday,*' but will always be Long Island's—but, except for press agents, those who hire press agents, news junkies, inveterate letters-to-the-editor writers and coupon clippers, no one who reads one of them reads the others."

Niles paused to give a fractional adjustment to his bow tie—his *inevitable* bow tie, the writer of his obituary would inevitably call it—using as a mirror the glass of his office door. He ran his hands over his head as if there were hair there, when there was none. "But, to dispel your delusion, everyone reads the *Dispatch*—or at least knows what the *Dispatch* said, which amounts to the same thing. The reason is very simple: The *Dispatch* is interesting. The reason it's interesting is also simple: It takes the one story every day—and every day there's usually only one story—the one story everyone who reads a newspaper is going to read; it puts it on the front page with an eye-catching headline—a breathtaking headline, someone once called it; it puts as many reporters on it as are necessary to answer every question about it. It beats it to death, some people say; I say it makes it come alive." Niles picked up the paper and admired it as if it were an Old Master. " 'Nowhere Man.' Beautiful. In a day or two, at most, everyone in town'll be calling him that—even the police. What *are* the police calling him, your pals at Homicide? And how's your movie coming?"

"I haven't shot a foot of film. They're interested in the idea of a movie, but they're reluctant to have cameras following them around. And anyway, they're consumed by Dimanche."

Niles lifted an eight-by-ten glossy of Dimanche off his desk and held it out as he had held the paper. "Interesting, don't you think? Two people murdered in the same city on the same day—one so anonymous, so solitary, he doesn't seem to be missing from anyone's life; the other so famous, so celebrated, that to hear people talk you'd think everyone in the world had been her closest friend." He put aside the picture and picked up a piece of wire service copy. "You should see the tributes—from Cher to Chernenko."

"Who's Chernenko?"

"More to the point is that he's dead. Too bad. It would've been a nice alliteration. World leaders, living or dead, are about the only ones who haven't expressed a terrible feeling of loss at the passing of the charismatic rock star."

"You sound cynical, Ter. Not like you."

Niles smiled. "A cynic, Oscar Wilde said, is a man who knows the price of everything and the value of nothing. I give full value to the place Dimanche occupied in people's lives, but what was her place in her own life? Who did she think she was, and what did she think of herself? I interviewed her last spring —or late winter, I guess it was. Did you read my piece?"

"I don't read the *Dispatch,* Terry. It gives me nightmares."

"Too bad. She was right on about one thing—though her diction was such that I was unable to quote her directly, the *Dispatch,* nightmarish or not, being still a family newspaper. She said, apropos of her celebrity, 'Fame sucks.' Right on, you see, for celebrities, by definition, are people whose view of themselves is perpetually skewed by other people's view of them. They take themselves for what others take them to be. When they die, it's almost redundant, for the famous are already posthumous."

Nell laughed. "You mean immortal, don't you?"

"Fame is a kind of dying," Niles said. "Any journalist can tell you that the famous are those who need no parenthetical phrases after their names explaining who they are. The famous have no apposites. Some famous are so famous that just one name suffices—a first name or a last name or a nickname: Reggie, Sinatra, Doctors J and K. Dimanche. Some can be reduced to their initials: FDR, JFK; they're the favorites of headline writers. To have your personality encompassed in a few bits of alphabet is to be rarely famous.

"Most of us spend our lives accruing to ourselves words, phrases, ranks, serial numbers that distance us from the implications of our names. But whereas we can thereby modify our personalities, the famous cannot—any more than they can alter the footprints they leave behind in the wet cement of Grauman's Chinese. Those footprints do more than commemorate a visit; they testify that there's been no trail from the past, no trail into the future. To be famous is to forever march in place, for the public demands of the famous that they be consistent. The public appreciates the famous because it can hold them in the palm of its hand. It doesn't brook complication, whimsy, experiment—and certainly not, since the palm is a limited space, growth.

"The famous are like sharks. Just the mention of them stirs up the ocean. Their shadows fall full length even at noon and the public gambols in those shadows and doesn't feel deprived of light, for the shadow is light itself. The shadow is more than light: It's substance. The public chips away at it for fragments —the way fans cut chunks of turf from the field of a pennant winner. And the public is sustained by those chunks the way medievals were by locks of holy hair, by bits of bone. Those chunks are mnemonic props, by which the public memorizes the famous. And, having memorized, the public never forgets. Everything the famous do stays done. It's as if their lives were those sashes that Boy and Girl Scouts wear, from which badges of both merit and demerit hang immutably. There's no forgetting their honors, but neither is there any erasing their mistakes—any redeeming or correcting. Those sashes are encrusted with dates, places, people—with steps that though false are frozen forever, with lovers who though dismissed stay loved, with gestures that though contradictory are the arabesques of one long dance. And when they die, it isn't an end; it's another accretion. They die forever."

"Jesus."

"A perfect example."

Nell laughed. "Tomorrow's column?"

Niles grinned immodestly.

"Do I detect a certain bitterness there, Ter? Some sour grapes?"

He waved at the idea. "You wouldn't have a cigarette, would you?"

"I quit. So did you, remember? We did it together—for 'us,' such as we were."

"We were a golden couple; many people said so. Don't be smug about kicking *one* of your addictions, Nell."

Nell took her hat off the desk, wrapped her hair around her hand, and tucked it under the hat.

"Can you tell me now, now that we're just, uh, friends, why you insist on dressing like that?"

"It's comfortable," Nell said. "Do you think your readers know what arabesques are? You don't think they'll think they're some terrorist group?"

"Send the bastards to the dictionary, I always say. What're

you doing here, anyway? You've finally decided that you really
do love me after all, that all that talk about freedom and inde-
pendence and—how did you put it?— 'carving out your own
territory' was just so much talk? I could take up with you again,
Nell—even if you do dress like Charlie Chaplin, even if you
don't know who Chernenko is, even if you do do so much cocaine."

"I left you, Terry, as you would've heard if you'd shut up,
because you talk too much. But I came to make you talk—about
Lieutenant Jacob Neuman."

"Neuman? Neuman's retired."

"Maybe, but he's working on the Dimanche case."

"Jake Neuman's working on the Dimanche case? I might
have the first opportunity in my long, ink-stained career to yell,
'Stop the presses.' "

"You didn't hear it from me," Nell said. "Tell me about
Neuman. I want him for the movie. Every movie needs a star.
Neuman's famous. Posthumous."

. . . twenty-six, twenty-seven, twenty-eight, twenty-nine,
thirty, thirty-one. Thirty-one Valiums—one for each year of
her life. More than enough.

So much to do. So much to do. So much to do.

B.G. Harris swept the Valium back into the bottle and put
it in a drawer of her apothecary's desk—the desk she'd bought
at Bloomingdale's to treat herself on receiving the first check
of her advance for her first Broadway play. Her last Broadway
play. She pulled her Olympia portable toward her and rolled a
piece of white twenty-pound bond into it. Maybe that was the
problem. She'd written the play on a manual typewriter—this
very one—on the kitchen table of an apartment in Bloomington, Indiana: ferns hanging in the window, a cat curled on the
sill, Liszt and Brahms on the tape deck, bread baking in the
oven, the car in the driveway for when she needed to get away
from what she was making up and have a look at what was real.
The rewrites she did on a leased IBM Selectric III in a backstage room at the Kean Theater: no windows; no other living
things; photographs of dead actors and actresses and play-
wrights on the walls; no music; the only smell that of disinfec-
tant in the bathroom that was too close to the desk, which

couldn't be moved for it wasn't a desk but a ledge in front of a mirror, for the room wasn't a place to write but a place to put on makeup; the only transport to make a getaway in taxis or buses or subways that had odors of their own and could take her nowhere very different from where she was, for there was no reality in New York: everything was artificial. The rewrites she wasn't able to write—not well.

Yes, that was the problem. She wasn't blocked; she was stymied. She had the wrong equipment and the wrong ambience: She'd written a play, a play that was being produced for the Broadway stage, but she wasn't . . . theatrical; she'd never had fantasies about the excitement of all-night rehearsals, the butterflies of opening night, the high of walking in triumph into Sardi's, the interviews, the talk shows, Tonys, Pulitzers; she couldn't write in the cramped little backstage room, on the electric typewriter (leased at great expense, Martin Klein liked to remind her) that hummed at her while it waited for her to hit it again, with everyone sitting around waiting to see what she'd done to make the play better. She wasn't theatrical; she was a homebody: not a shut-in, not a hermit, but a loner—a writer. She'd written many drafts of the play, on the Olympia, in the kitchen, for herself—and for the cat, to whom she read them—each draft better than the one before. What she'd written in the cramped little backstage room on the electric typewriter, while others paced and smoked and drummed their fingers, hadn't made the play better, only different.

She'd tried doing rewrites at home. ("At *home?*" Martin Klein had said when she'd asked if that would be okay. "You mean Austral*ia?*" Her new home, she'd told him, her dear—in every sense—Chelsea apartment, sublet from an actor who was doing dinner theater in Neptune, Florida, with some plants, oversized but alive, and a view of some rooftops that if you squinted looked like Paris, or what she imagined Paris looked like, her Olympia on the apothecary's desk she'd bought for herself and crammed in among the found objects the actor considered furniture. No cat for the actor was allergic to cats.) But nothing came to her there, either—not even something different.

She stared at the paper. It said nothing. The sphinx.

Ironic. An apothecary's desk and she was going to kill herself with an apothecary's potion.

Too ironic. Rewrite it, B.G.

The killer threw the *Dispatch* across the room. It was all wrong; it made the dead man sympathetic, tragic, almost heroic. It made him the victim of a senseless urban tragedy when the truth was that he was—had been—the villain of his own. Nowhere Man. How about Everywhere Man? How about Anytime–Anyplace–Anywhere–With-Any-Woman-at-All Man?

She made a list: January—she met him at a party and he got her number and later she found out he went home with another woman at the party. February—he told her he had to go to California on business and later she found out he'd gone to Vail with a woman. March—he told her he couldn't go to Vermont with her for a weekend because he had the flu and later she found out he spent the weekend in Sag Harbor with a woman. April—she found a camisole in his bathroom and he said it was a platonic friend's who had spent the night because her boyfriend had kicked her out and later she found out that it was the platonic friend's menstrual blood that had stained his carpet, where they'd fucked. May—

She crumpled the list up and threw it after the newspaper. *Later she found out . . .* Later he *told* her, for he was incapable of keeping his duplicity to himself. He called it honesty and called it a virtue and said when she got upset that she was too sensitive, too insecure—crazy.

She made another list. She would treat herself—she would go to Elizabeth Arden for a facial and Bumble & Bumble for a shampoo and conditioning. She would buy a watch at Tourneau, some underpants and bras at Victoria's Secret, a pair of boots at Knoud.

It was her apartment that really needed treating; she'd been just a visitor there for a long time now, breezing through to pick things up or drop them off, sleeping there maybe one night every two weeks, never eating a meal except for yogurt from the refrigerator—until it ran out.

She would buy a Queen Anne sofa at Sloane's, a high-tech lamp at D. F. Sanders, a bed at Wim & Karen, a limited-edition rug at Modern Age, a tea set at Hot House, dishes at Sointu.

56

She would buy food at places too chic to have names, buy caviar as if it were jelly beans, loins of meat from animals as pampered as royalty.

She would never look at price tags, she would pay cash for everything, which would cause a buzzing, a bringing together of bewildered heads. Some of the places would never have seen cash before, and would be unable to make change; she would tell them to keep the change.

She'd kept him a secret from her friends, so she didn't have to tell her friends that she'd stopped seeing him. She would keep the next one a secret too, and the one after that. She should have kept all of them secret, all her men. They had never made her part of their lives; she should never have made them part of hers. They'd shaken their heads despairingly when she'd talked about commitment, work, sharing, shaken their heads and wondered why she wouldn't just settle for what they had, which was something. Wasn't it? She should have killed them all. The assholes.

7

Thousands of teenage girls, all with blond hair cut short and blunt, black leather miniskirts, black camisoles, blue denim jackets, purple lace fingerless gloves, purple stiletto heels, one bracelet of elephant hair, one of copper, rhinestone chokers around their necks, gathered outside the Kean Theater on West Forty-ninth Street and marched down Seventh Avenue to West Twelfth Street. They made a right for one block to Greenwich Avenue, a left on Greenwich to Bank Street, a right on Bank. They filled the block of Bank between Waverly Place and West Fourth Street, the block on which Dimanche had lived.

The march south had been a silent one, but on Bank Street they sang Dimanche's songs, every one of them, again and again, a cappella.

Afterwards, they chanted: "We want Dimanche. We want Dimanche. We want Dimanche." Wanted, presumably, to see her body, for they were under the misapprehension that it was her town house to which it had been taken from the Bellevue Hospital morgue. A few of their number had stood vigil there, and had seen an ambulance, its windows mysteriously curtained, bear away some unnamed cargo, heading west on Twenty-ninth Street, then south on Second Avenue. To them that had signified that it was carrying Dimanche to Bank Street.

In fact, the ambulance had turned west on Twenty-third Street, north on Third Avenue, east on Thirty-fourth to the Queens-Midtown Tunnel to the Long Island Expressway to the Brooklyn-Queens Expressway to the Grand Central Parkway to La Guardia Airport. A chartered Falcon jet flew Dimanche's coffin to Providence, Rhode Island. Dimanche's father, a plumber, and her brother, an accountant, loaded the coffin onto the bed of a Dodge Ram pickup and drove it to a crematorium, where Dimanche, according to the terms of her will, was returned to ashes, which her brother, also following his sister's wishes, scattered in a favorite cove of Narragansett Bay.

Word would get out, and for weeks to come the waters of the bay would be dotted with rented boats full of teenage girls, all with blond hair cut short and blunt, black leather miniskirts, black camisoles, blue denim jackets, purple lace fingerless gloves, purple stiletto heels, one bracelet of elephant hair, one of copper, rhinestone chokers around their necks. The police and the coast guard, fearful of a catastrophe, would finally prevail on local marina operators to stifle their understandable instinct to make a buck and forbear from renting water craft to such patent landlubbers.

"Listen to this, Lieutenant."

Neuman thought about shooting Federici in the foot, say, by way of making the point that he was retired, to call him Jake. But he wasn't carrying a gun, because he was retired. But if he was retired, why wasn't he at home, watching his tape of the Mets against the Dodgers, Gooden against Valenzuela, instead of in the lobby of the Daily News Building (the former Tiger Paper, now a schizophrenic pussycat full of redundant gossip columns), his elbows on the railing around the big world globe, trying not to look at the sports-page headline of the newspaper Federici had bummed from a security guard and was flipping through? Federici, fortunately, was strictly a football and hockey fan, and didn't care who'd won.

"This is a letter to the editor from the head of the biology department at Brooklyn College. You went to CCNY, didn't you, Lieutenant?"

59

"Yeah, I did. I don't think I ever took biology. No, I didn't."
If he had, maybe his wife wouldn't need a vibrator.

"Listen. 'In a recent editorial, you say that bears hibernate.
Small mammals such as the hamster and dormouse hibernate,
but a bear's deep sleep is not a true state of hibernation. It is
a more superficial torpor, generally interrupted by periods of
wakefulness.' " He laughed.

"I don't get it, Steve."

"Sounds like a description of Matt McGovern. 'Superficial
torpor, generally interrupted by periods of wakefulness.' " He
laughed again.

Neuman read the legend on the base of the globe: *If the SUN
were the Size of This Globe and Placed Here Then Comparatively: The EARTH Would Be The Size of a WALNUT and
Located at the Main Entrance to Grand Central Terminal.* If
the earth were the size of a walnut, how big would a bear be?
A hamster? A dormouse? What exactly was a dormouse?

"Steve, how long is this list?"

"What list? Oh—Bobby's list. Fifteen, twenty names. Well,
eighteen—exactly."

"Any of them dead, besides this Dimanche?" Neuman pronounced it De-mon-*shay*.

Federici nodded. "Two of the women Bobby killed. The other
one he killed—I don't know if you remember, but she—"

"I remember. He killed her because she knew he'd been going
out with the second one he killed. She wouldn't be on any list."

"Right. She's not on it."

Neuman turned and leaned his back against the railing.
"Anyway, the point is, even though Bobby went out with this
Dimanche and I was Bobby's partner and therefore I might
know something about her, the fact is I don't know anything
about her, 'cause Bobby never said anything to me about the
women he went out with. Never even said whether she was a
blonde or a brunette or a redhead, what kind of work she did,
where she lived, let alone named names. Let me ask you something else, Steve."

Federici closed the paper and folded it in such a way that
Neuman couldn't help but read the headline: LA KAYOS DR. K.
"Yeah?"

"When you found this list, when it looked to you like a hit

list, how come you didn't tell anybody about it, in particular the women on it?"

Federici shrugged. " 'Cause Bobby was dead."

"That's what I thought you were going to say. So why, since Bobby's dead, does this woman's name being on a list of his that looked like a hit list have anything to do with anything, and in particular with me? Put it another way: Why should I come out of retirement just because somebody my ex- and dead partner was maybe thinking about killing happened to get killed? Am I making myself clear? I don't feel like I'm making myself clear. I haven't had to think this way in a long time. I watch cop shows on TV now and then, and try to think the way they think, but there's usually nothing to think. I mean, most of the time they show you who the bad guys are, and it's just a question of whether the cops're going to catch them before the show ends, which they always do, except sometimes when they have a two-part special or something, continued next week."

"Ever watch *Miami Vice,* Jake?" Federici said.

"I don't think so. No. Now why haven't I? I've heard about it."

"It's on Fridays at nine. It's pretty good, sometimes, on, you know, what it's like, police work."

"Fridays at nine. Well, the Mets're usually playing Fridays at nine, during the season, I mean, and when they're not I guess I watch something else."

"I forgot to tell you something, Jake," Federici said. "I forgot to tell you about the message on the mirror in Dimanche's dressing room. It hasn't been in the papers because Klinger and Easterly figured it was one of those things you don't tell the papers because only the killer knows about it. That's not quite true, because the people who found Dimanche's body know about it, but Klinger asked them not to say anything to the papers and they haven't—so far, anyway."

"What message, Steve?"

"It was printed with red lipstick on the mirror—the same lipstick Dimanche was wearing. It said, 'There's a needle in your arm and it makes you breathless.' We think it's words from a song, a punk rock song, but nobody's been free to track it down."

"Printed, meaning you couldn't tell if the handwriting was a man's or a woman's?"

"Right."

"Hunh. A song about drugs, you think?"

"Yeah."

"She do drugs?"

"She's in the entertainment business, Jake. It comes with the territory. But not horse. Everyone who had anything to do with the play says she was always on time, never strung out."

"*Dallas,*" Neuman said.

Federici gave him his gun-eating look again. "What?"

"Fridays at nine, Maria likes to watch *Dallas.*" He could tape *Miami Vice* while Maria was watching *Dallas,* and hope that no one would tell him how it turned out. Shit. Oh, well. Even Doctor K had to get kayoed once in a while. But by L.A.—shit. Dodger blue—shit, shit, shit.

"There she is," Federici said.

Neuman stood up straight, then laughed when he followed Federici's point. "For a sec, I thought you meant there's Maria. Jesus. Scared the crap out of me. . . . Uh, 'scuse me, Miss Johnstone." He tipped his hat—a straw snap-brim, for it was a new day, a summery day, and he had on different duds, summery duds: brown Wallabies, lime green socks, slacks with light and dark brown checks, the coat to an olive green summer suit whose pants didn't fit him anymore, a light blue shirt, a dark blue tie with white polka dots and a pink bloodstain (from a nosebleed he'd had over the winter from taking too many nosedrops for a cold). Maria hadn't said anything about how he looked when he left the house. Maria hadn't said anything at all. Shit. He'd just realized: He'd slept last night on the couch in the living room—slept badly: a superficial torpor generally interrupted by periods of wakefulness; he could've watched the ball game live instead of taping it. He could've been depressed at the time Doctor K was getting kayoed—depressed live instead of on tape. Except he wouldn't watch the game now because he knew the score. Shit.

Charly Johnstone looked him up and down. "You look like Dave. You're not, are you?"

"I don't think so. No. Dave who?"

"A Broadway denizen. He hangs around stage doors and collects autographs."

Neuman shook his head. "I got Tom Seaver's autograph once, when I was working in uniform out at Shea. But no, I'm not Dave."

Charly sniffed. "You're the cop who just phoned and asked to meet me here."

"Yeah. Well, actually, he's the cop who phoned"—Neuman wagged his thumb over his shoulder—"Detective Federici. He's got a better telephone voice, so he made the call. I'm Jake Neuman."

"Detective Neuman?"

"Yeah. Well. No. Lieutenant, really, but, well . . ."

Charly's laugh whipped several times around the lobby, bouncing off the walls. "Of course. *The* Lieutenant Neuman—of Newman and Redford. I thought you were retired."

"Yeah, well."

"And you want to talk about Dimanche?"

"About who killed her, yeah."

"You want to talk here? My office is right upstairs. I find it so handy to be just an elevator ride away from the editorial offices of one of America's largest newspapers. But then, you know where my office is."

"Yeah, I do. I mean, that's why we came over. And this is as good a place as any. I mean, there's no place to sit down, but that's just as well, 'cause you don't waste any time when you have to talk standing up, if you know what I'm saying."

Charly took a reef in her shawl. "I've already spoken to the police at some length. A Lieutenant McIver."

"Yeah, I read his report," Neuman said. "His report said that when, uh, Dimanche—which I understand is French for Sunday, the day of the week, not an ice cream sundae; but she's not French, she was born in Providence, Rhode Island—when Dimanche was killed, which was sometime between a few minutes after three P.M. Tuesday, when there was a break in the rehearsal, and three-thirty or so, when her body was discovered, there were twenty-two people in the theater—the Kean, on West Four-nine. *Dying Is Easy* is the name of the play, Lieutenant McIver's report said, which is kind of hard to believe—"

" 'Dying is easy, comedy is hard,' Lieutenant. It's an old theater maxim, first uttered, some allege, by Sir Edmund Kean, the theater's eponym. There are others who attribute the apothegm to Edmund *Gwenn,* Santa Claus in *Miracle on 34th Street* to you, Lieutenant. I always thought it was Kean, myself, probably said so publicly, recall Peter O'Toole crediting it to Kean in *My Favorite Year*—not *my* favorite year, Lieutenant, a, uh, film of that name. Then I read something in the *Times,* a symposium of comedians, comic writers and assorted wits, in which Carl Reiner said the observation was Kean's and Larry Gelbart leapt in to say, *au contraire,* it was Gwenn's. Mentioned it recently to Harry Haun, who writes for the *News,* and *he* said he once interviewed George Seaton, who wrote and directed *Miracle on 34th Street,* and *Seaton* said he'd gone to the hospital on hearing Gwenn was mortally ill and said, 'Oh, Teddy, it must be terrible,' and *Gwenn* said, 'Dying is easy, blah blah blah.' Of course, Gwenn could've been quoting *Kean.* In any case, it's the title of the play, which is a mystery involving a murder in a theater."

"That's pretty hard to believe too, isn't it?" Neuman said. "Or maybe it's not. I don't know. Anyway. So. The director, uh, Jay Dillen, the producer, Martin Klein, you, and Mindy Vezetti, Dillen's secretary, were in Dillen's office between a few minutes after three P.M. Tuesday and three-thirty or so; the five other actors in the show—two men, three women—were in their dressing rooms backstage: Each one has a separate dressing room. The writer, B.G. Harris, who I'm told is a woman, was also backstage, working on a new scene for the play.

"So that's ten people involved with the play, and twelve others—stagehands and theater employees—makes twenty-two. Twenty-two people were in the theater between a few minutes after three P.M. Tuesday and three-thirty or so." Those could be Lotto numbers: 3, 10, 12, 22, 30. Except 10 and 12 were kind of close together. And he needed one more number.

"Dillen, Klein, Vezetti and you, Miss Johnstone, are alibis for each other—but not for every minute of the time in question, because you and Dillen went out to the toilet during that time and Vezetti was in an outer office. Two of the actors—a man and a woman—went out to do errands—separate errands—and're each other's alibis for part of the time they were out; for the rest

64

of the time, neither one has an alibi. The three actors who stayed in the theater—one man, Kevin Last, who it turns out was Dimanche's boyfriend, and two women—have alibis for some of the time but not all of the time. The stagehands and the theater employees have alibis for just about the whole time 'cause they were drinking coffee together. The writer has no alibi. She was working in a room right down the hall from Dimanche's dressing room and there's nobody who can swear she was in that room the whole time. Except her. She swears it.

"So Lieutenant McIver found out just about everything anybody'd want to know, except he forgot to ask you one thing, so I thought I'd ask you. Did you kill Dimanche, Miss Johnstone?"

Charly roared. "Of course not."

"Know who did?"

"Of *course* not."

"Who do you think did?"

Charly sniffed.

"Yeah, see. Sometimes that's a hard question 'cause there're so many possible answers to it. I mean, who would kill somebody, right? Just about anybody who had the opportunity is what it comes down to, sometimes. A woman like this, good-looking, smart—she was smart, wasn't she? I get the feeling she was smart—successful, rich . . . there must've been a lot of people who wanted to pop her."

Charly puffed herself up. "Not a lot of people carry guns, Lieutenant."

"You'd be surprised. You'd be really surprised. It's interesting about the gun, isn't it? I mean, there's a thirty-eight Special in her dressing room she used as a prop in the play and she gets shot with a thirty-eight Special. A coincidence? Somebody's idea of a joke? I don't know. Do you know?"

"No."

"Right. Well. Thanks."

Charly swallowed. "That's it?"

"For now. You were going out to lunch, I guess. Sorry to hold you up."

Charly made a move to shrug off the web of words he'd woven around her, then stopped. "You don't have a prior engagement, do you, Lieutenant?"

Neuman looked at his hands, as if she were talking about a disease. "Uh, well, Detective Federici and I were thinking about finding a Chock Full o'Nuts or something, maybe having some soup, a hot dog. I used to like those places—what were they called? Those German places? They had good soup, good knockwurst. They went out of business, I guess. Zum-Zum."

"Indeed. Yes. Well. I have a regular table at Sardi's and I'd be honored if you would be my guest. I think there're a few things you should know about the, uh, rialto, and what better place to enlighten you than at Sardi's, which a late colleague of mine once described as 'the club, mess hall, lounge, post office, saloon and marketplace of the people of the theater'? Detective Federici's welcome to join us, of course. Tell me, Lieutenant, does Detective Federici ever *speak?*"

"Who? Him? Oh, yeah, well, he speaks sometimes. Not as much as I do, but almost nobody speaks as much as I do. It's this thing I got. I was retired, you were right. Still am, sort of. I didn't realize it, but the whole time I was out of work I hardly spoke at all. I've been speaking so much the past twenty-four hours or so, my mouth hurts, my jaw, my cheeks, like. Not even twenty-four hours. Less."

8

Three hours later, Neuman's ears hurt too, from listening to Charly talk. And his ass, from sitting so long in one place; and his chin, from propping it up on his hands so it wouldn't come crashing down on the table if he fell asleep, for the talk induced a superficial torpor, occasionally interrupted by periods of attentiveness; and his elbows, from supporting his hands and chin; and his stomach, from too much lasagna; and his nose, from inhaling too much acrid smoke from Charly's Sherman's cigarettes; and his right hand, from shaking the right hands of too many other diners who stopped by to say hello to Charly (expressing condolences but never saying what for, as if it was bad luck on the rialto to say what you were sorry about, the way it was bad luck to say good luck or to quote from *Macbeth,* which was something Neuman had learned at CCNY when he should have been learning biology so his wife wouldn't need a vibrator) and whom she introduced, after a fashion—not always saying their names, as if their faces were nominal; and his brain, from being rialtoed.

He put the pain out of his mind to attend to Charly's peroration:

"Who had the opportunity to kill Dimanche, you asked, Lieutenant. That's what it often comes down to, you said: Who had

67

the opportunity, given that so many, many people had the motive? A woman like Dimanche, as you said, good-looking, smart—she *was* smart, Lieutenant, extremely smart, shrewd—successful, rich . . . mustn't, as you asked in your inimitable argot, mustn't there have been a lot of people who wanted to pop her? Indeed, there must have been, Lieutenant. Indeed, there were." Charly put an elbow on the table with such force the china sang and the cutlery danced; she made a fist and from it thrust a spatular thumb. "Martin Klein. Once the Midas of the Great White Way, now just another name in the Business-to-Business Yellow Pages—Theatrical Managers and Produc-ers. A man in search of one more success to close out a career in which the misses of yester*day* threaten to eclipse the hits of yester*year*. Why would Martin Klein kill Dimanche? Quite simply, to keep from opening a show that in all likelihood would, on its opening night, have posted its closing notice. How does it happen? is the question I can see in your eyes—you have extraordinary eyes, Lieutenant; questing eyes—how does it happen that a play is mounted by intelligent, experienced peo-ple and yet has no chance on earth of being commercially or critically successful? How does money and time and creative energy get spent on a bomb, a turkey, a loser, by people who if the product were someone else's would know from the briefest glimpse that a bomb, a turkey, a loser is what it was? One of life's great mysteries, Lieutenant, one to which I have not even a *soupçon* of an answer, except perhaps to suggest that beneath the cynical exterior of even the most hardened Broadway vet-eran there beats the heart of a small child who fervently be-lieves that wishing something makes it so."

She catapulted her forefinger up to join her thumb. "Jay Dillen. The next Mike Nichols, *Variety* once called him, to which John Simon retorted, 'the last, I fervently hope, Jay Dillen.' A director lauded for his skill at directing women, when a more precise action word would be manipulating; a lothario who has his casting couch reupholstered thrice yearly, such a beating does it take; married four times to three women—yes, he tied the knot with one of them twice, Lieutenant—divorced four times, a three- or four-time loser, depending on how you look at it, in the marital lists. Why would Jay Dillen kill Dimanche? Quite simply, because she wouldn't sleep with him and because waiting in the wings was another starlet who would, who had, who does. Amanda Becker. Jay Dillen wanted Amanda Becker to play the lead in *Dying Is Easy*, Lieutenant, notwithstanding that the part was conceived with Dimanche in mind. 'A Monroe for the Eighties,' the stage business reads, and Dimanche was just that, while Amanda Becker is more Hepburn—Kate *or* Audrey—than Monroe.

"Jay had the taste, the discretion, the sense—remarkable, since those are three traits in which he is altogether deficient —to defer to the choice of the producer and the principal backer, but there's no question in my mind that the choice rankled. Jay was misdirecting Dimanche—he was giving her free rein when her relative inexperience required that she be held in close check. He was letting her look bad, in the hope, I believe, that the producer and the principal backer would see the mistake they'd made and raise the alarum—send out an emergency call for the lovely Amanda. But they weren't about to do that; they'd crossed their bridges and burned them behind them. There was nothing for it, if Jay wanted Amanda on stage on opening night—and he wanted it with all his heart, and it now looks as though he will get his wish, because the show *will* go on, Lieutenant, and Amanda has been summoned to hurry here *toute de suite* from California, where she'd been taking meetings, and I'm sure, knowing Amanda, giving a few, with some important helmers and dealmakers (she'd be a suspect too, Amanda, if she'd been in town)—there was nothing for it but to eradicate Dimanche . . . Dimanche, I repeat, who had spurned Jay's advances, quite publicly, at this very table once, in fact, before *tout* New York—or a part of it that counts for a great deal, at any rate."

Neuman wondered: If the sun were the size of the globe in the lobby of the Daily News Building and the earth, comparatively, were the size of a walnut and located at the main entrance to Grand Central Terminal, how big would *tout* New York be, and how big the part of New York that counted for a great deal?

Charly added her middle finger to the group. "Kevin Last. A supporting player in *Dying Is Easy,* but Dimanche's main squeeze and her discoverer, just a few short years ago a bass guitar player in a fifth-rate rock-and-roll band in search of a gimmick and possessed of enough savvy to know that her sex appeal was it; an opportunist *extraordinaire,* not a Svengali, exactly, for having achieved top billing, Dimanche was her own person, made her own decisions, thought for herself and with herself in mind; more a . . . a . . . Well, I don't know that there is a literary precedent. Why would Kevin Last kill Dimanche? Quite simply, jealousy. He made her a star; she shone with an incandescence that subsumed the light of his puny talents. He'd been relegated to the role of camp follower, Kevin; he got a part in the play because Martin Klein sagely figured that the female fans of Dimanche's band would enjoy seeing one of her leather-clad janissaries strutting his stuff in another medium. Dimanche, according to the grapevine, was about to dump Kevin; perhaps she already had. She had a new fellow; nobody seems to know who he was—an outlander, somebody from the other side of the deep, deep moat that surrounds the tight little island that is Broadway. Kevin beat her up—you *should* write this down, Detective Federici; you should check with the Sixth Precinct's Detective Winger—like Debra Winger, but no relation."

"Beat her up when?" Neuman said.

"Last week."

"Where?"

"Chez elle. Her fashionable Greenwich Village town house."

"She report it?"

"After a fashion. She told Detective Winger she'd been, uh, mugged—"

"Mugged in her house?"

"She *told* him she'd been mugged on the street out*side* her house, by a fictive Hispanic youth."

"My wife's Hispanic. Puerto Rican. I don't know what a fictive His— Oh. You mean she made him up."

"Indeed."

"You know about this, Steve?"

"Yeah." Federici didn't look up from his notetaking.

"Yeah, what?"

"Sorry, Lieutenant. I mean, I read about it, the mugging, and then I just forgot it, I guess. You think there might be a connection?"

Of course there was a connection; the earth was the size of a walnut, or might as well be. "So Dimanche told you—what?"

he said to Charly. "That Kevin Last beat her up and—what?—talked her into calling it a mugging?"

Charly waved away the cloud of smoke from a new cigarette. "I must confess that I've been speculating. Dimanche *was* the recipient of some blows about the face and eyes; she *did* tell Detective Winger that she'd been mugged. *I* deduced from certain hints that she gave that she'd concocted the mugging story to cover up the truth—namely, that she'd been abused by one of her boyfriends."

"You just said Kevin Last. Now you're saying *one* of her boyfriends."

Charly shrugged. "Perhaps this new chap beat her up. Isn't that what a certain kind of man does—to get a woman's attention, as it were?"

"Maybe her ex-husband beat her up," Neuman said. "Detective Federici tells me she has one."

"From her days as Juliet Marko, one of the pioneers of the Hoboken Sound, just another rather tuneless songbird in the verdant bush that is the New York pop music scene. That was a long time ago, Lieutenant, as things are measured in our disposable society; her ex- hardly figures in her present."

"Yeah, well. That might be a good reason he'd want to beat her up, even kill her. You were telling me all the reasons some other people had to kill Dimanche. You think of anybody else who had a reason—offhand, I mean?"

Somehow, Charly got her ring finger to stand up by itself, something that made Neuman's hand hurt just to watch. "Vivian Thibault Wyndham. The principal backer of *Dying Is Easy,* a resident of Park House, Lloyd Harbor, Hyannis Port, Lyford Cay, Palm Beach, Aspen and Juan-les-Pins; widow of Hubert Kraven Wyndham, whose father invented a doodad about yea big"—she held the thumb and forefinger of her nonsmoking hand an inch apart—"that apparently one simply cannot drill for oil without; an heiress in her own right, to the Thibault insecticide fortune—an oxymoron if ever I've heard one; a member of more clubs than I have fingers—*knuckles* on my fingers; a—"

"She's a hundred years old," Neuman said. "Isn't she?"

Charly laughed. "Eighty-two, if she's a day."

Neuman sighed. "Why would she want to kill Dimanche?"

"Because she's eighty-two if she's a day, Lieutenant. Because she'd bet a piece of the Thibault-Wyndham fortune on the head of a beautiful, sexy, thin, young thing who it was beginning to look didn't have the stuff to give the play legs—another theatrical term, Lieutenant. Do I think Viv Thib Wynd, as I like to call her behind her back, killed Dimanche? Of course not; she's eighty-two if she's a day. Do I think she *had* her killed? *Pourquoi pas?* The rich don't get richer by throwing good money after bad, Lieutenant."

Charly waggled her pinkie. "B.G. Harris. The author of *Dying Is Easy,* a novice, a tyro, a rank beginner, a housewife, practically, although the house she kept—in Bloomington, Indiana, if you can imagine that; or is it Bloom*field,* or -berg or -ville or -town? in any case, it's not Blooms*bury*—the house she kept was a solitary one: no husband, no boyfriend, no, uh, best friend of the female gender, no roommate, no decrepit mother or dysfunctional brother; just a cat, and B.G., tap, tap, tapping at her typewriter, for four . . . solid . . . years, working nights as a room clerk at a Howard Johnson's or something similarly grim, and turning out, *mirabile dictu* and *lectu* and *visu,* a play that was not half bad, a play with wit and charm and 'a palpable suspense,' as one of the out-of-town critics put it, whatever that means; sending it over the transom to Howard Lessik, this here town's premier theatrical literary agent, a man so protected against such upstart outpourings from the hinterlands that his secretary is armed with a rubber stamp that says 'refused by addressee'—they don't even open the stuff, Lieutenant—but somehow penetrating the laager's defenses, somehow getting it read, and, the most wonderful of wonders, not only getting it read but getting it appreciated, enthused over and, last but not least, produced, by the aforementioned Martin Klein. Why would B.G. Harris kill Dimanche? Quite simply, for the same reason as the aforementioned Martin Klein: to keep the show from going on. There's something you should know, Lieutenant: There were problems with the play, as you've already noted; some of them were technical—having to do with staging and blocking and interpretation; some of them were textual. B.G. had never written a play; she'd never really even *seen* a play; she's a great reader, but of novels, which don't have the exigencies of plays. A novelist can, if he wishes, order the entire Red Chinese Army to appear on his protagonist's doorstep; a playwright—"

"Uh, Miss Johnstone. We're kind of running out of time."

"Yes, quite. All right, then. Well. All I wanted to say, and I'll say it briefly, is that on Tuesday, between three and three-thirty or so, when Dimanche was killed, B.G. was backstage working on a rewrite of a problematic scene. As you've noted, she has no alibi, other than her own word that her backstage office is where she was and writing is what she was doing. She swore to it, is what you said. Well, I'd just like you to know that it was I who went to that backstage office to tell B.G. what had befallen the leading maiden of her maiden play. B.G. was shocked, horrified, dumbstruck—all of the appropriate emotions. She had also—and this is the point, Lieutenant—not written word one on her IBM Selectric typewriter; the page before her was a *tabula rasa;* there were no pages—I should be a detective, Lieutenant; what questing eyes I have—no pages crumpled up on the floor around her or in the wastebasket alongside her chair. She'd been procrastinating; she was blocked; or . . . she'd been busy elsewhere. . . . There is one more suspect, Lieutenant."

Neuman propped his chin in his hands. "Yeah? Who?"

Charly sat up straight and beamed, setting all her fingers to doing a samba. *"Moi.* Me, myself, I. The Big Apple's press agent's press agent, the *ne plus ultra* of the—"

Neuman semaphored his hands. "Yeah, well. Okay. Look. Miss Johnstone. I appreciate you taking the time to tell us all this stuff. And I understand that you're bending over backwards to be, you know, fair by including yourself among the suspects—"

"But I *am* a suspect, Lieutenant," Charly said. She pouted. "Am I not?"

"You want to be a suspect, you're a suspect. What I want to ask you, and I don't want to sit here all day waiting for it to come up in the, uh, course of the conversation, is what about the stagehands?"

Charly sniffed, as if she could smell them. "What about them?"

"Sometimes they kill people. At least once, anyway. A couple of years ago, that young woman in the New York Philharmonic—"

"It was the Metropolitan Opera orchestra, Lieutenant, and, yes, she was killed by a stagehand, one whose overtures, if you'll pardon the expression, she had rebuffed, but I hardly think that's reason to condemn the entire profession. Stagehands, well, they're a lot more loyal bunch than most people give them credit for being. They take a lot of flak for being members of a union that has, very cleverly, I think, devised ways for its members to get paid even when they don't work, that has—"

"Okay. Well. Yeah. Look, Miss Johnstone, thanks very much for the info and the feed—that's great lasagna. We got to get moving. Steve, give her our numbers, will you, please? Anything comes up, Miss Johnstone, give us a call, okay? Nice meeting you. Steve, I'll meet you outside. I got to go to the head."

In the men's room, Neuman splashed water on his face and scrubbed it and dried it, not looking with those questing eyes of his in the mirror at the reflection that waited to ask him what the fuck he was doing there, he was retired, wasn't he? Bobby was dead, wasn't he, so what did Dimanche's name being on a list of his that looked like a hit list have anything to do with anything, and in particular with him? Why should he come out of retirement just because somebody his ex- and dead partner was maybe thinking about killing happened to get killed? He had a Hispanic wife who wasn't fictive, didn't he, who wasn't dead, and she had a problem, didn't she, and her problem was his problem, wasn't it?

And, he wondered, *did* Steve Federici ever speak? He'd spoken the other day, around the corner from Neuman's house, but he wasn't speaking now—just the way Bobby Redfield, after a time Neuman could point to only in hindsight, hadn't spoken.

Neuman finally looked at himself with those questing eyes and told himself to stop thinking that way.

"Are you going to spend another night on the sofa, Jacob?"

"Yeah, well. I mean, no, not necessarily. I just thought, well, that you're probably still mad."

Maria leaned against the living room door, her arms crossed under her breasts. She wore a quilted robe; her hair was down and brushed to a sheen. "I'm very sad, Jacob. I'm disappointed. I'm confused. I have always thought that we were everything to each other—"

"Hey, babe, you're everything to me."

"Let me finish. Please. That we were husband and wife and lovers and friends and confidantes and helpers—that you were even a little bit of a father to me and I was a little bit of a daughter to you. But I think perhaps—and I do not think it is a bad thing—I think perhaps no one can be all of those things to another person. Especially, no one can be another person's therapist." She paused, anticipating an explosion; somehow, he managed to squelch it. "In working with Morton, I have come to understand that, very simply, a person's physical health is a reflection of his or her mental health. Headaches, backaches, respiratory problems—they are all in some way related to emotions. I am overweight; so are you. It is not just metabolism that makes us that way; we are protecting ourselves against the world. With so much protection, it is difficult for us to be as intimate as we might; it is difficult for us to get as close as we might. We have orgasms, but they are not as complete as they might be. Your face says you think an orgasm is an orgasm."

And that there's no fat on a vibrator, you can get as intimate with it as you want. "Hey, babe. I'm just listening, okay?"

"In the work I do with Morton there exists the possibility of a complete orgasm—"

I'll break his fucking legs.

"I intend to do the work—"

And his arms.

"And I would like you to do it too—not along with me but on your own—"

I get him on his own, I'll cut his balls off.

"Otherwise, there is the danger that I will be making demands on you that you cannot fulfill—"

Can a vibrator kiss you? Can a vibrator lick you?

Maria stood up straight. "You have nothing to say."

He shrugged. "What difference does it make? I mean, you've got it all figured out; it doesn't sound like you're looking for any, you know, input."

After a long time, Maria said, "There were some phone calls."

Good. "Yeah?"

"Miles Easterly called. He wants you to go to the Personnel Department first thing in the morning."

"Yeah."

"Something about getting your badge and taking a marksmanship test."

"Umm."

"And a woman named Nell Ward called. She wants to have lunch."

"Don't start in, babe. Don't make it into something it isn't."

"Don't make what?"

"She's making a movie—a documentary—about cops. She wants to film me walking down the street or something, probably, looking in garbage cans, knocking on doors."

"She sounded very attractive—and very intelligent."

"Yeah, well. She's a kid."

"I am going to bed now, Jacob. I am very angry with you and I want you to spend another night on the sofa. That is what I *want,* and having what I *want* is what all of this is about. You should try and decide what it is that you want, Jacob. When you are ready to talk about what it is you want, I will be ready to listen."

How about next year? I have some free time in March, I think.

"Yeah. Okay."

"If you are in this woman's movie, Jacob," Maria said, "I hope you will wear some decent clothes."

9

"Hi."

Artie held his hand out but didn't look up from his newspaper. "Ticket?"

"No. No ticket."

"Cost you ten bucks, you lost your ticket."

"My car's not parked here."

"You want a space, read the sign: We're full up."

"I want to ask you some questions."

"My mother taught me never talk to strangers."

"Your mother teach you to be an asshole, or did you pick that up on your own?"

Artie closed the paper and folded it and put it in his hip pocket. "Who's calling who a asshole?" He almost added *skinhead,* but the effect of the man's total baldness was more menacing than Milquetoast.

"I'm calling you an asshole—Artie. And it's your asshole you're going to have to start worrying about—Artie—in the joint."

Artie felt a twinge there, and moved around on the metal folding chair. "You a cop?"

"A reporter."

"We already talked to the cops."

77

"I know. Were you sitting outside like this on Tuesday morning, or did you hear the shot and come outside?"

"What's it to you?"

"What it is to me is I wonder what you're hiding."

"Hey, man, I tolja—"

"You told me you talked to the cops. If you talked to the cops and you're still out on the street, you must not have anything to hide."

". . . That's right."

"If you told them the truth."

"Hey, man, you saying I'm a liar?"

Terry Niles opened his notebook. "Are you, Artie?"

"Come you know my name, man?"

"It's on your jacket—man."

"Oh." Artie fingered the embroidered script on his breast. "I don't want my name in the paper, man."

"Okay."

"So put the notebook away, man."

"Look, Artie—Artie Fenestra—your name's not only on your jacket, *man;* it's on pieces of paper at police precincts all over town, which is what happens when you talk to the cops. Those pieces of paper have a way of getting left out on desks where people who're interested in such things can have a look at them, if they're of a mind to. If I'm the first reporter to find you, I won't be the last. There'll be TV cameras, lights, microphones; you're liable to get nervous, say something you shouldn't say. I'm giving you a chance to say it in a relaxed situation, no pressure. You don't want your name in the paper, I won't put your name in the paper. But I still want to talk to you—because you know some things I'd like to know, things you didn't tell the cops. Not because you're a a liar but because you're a smart guy, you don't tell anybody any more than you have to; they ask you a question, you give them an answer to that question—nothing more. Am I right?"

"Well, uh, yeah. Yeah, you're right."

"Of course I'm right, Artie. So tell me, Artie, were you sitting outside like this on Tuesday, around four-thirty, five o'clock in the morning?"

Artie cocked his head. "Tuesday. Tuesday. I don't remember. I might a been, I might not a been."

"See anything unusual?"

"Whattaya mean?"

"I know you saw a guy get shot, Artie, and I know—"

"Hey, man, we didn't *see* him get shot, you dig? We saw he *was* shot, you know what I'm saying? But we didn't *see* him get shot."

" 'We,' meaning you and"—Niles looked back through his notebook—"Jerry Marder?"

"Come you know so much, man?"

"I'm a reporter, Artie. It's my job to know things, like it's your job to park cars. Okay, so you didn't see the guy get shot. That's not what I'm asking you, anyway, Art. I know it's unusual to see a guy die—even a guy you didn't see get shot— but what I'm asking you is did you see anything else unusual? In particular, did you see anyone else—anyone other than the guy who died?"

Artie shrugged. "No. Like who?"

"You tell me, Artie."

"I tolja—no."

"I take it back, Artie. I think you are a liar."

"Yeah? Well, go fuck yourself."

Niles took a step inside the garage. "Jerry around?"

"He went to— No. No, he's out sick. The flu."

"A bad liar, Artie. How big was the guy?"

"What guy?"

"The shooter. *You* didn't shoot him, did you, Artie?"

"No, man. Hey."

"I didn't think you did. But you *did* see the shooter."

"You axing me or telling me, man?"

"I'm telling you. Are you blackmailing him, is that it, Artie? Are you leaning on him to pay you to keep quiet?"

"I don't know what the fuck you're talking about, man." *"Artie?"*

Artie startled at the sound and saw Jerry standing in a pool of light thirty feet from the garage entrance, knees bent, arms spread out like a runner leading off first. Except that he had a paper bag in one hand. Except that, the pitcher having seen him, there was nothing to do but run away forever or come back to the base. The dumb fuck.

"Hello, Jerry," Niles said.

"Who's this guy, Artie?" Jerry whispered, tiptoeing, with the wild illogic of the dumb and the fucked, toward the garage.

Niles waited until Jerry sat on the front edge of the folding chair next to Artie's. "How big would you say the guy was, Jerry?"

"You *told* him?"

"You schmuck, Jerry."

"Told me what, Jer?"

"Shut the fuck up, Jerry. Don't say anything."

"My size? Or bigger? Or not as big?"

"I tolja, Artie. I tolja we should a told 'em."

"Why didn't you, Jerry? Is the guy someone you know?"

"We don't even know if it was a guy. I thought—"

"Jerry."

"Thought what, Jerry? That it was a woman?"

"Well—"

"Jerry."

"What the fuck, Artie? I mean, if they know, they know. We should a told them in the first—"

"This guy's not a *cop,* Jerry. He's a fucking reporter. We don't have to tell him *noth*ing."

"You really do, Jerry," Niles said. "You really do. It's not just your civic responsibility. You'll sleep better if you tell me. How're you sleeping these days, Jer?"

"Well—"

"Jerry."

"Bad, hunh, Jer? Nightmares, right?"

". . . Yeah."

"You scumbag, Jerry." Artie got off his stool and stalked inside.

Niles put a hand on Jerry's shoulder. "What'd this woman look like, Jer? Tall? Short? Fat? Thin?"

Jerry looked over his shoulder.

"You have a cigarette, Jer?"

"Don't smoke."

"You're smart. What did she look like?"

"It was dark."

"Tall?"

"Medium."

"Fat?"

"Medium."

"Hair? Long? Short? Blond? Brunette?"

"I . . ."

"What, Jerry?"

"I think she had a hat on."

"What kind of hat?"

"I don't know what it's called."

"Draw it." Niles held out his notebook and pen.

"I can't draw, man."

"A woman's hat? A man's hat—with a brim? A baseball cap? Come on, Jerry, this isn't a contest."

Jerry drew a lumpy oval, then a small semicircle under it.

"That looks like a blimp, Jer—not a hat. Unless . . . You mean it was like a newsboy's hat, they used to call them? A golf cap?"

"Yeah. Yeah, that's it."

Niles took the notebook and pen back and improved the drawing. "Clothes? What kind of clothes was she wearing? A dress? Pants?"

"A coat. A big coat."

"It was warm, Jerry. Like right now. Indian summer."

"She's a *bag* lady."

"Oh?"

"You know—they wear coats all a time."

"Right, Jer. I know. So she might've been thin, and wearing a big coat—or maybe a couple of coats—made her look medium."

"Yeah. She might a."

"Shoes, Jer? Boots? Sneakers? Heels?"

Jerry turned and looked into the garage. "Did he tell you about . . . ?"

"About what, Jerry?"

"The . . . the ticket."

"No. What ticket?"

"I shouldn't tell you, he didn't tell you."

"They're your nightmares, Jer."

". . . The Lotto ticket."

"She dropped a Lotto ticket?"

"No. He did. Nowhere Man. He didn't drop it, he . . . he had it, in the pocket a his shorts, like."

"That's funny, don't you think, Jer?"

"Yeah."

"Would you carry around a Lotto ticket in the pocket of your shorts when you went out jogging?"

"No. No, I wouldn't. I mean, I don't jog. I play handball, I don't jog, but I wouldn't carry a Lotto ticket in the pocket a my shorts when I was out jogging, no. No, I wouldn't."

"Especially when you weren't carrying any other ID, right, Jer?"

"Right."

"You didn't—you and Artie, I mean—you didn't take the guy's ID, did you, Jer?"

"No. We told the cops, man. No."

"I believe you, Jer. You didn't take his keys, his wallet, his money?"

"We didn't take nothing, man."

"Except the ticket." Niles waited for a moment, then went on. "The way I see it, Jerry, the only explanation for a guy carrying a Lotto ticket in the pocket of his shorts when he's not carrying a wallet, money or keys is he'd just bought the Lotto ticket."

"That's what I said, man. That's what I told Artie. I told him we should a told the cops about the bag lady 'cause when the guy who sold the winning ticket, the newsstand guy or the guy in the candy store, when he re*mem*bers he sold the winning ticket to the guy in the jogging shorts, re*mem*bers because he *was* in jogging shorts— I mean, how many guys in jogging shorts stop to buy a Lotto ticket at four in the morning, which was what he must a done, 'cause otherwise why carry it around on him? Thirty-six million, or whatever Artie said? No. One— Re*mem*bers because he *was* in jogging shorts, recognizes from seeing his picture in the paper that he's the guy got offed, tells the cops that's the guy he sold the ticket to, not us, the cops figure we must a offed the guy, took his ticket, the cops come around, say you took his *tick*et, didn't you, you *offed* him, didn't you? We say we took his *tick*et but we didn't *off* him, maybe the *bag* lady offed him, they say what *bag* lady, we say the *bag* lady we saw 'cross the street, they say you didn't tell us about no *bag* lady, we say there was one, they say, yeah, sure, what you mean, you murderers, is you're telling us there was one *now*, but you didn't tell us *yes*terday, you're just trying to get off the

82

hook. *That's* why we should a told them about the *bag* lady, I told Artie. *That's* why. And not only that—the guy in the jogging shorts who got offed is the guy me and Artie seen running by here every day, just about, every day for, I don't know, a year, just about. Around six, six-thirty, usually, 'cause I remember once I almost backed into him with the blue Marquis."

Niles stood up and rubbed his thighs. "What makes you think it's the winning ticket, Jerry?"

"Artie thinks so."

"What're the numbers?"

"I . . . I don't know if I should tell you."

"Jerry . . ."

"Uh, 2, 5, 8, 9, 42, 44."

"Mean anything special to you, Jer?"

"Nah. But Artie, Artie thinks it's the winning ticket."

"Artie's a thinker, isn't he?"

"Yeah. Like Jackie Sharps."

"Who's Jackie Sharps."

"Friend a ours doing points in Rahway."

Niles laughed. "I have to go now, Jer, but I'm going to come around again in a couple of days." He took out his wallet and handed a card to Jerry. "If anything comes up, Jerry, call me, okay? That's my number at the paper, and if I'm not there the switchboard'll pick up and'll know how to reach me. I'll make sure they know you might be calling."

"Terry Niles?"

Niles shrugged.

"I read your stuff all a time, man. I mean, I seen you on TV talking about how you was the first guy to call him Nowhere Man, man. I should a recognized you, man, on account of, you know, the hair, man."

"Call me, Jer—okay?—if anything comes up. And see if you can't talk some sense into Artie. Artie the thinker."

Jerry laughed. "Yeah. Artie the thinker. Like Jackie Sharps."

"Want to crack it up, babe?" The fat man handed Nell Ward a glass pipe and a gold Dunhill lighter. Bob Seger sang on the tape deck: "Fire Lake."

She flicked at the black cat to make a place for herself on the

83

worn sofa and sat, holding the pipe far from her—that fateful moment between contemplation and commission. "Do you ever clean this place?"

The fat man looked around the apartment, which was like a cave—dark, damp, littered with detritus. "Since when're you an uptown girl? Crack it up, babe, you'll think you're in a Park Avenue penthouse."

She'd been bred in a Park Avenue penthouse, but he didn't know that and wasn't being ironic. She flicked the lighter and held the flame under the bowl.

"So what's new, Nellie?" The fat man sat in a sprung armchair, pulling a copy of *Oui* out from under him and tossing it onto the midden in a corner of the room. "Who you fucking these days?"

"My hand."

He laughed. "I heard you were seeing someone."

"It didn't work out."

He grinned. "You do my blow, it'd be a friendly gesture to fuck me, don't you think?"

She shivered.

He put his hands on the chair arms, a regal slob. "So what's new? Still making movies?"

"A movie about cops."

"Bullshit."

"Homicide cops."

"Bull*shit.*"

The rush came and went so fast she wanted to ask for her money back. Except that she hadn't paid him. She was about to pay him. But first she had to assuage the hunger. She got up and went to the refrigerator, which nearly toppled when she opened it.

"You got to be careful with that," the fat man said. "The floor tilts, or something."

The refrigerator was empty, except for a six-pack of Rolling Rock. "God."

He laughed, and unzipped his jeans. "You're hungry, Nellie, eat this."

Maybe it didn't go so perfectly.
Of course it did.

Maybe somebody saw me.

Who?

The doorman.

The doorman was asleep.

I didn't know he was going to be asleep. That was too risky.

It was always a risk; that's why you wore the coat and the hat. All the doorman would've seen, if he had been awake, was someone leaving early in a big coat and hat; he wouldn't've asked any questions—you were leaving the building, not trying to come in.

He got up before the alarm went off.

The doorman?

Nowhere Man. Ha ha.

Ha ha.

If I hadn't heard him in the bathroom, I wouldn't've waked up.

Don't be ridiculous. You were awake all night.

I was nervous.

You were wired—that's different from nervous.

Maybe somebody saw me on the street.

Being seen and being recognized, identified, are very different things.

I left some things at his apartment.

What kinds of things?

A leotard. Some tights. Exercise things.

Do they have your name in them?

No.

So? Besides, remember, they don't know who he is.

He's nowhere.

That's right.

He's nothing.

Exactly.

God, I feel good.

You bet we do.

10

If the sun were the size of the globe in the lobby of the Daily News Building and the earth, comparatively, were the size of a walnut and located at the main entrance to Grand Central Terminal, would the walnut's inhabitants be as predictable as the real thing's? Would they, in particular, to a man and woman, unswervingly, without fail, like clockwork, so you could bet on it, bank on it, write home about it, always—*always* —tell a cop who came to ask them a few questions about a murder that they'd already talked to the cops?

"His name was McSomething," Vivian Thibault Wyndham said.

"Iver." Neuman said it loudly, for she sat at one end of her living room on the thirty-fifth floor of Park House and he and Federici sat at the other; the ceiling was somewhere overhead and the walls somewhere to the left and right of him and he felt the size of a walnut. "Look. Mrs. Wyndham. We won't take a lot of your time. We don't have a lot of time. We've got a lot of people to talk to—twenty-two people who were in the Kean Theater around the time Dimanche was killed sometime after the rehearsal break on Tuesday afternoon. And it turns out you make twenty-three, because you were at the Kean Theater and left just before the rehearsal break. In fact, it was on account

86

of you there was a rehearsal break, they tell me, because you didn't like the way things were going on stage. You told the producer, Mr. Klein, you didn't like the way things were going, they took a break. Is that right?"

Vivian Thibault Wyndham sniffed. "What did you say your name was?"

"Neuman."

"Detective Neuman?"

"Sure. Why not. Look. Mrs. Wyndham—"

"And your partner's name?"

Neuman waited, but Federici didn't speak, so he did. "This is Detective Federici."

"Freesi?"

"Fed-er-ici. Mrs. Wyndham, did you kill Dimanche?"

Vivian Thibault Wyndham moved her foot in a peculiar way. When a door several light-years away to the north-northeast opened, Neuman realized she'd pressed some sort of button under the carpet that summoned the butler, who must have been waiting pretty close by, for he had the door open in a few seconds, even if it did take him a couple of weeks to get to where she was sitting to see what she wanted. Not that he was as decrepit as his mistress, or the furniture; he was in good shape, the shape of an ex–football player or wrestler, one who still worked out, one who wouldn't mind throwing somebody out on his ear, who would probably enjoy it. "Evans, would you be so good as to see these gentle—"

"Just hang on a sec, Evans, okay?" Neuman said. "You put your meathooks on either of us I'll see you spend the rest of the day in the Tombs for obstructing a homicide investigation. You won't like it there, Evans. The people aren't your kind of people, they don't ask you would you be so good, they tell you to bend over and spread your cheeks. They have a women's lockup there too, Mrs. Wyndham." Interesting, that he could talk like that (he'd almost called her Viv Thib Wynd), being retired and not carrying a gun and a badge and all. When he'd been on the force, carrying a gun and a badge and all, he'd hardly ever talked like that. That was the way cops talked in the movies and on TV, cops whose lines were dreamed up by writers who'd never been face-to-face with psychotic killers or strung-out junkies or arrogant mobsters or mean crowds or an ex–football player or wrestler who would probably enjoy throwing somebody out on his ear. Or maybe they had. What did he know? Why didn't Federici talk like that? He had a gun and a badge and all. Why didn't Federici talk at all?

Vivian Thibault Wyndham flicked a finger and Evans began the long trek back to where he'd come from, but not before giving Neuman a look that tickled the hairs on the back of his neck.

"So, Detective Neuman," Vivian Thibault Wyndham said.

Neuman said, "Yeah."

She got out of her chair and went to the window overlooking Fifth Avenue, Central Park, California. "I have many houses, gentlemen."

"Right. Park House, here. Lloyd's Harbor. Hyannisville. The Florida Keys. Palm Springs. Aspen and One Lay Pan."

She laughed an affectionate laugh at Neuman's ingenuous gazetteer. "Indeed. And do you know that sometimes I wake up in the morning with some uncertainty as to where I am?"

"Must be rough. I have mornings like that too, and I got just one house. In Rego Park."

"Except for New York," Vivian Thibault Wyndham said. "When I wake up in New York, I have no doubt where I am."

"Yeah. Well. It's pretty noisy in New York. I mean, you're pretty high up here, you can still hear the traffic."

She turned to faced them, a wraith against the bright window. "The reason, Detective Neuman, that I know I'm in New York is not the noise of traffic. It's the sound of the cocks crowing in the Children's Zoo in the park."

"Hunh," Neuman said, and wondered if she had ever heard the bears growling, or, during their superficial torpor, generally interrupted by periods of wakefulness, snoring. Except there were no bears in the Children's Zoo, and the main zoo was closed for renovation. Wasn't it? What did he know?

"No, I didn't kill Dimanche," Vivian Thibault Wyndham said. "I could have, figuratively. I could have slapped her and shaken her and upbraided her and, figuratively, killed her, for treating the play—my investment—as though it were some . . . some vanity production mounted for the delectation of her admirers and, in particular, herself. I did none of those things, especially the last."

"Un hunh. Well. Any idea who did?"

"As I explained to the other police officer—a lieutenant, I believe he was, Lieutenant McSomething—"

"Iver."

From the way she looked at him, with a glint of exasperation in her eye, it was clear she thought the word was police-ese: *"Unit Six, report of shots fired on West Four-two between Eight and Nine. K." "Iver, Central. Unit Six responding."* "As I explained to Lieutenant McSomething, I would imagine that someone with Dimanche's upbringing and background, someone from her social milieu, someone in her line of, shall we say, work, would have accrued to herself over the course of even a brief lifetime a considerable number of enemies."

And if the sun were the size of the globe in the lobby of the Daily News Building and the earth, comparatively, were the size of a walnut and located at the main entrance to Grand Central Terminal, would the walnut's inhabitants ever tire of reminding you that everyone has enemies? "Right. Well. You got an alibi, Mrs. Wyndham?"

She smiled, or so he thought; the backlighting obscured her features. "No."

"No?"

"As I explained to the other officer, I was rather distraught after the display Dimanche put on at the rehearsal. I didn't fancy being cooped up in my car in traffic, so I gave my chauffeur the afternoon off and walked home."

"Un hunh. That's what he said—the other officer. That's what your chauffeur said too. And from what the doorman says, that sounds about right, 'cause you left the theater a little after three and didn't get home till a little after four. That's about how long it would take for someone to walk from West Four-nine, where the theater is, to East Six-three, which is where we are."

"Someone my age and with my various afflictions, you mean, Detective Neuman." As if to demonstrate some of them, she walked back to the chair, limping slightly, and sat, slowly.

"Yeah. Well. But you see, the thing is, that's also how long it would take for someone to leave the theater on West Four-nine, tell their chauffeur they were going to walk home, walk down to Broadway, say, look to see that he'd driven off—West

Four-nine's one-way westbound, so he'd've gone the other way, toward Eighth Avenue—walk back to the theater, go backstage, knock on the dressing room door, shoot Dimanche— whatever afflictions you got, Mrs. Wyndham, they don't look like they'd keep you from pulling a trigger—go back outside, walk a little ways, just so when you got in a taxi the cabbie wouldn't think you were coming out of the Kean, get in a taxi, drive around a little bit, maybe do some shopping, get another taxi, have him drop you off down at the Plaza, say, walk up here, get here a little after four."

"You're quite impertinent, Detective Neuman," Vivian Thibault Wyndham said. "And quite delightful."

"Yeah. Well." *Tell it to my wife. My wife thinks I'm a pain in the ass lately.*

"Of course . . ." Vivian Thibault Wyndham held up a forefinger, then let it die.

"Of course, what?"

"Well . . ." She let her head droop too.

He knew what was coming, but he had to encourage it. "Yeah?"

"I don't know if I should say this."

"Say it."

"It's really none of my business."

"Yeah, well. That's okay."

"Martin Klein . . ."

"What about him?"

"Well, one hears talk . . ."

"Yeah, one does."

"Talk of, well, debts."

That would be all she knew about debts—talk of them. "What kind of debts?"

"Debts incurred as the result of some ill-advised real estate speculation. The market is—"

"Yeah, I know, it's soft; or maybe it's hard. What do I know? What're you saying, Mrs. Wyndham? That Klein killed Dimanche to—what?—collect the insurance or something? There must be insurance against your leading lady getting bumped off."

"Indeed, there is. And indeed, I . . . Well, I would just be speculating."

90

"Speculate. This is just between us."

"Well, I don't actually think Mr. Klein *killed* Dimanche. He has, after all, as I understand it, an alibi. That is to say, his whereabouts are accounted for during the time in question."

"Yeah. So? You saying he had her killed? You saying he put out a contract on her?"

"That is, I believe, the vernacular."

Neuman got up and moved toward the door. Federici got up too, and followed, silently. "We'll want to talk to you again, Mrs. Wyndham. You decide to go anywhere, you let us or the other officer know, okay? You know, to Palm Springs or whatever."

"Debts? Sure, I've got debts. Who doesn't have debts? You have debts, Neuman?"

If Klein said it one more time, Neuman decided, he'd get up out of his chair, throw it through the plate-glass window, and throw Klein out after it. Fifteen flights, 1500 Broadway, 15:15 in the afternoon, according to the goddamn twenty-four-hour digital clock on Klein's desk. More Lotto numbers: 15 and 15 again is 30 and 15 again is 45 and 15 again is 60, except the numbers don't go up to 60 so make it 6. Six, 15, 30, 45, and still two numbers short. How about 24, for the hours on the digital clock, and 3 for 3:15, which was what 15:15 was on a twenty-four-hour clock. Wasn't it? 3, 6, 15, 24, 30, 45. Not bad numbers. "Yeah, Klein, I got debts, but none that if I killed somebody would be forgiven, if you know what I'm saying. Did you kill Dimanche, Klein?"

Klein rolled his eyes. "I already talked to the cops, I already told them I got an alibi."

"A pretty good one too, I got to say. You were in Dillen's office from three to three-thirty, at one point Charly Johnstone went to the toilet, at another Dillen went to the toilet, but you weren't alone for more than a couple of seconds. I'd say you couldn't've done it, except you used the word *alibi* and people who use the word *alibi,* a lot of the time they need one, if you know what I'm saying. You didn't kill her, you know who did?"

Klein leaned across his desk. "Yeah. A nut."

"How'd he get in the theater?"

"He climbed. He flew, maybe."

"Meaning he wasn't a nut you know, he was a nut off the street."

"The Kean's in Times Square, for Christ's sake, Neuman."

"In which case you ought to have bars and nets and stuff to keep the nuts from climbing in, flying in."

Klein laughed. "It's not my theater, Neuman."

"You didn't like Dimanche, I hear," Neuman said.

"Who says?"

Neuman shrugged. "I heard it on the rialto."

Klein laughed. "I *loved* her. Oh, fuck. Sure. Okay. No, I didn't like her. How could you like her? She wore purple gloves. Look, Neuman. I'd love to talk to you some more, you and your pal here, Detective Federici—you ever say anything, Federici? —but I got an insurance adjuster coming in here in about two minutes. You want to find who killed Di*manche*, Neuman, find somebody with a motive that doesn't bring insurance adjusters breathing down his neck. I'm thinking about killing myself rather than face this insurance adjuster, doing a Brody right out this window—fifteen floors straight down to the Great White Way. Fifteen floors, Fifteen Hundred Broadway, fifteen-twenty in the afternoon. What time is fifteen-twenty? My accountant gave me this clock for my birthday, which is April fifteenth, which he thinks is funny, being an accountant. I never know what time it is; I have to count on my fingers. Fifteen-twenty is twenty after three, isn't it? The insurance adjuster should've been here five minutes ago; that's what they like to do, they like to sweat you."

"You should play some of those fifteens in the lottery," Neuman said.

"Fuck the lottery."

"You don't play the lottery?"

"Don't tell me you play the lottery, Neuman. You look like a smart guy, except you're not that smart if you're wasting your time talking to a guy who on account of Di*manche* is dead has an appointment with an insurance adjuster."

Neuman stood. "We're going to want to take a look at your books, Klein."

Klein shrugged. "Sure. Why not? They're good for a laugh. I've been thinking I should get somebody to write a score, mount a show based on my books. The critics say musical com-

92

edy is dead; I'll give them a look at my books. But I'll say it again, Neuman—'cause my books're good for a laugh doesn't mean I killed Di*manche.*"

"Is that how you pronounce it?" Neuman said. "Di*manche?*"

"How do I know?" Klein said. "She wore purple gloves."

"Who's there?"

"Kevin Last?"

"Who is it?"

"Kevin Last in?"

"Who wants to know?"

"Santa Claus. You been a good boy?"

"Who?"

Neuman nodded and Federici kicked open the door of the fifth-floor walkup on St. Mark's Place.

Kevin Last backed toward the window, his arms spread behind him, fingers splayed, the classic pose of a man out of room. "What the fuck?"

"Yeah, well. That's what comes of living in a neighborhood like this, Kev. What do they call this neighborhood these days? They still call it the East Village, or they call it something else? Northeast SoHo or something? What would that be—No-EaSoHo? You know what I call it, Kev? I call it the Lower East Side. What comes of living in a neighborhood like this, Kev, is you learn from experience you can't be too careful, you can't go opening the door to anybody who knocks. But I got another point of view, Kev. My point of view is I want to talk to you, I can't be standing around in the hall while you try and decide whether I'm on the up-and-up, whether I'm here to collect something you owe me or try and sell you an encyclopedia or beat the shit out of you. How come you live in a dump like this when your girlfriend had that nice little town house over on Bank Street?"

Last smiled. "Don't you read the papers, man? This is where it's happening, man. The *New York Times* said so, man—'A Different Bohemia,' man."

"Yeah, well. No, I didn't read about it, Kev, and even if I had, I'd still think you live here 'cause it's convenient to Alphabet City, all the dealers. Sit down, Kevin. Oh, I forgot to tell you, we're cops—"

93

"I already talked to the cops."

Neuman rubbed the bridge of his nose. "Tell me something, Kev. You're in a play, right? You probably had a little chat with the producer, right, about being in it? He probably said he had to talk it over with some other people, get their, you know, input, he'd get back to you. A couple of days later he got back to you, the producer, did you say, 'I already talked to you'? No. You were glad to hear from him, you talked nice to him, you listened to what he had to say, you answered his questions. So you already talked to the cops, so what? I'm the cops and I got more questions to ask you. Like, did you kill Dimanche?"

Last snorted. "No. Did you?"

"No. No, I didn't. And you say you didn't, either, Kev, so that makes us—what?—blood brothers, birds of a feather, a couple of wild and crazy guys? Okay, question number two: Did you beat up Dimanche on the afternoon or early evening of September seven?"

He laughed, a high-pitched giggle that didn't go with his wasted good looks, his purple brocade Edwardian coat, ruffled white silk shirt, red leather pants, yellow snakeskin boots; with the death's head earring in his left ear or the black-lacquered mandarin nail on his left little finger. "Christ. You're just fishing."

Neuman moved his head and Federici lifted Last onto tiptoe and pushed him back on the couch. "He said sit."

Neuman sat on the coffee table in front of the couch, moving aside some books and magazines and an ashtray full of butts. He poked at the butts with a fingertip. "Tsk, tsk. Marijuana. Marijuana's a no-no, Kev. You're thinking possession for personal use is a misdemeanor, I can shove my misdemeanor up my ass, but it's grounds for a search warrant, Kev, and the search turns up a quantity of marijuana that's for more than just personal use, not to mention some blow, some snow, some 'ludes, some whatever it is that makes your eyes look like that, Kev, that makes it sound like you got a saxophone instead of a nose, you're looking at a few points, Kev, I don't know how many—I leave that to the D.A., the judge—but a few." He leaned forward and patted Last's cheek. "So you want to tell me how you knocked her around, Kev?"

"I didn't," Last said.

"I say you did, Kev. I say you knocked her around, the two of you figured it wasn't going to look good for either of you, you made up a story about a mugging. I wish you hadn't done that, Kev. You know how much taxpayers' money you wasted, sending cops out into the street looking for a mugger who didn't mug anybody? What was it, a lovers' quarrel? Something about money? Something about she was a star and you're just a star-fucker?"

Last came out of his seat—or tried to. His chest hit Neuman's outstretched left hand and he ricocheted back.

Neuman was quiet for a moment, thinking that now his left hand and wrist hurt, as well as his mouth, his jaw, his cheeks, his ass, his chin, his elbows, his stomach, his nose, his right hand, his brain. He was out of practice in every respect. And he was retired. Why wasn't Federici doing the dirty work?

"Here's the deal, Kev. You're a suspect in the murder of Juliet Marko, a/k/a Dimanche. A Lieutenant McIver and a Detective Bloomfield're going to be here in a little while with a warrant to search your apartment. In particular they're look-ing for a Smith and Wesson thirty-eight-caliber double-action revolver, like the one Dimanche used in the play, s'matter of fact, so I hope for your sake you got rid of it. I also hope for your sake you don't have more than a lid or so of that grass, that you don't have more than a couple of grams of blow, that you don't have a free-basing chemistry set in your closet somewhere, Kev, 'cause if you do it's points you're looking at and I got to tell you from what I hear lately things're getting tough in the joint for pretty white boys. I mean, I hear stories that they're making them wear wigs and dresses and—"

"What do you want to know?" Last said. He took a cigarette from a wooden box on the coffee table and put it in his mouth.

Neuman reached over and took it out of his mouth. "Roth-man's. We found Rothmans in the ashtray in Dimanche's dress-ing room."

Last smiled. "Did you find the pack they came out of? That's what she smoked."

"Yeah, as a matter of fact, we did. And, yeah, as a matter of fact, we know that's what she smoked. But it's kind of interest-ing, don't you think, Kev, that some of the Rothmans we found had lipstick on them and some of them didn't?"

Last shrugged. "So some of them were mine, so what? Yeah, I've been in her dressing room. Yeah, I smoke them too."

"I can see that, Kev. What am I, a tourist? I got off the Gray Line, I thought I'd take a look at how real New Yorkers live, I climbed up five flights and kicked your door down and read the name on your cigarettes and I didn't see they're Rothmans? . . . You're not going to start crying on me, are you, Kev? You're not going to get all sentimental and tell me how you saw her just a few minutes before she died and how beautiful she looked, how alive? Are you?"

Last burbled for a while.

Neuman rolled his eyes at Federici, who looked away. Maybe things had changed since he'd been away; maybe nobody talked tough or acted tough anymore—except the cops on TV, in the movies.

"Saturday was eight years, exactly," Last finally said.

"Was what, Kev?"

"Since we met."

"Tell me about it."

"We met at Maxwell's—in Hoboken. It's a . . . a club."

"Oh, yeah? Hoboken's where they make Maxwell House coffee, isn't it? I know it is. I went out with a girl once, a hundred years ago, lived in Hoboken, right across from the Maxwell House coffee factory. I still remember the address—ten-oh-four Hudson Street. I remember her name too. Mira Esterowitz. We had a joke: She'd say, 'You want to come in for a cup of coffee?' I'd say, 'Let's just get some cups, walk over to the Maxwell House coffee factory, ask them to fill them up.' Funny, her name being Mira and my wife, who I married, saying *mira* a lot, 'cause she's Hispanic. You know, it means 'hey,' like. Anyway, for a second I thought you were going to say you worked there, or something, at the Maxwell House coffee factory, met her on the assembly line, sorting beans or something."

"I had a band. She was looking for a gig. We hooked up. It was strictly professional at first, then we, you know."

"Yeah. I mean, no. No, I don't know. But I can guess. So?"

Last shrugged. "We were together a long time."

"That depends on how you look at it, Kev. I mean, I'm fifty-four years old, Kev. I was a cop for thirty-three years. I still am,

I guess, kind of. Been married fourteen years—I married kind of late." Maybe those should be his Lotto numbers: 14, 33, 54 —except the numbers only went up to 48. He could turn 54 around to 45, the way Federici turned one of his numbers around, but he still needed three more numbers. He looked at Federici. He was still there. "So eight years doesn't sound like a long time to me, Kev. But maybe it is to you. I don't know. So how'd you two get along, Kev? What I mean is, how'd you take the fact that you were the guy had the band, she was the girl looking for a gig, you hooked up, she was the one who got famous?"

Last drew himself up, trying to attain some dignity and almost making it. "I handled it. I don't get professionally jealous."

"What about, you know, jealous jealous?"

Last sniffed. "That was harder. A lot of guys wanted to say they'd made it with her."

"Did a lot of guys? Make it with her, I mean."

". . . Yeah."

Guys like Bobby, who'd put her on his list. Should he ask if Last had known about Bobby, who would've had to make it with Dimanche after she hooked up with Last? Wouldn't he? What did it matter? Bobby was dead. "And?"

"I kept my mouth shut."

"That must've been hard."

"Yeah."

"So hard you must've wanted to pop her every once in a while, hey, Kev?"

"I never touched her."

"Umm."

"He did, though."

"Who's he, Kev?"

"The guy she's been seeing. She's been seeing a new guy."

"I heard about that guy, Kev. It's all over town. Who is he?"

"The guy who beat her up, that's who. The guy who killed her."

"Why did I know you were going to say that, Kev? I knew you were going to say that the way I knew you were going to say when I told you we were cops you'd already talked to the cops. You know his name?"

Last shook his head. "She wouldn't tell me."

"Why not?"

"Because she was a cunt, that's why."

"A bitch."

"Yeah."

"A ball-breaker."

"Yeah."

"A castrater."

"Yeah."

"You sound like a guy I used to know, Kev. He talked about women that way a lot. You know what he did, Kev? He killed three of them. He wrote letters to the papers telling why he'd done it and that he was going to do it again."

"Hey, man. I told you, I didn't kill her."

"Yeah, and I told you I didn't, either, Kev, and you know what my telling you that's worth? Coffee grounds. So you just sit tight and wait for Lieutenant McIver and Sergeant Bloomfield and a couple of other guys to get here with that search warrant. And in case you're thinking that while they're on the way over you're going to dispose of your thirty-eight Special, your lids, your blow, your chemistry set, there's a Patrolman Rohter out in the hall's going to baby-sit. I hate to just up and leave you like this, Kev, but we're running on a tight schedule, lot of people to talk to, uptown, downtown, all over town. But we'll be back. Oh, and, uh, next time, open up when we knock, okay?"

Neuman stopped on the fourth-floor landing. "You okay, Steve?"

"I think I'm getting a little cold."

"You look worried about something."

Federici smiled. "I guess I'm worried that I might have to cut down on my training—for the marathon."

"That's what you're worried about—whether you'll feel good enough to run two hundred sixty miles?"

"Twenty-six miles, Lieutenant."

"Whatever. Anyway, go home."

"Hey, it's just a cold. I'm not going to die."

"Yeah, well. The thing is, Steve, you're no use to me this way. You're not asking questions, you're not saying anything, for all

I know you're not thinking. I mean, sometimes you got a cold you can't think, all you can do is have it, it's understandable. So go home, take a nap, drink some juice, take some vitamin C, have some soup, watch some TV, sweat a little, I'll see you tomorrow, or the day after. I'll even tell you my remedy for a cold; you want to try it, you're welcome. You get in a bed with a lot of covers, you drink hot tea with whiskey and honey in it, when you can't see your feet anymore you go to sleep; you wake up, you're better."

Federici poked at the sidewalk with the toe of his loafer. "Does this mean—"

"I told you, Steve, it doesn't mean anything. I just want you sharp, that's all."

Federici smiled. "I started to say—"

"I'm sorry, Steve. I shouldn't've interrupted. What?"

"Does this mean you're back on the force, Lieutenant. I mean, we haven't talked about it. So far, you've just been helping out, you know?"

"Yeah, I know. I don't know if that's what it means, Steve. I have to talk to Klinger, and the truth of it is I don't feel like talking to Klinger. I also have to talk to the wife, and the truth of it is—and this is just between us, Steve, okay?—things're a little out of whack at home. Nothing serious, I hope, but, well, we'll see."

"I'm sorry to hear that, Jake."

"Yeah, well. Me too. But now that I've said something about it, maybe I'll do something about it. Sometimes that's the way it works, isn't it? Something'll be bothering you and you won't say anything about it and it keeps on bothering you until finally you say something about it and then it stops bothering you, you know?"

"Yeah. I know."

"Anything bothering *you*, Steve? Other than your cold, I mean."

"I'm okay, Jake. Except for the cold. I'll see you tomorrow."

"See you, Steve."

11

Uptown, downtown, all over town, all over *tout* New York.
From the old-money shabby elegance of Park House to the
fuck-money drear of St. Mark's Place to the fast-money back-
talk of 1500 Broadway to the new-money sterility of La Rive
Gauche in what Neuman called Yorkville-verging-on-El-Barrio
but others probably called the New Upper Upper East Side.
The *Nouveau Haut Haut Côte d'Est.*

"Whom do you wish to see?" The doorman, who he had
thought from a distance was a moonlighting jockey, was a
woman, a cute woman. (Another case of mistaken gender, the
second this week. The result of society's slip-slide toward an-
drogyny or his myopia? Except that he wasn't myopic: He had
questing eyes, eyes sharp enough to read a newspaper headline from a second-story window, though not to be sure about
the sex of the reader.) This one had long red hair tucked up
under her cap, the way Nell Ward had had her long blond
hair tucked up under her fedora. Nell Ward. Was she cute?
No. She was more . . . What? Or maybe she wasn't. What did
he know?

"Dillen. Jay Dillen."

"Whom shall I say is calling?"

"Neuman. Mr. Neuman."

"Mr. Dillen isn't in just now, Mr. Neuman. If you'd care to—"

"Yeah, I know, he's playing tennis. He said he'd meet me here when he's through. Maybe I'll get some coffee. Is there a good place around here?"

The woman cracked a piece of gum, which went with her cuteness, but not with her whoms and her formality. "You a cop?" She dropped her midatlantic accent for an Atlantic Avenue one.

"Uh, yeah."

"Got some ID? Never mind, you look too much like a cop to be anything but. What'd Dillen do? Oh, yeah—Dimanche. You want to talk to Amanda? I would, if I were a cop. She just went up."

"Amanda Becker?"

"The one and only."

"I got an address for Amanda Becker on Riverside Drive."

"I wouldn't know. This is where she shacks up."

"At Dillen's?"

"At Dillen's."

"And she just went up?"

"Five minutes ago."

"Alone?"

"No. With three or four Bloomie's bags. I'm surprised it's taken this long."

"What?"

"For the cops to talk to Amanda."

"Yeah, well, she's been in California. She wasn't supposed to be back till tomorrow."

"Says who?"

"Her answering service."

The woman leaned toward him, her left hand backhanded alongside her mouth. "Amanda came back from California the afternoon Dimanche died."

"Says who?"

She tapped her chest with a thumb.

"What time the afternoon Dimanche died?"

"Three thirty-three."

Neuman laughed. "More or less?"

"Exactly." She pointed to the digital clock in the center of the building's intercom board. "Three thirty-three's one of those times you notice when it comes up on a digital clock. Like eleven eleven. Eleven eleven comes around only twice a day, and some days I'm looking right at a digital clock both times. Also, three thirty-three was my time in the marathon last year."

"I never ran in the marathon," Neuman said, "but I know what you mean about digital clocks. She came in a cab, Amanda?"

"All-Over."

"All over what?"

"That's the name of the cab company."

"Oh. Any special reason you remember that?"

"You ever worked a door?"

"No. No, I haven't. Well, maybe I have. In college, once, I worked in the library for a while. I used to sit at the exit and check to make sure people weren't walking out with books."

"Pretty boring, right?"

"Superficial torpor, generally interrupted by periods of wakefulness," Neuman said, and got back a laugh like a shower of jewels, a laugh he was startled to experience a response to in his gonads. Careful, Jakala—you're not only retired, you're married. Or was it the other way around?

"So to make time pass," she said, "you notice things like the names of cab companies. At first, I thought it was Fall-Over. I thought that was pretty funny."

Neuman thought it was kind of funny too. Anything she thought, he'd be inclined to think. "The driver—was he white, black, Hispanic, Greek, Israeli, Indian, Arab, Korean, what?"

"White. Out of Central Casting."

"You mean, you wanted a guy to play a cabdriver in a movie, you'd get this guy?"

"Yup. Except I just read in the paper that there are more foreign cabbies than any other kind, which I didn't have to read the paper to know, all I had to do was get in a cab."

"You an actress—when you're not working the door, I mean?"

"Isn't everybody? I'm giving it up, though—acting and working the door. I'm going to win the lottery and move to Gloucester, Mass."

"What's in Gloucester, Mass?"

"I don't know. I just like to say it: Gloucester, Mass. I thought it'd be funny, actually, to open a restaurant up there, a seafood place, so I could put on the menu l-o-b-c-e-s-t-e-r. Get it?"

"You win the lottery, you won't have to work. What numbers did you play, you don't mind my asking?"

Her eyes got hard. "Have you bought a ticket yet?"

"Uh, well, no. But I won't play your numbers."

"Why do I believe you?"

"I've got an honest face, I guess."

She laughed. "One, 2, 3, 4, 5, 6."

"Really?"

She shrugged. "Think it's a long shot?"

"Yeah, well, I do. But, well, what isn't?"

"Thirty-six B."

"Sorry?"

"Amanda Becker's in thirty-six B."

If Amanda Becker killed Dimanche, he'd make 36 one of his numbers: What numbers did he have so far? Lots of numbers: 3, 6, 15, 24, 30, 45—for stuff at Klein's office that he'd already forgotten. And before that, 3, 10, 12, 22, 30: 3 and 30 for the time, 10 for the people involved with the play, 12 for the stagehands and theater employees, 22 for the total number of suspects, except now Viv Thib Wynd made it eleven people involved with the play and twenty-three total suspects, and come to think of it, her chauffeur was a suspect, wasn't he, because she was eighty-two if she was a day but chipper enough to order a flunky to do a little murder for her and make up the gave-the-chauffeur-the-afternoon-off-and-walked-all-the-way-home story.

And before that, 14, 33, 54—fourteen years married, thirty-three years a cop, fifty-four years old—except the numbers only went up to 48, so he'd have to turn 54 around and make it 45. So: If Amanda Becker killed Dimanche, he'd play 3, 10, 12, 22, 30, 36, because it wouldn't matter if he didn't count Viv Thib Wynd or her chauffeur. Or should he play 14, 33, 36, 45 (54 turned around) and two other numbers? Which two? How about 4 and 8? Why those two? Four for the number of letters in Nell, 8 for the number in Nell Ward.

Nell Ward? What're you thinking, Jake?

I'm thinking about having coffee, that's all.
What about this girl?
What about her?
You seem to like her.
So? I'm retired and married.
You mean married and retired, don't you, Jake?

"Amanda Becker?" She had the biggest eyes Neuman had
ever seen, set in a face not quite wide enough to accommodate
them—a funny face, with those big eyes, but also a beautiful
one. Not the face of a Hepburn for the eighties—Katharine or
Audrey—as Charly Johnstone had said; Nell Ward had more
that kind of face. *Stop it, Jake.* "I'm Lieutenant Neuman. Police." At least she wouldn't say she'd already talked to the
police.

"How did you get up here?"

"Elevator."

"Who let you in?"

"Doorman. Doorperson, I guess I should say. I never saw a
woman doorman before. Not that I can recall. No, I haven't.
Saw a woman sanitation man the other day—a sanperson. I
asked the doorperson not to buzz you. I didn't want you running
down the back stairs while I was riding the elevator up, although I probably could've ridden back down again and caught
you. That's one of the fastest elevators I've ever been on."

"Jay's not here," Amanda Becker said.

"I know that. He's playing tennis."

"He's already spoken to the police."

Neuman sighed. "Right. I come in?"

She tapped her back teeth together, once, and stepped aside.
"I assume you have a warrant."

"Don't need one to talk to you." Neuman went through the
door and right into the living room, minimally furnished in
leather and glass and steel, without benefit of foyer; for the rent
Dillen must pay for the French name and the supersonic elevator and the abstract paintings on the hallway walls, Neuman
would've thought he'd get a foyer. He took his hat off and
walked over to the picture window looking the other way from
Viv Thib Wynd's, out over the East River, Queens, Europe.

104

"I'm confused." Amanda Becker was right on his heels. "Talk to me about what? Jay's the—"

Neuman turned. "Jay's the what?"

She bit her lip—not cutely, hard.

"The suspect? Yeah, he's a suspect. And guess what—so're you."

She laughed.

So did Neuman. "I know. It's corny, isn't it? If I were writing a book or something, or a play, I wouldn't put it in. An actress gets bumped off just a couple of weeks before making her Broadway debut in a play about an actress getting bumped off a couple of weeks before making her Broadway debut in a play about an actress getting bumped off, and so on, an actress who got the part over another actress who's the director's girlfriend and who everybody figured because she was the director's girlfriend was a shoo-in to get the part.

"What else is corny is this: The actress who's the director's girlfriend went to California after she didn't get the part, but she came back the very afternoon the actress who got the part over her got killed, only she didn't tell anybody that, didn't tell her answering service, anyway. What I know about actresses, which isn't a whole lot, is they go anywhere, or come back, their answering service is the first to know. What's so funny?"

Amanda laughed till tears came. She wiped them with the heels of her hands and put her hands on her hips. She had nice hips. "Jessie told you that, didn't she?"

"Who's Jessie?"

"The door*person*. She hates me."

"Oh?"

"She's an *ac*tress."

"Isn't everybody?"

Amanda laughed again, one bitter note. "No, Lieutenant Neuman. Everybody isn't. A few of us are; many, many thousands more aspire to be. They wait on tables or drive taxis or clean apartments until their ship comes in or their dream evaporates."

"Or work as doorpersons."

"Yes."

"There's another kind of actress, isn't there?" Neuman said.

"I mean, like I said, I don't know much about actresses, I don't go to shows or anything much. I did see *42nd Street*. One of my wife's sisters was in town and she wanted to see a show so we went to see *42nd Street*. It was okay. Isn't there another kind of actress who isn't really an actress but isn't waiting on tables, either, or driving a cab or cleaning apartments or working a door until her ship comes in or her dream evaporates? Isn't there another kind of actress, who's sort of—how would you put it?—a personality, who gets to be in a show because of, you know, who she is? It must be hard on someone like you, an actress—you probably studied and everything, paid your dues in summer stock or whatever it's called, off-off-Broadway—to handle someone like that getting a part in a play, harder than handling all the people waiting on tables or driving taxis or cleaning apartments or working doors until their ship comes in or their dream evaporates."

Amanda Becker's nostrils contracted. "I didn't kill Dimanche, Lieutenant."

"Know who did?"

"I know Jay didn't."

"Because you did, so he didn't have to?"

"I told you, I didn't."

"I've been a cop for thirty-three years"—*Shut up, Jake. Jesus*—"and you know how many people've lied to me out of one side of their mouth while telling me out of the other they were telling me the truth? A lot, that's how many, so pardon me if I don't fall down on the floor thanking you for being so, you know, honest with me. What airline did you fly on Tuesday?"

"American. I have the ticket receipt."

"Good. You'll need it. What airport?"

"Kennedy. I took a cab."

"Straight here?"

"Yes. There was a lot of traffic. It took over an hour. The plane got in at two and I didn't get here until after three."

"You got here at three thirty-three, which was time enough to stop by the Kean Theater and kill Dimanche."

She smiled. "Except that I didn't kill Dimanche."

"What cab company?"

"I didn't notice. It would be *more* suspicious if I *had* noticed, don't you think?"

"I'll be the judge of what's suspicious, Miss Becker."

She laughed. "God, you're right out of some bad movie."

That hurt. To be out of some movie would be bad enough, but a bad movie . . . "So you didn't notice the driver's name, either?"

"No."

"Remember anything about him?"

"No."

"You must remember something. Was he black, white, Hispanic? Was he a she?"

"He was white. Oh, yes, and I remember Elliott Gould."

"He's driving a cab, Elliott Gould?"

"The cabdriver recognized me, or thought he did. He said he'd recently driven Elliott Gould . . . I wasn't Dimanche's only enemy, Lieutenant."

He slumped. "Right."

"Have you . . . ?"

"Have I what?"

"Have you talked to Charly Johnstone?"

"Yeah, I've talked to Charly Johnstone." And wore out my ass, my chin, my elbows, my stomach, my nose and my right hand in the process. "Why?"

A long pause.

"Why?"

"Charly was in love with Dimanche."

"Charly Johnstone?"

"Yes."

"In love with Dimanche?"

"Yes."

"Meaning she's . . . ?"

"Yes."

"Well, so? I mean, Dimanche isn't, is she? I mean, wasn't. Was she?"

"Dimanche was a hedonist. She took pleasure where she found it."

"Right. I mean, okay, but . . . Charly Johnstone is, uh . . ."

"Old and fat and ugly—compared with Dimanche. I'm not suggesting her love was requited. I'm suggesting, on the contrary, that it wasn't, and that, well . . ."

"This is dirty pool, Miss Becker."

"Indeed, Amanda. I'm shocked." Jay Dillen had come in on

little cat feet—or rather, Reebok sneakers. He wore a royal blue Fila warm-up suit, had sweatbands on both wrists and around his forehead, and carried four Prince rackets. He didn't look shocked; he looked fit and flushed and not a little titillated by what he'd overheard. The sparkle in his eyes said there was no business like show business.

Amanda Becker took her cue from him. "Isn't this how the police find things out, Lieutenant—from informants?"

"Yeah, well. There're informants and there're informants. There're informants you did a favor for—maybe kept their brother-in-law out of the joint, or them—and they owe you one; there're informants who'd like to keep their brother-in-law out of the joint, or them, so they do you a favor hoping you'll do them one back; there're informants who figure the time'll come they'll want to keep their brother-in-law out of the joint, or them, so they do you a favor, as an investment, like; there're informants who don't want anything for themselves, they're just, I don't know, concerned citizens or something who just happen to have a circle of friends who know things most people don't know—who wants who killed, who's delivering what where, like that—they tell the cops 'cause they think the cops shouldn't ought to be in the dark about things like that; and then there're informants who're weasels, who talk 'cause they like the sound of their own voice, who can't keep a secret, who think it's funny, somehow, that some of us aren't like the rest of us—have vices or quirks or, uh, hobbies that're a little out of the ordinary—like to dress up weird or do weird things to other people. You're still a suspect, Miss Becker. In a funny way, you just made yourself more of one than if you'd kept your mouth shut. I'll be talking to you again, so don't go anywhere —back to California or anything. Stick around. Stay put. Dillen, let's talk sitting down somewhere."

They sat in the kitchen, which maybe had had water boiled in it, but had never endured any serious cookery. Dillen drank from a bottle of Gatorade that shared the refrigerator with the last of a six-pack of Tab and two Chinese-food containers, and said the usual things about having talked to the cops and Dimanche's having had enemies. He praised himself for giving the part to Dimanche despite his arrangement with Amanda and rejected—having also anticipated it—the allegation that he had tried to sabotage Dimanche's acting debut by giving her her head.

"You went out to the toilet during the time Dimanche was killed," Neuman said. "How long would you say you were gone?"

"A minute or two, at most. I urinated, Lieutenant, if you want to be clinical about it."

"I don't especially, no. You see anybody while you were in the head?"

"It's a small facility, Lieutenant. One customer at a time."

"Un hunh. Well. You see anybody in the halls, then? Anybody you know, anybody you don't know?"

"As I've already told your confreres, I saw no one."

"How about, you know, personally? You seeing anyone personally? Anyone else, I mean?"

Dillen shook his head. "I don't follow, Lieutenant."

"Are you fucking anyone besides Amanda? Anyone who maybe didn't like Amanda, thought maybe if she killed Dimanche people'd think Amanda did it, Amanda'd be out of the picture."

Dillen laughed. "Lord, Lieutenant—what a vivid imagination."

"Yeah, well. Are you?"

"I don't see that that's any of your business."

"Meaning you are."

"Meaning I wouldn't tell you if I were."

"Meaning you're protecting someone."

"Meaning that's for you to find out."

"Meaning you'll be coming with me, Dillen, and meeting a few more of my, uh, confreres, the ones we have to keep in the station house, they have a way of throwing people through plate-glass windows if we let them work in the streets."

Dillen laughed. "It always comes to that, doesn't it? The threat of violence versus the citizen's right to life, liberty and the pursuit of happiness."

Neuman shrugged. "Yeah, well."

Dillen moved the Gatorade aside and leaned over the table. "Can I trust you, Lieutenant, to use this information only insofar as it pertains to Dimanche's murder? That is to say, when you find that my, uh, relationship with this particular woman has no bearing on Dimanche's murder—which is what you will find—can I trust you to file the information in that part of your mind that forgives and forgets?"

Was that anything like the part of New York that counted for a great deal? "Sure. Yeah. Why not?"

"Perhaps you noticed on your way in—you couldn't've helped but notice; Jessica's an extraord—"

"No." Neuman sat back and waved his hands. "Don't tell me about it. I don't want to hear it. You're right—it's none of my business. Forget it. I'm sorry I asked. Never mind."

This time, Dillen looked shocked. "I hope Jessica's not . . ."

"No. She's not my girlfriend, my daughter, my niece, my anything. She's just a nice kid I had a nice talk with and it pisses me off, it gives me a pain in the gut—or maybe it's my heart; anyway, *here*—that she's mixed up with a bunch of ass-holes like you and the rest of your crowd, Dillen. I've got more questions to ask you, but they can wait, 'cause you're not going anywhere, either. Understand? You're grounded, Dillen, till I tell you otherwise. If I hear you hurt that kid downstairs in any way at all; if I hear she lost her job 'cause of you, or didn't get some acting job she should've got 'cause Amanda found out about her and used her clout to keep her from getting it; if I hear *any*thing I don't like the sound of and you're the reason it stinks, I'll come back here with my, uh, confreres and throw you out the fucking window. Don't get up. I can find my own way out."

"You say your name was Neuman?" Jessie didn't look at him, as if she knew he knew.

"Uh, yeah."

"Couple of guys waiting for you. They look like good guys, but then again, they could be bad guys."

Neuman followed her point and saw another unmarked squad car painted a utilitarian brown that might as well have been Day-Glo orange with COPS in bright blue on the sides. Tim McIver was behind the wheel; a small man rode shotgun, reading a thick book. "Yeah, they're good guys. You're right, though; they could be bad guys. A certain time of day, a certain kind of light, a certain frame of mind, they could be bad guys."

110

Jessie laughed. "You a poet—when you're not a cop?"

"Who isn't?" Neuman said, and tried to think of something more to say and couldn't and went out the door and down the steps of La Rive Gauche's expensive entryway and across the street.

"Jake, long time no see." McIver had made him and gotten out of the car.

"Tim. You finished going over whatshisname's place—Last's?"

"Bloomfield's still over there, Jake, with a bunch of other guys, whose names I don't know. You know how many guys there are in the Department whose names I don't know? Sometimes I think I showed up for work at the wrong place or something. Turnover. Lot of turnover. . . . They asked me to tell you, Jake."

Neuman didn't have to ask who *they* were; *they* were the good guys who at a certain time of day, in a certain kind of light, with a certain frame of mind, could be bad guys. He didn't have to ask tell him what? What? was bad news, which was the only kind of news people found you out on the street to tell you. How *had* McIver found him? Just by looking around, he supposed—cruising around the part of New York that counted for a great deal. Or was this the part that didn't count for anything at all?

"You read the paper today, Jake?" McIver said. They'd moved onto the sidewalk and the small man, who wore a large suit, had gotten out of his side of the car, the thick book—*Texas*—still in his hand, a finger marking his place. Neuman supposed that since the small man was riding shotgun with McIver and since McIver was talking in front of the small man, the small man was with McIver, but McIver didn't introduce him, as if someone who read thick best-sellers didn't need an introduction.

"Yeah. I mean, kind of." He hadn't read the sports page, for he'd taped the Dodgers and the Mets again and was hoping to watch it at home—if he ever stopped going uptown, downtown, all over town; if he went home. But McIver hadn't cruised around this part of New York to find him and tell him the ball scores. McIver liked boxing.

"There was a murder downtown Tuesday morning. SoHo. A

111

guy wearing running clothes. No ID, no keys, no nothing, just a pair of shorts and a shirt and socks and shoes. Papers're calling him Nowhere Man. He was shot in the face with a forty-five, so he doesn't look too pretty, if you know what I'm saying."

"I'm retired, Tim," Neuman said. "I'm just sort of, uh, helping out on this Dimanche thing. Matt McGovern's got something wrong with his gut and I guess they're kind of shorthanded. You working on that case too, along with this Dimanche thing? They must be shorthanded."

"The M.E. got a good slug out of the guy, Jake, and Crime Scene got some good ballistics. Then we got real lucky, Jake: Some guys working on a construction site at Thompson and West Third, which isn't too far from where the jogger was iced, found a gun in one of their cement mixers—not the big ones, the trucks, but those little ones you see them making cement in. A Colt forty-five. Yeah, it's the same gun, Jake, and here's the thing—"

"Who's this guy?" Neuman said, as if it was suddenly the most important thing in the world to put a name to the little man who read thick best-sellers.

"Detective Winger, Lieutenant." The little man tucked the book into his left armpit and put out his right hand. "Sixth Squad, Lieutenant."

Neuman ignored the hand.

"Jake." McIver put a hand on Neuman's shoulder. "It may not be anything. Look. Here's what happened. Steve Federici lost one of his pieces—or it was stolen; he doesn't know which. He reported it. Said he had it in the glove compartment of his car and then he didn't have it. About a month ago. He said maybe he did put it in the glove compartment and forgot to lock the car and somebody took it, or maybe he didn't put it in the glove compartment, he put it somewhere else, but he couldn't remember where, or maybe wherever he put it, somebody took it from there. I don't know. He didn't know; I don't know. But he reported it. And it turned up. In a cement mixer. And it killed a guy. Nowhere Man."

The sidewalk wasn't a sidewalk anymore; it was a room in a funhouse, with a distorting mirror and tilting floor and weird music and a jack-in-the-box popping out at you. Neuman leaned his hands on the fender of the car and after a while got his breath back and his balance and the sidewalk was a sidewalk again; the mirror was just a store window and the ground was true and the music was the sound of a garbage truck down the block and the jack-in-the-box was the little man in the big suit, who was smiling a big smile. "A forty-five?" When you've got nothing to say, ask a question you already know the answer to.

"A forty-five," McIver said.

That could be another Lotto number, except he already had 45—54 turned around, 54 being his age; fourteen years married, thirty-three years a cop, fifty-four years old.

"What's he doing here?" Neuman tipped his head toward Winger. "He's working on the Dimanche mugging, right?"

Winger snorted. "Dimanche didn't get mugged, Lieutenant. You know that, and I know that, so what're we calling it a mugging for, Lieutenant? She got knocked around by one of her boyfriends, Lieutenant. Guess which one, Lieutenant."

Neuman cocked his arm to knock the lieutenants out of Winger, but McIver caught his fist in his hand. "Easy, Jake. It's just guesswork we're doing here. Nobody knows anything for sure. But Steve knew her. His name was in her phone book. So're the names of a hundred other guys, but his is one of them."

"Steve Federici?"

"Yeah."

"You're saying Steve Federici killed Dimanche too?"

"We're not saying that, Jake, but we got to take a look at the possibility."

"And killed this guy Nowhere Man?"

"It was his gun, Jake. No doubt about that."

"Steve Federici killed *two* people?"

"Jake—"

"Steve Federici, my partner?"

"Oh, hell, Jake. Why do you want to look at it like that? I mean, you're just sort of helping out on this Dimanche thing, is what I hear. Matt McGovern's got something wrong with his gut and we're kind of shorthanded. You're retired, right?"

12

"Jacob?"

"Yeah, babe?"

"Are you all right? I did not hear you come in."

"Yeah, I'm just watching this TV show."

"Oh? I will not disturb you then."

"It's okay. It's over, I think. Yeah. *Miami Vice*. You usually watch *Dallas* Fridays at nine, but a lot of people watch *Miami Vice*. I thought I'd watch it. I guess I should've asked you if you wanted to watch *Dallas;* I could've taped *Miami Vice* and watched it later."

"Dallas was a repeat tonight. The new season begins in a couple of weeks. Anyway, I have been reading."

"Yeah, well. I think this *Miami Vice* was a repeat too. It said *R* after it in the paper. That means *repeat,* doesn't it? Or maybe it means *recommended.* I don't know."

"Jacob, I heard about Steven on the radio."

"Yeah, well, it shouldn't be on the radio, 'cause all they've got is a gun he says was stolen from him, they don't have anything else, except he kind of knew this woman, Dimanche, who also got killed, but not with his gun. It looks like a cop does something wrong, the Department's about as loyal as a boa constrictor, just in case the politicians and the press and the civil liberties types start screaming and moaning that he's getting special treatment. They forget cops have rights too. I'm surprised they didn't shoot him."

"Jacob."

"Yeah, I know. Steve likes *Miami Vice;* he says it's pretty good on what it's like, police work. I don't know. At first I thought the cops were the bad guys, they were all dressed up in white pants and stuff, and T-shirts and those slippers, like, with no socks—the white guy, anyway, and he lives on a sailboat and has a pet alligator, or maybe it's a crocodile, and drives a Ferrari. I didn't know it was a Ferrari—I mean, I don't know one sports car from another—but he kept calling it the Ferrari, the white guy, who also carries a Bren ten, which is a serious piece. Is that what it's like, police work? I don't know. I wore white pants on the job, they'd be dirty just from sitting down in the squad room, forget about crawling around on my gut looking to see if some bad guy dropped his American Express card or something, so I'd know who he was. I carried a Bren ten, I'd probably shoot a lot of people, just to, you know, justify having such a serious piece. The black guy wears suits and ties.

"In this show the cops're trying to nab this coke dealer, pretending they're big spenders from New York, looking to buy a hundred fifty keys—a lot of keys. They tell their boss— His name is Lieutenant Castillo; he wears regular suits, regular ties, almost looks like a real cop, has bad skin, hardly talks at all, kind of like me. Hah. I kind of liked him, except I wouldn't want him mad at me— They tell him they need the money for the keys *and* they need twenty-five large to ante up for this boat race the coke dealer's going to have to Bimini and back— those big, noisy boats like we saw that time we went out to Greenport, stayed at that motel where everybody was Greek, we joked we were finally having a vacation on the Mediterranean; cigarette boats—'cause if they're in the boat race they look like big spenders, the dealer doesn't get suspicious. Their boss says—I laughed out loud at this, I swear, Maria—he says, 'You get in the race, let me worry about the money.' I can just hear Lou Klinger or Miles Easterly saying, if I went to them and asked for money for a hundred fifty keys of cocaine and ante for a boat race to Bimini and back, 'Sure, Jake. You go ahead and set it up. Let me worry about the money.' That isn't what it's like, police work; police work is somebody saying, 'You want to buy some cocaine, Jake? Sure, here's two yards, buy a couple of grams. You want to take a boat ride, Jake? Sure, go to Staten Island and back.' Where's Bimini? Bermuda? I didn't know Bermuda was so close to Miami.

"Anyway, Castillo *can't* get the money for the ante for the boat race, which *is* what it's like, police work. He says to the white cop—his name's Sonny; he's supposed to drive the boat —he says, 'Downtown doesn't have enough confidence in your racing ability, Sonny.' And Sonny says, 'That hurts.' I laughed at that too; I don't know if it was supposed to be funny. But then Castillo says there're these two women cops who just happen to have twenty-five large they're going to use to make a drug bust and if Sonny and the black cop should happen to borrow the money for a while, between the time the women cops make the bust and the time the money's supposed to be back at Property or wherever the hell you get twenty-five large, he won't ask any questions, Castillo. So Sonny and the black cop hang around this motel where the drug deal's going down and as soon as the women cops make the bust, they grab the money and take off. Somebody like Tim McIver or somebody had authorization to carry around twenty-five large to make a buy, I tried to borrow it from him, you know what he'd do? He'd shoot me.

"So they race to Bimini and back and it turns out the dealer's using the race as a cover to smuggle in coke. He's got this other boat, see, just like the boat he starts out in, same numbers and markings on it and everything, the guys on it're wearing the same crash helmets and everything, and on the way back from Bimini he goes behind this little island and the other boat comes out the other side, all loaded with cocaine, and when it gets back to the dock nobody'd ask any questions. But Castillo's there and a bunch of DEA guys, I guess they were, and they bust the dealer and also this black woman I forgot to mention who's the dealer's girlfriend and even though she's the dealer's girlfriend the black cop went to bed with her, which isn't what it's like, police work."

Maria had moved to the arm of the easy chair. "Jacob?"

"I know, babe. I talk too much."

"Have you gone back to work, Jacob? You have not said a thing about it."

"Yeah, well. I don't know if I have is the reason I haven't. I was supposed to call Easterly, but I didn't. I was supposed to see Personnel, but I didn't. I was supposed to set up a marksmanship test, but I didn't. So I don't know. I mean, there was this weird thing: This woman, Dimanche, was murdered and her name was on a list Steve found in a desk Bobby used to use, so it looked like, I don't know, there was some connection to Bobby, except how could there be—Bobby's dead, right? But I had to find out if there was a connection. I had to 'cause—I don't know—'cause if there *wasn't* a connection, which there couldn't be, 'cause Bobby was dead, then at least Bobby could maybe rest in peace. Then this thing with Steve happened. I mean, he's not really my partner 'cause I'm not really working, am I? But all of a sudden it looks like he might've killed a guy, or at least his gun did. And . . . Shit, I don't know. I don't know, I don't know, I don't know."

"Jacob?"

"Yeah, babe?"

"Have you ever slept with a woman on a case?"

Neuman laughed. "Hey, babe, I know things're kind of, you know, awkward between us right now, but if you're talking about this thing on *Miami Vice,* this black cop's a good-looking guy, you know? He's young, he's got a nice build, he's a good dancer and stuff. I'm just a fat slob who talks too much."

"Would you, if you thought it would help solve the case?"

"Hey, babe, if I had a million dollars I'd be a millionaire, but I don't, so that's a big if. Which reminds me, did you buy a Lotto ticket? The drawing's tomorrow night, I think. Yeah. Saturday. If we win, we won't have to worry about anything again."

"If," Maria said.

"Yeah, well."

"Nell Ward called again tonight."

"Christ, Maria. I met her once, for like thirty seconds."

"She is very persistent—and very engaging. We had a long talk."

Christ.

"She said it is very important that she have a famous detective such as you in her film."

"Yeah, well."

"That is a very flattering thing to say. I thought perhaps—"

"Maria, Christ."

"—that perhaps that was why you have not been interested—"

"Can we talk about something else, Maria? Okay? It's not that I don't want to talk about it sometime. It's just that there's this thing with Steve and I don't know if he's my partner or not 'cause I don't know if I've gone back to work or not, but it's on my mind, which is why I watched *Miami Vice*, I thought that'd take my mind off it."

"Miles called again, as well," Maria said.

"Yeah, well. I figured he would."

"He gave me a message for you. He said he doesn't like to involve wives in police matters, but he was afraid you wouldn't call back unless he did."

"Yeah, well. Miles does everything by the book; Miles goes to the can by the book. And he's probably right; I probably won't call him back."

"He said to tell you that the Dimanche case is closed."

"Oh?"

"He said B.G. Harris killed Dimanche."

"Who? Oh, right—the playwright. I was going to talk to her tomorrow. I guess somebody saved me the trouble. Miles say who she confessed to? He probably didn't—that wouldn't be by the book."

"He said she wrote a note, before killing herself."

13

"Holy shit."

"Maybe we should go straight to Maui, forget about Honolulu. I mean, we seen Honolulu lots a times, right—on *Hawaii Five-O, Magnum?*"

"Artie, look at this. That guy, that reporter, who came around the other night, Terry Niles? He found the newsstand guy."

"Honolulu's just another crummy city. Like New York. It's got crime, it's got junkies. Who needs it?"

"Artie, he found the *news*stand guy."

"Will you stop reading the papers, Jer, making yourself crazy? 'Specially that skinhead, Niles. You keep reading the papers, 'specially that skinhead, Niles, thinking you're gonna see something about we took the dude's Lotto ticket, you're making yourself crazy. Think about it for a second. If we don't tell anybody—and we'd be crazy to, right?—then who's gonna know we took the dude's Lotto ticket?"

"I . . . I told him."

"Told who?"

"The reporter. Niles."

"Told him what?"

"We took the dude's Lotto ticket."

"No."

"Yeah."

"No, Jerry, no. Say you didn't tell that skinhead, Niles, Jer."

"I told him."

"Say you didn't. Say you're putting me on."

"I told him. *Ow!*"

"Say you're putting me on, Jer, or I'll break your nose."

"Shit, man. I can't hear anything. You broke my eardrum."

"I'll break your nose, Jerry, 'less you say you're putting me on."

"I already told you. I— *Ow!*"

"You are a scumbag, Jerry. A motherfucking scumbag."

"He didn't write nothing about it."

"I can't hear you, Jer, when you got your head between your knees."

"He didn't write nothing about it."

"Shoved up your ass is where you ought a put your head, you scumbag."

"Here. Here's what he wrote. He didn't write nothing about it. He wrote how he found the newsstand guy."

"Gimme that.... *'On the Trail of Nowhere Man.'* Shit. *'By Terry Niles.'* Another scumbag, a skinhead scumbag. It takes a scumbag to talk to a scumbag.... *'Who he was, no one knows. Where he lived, no one knows. Where he worked, no one knows.'* What is this, a poem or something? *'Whom he lived with'*— whom?—*'worked with, hung out with, shared ideas with, loved, envied, idealized—no one knows. Or no one is saying.'* Fuck does he mean by that?"

"He means us, Artie, that's who he means."

"Shut the fuck up, scumbag. I'm trying to read this, so gimme a little quiet, okay? *'He is known only as Nowhere Man, and he died early Tuesday morning on a deserted SoHo street from a forty-five-caliber bullet in the brain, died while the city still slumbered, turning over one last time, fighting off consciousness, the slim awareness that a new day was about to break, that sweet dreams were about to give way to harsh reality.'* This guy is a skinhead fag poet.... *'No, not quite, not entirely.'* Fuck does he mean by that? *'The whole city was not asleep, for the whole city never sleeps—not simultaneously, not en masse.'* Fuck does 'en massay' mean? Like a massé shot, in pool? *'No, New York,*

120

*as Sinatra says in that adulatory television commercial, is open
all night*—all *night*'— Adulatory is when you fuck another
guy's wife, right? I seen that commercial; there's nothing in it
about fucking another guy's wife. Fuck's the skinhead talking
about? *'Open for revelers, gamblers, con men, prostitutes and
pimps, grifters, muggers, murderers, the homeless, the shiftless,
the sleepless, its swells and its predators; and open, too, for its
honest, hard-working night laborers—its bartenders and barmaids; its sandhogs and its police officers; its firefighters and its
cabbies; its newspaper reporters, photographers, printers and
pressmen; its conductors and its motormen; its bus drivers and
its night watchmen; its doormen and its milkmen . . .'* Yeah,
okay, I think we get the point, Niles, you skinhead. It's open for
the stiffs on the fucking graveyard shift. What about its garage
attendants?"

"We're there."

"What?"

"We're there."

"I heard you, Jerry. Fuck do you mean, 'We're there'?"

"Keep reading. We're there."

*"'. . . its doormen and its milkmen; its sanitmen and its
porters; its news vendors and its garage attendants—'"*

"See? That's us."

"It ain't *us,* Jer. It's what we do, maybe—*use* ta do, in a
couple of hours from now, after we throw these crummy jackets
on the floor and spit in Leon's face, *use* ta do before we went
Hawaiian—but it ain't *us.*"

"Read the rest of it."

Artie tossed the paper aside. "I don't want to read it, Jer. You
know why? 'Cause I'm bored with it, that's why. I got better
things to do, like figure out whether we should go straight to
Maui, forget about Honolulu, 'cause we seen Honolulu lots a
times on *Five-O,* on *Magnum,* it's just another crummy city like
New York; crime, junkies, who needs it?"

Jerry picked up the paper and flattened the creases with the
back of his hand. *" 'It's hard to walk the streets of New York at
midnight, at two, at four, at six, and not see someone—and not
be seen. For the past two nights, this reporter has done just that
—walked the streets of New York at midnight, at two, at four,
at six—and has seen, if not millions of people, if not thousands,*

certainly hundreds, many of whom, dozens at least, have seen him, noted him, remarked him—scrutinized him, sometimes, to make sure whose side he was on, on which side of the law. Does any one of them remember seeing this reporter? Can any of them accurately describe him? Could any of them say with a certainty where he was coming from when they remarked him, where he was going? Impossible, without soliciting their letters and phone calls, to know. But this reporter certainly remembers seeing quite a number of them. Some of the memories are indelible, for this reporter momentarily feared for his wallet, even his life on two or three occasions; some are like wisps of smoke—reach for them and they will disappear altogether. But confront this reporter with the grim fact that on a street he walked someone was murdered; ask him to dredge his memory for any other fact, however slight, however fragile, that might illuminate that dark tragedy, that might help bring to justice the wanton taker of a life, and the likelihood is strong that his memory would be up to the task. With that in mind—' "

"I really don't fucking care, Jerry. You know that?"

" 'With that in mind, this reporter, in his walks through the city's streets, at midnight, at two, at four, at six—' "

" 'At midnight, at two, at four, at six,' " Artie singsonged. "The guy is a fag poet, no doubt about it."

" '—has been asking questions of bartenders and barmaids, firefighters and cabbies, bus drivers and night watchmen, doormen and milkmen and sanitmen and porters—even of revelers and prostitutes and pimps, of the homeless, the shiftless and the sleepless, of news vendors and garage attendants—asking them if they know anything or saw anything of the man known only as Nowhere Man. Interestingly, curiously, almost inexplicably, this reporter was the first to talk to the people he approached. Except for the two parking attendants who discovered Nowhere Man's body on the deserted SoHo street near the all-night garage where they do their honest labor'—meaning us, Artie."

"I know it means us, Jerry. Fuck am I, a retard?"

" 'Except for the two parking attendants who discovered Nowhere Man's body on the deserted SoHo street near the all-night garage where they do their honest labor, not a single one of them had been previously approached by any of the police officers or detectives assigned to Nowhere Man's case; not a single one of

them had been previously asked to dredge his memory for any other fact, however slight, however fragile, that might illuminate that dark tragedy, that might help bring to justice the wanton taker of a life—'"

"Wonton is soup. Fuck is he writing about soup?"

"'Why haven't the police done what this reporter did? Because they have a suspect, one of their own, Detective Second Grade Steven Federici, thirty-three, an eight-year veteran of the force, the owner of the forty-five-caliber pistol that killed Nowhere Man, a pistol Federici contends was stolen from the—'"

Artie grabbed the paper and hurled it, flapping, like a crashing bird, into the gutter. "I *tolja,* Jerry, I don't give a shit."

Jerry rubbed newsprint from his fingertips. "Anyway, he found the newsstand guy. The newsstand guy who sold Nowhere Man the Lotto ticket. He remembered him, like I said he'd remember him, 'cause he was wearing jogging shorts."

Artie took a travel brochure from his hip pocket. "Maybe soon as we get off the plane we should just get a boat, one of them big cabin cruisers, like, and cruise the islands, not have to worry about taking planes, making reservations. We could hire a couple a broads to drive it for us, a couple a blondes."

"I'm going to the cops, Artie."

"Or maybe a sailboat, like Crockett's got on *Miami Vice.*"

"I'm gonna tell them about the bag lady. They're questioning this cop, for chrissake. They think he did it. I don't think he did it. I think the bag lady did it. They ought a know about the bag lady."

"Or maybe a couple a Hawaiian broads. You know, a little dark meat."

"I'm going soon's we get off work, Artie."

"Think about something, Jer. Think about what if the guy *dropped* the Lotto ticket? What if Nowhere Man didn't get shot or nothing, he ran by here the way you say he ran by here every morning—I don't remember him, but you say you almost backed into him once with the blue Marquis—he ran by here and he *dropped* the ticket, it came out a his pocket? It's finders keepers, Jer. Possession is nine-tents of the law, Jer. You seen that on TV, right? Possession is nine-tents of the law."

"He didn't drop it, Artie. We took it."

"Who's to know, Jer, if he dropped it or if we took it? If he

123

dropped it and we found it, we might not even know who dropped it, 'less we saw him drop it, which we might not a, getting the blue Marquis, the gray Fleetwood and all."

"Niles knows."

"Thanks to you, you scumbag."

"The cops're gonna read this, Artie. They're gonna read it, they're gonna talk to the newsstand guy, they're gonna wonder what happened to the Lotto ticket, they're gonna ax us, 'cause we found the body, if we took it. They're not gonna *ax* us, they're gonna *tell* us—you murdered the guy, you took his Lotto ticket—"

"Jerry."

"You lied to us when we axed you if the guy had any ID, if you found any ID on the floor where the guy was laying—"

"Jerry."

"What?"

"You're a scumbag. So the cops read it, so what? So they talk to the newsstand guy, so what? So he told skinhead Niles he sold Nowhere Man a Lotto ticket, so what? Does he know what numbers Nowhere Man bet on? He know he bet on the winning number?"

"We don't know it's the winning number, Artie."

"Ten o'clock tonight, Jer, we'll know. Ten o'clock tonight, the whole town'll know. Me, I know now. I been reading the papers too, Jer, and you know what I read? I read Will Wynn's Lotto Info in the *News*, where they do that computer analysis a the winning numbers. And guess what, Jer? The numbers we got —2, 5, 8, 9, 42, 44—they been winning numbers a total of fifty-four times. Two's won eleven times, 5's won ten times, 8's won eight times, 9's won six times, 41's won eleven times, 44's won eight times. I'm telling you, Jer, 2, 5, 8, 9, 42, 44's the winning number, which is good for sixty million dollars, Jer, at least, 'cause that's what the pot's up to, on account a so many people bought tickets the last couple a days, thirty million for me, thirty million for you, at least. Two, 5, 8, 9, 42, 44, and we got it. The newsstand guy know Nowhere Man bet on those numbers?"

". . . No. Niles says he don't know that."

"Course he don't know, Jer. The fuck could he? He sells hundreds a Lotto tickets. Thousands. He don't know what numbers people bet on, he just takes their money, the slip they mark the numbers they're betting on, he puts the slip in a machine, the machine coughs up a ticket. He don't know what numbers they're betting on. Sure, he might remember he *sold* a ticket to Nowhere Man, same way he might remember he sold a ticket to a good-looking piece a ass, a guy with no leg, a woman with one eye or something, but he don't know *what* numbers they bet on. He knew that, he remembered them, he had a pornographic memory like that, he'd be working for the FBI or something, the CIA, remembering things about the Russians, the Chinks."

"He's a I-ranian."

"Who?"

"The newsstand guy."

Artie spread his hands. "So that's perfect then, isn't it, Jerry? I mean, who the fuck's gonna believe a I-ranian he says he sold a ticket to Nowhere Man? You think people don't still remember about the hostages, Jer? You think they don't remember what it was like every night for—what? a year?— watching a million a those I-ranians jumping up and down on TV, yelling and waving signs and pictures of Itolja Howmany? You think they don't remember? They remember. *I* remember. I mean, who the fuck's gonna believe a I-ranian? So skinhead Niles writes it in the paper a I-ranian sold Nowhere Man a Lotto ticket, so what? That don't make it true, Jer. All it makes it is something a I-ranian told skinhead Niles and Niles wrote in the paper. A I-ranian. It's perfect. It's really perfect."

"Steve Federici, please."

"Who's this?" Another reporter, undoubtedly. Or maybe his yuppie lawyer, reminding him not to talk to any reporters.

"You don't know me. I'm surprised you're home, you're not in jail or something. I'm surprised your number's listed. I didn't wake you, did I? I know it's kind of late, but I just got off work."

He smiled at her pell-mell giddiness. She sounded cute— short and cute. "It is late, yeah, so if you don't mind—"

"I want to help you, Steve."

His yuppie lawyer had said there'd be calls from women like this—maternal types, nurse types—said it by way of suggesting

125

he get an unlisted number, or at least an answering machine. "Right. Thanks for calling."

"This guy—Nowhere Man?—maybe I know him."

Crackpots too. His yuppie lawyer had said there'd be crackpots. "Who is this?"

"I'm not going to tell you my name, Steve. That's just the way it has to be."

"You going to tell me his name?"

"I don't know his name."

"Right. Good night."

"Okay, I don't *know* him, but I think I know something a*bout* him. He's a runner; I'm a runner."

Federici snorted. "I'm a runner too. So what? There're a million runners out there."

"Not at four-thirty in the morning, Steve. You're a runner? It didn't say anything about that in the paper. You run in the marathon?"

"This is my first year. I hope."

"I'm sure it will be. This is my fourth. I did three thirty-three last year."

"Pretty good. I'm shooting for four hours."

"Shoot for three thirty. If you can run it in four, you can run it in three thirty. You're thinking nines, you should be thinking eights. You probably run eights in practice, right?"

He ran sevens in practice, but he couldn't imagine running twenty-six of them in a row, or twenty-six eights. "Where do you run? Downtown?"

"It's not important. You must, though, living on Perry Street."

"I run at the McBurney Y, on Twenty-third Street."

"On a track?"

"Yeah. A banked track."

"How many laps to a mile?"

"Sixteen."

"I couldn't do that, Steve. I'd go nuts. I like to run somewhere and back. That way, I'm not tempted to stop."

"You run at four in the morning?"

"I get off work at one. I get home about one-thirty, quarter to two. I'm too wired to sleep, so I usually watch an old movie. If I'm still not sleepy when it's over, I go for a run."

"Downtown?"

"It's not important."

"What kind of work do you do?"

She laughed. "You're trying to find out who I am, Steve. It's not important who I am. Just whom I know."

Whom? His yuppie lawyer hadn't said there'd be calls from people with good grammar. "Know a*bout,* you mean."

"Did you see the *Dispatch?* There's an article saying Nowhere Man bought a Lotto ticket at a newsstand on Sixth Avenue and Fourth Street, at the beginning of his run."

He hadn't seen it, for though he was free to come and go, he didn't like walking around with a tail, which he was sure he had, although he hadn't made him. Or her. But his yuppie lawyer had read it to him. "Beginning?"

She giggled. "I guess the reporter who wrote it's not a runner. Where is it? I have it here. Terry Niles. If Terry Niles were a runner, he'd've asked the newsstand guy if Nowhere Man was sweating a lot, meaning he'd already run a long way. He wasn't, and it was warm that morning. I worked overtime that morning, and I remember wishing I wasn't, so I could get in a run before it got too much warmer."

"If Terry Niles didn't ask if Nowhere Man was sweating, how do you know he *wasn't* sweating?"

"I asked the newsstand guy."

"Oh?"

"He's getting his fifteen minutes' worth of fame. Picture in the paper and everything. There were a whole bunch of people talking to him, so I stuck my head in and asked if Nowhere Man was sweating."

"Asked him on the way home from work?"

Another giggle. "All right, Steve, I live downtown. I got off the subway at Eighth Street, I walked past the newsstand. Let me tell you what I figure, Steve. I figure Nowhere Man lived somewhere in the Village, say between Eighth Street and Fourteenth Street and between Fifth Avenue and the river—"

"That's a big figure."

"Just listen to me. He ran downtown, heading for the newsstand, knowing it's open all night, thinking he'd buy a Lotto ticket without having to stand on line. He wasn't sweating when he got there, which the newsstand guy says was around

127

four-fifteen, 'cause he gets a delivery right around four-fifteen every day, and the truck pulled up when he finished selling the ticket, so he probably hadn't run more than half to three-quarters of a mile. I start sweating after three-quarters of a mile, almost like clockwork, no matter how hot or cold it is. After Nowhere Man bought the ticket he headed downtown. I figure if he's out running at four in the morning he's a serious runner, he runs sevens, at the slowest. He was found dead by those garage attendants at four-thirty, meaning he'd run another fifteen minutes, or just over two miles. He could've gone anywhere once he headed south, but if he'd only run two miles—he was heading north on Crosby Street, don't forget—he didn't go that far south, probably only as far as Canal Street, which is three-quarters of a mile from West Fourth, if he went straight down Sixth Avenue. He went east to Crosby, which is just over a quarter of a mile, then headed north to just south of Houston, another thousand meters or so, for a total of a little under two miles, meaning he was either slower than I figure or he went farther west than I've figured, or farther south. Another factor is that there's traffic on Canal even at four, so more likely he ran east on Broome or Grand—Grand, probably. When I run down there at four I run on Grand; I go all the way to the Bowery, then head uptown. I'm not going to tell you how far, 'cause if I do, you'll start trying to figure out things about me again, such as where I live, which isn't important. What's important is this, Steve: If a guy goes out running, at any hour, without any keys, what does that mean to you?"

"It means he lives with somebody, somebody who'd let him in when he got home. That's what I keep coming back to." Federici was relieved to have someone to say it to, someone other than his yuppie lawyer, who when he said it just chewed on the earpiece of his horn-rimmed glasses and made notes on a yellow pad and said nothing back.

"I don't think so, Steve. I mean, nobody's reported him missing, have they? If he lived with somebody, they'd surely have reported him missing by now, wouldn't they?"

"Yeah. Yeah, you're right."

"I know I'm right, Steve. I've got it figured. He could've stashed his key, in one of those magnetic things, or in a flower box, or under a doormat—but that's risky. It's something people do in small towns where they don't really need to lock their doors in the first place, not something people do in New York City. No, what I figure is this—he lived in a building with a doorman, so he didn't need a front door key, and he either left his apartment door unlocked or he stashed *that* key under the doormat or something. That's not so risky, if you've got a doorman, if you're only going to be gone for a while. So all you have to do to find out who he was is check the buildings with doormen between Eighth Street and Fourteenth Street and between Fifth Avenue and the river. And before you say, 'That's a big figure,' it's not; there're mostly brownstones; there can't be more than fifteen or twenty buildings with doormen, and most of them're on Fifth."

Federici shook his head, as if she could see him. "Doormen know everything that goes on in a building. If a tenant was missing, they'd know about it."

"I thought about that. You see, I live in a doorman building —don't try to figure out which one, Steve; it's not important— and, yes, the doormen know a lot about what goes on in the building, but the doormen also goof off: They sleep, they go down to the basement for coffee, to watch TV, to go to the john. In some buildings, the overnight doormen have other work besides the door; they have to mop floors, haul garbage, do shit work. I told you, I get home around one-thirty, quarter to two. A lot of the time, my doorman's not there; if the door's locked, I have to let myself in; but sometimes it's not locked, I just walk in. This is the overnight doorman I'm talking about, so he doesn't know if I'm in or out because I leave for work at two-thirty or three and he doesn't come on till eleven-thirty or twelve. And if he's not there when I come back, whether I let myself in or just walk in, he doesn't know about it. I'd say four or five days sometimes go by without my ever seeing my overnight doorman—and there's not just one overnight doorman, there're two, because the regular guy's days off are Tuesday and Wednesday and there's a relief guy on those days, and it's not always the same guy, there's a kind of rotation. So I figure Nowhere Man lived in a doorman building between Eighth Street and Fourteenth Street and between Fifth Avenue and the river and he went out and left his apartment door unlocked and didn't see the doorman on the way out 'cause the doorman

129

was goofing off in the basement or sleeping or using the john or doing shit work and didn't know that Nowhere Man left and still doesn't because it might not even have been the regular doorman, it might've been the relief guy."

Federici laughed. "You sound like you're a doorman. Doorperson."

"It's not important what I am, Steve. Or who. What's important is—"

"You want to meet? You want to have a cup of coffee, talk about this some more?"

". . . I don't think so, Steve. I think the best thing'd be for you to get on a stick and start checking out doormen buildings between Eighth Street and—"

"Why're you doing this? Why're you telling me this?"

"I told you, Steve. I want to help. Good night, now."

"Hey, wait. No . . ." Federici clicked the disconnect button several times, the way they did in bad movies, but it didn't matter; she'd hung up.

While Nell Ward slept, the fat man went through her Hunting World shoulder bag: a Lamston's bag with a picture frame inside; copies of the *Voice, American Cinematographer, Vanity Fair;* a cassette of *The Flamingo Kid,* rented from Video Vault; an audio cassette by Tom Petty and the Heartbreakers; a bottle of vitamin C capsules; a plastic 35-millimeter film can with some kind of skin cream inside—Noxzema? another with some pills—Bufferin and some marked with an *M;* another, empty; a plastic zippered makeup case; a Sanyo answering machine remote beeper; two key rings, one with two keys on it, the other with a dozen; a Day Runner organizer with a purple vinyl cover.

She stirred. "Mark?"

He added some Jim Beam to what was in his glass, took a sip, and waited.

The Day Runner's phone index was a palimpsest of names and numbers: There were names and numbers in the top and side margins, names and numbers squeezed between other names and numbers. He looked for his name and number and found them under the next letter of the alphabet.

The calendar was testimony to a full life: *Pukit/4. Lily/6.*

Call Dan T. Brenda due. Costello/1. Susan Price/McBell's/8:30. Call Computer Era. Call Jill G. Watch Nova/9. Return movie to VV. Post office. Ceco. Trans-Audio. Laundry. MARK'S BIRTHDAY MON!!! That was a typical day.

Mark, Mark, Mark. He turned slowly through the phone index, looking for a Mark. Mark, Mark, Mark. When he found him, he'd call him and whisper in his most horrifying voice to stay away from Nell or he'd cut his nuts off. Not that the fat man loved Nell Ward; he didn't know what love was. But possessing her nose as he did, and sometimes invading her body, he was ever frustrated at his inability to control her mind.

Mark Follett, 42 Fifth Avenue.

The fat man took the phone into the bathroom and dialed the number. There was no answer. Funny for a friend of Nell's not to have an answering machine. Funny not to be home at four in the morning.

14

"Sometimes, it looks like suicide, it's just someone trying to, you know, get someone else's attention." Neuman picked things up off B.G. Harris's desk and put them down: a glass paperweight shaped like an egg, with a low relief of a merman with a crown, a beard and a trident; three tiny acorns, one with a stem, one with a hat, one bareheaded; an autographed baseball. "You don't really want to go the whole way."

"She put a thirty-eight Special in her ear, Jake." Miles Easterly put a fingertip in his. "You put a thirty-eight Special in your ear, you're not buying a round-trip ticket."

Neuman read names off the baseball: *George Kell, Judy Johnson, Ralph Kiner, Lloyd Waner.* "Where's the note?"

"Lab. So's her typewriter—an Olympia portable, which I don't have to be a forensics expert to know is what she typed it on. The little doohickey on the right side of the capital *T*'s worn off."

Ted Page, Buddy Lindstrom. "Which doesn't mean she typed it."

"Meaning what, Jake?"

Bill Terry, Charlie Gehringer, Warren Spahn. "What'd it say?"

" 'I killed Dimanche to save my play. I'm sorry.' " Easterly pronounced Dimanche to rhyme with *paunch*.

Neuman put the ball down and opened and closed some of the desk's many small drawers, finding nothing. "No capital *T*'s in that."

"It was in an envelope addressed 'To whom it may concern,' with a capital *T* in 'to.'"

"Who found the body?"

"Super. A neighbor complained about the music. The stereo was going full blast all day long."

"How's that possible?" Neuman went to the stereo and bent over it. "I mean, there's only one record on here, a record plays for—what?—a half hour, right? Forty-five minutes, max."

"Fireman figured it out. See that arm there, that—"

"What fireman? There was a fire?"

"Jim Fireman. A new guy in Uptown West. Used to work in Jersey—Trenton, I think."

"A cop named *Fire*man?"

"Jake, I've known a cop named Nurse, a cop named Doctor, a cop named Outlaw. Someday I'll meet a cop named Certified Public Accountant, it won't surprise me. Fireman figured it out. See that arm there, that plastic thing? It's for holding a stack of records."

"There's only one record on here," Neuman said.

"That's what I'm trying to tell you, Jake. There was only one record on there, she pushed the arm over to the side, the way you see it; when it's like that, Fireman figured out, the needle gets to the end, it lifts up and swings back to the beginning, the record plays over and over. That's why the neighbor complained—one record, playing over and over, full blast. I thought it was pretty good, Fireman figuring that out. I mean, we might've spent a lot of time, since the M.E. says she died around six-thirty, seven, yesterday morning, and it was two-thirty, three, before the super opened the door—we might've spent a lot of time trying to find out who was hanging around here playing the same record over and over full blast while she was sitting in that chair with what was left of her head on the desk."

"This stereo been dusted?" Neuman said.

Easterly made a wet noise. "Yeah, it's been dusted, and you know what, Jake? There're prints on it. Hers and a lot of other

133

people's. This apartment's a sublet; guy who rents it's out of town, Florida; he's an actor, we talked to him on the phone, he says when he's here he has lots of people over, they play records, watch TV, the place is crawling with prints. It's wrapped up, Jake. What're you asking for? You called me up and said you wanted to see the place, I came over here with you, I figured you ought to see it since you were kind of working on the Dimanche thing, now you're asking did we dust the place. What gives?"

Neuman went back to the desk and opened and closed some more drawers. "Hello."

Easterly laughed. "I know, Jake. You just found the evidence card that that's where we found the empty Valium bottle. You're going to ask me how it fits. You're right, it doesn't fit. You know why it doesn't fit? 'Cause this is real life, not some TV show; in real life things don't always fit. The bottle was empty because she emptied it, is the way I see it—not in one belt but a couple at a time. The prescription was six months old. She was under a lot of pressure—small-town girl in the Big Apple, a Broadway play opening, her folks both died when she was a kid, no friends who've come out of the woodwork. Yes, we called the pharmacist, yes, we called the doctor—both of them in wherever she's from, Iowa."

"Indiana."

"Whatever. They said she wasn't a pill-popper; she was your basic, average neurotic who needed a downer once in a while. They were blues—five milligrams per—not yellows, not heavy-duty."

"When're they doing the autopsy?"

"When they get around to it. Some Haitians chopped each other up with machetes in Washington Heights last night, they've got stiffs standing on line around the block at the M.E.'s. Jake, she put a thirty-eight Special in her ear, the same thirty-eight Special that killed Dimanche, she pulled the trigger, her prints're all over the gun—the way her head was all over this desk. You're lucky I had it cleaned up; it was fucking grim."

Neuman put the evidence card back in the drawer, but not before noting that Dr. Daniel Rooker's prescription had been filled by the Addison Pharmacy—noting it but not writing it down, for this was what it was like, police work; sometimes you had to go back over old ground without stepping on the toes of those who had gone before you. "Just one neighbor complain, or a lot?"

"One. Ten. I don't know."

"Wonder what people were doing home in the daytime."

"Jake, this is New York City. What does Sinatra say in that commercial? 'It's open all night—*all* night.' So maybe it was a night owl trying to sleep who complained. A night watchman. Some retired guy. Don't look at me like that, Jake. I know you're touchy about retirement."

"What I want to know is," Neuman said, "she ever play the stereo full blast before?"

Easterly just sighed.

"This the record that was playing?" With a knuckle, Neuman spun the record to read the label: *The Last Waltz.*

"Yeah, it's the record that was playing. You think we came in and put on another record 'cause we thought it'd be funny if the record she was playing was *The Last Waltz?*"

"It is funny, don't you think? I mean, I never heard this record, but it's funny, you decide to kill yourself, to put on a record called *The Last Waltz.* Not funny, but ironic—ironic like an actress getting bumped off just a couple of weeks before making her Broadway debut in a play about an actress getting bumped off, and so on; ironic like the actress who got killed getting the part over another actress who's the director's girlfriend and who everybody figured because she was the director's girlfriend was a shoo-in to get the part. Ironic like the actress who's the director's girlfriend going to California after she didn't get the part, but coming back the very afternoon the actress who got the part over her got killed. Ironic like the actress who got killed getting killed with a thirty-eight Special and a thirty-eight Special being the gun she used as a prop in the play. Ironic like the play the actress who got killed was in being called *Dying Is Easy.* Ironic, you come right down to it, 'Dying is easy' being something that was once said by Sir Edmund Kean—'Dying is easy, comedy's hard'—and the play being at the theater named after Sir Edmund Kean. Except maybe it wasn't Edmund Kean who said it, maybe it was Edmund Gwenn, Santa Claus in *Miracle on 34th Street.* Don't look at me like how do I know about this stuff; I've been rialtoed, that's how I know. Ironic, this woman who wrote *Dying Is Easy* killing herself with a thirty-eight Special and also having a bottle of Valium in this desk, which I happen to know—don't ask me how; I saw it in a magazine or something—is called an apothecary's desk, apothecary meaning druggist. I called it corny before, I said if I were writing a book or something, or a play, I wouldn't put it in. But it's not corny, it's ironic. Is this the name of the band—The Band? It says The Band on this record. Is that the name of the band—The Band?"

"Fireman says it is. He's a young guy, knows music."

"Yeah? He know the song about 'There's a needle in your arm and it makes you breathless,' or however it goes?"

"What? Oh, yeah—Dimanche's mirror."

"You give the press B.G. yet?"

Easterly shook his head. "We've been trying to find next of kin. We'll probably give her to them this afternoon, except it's Saturday and the Sunday papers go to press early. So maybe we'll give her to them tomorrow, 'cause there's not a lot of news on Sunday for Monday's papers, except maybe there'll be a lottery winner. You got your ticket yet, Jake?"

That was what it was like, police work—always angling for the front page even if it meant holding off on tooting your own horn. And, no, he didn't have his ticket yet; all he had was a lot of numbers he might or not might play. "When you give them B.G., don't give them the song."

"What song?"

" 'There's a needle in your arm and it makes you breathless,' or however it goes."

"What gives, Jake?" Easterly said.

"What gives is I don't think she killed herself. If she didn't kill herself, there's a good chance she didn't kill Dimanche. If she didn't kill Dimanche, it's still just us and the killer who know about the song."

"Jake. Buddy. Listen. I mean this from my heart: You've been away for a while; you've forgotten what police work's like; it's a bitch to stage a suicide. This was the genuine article."

Neuman shook his head. "Don't get me wrong, Miles. I wish

it was the genuine article. Whatever, you know, bad feelings I've got about the Department, I don't get a kick out of seeing cops going around in circles looking for killers they can't find. If this was the genuine article it'd clear the air; but the air's still cloudy as hell. Like I told you on the way over, everybody I've talked to's got a reason why somebody else killed Dimanche, and I haven't even talked to everybody yet. Also—"

"Come on, Jake, give me a break."

"Also, if you're giving the press B.G., you going to let Steve walk?"

"Steve who? Oh—Federici." Easterly patted his pockets, looking for the cigarettes that hadn't been there since January. "Are you retired, Jake, or what? I asked you to stop by Personnel, they tell me you haven't stopped by. I asked you to set up a pistol test, they tell me you haven't set one up."

"Let him walk. Let him work with me."

Easterly slumped. "Jake, I never said Federici killed Dimanche. B.G. Harris killed Dimanche, and wrote a note saying so before she put a thirty-eight Special in her ear, a note that's good enough for me, and by the way, good enough for Klinger, good enough for borough D's, good enough for chief of D's, good enough for the chief, good enough for the commissioner, good enough for the mayor. Good enough means enough is enough, Jake. I never said Federici killed Dimanche. I said I thought it was funny his name was in her phone book—"

"Along with a hundred other guys', McIver tells me."

"Exactly, Jake, which is what I'm saying. I'm saying it looked funny that Federici's name was in her phone book, but since it was along with a hundred other guys', it doesn't look all that funny, except it does look funny that he didn't tell us when we put him on the case that we might find his name in her phone book, along with a hundred other guys', or not, but now that we got this note it doesn't matter one way or another whether his name was in her phone book, or the hundred other guys'. But that doesn't mean I'm going to let Federici walk, 'cause what I still want to know is how come his gun killed the guy in SoHo? Nowhere Man. Notice I didn't say how come *he* killed the guy in SoHo, Nowhere Man. I've still got an open mind about it, he's not locked up, he's at home, so it's not even a question of walking, but until I know for sure one way or the other, no, I'm not going to let him walk, if he was locked up, if it was a question of walking, and, no, you can't work with him. You're not retired, you're back on the force, I've got something you can do: You can go up to Washington Heights and find out why these Haitians chopped each other up."

"This her baseball or what?" Neuman picked up the ball and tossed it.

"I told you, Jake, it's a sublet—some of the stuff's hers, some of it's the guy's who rents it. What difference does it make, Jake? There was no foul play; there was no B and E; there was nothing taken—"

"You don't know that, Miles. Maybe she had an autographed football too. There was no B and E, maybe she let the guy in, or the woman, 'cause she knew him, or her. The super found her, I guess that means the door was locked."

"Yes, it was locked, Jake. It was locked 'cause she locked it. This is New York *City,* not Iowa. People go inside, they lock the door."

"Was there a chain on?"

Easterly pointed. "You see the chain, Jake? Does it look broken? If the chain was on, the super would've had to break it, right?"

"There was no chain on, it could mean whoever she let in had to let himself out and couldn't put the chain on. Or herself. Is she missing a key?"

Easterly sighed. "Keys accounted for. Fireman's a good cop, Jake. He's thought of all this."

"Maybe there was a spare key. He think of that?"

Easterly laughed. "You been watching too much TV, Jake. I bet you watch *Miami Vice* a lot, don't you? You think that's what police work's like, dressing in fancy clothes, driving in fancy cars, climbing into the rack with fancy broads."

No. This was what it was like, police work—beating your head against the stone wall of your superior's obdurateness. Neuman read from the ball: *Billy Herman, Bob Lemon.* "You know what I bet this is from—all these players from different generations? Some kind of Old-Timers' Day, or maybe one of those games at Cooperstown—you know, the Hall of Fame game. You have a key to Dimanche's place?"

Easterly breathed in and out through his nose. "You're a ballbreaker, Jake, you know that?"

"I just want to have a look around. I've never been in, you know, a pop star's house."

"What you should be in, Jake, is the ballbreakers' hall of fame."

15

"Can I buy you a beer?" Nell Ward leaned on the fender of Neuman's car outside B.G. Harris's apartment building, wearing a Ben Hogan golf cap, round-collar white shirt, a string bow tie, argyle V-neck sweater, baggy pleated brown slacks, brown-and-white saddle shoes. She looked ridiculous—and terrific.

Sonny of *Miami Vice* would say something clever, or the black cop. Neuman said, "I don't drink beer in the daytime."

She sighed. "You know, when I was in college a guy came over to me in the library once and asked me if he could buy me a beer and I said, 'I don't drink beer,' and he went away mad and humiliated and never said a word to me again, although I used to see him around a lot. He was a very cute guy; he had a nice voice; he smelled nice. I'd've loved to get to know him, but I was a feminist and independent and a ballbreaker and I had to take him literally and what did it get me? A missed opportunity."

"So you drink it nowadays, beer?"

"Not in the daytime. And neither do you. So let's go have a cup of coffee or a glass of milk or whatever it is we drink."

On *Miami Vice,* Sonny would have said that, and said something with innuendo about what they'd do later. Neuman said,

"Okay." After all, if she was a ballbreaker too, why miss an opportunity?

There was a place at the end of the block with a sidewalk café. They sat outdoors and she ordered an espresso and Neuman a Pellegrino water. Before the waitress brought them, Nell went inside to the bathroom and Neuman played with the place mat and wished he smoked, like Sonny, to have something to do to keep from thinking about what he ought to be doing—and about what he was doing.

"September's always the nicest month in New York," Nell said when she came back.

Especially now that you showed up, Sonny would say. Neuman said, "How'd you know where to find me?"

She cocked her head, a little proudly. "I followed you. I was at the precinct, trying to talk to Steve. I saw you leave with Easterly. I followed you. I'm not *fol*lowing you. You never return phone calls. I want to talk to you. If you'd return phone calls, I wouldn't've had to do this."

"Talk to Steve about what?"

She shrugged. "To see if he's okay. To see if he needs anything."

"You a, uh, friend of Steve's?"

"A better friend than you. You haven't been to see him at all. You're afraid people're going to start saying you're a jinx to your partners. Team up with Neuman and you start killing people. I know all about you, Lieutenant, about you and Bobby Redfield. You were working on the Samaritan Killer case: A kid pulled a knife on a woman on the subway and a passenger shot him, got off at the next stop and disappeared. The newspapers made him a hero—Charles Bronson, Bernhard Goetz, except it was before Bernhard Goetz—but what nobody knew till later was that he was carrying a gun because he was hunting down some guys from his old army outfit—to get revenge for something that happened in Vietnam.

"Around the same time, some women were murdered and their killer wrote notes to the papers threatening to kill more. He called himself the Cunt-Bitch Killer, although the papers never printed that; they bowdlerized it to Lady Killer. It turned out that the hunted was hunting the hunter: Redfield was one of the guys the guy on the subway was looking for, and Redfield was also the guy who was killing the women—a bad case of post-traumatic stress disorder with a side of misogyny. You finally put it together and trailed Redfield to an apartment up on the West Side where he'd taken a woman hostage; you were trying to talk him into giving up when a bunch of Special Services guys kicked in the door and killed Redfield. You quit; you said the Department'd ordered Redfield assassinated to avoid the embarrassment of a trial, of the papers asking how they could have a murderer on the force and not know it. You said Redfield deserved a chance to tell his side of it. My movie's a chance for you to tell his side of it by telling your side, Lieutenant. Spend an afternoon with me; that's all the time I need."

Neuman looked up from his glass of water, in which he'd been making a tiny maelstrom with a swizzle stick. Nothing like hearing a nice, tidy rendering of a part of your life that at the time had been a masterpiece of disorder and in retrospect was no less a mess. "Not too many people know that much about it. Who've you been talking to?"

She flicked a finger at that. "Figure three hours: two to do what we call a preinterview—I ask you questions, you give me answers, I suggest how you could maybe elaborate a little bit on some of the answers; we call it documentary filmmaking, but there's a certain amount of artifice involved—one to do the actual filming. I usually work with three people—camera, lights, sound; I can have the cameraman do the lighting and I'll do the sound if you'd be more comfortable. We can do it at your house, at the precinct, in a park somewhere—anywhere where you can relax."

"Is that what Steve says—that I'm afraid people'll say I'm a jinx?"

"I'm tempted to say you should let him say to you what he has to say to you, but, in fact, no. No, he doesn't say that. He . . ."

"He what?"

"Nothing."

"He thinks I'm out trying to clear him?"

"Are you?"

"Should I be?"

"Shouldn't you? He's your partner. Terry Niles's been doing

more than you have. Do you read the *Dispatch?* He's trying to find out who the victim was, which seems a logical way to determine if Steve killed him."

"Steve's not my partner. I'm retired."

"Then what were you doing at B.G. Harris's? She's dead, isn't she? She killed herself. I overheard McIver say so. Did she kill Dimanche? Is that why she killed herself?"

"McIver a friend too? Klinger? Easterly?"

She frowned. "What do you mean?"

"You know."

She shook her head. "No, they're not friends. I'm making a movie about homicide cops. McIver and Klinger and Easterly're homicide cops, so I know them. What exactly are you asking me, Lieutenant Neuman?"

He shrugged. "Nothing."

"You're asking me if I've slept with Steve, aren't you?"

"No."

"No, you are. You're jealous, aren't you? That's ridiculous. I mean, I'm flattered, but it's ridiculous."

He watched the traffic. "I don't know what you're talking about."

She giggled. "Men're the silliest creatures. I have a theory about it."

"I bet you do. Well, it's been nice talking to you, Miss Ward, but I have things to do, so if you'll excuse me . . ."

"What kind of things? If B.G. Harris killed Dimanche, why're you still working on the case?"

"You already asked me that."

"And you didn't answer."

"Meaning it's none of your business."

"I've got Klinger's approval to make this movie, Lieutenant. I've got the commissioner's approval. All I had to promise was that I'd stay out of the way if anybody started shooting. Do you want to see the letter the commissioner wrote requesting that 'all personnel give their fullest cooperation'?"

"No."

"I'm not trying to make the police look bad. I just want to make an honest movie. Will you do something for me? Will you look at another film I made? It's about the Marines. It won awards. It's an honest picture. There're some things in it the

143

Marines didn't like, that they wanted me to take out, but all in all they had to admit it was an honest picture."

"You like being around guys, is that it? Groups of guys in uniforms? I don't wear one. Sorry."

"Why're you so hostile, Lieutenant? Have we ever met before? Did I do something to you? The way you're acting, that's the only explanation for it."

No, there was another explanation: He *was* jealous—jealous of the commissioner, of Klinger and Easterly, especially jealous of Federici, for being someone she wanted to know was okay or in need of anything. He was even jealous of the Marines. "This movie—when does it come out?"

She laughed. "It's not that kind of movie, Lieutenant. It doesn't *come* out, not in theaters. It has an air date, which is very tentative, to be shown on PBS next fall. That's Public Broadcasting—Channel Thirteen."

"You mean like a year from now?"

"At the earliest."

"Who's paying for it? I mean, where do you get the money for film and stuff?"

"I beg. I have some grants; I have a little money from PBS; I have some money of my own."

"And you want to know what it's like, police work?"

"Yes."

"You just want to film me sitting in a chair telling war stories?"

She shook her head. "I'd also like to follow you around a little—"

"Looking in garbage cans, knocking on doors?"

Nell Ward smiled. "Look. I know I can't film you interviewing suspects, because they might turn out to be innocent. And I know I can't ask you to confide your suspicions, because they'd be only that. But I can show the process; I can show that a murder isn't something that's solved in an hour, not including commercials."

"Like on *Miami Vice?*"

"Or *Hill Street Blues* or any TV show or movie or detective novel."

Neuman sucked on his swizzle stick. "Problem is, I'm sort of retired." And married.

144

"Maybe so, but you're *sort* of working on the Dimanche case, even though B.G. Harris's dead."

Neuman wiped his swizzle stick on his napkin, then stirred up his water again. "Terry Niles a friend too?"

She frowned. "What is the *mat*ter with you?"

"He told you the stuff about Bobby Redfield, didn't he? He's the only one who knows that much. He never wrote about it, 'cause I asked him not to, so you must've talked to him, so he must be a friend."

She said something into her glass.

"What?"

"An old *lov*er." She looked up, moved her cup aside and leaned her elbows on the table. "Is it that you feel paternal about me? Men your age sometimes do. You feel you have to protect me from the big bad wolves prowling around out there. I can take care of myself, Lieutenant; I really can. And I resent the implication that I can't."

"Inference."

"What?"

"You made it, so it's an inference, not an implication, and since you made it, if you want to resent it it's your problem. Terry tell you about Bobby?"

"Yes. But don't get mad at him. I told him you were working on the Dimanche case and he didn't print it."

"Women find Terry, uh, you know, attractive?"

"You mean even though he's bald? Yes."

"Sort of like Yul Brynner, I guess."

She sat back, fingertips on the tabletop, smiling. "You're going to do it, aren't you? You're going to let me film you."

"Let's go for a ride. Where's your car?"

"I'll ride with you. Just let me go to the bathroom. Don't say 'Again?'"

He flipped his hand, Sonny-like. He watched her go back inside the restaurant, which Sonny wouldn't have done; he'd've smoked and looked around a little wearily, as if a good-looking woman was like his Bren 10—nice to have with you but at the same time a burden.

She came back to the table flushed with what he told himself was expectation and he made himself ignore the implication of what he'd seen through the window as another customer went into the ladies' room while Nell was still inside, of her standing before the mirror, scrubbing her nostrils over and over with a fingertip and brushing her gums with it. The inference.

Neuman found a parking place right in front of where he was going. Whatshisname, on *Mike Hammer,* always found a parking place right in front of where he was going, but Neuman rarely did, for that wasn't what it was like, police work. On the other hand, Mike Hammer was a private.

"This is Dimanche's house," Nell Ward said. "You don't think B.G. killed her, do you?"

"Like you said, you can't ask me to confide my suspicions, because that's all they'd be, but let's just say I've got them. I want to look around inside. Sometimes, when I'm going over a woman's place, I like to have a woman officer along. Sometimes they see something's not right that looks okay to me."

She hugged herself and sat lower in the passenger's seat. "That's why you asked me along—to get a woman's opinion on her taste."

"If you have an opinion, I'm sure you'll give it to me. What I want is for you to just tell me if there's anything that doesn't feel right. I'll give you an example. This is strictly confidential, it better not turn up in any movies: There was a record on the stereo at B.G. Harris's; I don't know anything about music so I don't know if it's the kind of record she'd listen to or if maybe somebody put it on the stereo as a way of, you know, leaving a signature, a mark, like."

"Who?"

"You ever heard of it? *The Last Waltz?*"

She laughed. "Of course. I mean, yes. Yes, it's one of my favorites. Or shouldn't I say that?"

"Not unless you killed her."

She sat up straight and stared at him. "Somebody *killed* B.G.?"

"Tell me about *The Last Waltz.*"

"It's a sound track of a film, a documentary, about a concert, a farewell concert, by a group called The Band. The Band plays on it, and so do a lot of other people—Dylan, Joni Mitchell, Neil Young, Neil Diamond, Van Morrison, Doctor John, Muddy Waters, Paul Butterfield, Emmylou Harris. It's a kind of eulogy,

I guess you'd call it, to a part of the sixties that lasted till the late seventies."

"And it's, you know, popular?"

"If you mean did it sell millions of copies, I'd be surprised. If I were making a fiction film and had a character who listened to *The Last Waltz,* he'd be someone who'd been a hippie and was now almost but not quite straight—someone who still wore blue jeans, but also a Rolex watch; someone who used a Macintosh computer."

The Band, Dylan, Joni Mitchell, Neil Young, Neil Diamond, Van Morrison, Doctor John, Muddy Waters, Paul Butterfield, Emmylou Harris, Macintosh computers: Things that had resonance for her were clinkers to him. A Rolex watch he knew about; it was what the astronauts wore. Wasn't it? "You said 'he.' Is it more likely a man'd play *The Last Waltz* than a woman?"

She smiled. "I said it unconsciously, but I guess I think it is more a man's album. The Band's definitely a man's band, although Robbie Robertson is one of the more beautiful men ever invented. Terry—Terry Niles—said after seeing the film *The Last Waltz* that he could have a crush on Robbie Robertson."

He'd forgotten to be jealous of Terry Niles, the bald son-of-a-bitch. Should he be jealous of the whole Band, or just Robbie Robertson? And what about Neil Young, Neil Diamond, Van Morrison, Doctor John, Muddy Waters and Paul Butterfield? And Dylan? Dylan was a man, wasn't he? And what about men who wore blue jeans and Rolex watches and used Macintosh computers? And what about the Marines? "But a woman might play it."

She shrugged. "Of course."

Having given her an example, he was no longer sure an example of what. "Yeah, well. Let's go inside, see what we can see."

"This is wrong." Nell Ward stood over a telephone answering machine in Dimanche's bedroom. "Well, not wrong—but curious."

To Neuman, the whole place was wrong—not curious, just wrong. It didn't look like a pop star's house; it looked like a grandmother's, his grandmother's, on President Street in

Brooklyn—not the Mafia part of President Street, the Jewish part, near Grand Army Plaza: full of chintz and brocade and plush and doilies and knickknacks; pictures on the wall of grandmothers and grandfathers and their grandmothers and grandfathers; sofas that didn't invite you to sit on them and chairs that did but didn't look as though anyone had ever accepted; high, narrow wooden beds suitable for convalescing, or dying, not for sleeping, or loving; dark carpets, dark drapes, dark paneling, vast chandeliers; halls that echoed, stairs that creaked; twice as many doors, it seemed, as there were rooms. The only traces that another generation than those grandmothers' and grandfathers' had occupied the place were a few current magazines and newspapers—no books—lying here and there, a high-tech stereo rig in the living room, televisions in the kitchen and master bedroom, and the answering machine.

"Yeah? What?"

She ducked her head shyly. "It's probably nothing."

"What?"

"I'm just playing cop."

"Play."

"Has anybody gone over this house? Any cops?"

"McIver went over it, mostly to make sure there wasn't anybody living here who was, you know, waiting for Dimanche to come home for dinner. She had a maid, but she didn't live in. Why?"

"This machine is on."

"So?"

She shrugged. "You're right. It's probably nothing."

"What?"

"I don't know. I just had this thought: What if whoever killed Dimanche had been calling her—to threaten her, maybe, or just to say hello, assuming whoever killed her was someone she knew, which is what I assume."

"Yeah, well. There were a bunch of people in the theater when she died. They all knew her in one way or another."

"That's not what I'm talking about. Steve took me through the theater so I could see if it was a place I wanted to film. Dimanche was killed in her dressing room backstage. To get backstage you have to go through the stage door; the stage

148

doorman there isn't the kindly old coot you see in movies about the theater—he's always called Pop and always gives the ingenue advice on how to get the part *and* her boyfriend back; this stage doorman's a young black guy who's very alert, very diligent—and who was very upset at the *implication*"—she looked up and smiled and Neuman smiled back—"that someone he'd let past him might've killed Dimanche. I don't think he let anybody past him. I think Dimanche went out to the front of the theater, through the orchestra, and let someone in through one of the lobby doors, which are locked but can be opened from the inside without a key. Someone she knew, someone she'd invited, someone she was expecting, someone she told to come in that way because *she* didn't want anyone to see him. I think that someone killed her, then left the way he came in; the door would lock itself: It's one of those—I don't know what they're called—locks with a metal bar you push from the inside."

"Panic locks."

Nell cocked her head. "Really?"

Neuman kidded himself that she'd fallen in love with him for knowing that, as she might if he wore blue jeans and a Rolex watch and used a Macintosh computer. He sat in one of the chairs, which groaned a little, surprised. "Yeah, well. The only trouble with that is this: There was a break in the rehearsal on account of Dimanche was having some problems with her lines, problems that didn't sit well with Dillen and Klein and Mrs. Wyndham, the, uh, money lady. The break wasn't scheduled, so it's not likely Dimanche was expecting anyone."

"Okay, so she called him because she was upset. She wanted him to comfort her; she was getting only grief from the people she was working with."

Neuman shook his head. "There wasn't enough time for her to make a phone call, for somebody to get to the theater, kill her, leave."

"Unless he lived or worked close by."

Neuman tipped his hat back on his head. "You're saying 'he' again. You saying it unconsciously, the way you did when you were talking about *The Last Waltz,* or what?"

She came and sat on the arm of the chair, which surprised the chair *and* Neuman. "Dimanche had a boyfriend, a new boyfriend, someone she was seeing but not being seen *with*. It'd been going on for a couple of months at least. She was still, for the consumption of the gossip columnists and the public, involved with Kevin Last, which probably explains her secretiveness. But it had to rankle—rankle the new boyfriend, I mean. Nobody likes to play second fiddle, especially when the first fiddle's getting his picture in the paper all the time with the conductor."

"You've been doing a lot of thinking about this," Neuman said.

Nell started to say something, but stopped herself and pursed her lips.

"What?"

"Oh, nothing. Oh, all right. I went to see Terry the other day to find out a little about you. We talked about Dimanche, about Nowhere Man—Terry's creation, practically—for a long time. It's Terry's favorite thing, talking. He loves to sit in his office with his door open and his feet up on his desk and have his cronies drop in and listen to him speculate, pontificate, elucidate. He's very good at it. He told a story about a venerable British actor—he thought it was Ralph Richardson but it might've been John Gielgud—who said, apropos of acting but also apropos of life, that every love affair requires a murder: The new lover has to kill—figuratively, of course—all of his new lover's old lovers. Terry thinks that because Dimanche's new lover couldn't do that—because she was famous, because her old love affairs were part of recorded history—he had to kill *her*—literally."

The speculating, pontificating, elucidating son-of-a-bitch. "Yeah, well. I'll have to look Terry up one of these days. I haven't seen him in a couple of years. I'll have to ask him to put his feet up on his desk and speculate, so I can take notes and maybe get a few pointers. I'll have to—"

"Jake?" Nell said.

". . . Yeah?"

"Kiss me."

They took their hats off to do it. She tasted like coffee: cocaine, caffeine—were they the same thing? What did he know? What *did* he know?

They took the tape out of Dimanche's answering machine and took it along with them to Nell Ward's loft, on Hudson Street, to play . . . afterward.

They didn't talk on the way downtown. They didn't mention that Nell's car was still parked up in Chelsea, near B.G. Harris's.

They found a parking place right in front of where they were going, just like Mike Hammer.

They didn't talk while Nell unlocked the street door.

Then Nell said, "Excuse the graffito. There's an after-hours punk rock club down the block and some of its customers broke in here a couple of weeks ago and did their thing."

"I've got to go," Neuman said.

"Jake?"

"I've got to go. I just remembered something."

"Oh, Jake. Don't be scared. I know . . . I know you're married, but it'll be all right. It'll just be between us."

"I'll be talking to you, I guess. Okay?"

"Jake."

He drove downtown, for no reason. He wound up in the Brooklyn-Battery Tunnel, for no reason. He came out on the Gowanus and stayed on it until it became the Belt and got off at Cropsey Avenue and drove over to Coney Island, for no reason. He found a parking place on Neptune Avenue, just like Mike Hammer, and walked down to the beach, for no reason, and along it, toward Sea Gate, for no reason. He picked up a stick and drew patterns in the sand, pointless patterns, then watched the waves erase them. He wished he could erase the implication, the inference, of what he'd read on the wall of Nell Ward's hallway:

> *There's a needle in your arm*
> *and it makes you breathless.*

16

"Hey, wait a sec. That ain't Angela. Where's Angela?"

"That's the guy runs the Lotto. They just said it while you were in the head."

"I don't want a see a guy in a suit pick the numbers. I want a see Angela."

"I just *tol*ja, Artie. That's the guy runs the Lotto. They just said it while you were in the head."

"You ever get tired a listening to yourself saying the same thing over and over, Jer? *I* get tired a listening to you saying the same thing over and over."

"Maybe Angela made a deal with somebody else, Art, for a piece a the fifty-two mil. Maybe she's already in Hawaii, waiting for the guy who's gonna give her a piece a it, some guy who already went out with her, not some guy like you whose sister knows her sister."

"Hey, I tolja, Jer, I wanted to go out with her, I could a. I decided I didn't want a, that's all, I didn't need a, that's all. Why give her a piece a the sixty mil—it's sixty mil, Jer, on account a so many people bought tickets the last couple a days—when I can have it all to myself?"

"When you can have half, you mean. I'm getting half too, don't forget."

152

"Hey, listen to you all a a sudden, Jerry, talking about making sure you get your half. Couple a hours ago, you were talking about going to the cops, telling them we took the dude's ticket, not wanting to have nothing to do with it. All a a sudden, you're talking about making sure you get your half."

"Shut up, will you. The guy's drawing the number."

"I wish Angela was doing it. Angela's good luck. Plus, she's got nice tits."

"Shut up, will you."

"It's about time. They tell you the drawing's at ten, you turn on the tube you got to watch the news first, a plane crashed in Guacamole, who cares?"

"Guatemala."

"Then you got to watch the sports, the weather, the Yanks lost, the Mets lost, who cares, it's gonna be nice tomorrow, nice for us, on account a we're gonna win sixty million— Five! All right! Five! I tolja, Jerry. We got the winning number. I tolja, man. Five! All right!"

"Come on, Artie. I can't hear. What'd he just say? Something about signing the ticket. You sign the ticket, Artie?"

"He's talking about after you win, so somebody doesn't cop your— Forty-four! Can you believe it, Jer? Five and 44! We got them both. Can you believe it?"

"I can't hear nothing, Artie. Stop jumping around. What'd he just say? Something about not knowing who won till tomorrow afternoon?"

"They won't know till tomorrow afternoon. We'll know in a couple a seconds— Nine! Holy shit! Nine! I can't believe it—5, 9, 44. And we got them—5, 9, 44."

"Get off a me, you asshole. I can't see a thing."

"Two! Two! Two! Two, 5, 9, 44! We got them! Two, 5, 9, 44!"

"Come on, man. The neighbors. You want the neighbors to know?"

"Forty-two! I can't believe it. We just need 8, Jer. We just need 8. Eight and we got it. Oh, shit. I can't believe it. Oh, shit, we're not gonna get it. I can feel it. Eight and 9're too close together, man. I never liked that 8 and 9're so close together. I never would a bet on 8 and 9; they're too close together."

"Shut up, Artie."

"We're not gonna get it."

153

"Shut up."

"We're not gonna get it."

"Shut up."

"We're not gonna get it. . . . Eight! Eight, eight, eight, eight, eight, eight, eight! We did it! We won, Jerry! We won! Sixty million dollars. We won, we won, we won!"

"Come on, man, the neighbors."

"We won, we won, we won!"

"Artie?"

"We won, we won, we won! Two, 5, 8, 9, 42, 44! We won, we won, we won!"

"Artie?"

"We won, we won, we won!"

"What'd he do, Artie? He drew another number. He drew 22. We don't got 22."

"That's the supple-mentry number. That's for the losers. They got it and they got a couple a other numbers, they win a few bucks. It ain't for us. We got the winning number—2, 5, 8, 9, 42, 44. I can't believe it."

"Artie?"

"Aloha, Waikiki."

"The phone's ringing, Artie."

"I can't believe it, Jer. When we just needed 8, Jer, when we just needed 8, I didn't think we'd get it. I thought, oh, shit, we're not gonna get it. Eight and 9're too close together, man. I never liked that 8 and 9 were so close together. I never would a bet on 8 and 9; they were too close together. But we did it, we did it, we did it! We won, we won, we won!"

"Artie, the phone's ringing."

"So answer it."

"It's your phone, Artie."

"Prob'bly for my sister, my mother."

"They ain't home."

"So what am I, their secretary? We won, Jerry. We won, we won, we won!"

"Maybe it's Terry Niles," Jerry said. "He knows the Lotto number."

"How could he know the number? They just drew the number."

154

"He was watching. He must a been. We were watching, right? He must a been watching too. He knows the winning number, he knows we got it."

"Knows from when?"

"When I told him."

"Let me get this straight, Jerry. You *told* Niles the number we bet on?"

"We didn't bet on it, Artie. Nowhere Man bet on it."

"You *told* him we took the dude's ticket *and* you told him what the number was?"

"He axed me."

"Right, he axed you. So tell me you didn't tell him, Jerry."

"I just—"

"Tell me you didn't, Jer."

"I just tolja, I— *Ow!"*

"You scumbag, Jerry."

"Ow! Hey, come on, man. *Ow!"*

"You scumbag. You *told* Niles we took the dude's ticket *and* you told him what the number was *and* you told him my phone number?"

"No, man. Hey— *Ow!"*

"Whattaya mean, *no,* Jerry? The phone's ringing, ain't it, Jer? You mean *yes,* don't you, Jer? You mean *yes* you told Niles we took the dude's ticket, *yes* you told him what the number was, *yes* you told him my phone number. You scumbag."

"Maybe it ain't Niles. Maybe you should answer it. It's still ringing. Maybe it's a emergency."

"The only emergency, Jer, is you. You're the only emergency. You're gonna need a ambulance for the rest a your life, Jer."

"I'm gonna answer it."

"Don't answer it, Jer."

"Maybe it ain't Niles."

"You said that, Jerry. First you said it *was* Niles, now you're saying maybe it *ain't* Niles. Don't answer it, Jerry."

"Hello?"

"You scumbag."

". . . Yeah. . . . Yeah, I figured it was you."

" 'I figured it was you,' " Artie singsonged.

". . . Yeah. Yeah, we got the number. . . . Yeah, 2, 5, 8, 9, 42, 44."

155

"Tell the whole world, why don't you, Jer? Tell the whole world."

". . . I don't know what we're gonna do. We don't know what we're gonna do. . . . When? . . . Yeah, I guess we could. . . . Okay, yeah. . . . Yeah, yeah, okay, yeah. . . . Yeah, I'll bring him." Jerry hung up the phone. "That was Niles."

"No shit, Kojak."

"He got your number out a the phone book."

"You gave it to him, you mean."

"He got it out a the *phone* book."

"That reminds me, I got a get a unlisted phone, 'cause people're gonna be crawling out a the woodwork hitting on me for a little scratch. I got a get a unlisted phone on my yacht too, in my Benz, in my plane. I'll only give the number to blondes. And maybe redheads."

"He wants to meet us."

"And you know what, Jerry? I'm thinking you been shooting your mouth off so much, maybe I'm not going to give you half a the sixty mil. I'm thinking maybe you could use a lesson in keeping your mouth shut."

"He wants to meet us, Artie."

"I mean, you talk too much, Jer. Let's face it."

"He'll call us back about when."

"Somebody who talks so much, it's not healthy, you know what I'm saying?"

"I think he wants a piece a it, Artie."

"I'm not saying I'll stiff you, Jer. I'll give you something. But I ain't gonna give you half, I don't think."

"A piece a the sixty mil, Artie. 'Cause otherwise he says he knows who Nowhere Man is, he's gonna tell the cops."

". . . He said that?"

"I just *tol*ja."

"He said he knows who Nowhere Man is?" Artie went to a closet and felt around on the shelf.

"What're you doing, Artie?"

"I can't hear you, Jerry. Don't you think I got my head in a closet maybe I can't hear you?"

"I said, what're you— The fuck is that?"

"Fuck does it look like, Jerry?"

"It's a gun. Where'd you get a gun?"

"I got it. Fuck difference does it make where?"

"Fuck're you gonna do with it?"

"I'm gonna pop him. Fuck do you think?"

"Pop who?"

"Fuck do you think, Jerry?"

"Niles?"

"Bingo. This must be your night, Jerry. First you win half a the Lotto, then you get bingo. This must be your night."

17

"Hello, Lieutenant."

"Hello, Steve. Thanks for letting me come over on such short notice. This is a nice place you got here. Small, but nice. And it's Jake, goddamn it."

Federici smiled. "What's up, Jake? I heard the Dimanche thing got wrapped up."

"Heard it where?"

"McIver. He's, you know, investigating this Nowhere Man thing, but he still treats me like a cop, not like, you know, ratshit. You want something to drink, Jake? Coffee? Booze? A beer?"

"No. No, thanks."

"Something to eat? I got chicken, you can have it cold, some eggplant parmesan, I can heat it up. Or some popcorn? I was just going to make some popcorn."

"I ate, thanks." Had he? No—just driven.

"I think I'll make popcorn anyway. Come on in the kitchen."

Neuman leaned against the kitchen door while Federici got a stainless-steel pan from under the sink, a bottle of safflower oil from a cupboard, a butter dish from the refrigerator, a jar of popcorn from the freezer.

"I've been eating a lot of popcorn lately," Federici said.

158

"Nerves, I guess. I'm glad I don't smoke. Did you ever smoke, Jake?"

"I don't think so. No, I never did. You always keep your popcorn in the freezer?"

"They say that keeps it fresh." Federici laughed. "Don't ask me who 'they' are. I just read it somewhere." He poured some oil in the pan and dropped in a single kernel. "So you're not retired anymore, Jake? You're working on this Nowhere Man thing?"

"Who? Oh—no. No, I'm not. Is that all you're making?"

"It's something else I read somewhere—on how to make the best popcorn. Put in one kernel and don't add the rest until it pops. That way you know the oil's hot and the kernels don't lie there soaking up the oil. I got a phone call, Jake—a weird phone call. I'm wondering if I should tell McIver about it or maybe do something about it on my own. From a woman. She wouldn't tell me who she was or anything, except that she's a serious runner, like Nowhere Man probably was, but she had some ideas about who Nowhere Man is, about where he might've lived. . . ."

He went through it all, but half of Neuman didn't listen. That half wondered: If the sun were the size of the globe in the lobby of the Daily News Building and the earth, comparatively, were the size of a walnut and located at the main entrance to Grand Central Terminal, would people whose job it was to unravel knots still give so much credence to the musings of cranks and crackpots? But then, Federici wasn't in the unraveling business just now; he was part of the knot.

"You think I should tell McIver about it, Jake?" Federici said.

"I don't know," Neuman said. "I mean, I guess you could, sure."

The kernel popped. Federici poured in enough kernels to cover the bottom of the pan, and put on the lid. "You sure you don't want any?"

"Yeah. I mean, no—no, thanks."

"I didn't win the Lotto, Jake. Did you?"

"I don't know. I mean, I don't think so. I didn't buy a ticket, so I guess I didn't. They have the drawing already?"

Federici lifted the pan off the flame and shook it gently.

159

"About an hour ago. Two, 5, 8, 9, 42, 44 were the winning numbers. They drew 5 first, which was one of my numbers, so for about ten seconds there I was thinking goodbye NYPD, hello permanent R and R, but I didn't have any of the others."

Just as well Neuman hadn't bought a ticket; he'd saved a dollar, for he wouldn't have played those numbers. Would he? He had been thinking about playing 8—for the letters in Nell Ward's name. Nell Ward—Jesus. "They're really popping, aren't they?"

"It's because the oil's nice and hot." Federici concentrated on the popping until it stopped. He dumped the popcorn into a big blue bowl and put it on the counter. He put the pot back on the burner and turned off the flame.

"Don't you use butter?" Neuman said.

"The pot's too hot for it right this sec. It'd burn. It'll still be hot enough to melt it in a minute. I won't need any more heat."

"You've got this down to, you know, a science, don't you?" Neuman said.

"Jake?"

"Yeah?"

"I'm sorry I didn't tell you about Dimanche, Jake. It was nothing, the thing I had with her. I mean, it wasn't a thing at all. I met her at this party Nell took me to— What's the matter?"

"Nothing."

"You look like somebody kicked you in the balls."

Somebody like you. "You're pals, hunh? You and Nell Ward?"

Federici gave him his gun-eating look. "Nell's a friend, yeah. I mean, since she's been hanging around, doing preproduction for her movie, I've gotten to know her. She was going to this party, some people in the film business, the business she's in, she asked me if I'd like to go. It was down in TriBeCa, a big loft. There were a lot of famous people. Not famous famous, but, you know—punk rockers, modern dancers, painters, writers, filmmakers like Nell. I don't know. I mean, I guess I've got a thing for that kind of people. I mean, I sometimes wonder if they aren't doing something that I ought to be doing. Not that I'm an artist or anything, but, well . . . Anyway, I met Dimanche, we danced, we talked, I liked her. She was a beautiful

160

woman, Jake. Jesus. She gave me her phone number. I was surprised. I mean, a woman like that, guys're hitting on her all the time. I called her up a few times. We talked. She was always busy, though. I mean, she couldn't go out or anything. It's funny, you know—she had this boyfriend, Last, but she never said he was the reason she couldn't go out, never said 'I can't go out with you because I'm seeing someone. . . .'

"It's just as well, probably. I mean, where would I've taken her? To the Blue Mill? That's where I usually take a date for dinner the first time. To a movie? I can't see her standing on line at the Waverly, can you? To McBell's? That's where I like to go for a drink. You know it, Jake? It's in the Village. I tell you I moved to the Village—from Bay Ridge? I think I did, when I told you about finding Bobby's list, and somehow we started talking about the lottery and you asked me what numbers I played and I told you 1, 5, 6, 12, 22, 35—1, 22, 35, which is 53 turned around, for my birthday, 12, 5, 6 for the sixth floor, 12 Perry Street—five letters—which is in the Village. What'm I saying? Of course I told you. You're here right now. In the Village . . ." He was weeping now. "Jake, I didn't kill the guy. Nowhere Man. Why would I kill the guy? I mean, who the fuck was he? Nobody's even missed the guy. People he worked with, people he lived with, neighbors, friends, family, the corner grocer. Nobody. Who'd kill a guy like that, Jake? I mean, he was already dead."

Where was Charly Johnstone now, to hear Detective Federici talking? "You ever tell Dimanche her name was on Bobby's list, Steve?"

Federici pulled a paper towel off a roller and blew his nose. "Why scare her? Bobby was dead."

"You ever talk to her about Bobby?"

Federici smiled. "You know how it is, Jake—or maybe you don't; you've been married a long time. . . ."

Fourteen years.

"You meet a woman, you like to think you're the first guy who ever rode through town, so to speak; you don't want to know a whole lot about the other guys who beat you to her."

Neuman knew how it was: He hadn't wanted to know a whole lot about Nell Ward and the commissioner, Klinger, Easterly, Federici, Terry Niles, The Band, Robbie Robertson, Neil

Young, Neil Diamond, Van Morrison, Doctor John, Muddy Waters, Paul Butterfield, Dylan, men who wore blue jeans and Rolex watches and used Macintosh computers, and the Marines. "Where is Bobby's list, Steve?"

"B.G. Harris killed Dimanche. What's the difference?"

"Where is it?"

"At the squad. McIver has it."

"You ever talk to Nell Ward about it?"

"No."

"Think, Steve. Did you?"

"Hey, Jake. Give me a break."

"Who did you talk to about it?"

Federici put some butter in the pan. "McIver, Easterly, Klinger—you know."

"Matty McGovern?"

"Matty's on sick leave. Something wrong with his gut."

"You found the list before he went on sick leave."

". . . I guess I told him. Yeah, I told him."

"You tell anybody outside the Department? Any reporters?"

". . . No."

"You're not sure."

"Shit, Jake, I don't know. I think maybe Matty . . ."

"Matty what?"

"He drinks with Terry Niles. I think he maybe told him about it. Niles never wrote anything, though. He's a pretty straight guy."

"You said Nell Ward took you to this party Dimanche was at. Were she and Dimanche friends?"

"Nell knew her. They were each part of crowds that overlapped that could wind up at the same party, but they weren't friends, no. Nell wasn't shaken up or anything when she heard Dimanche was dead."

"How about when you took her to the theater? She act funny then?"

"How do you know about that?"

"Did she?"

"No. How do you know about that?"

"She say anything to you about her front door theory?"

"What're you talking about, Jake?"

"You ever hear a song called 'The Last Waltz'?"

162

"It's not a song. It's a, you know, an instrumental, on an album called *The Last Waltz.*"

"So you know it."

"Jake."

"You ever hear it at Nell Ward's, by any chance? You've been there, right, to her loft?"

"Jake, I feel like I'm being sweated."

"Right?"

"I've been there, yeah."

"She ever play that record while you were there?"

Federici laughed. "I just remembered how I told you you should watch *Miami Vice,* that sometimes it was pretty good on what police work's like. If they ever had a scene like this on *Miami Vice,* people'd either turn it off or fall asleep over it."

"Yeah, well. You got a boat, Steve? We can take a little run to Bimini and back. Or maybe just over to Weehawken."

The gun-eating look again.

"How long since you were at Nell's loft?"

"A month. Six weeks."

"So the graffiti wasn't on the wall?"

"What graffiti?"

"When you took her to the theater, did you show her the message on Dimanche's mirror?"

"Hey, Jake. It was a crime scene. I let her walk through the parts of the theater that weren't a crime scene."

"The whole theater was a crime scene, Steve. Who knows what clues she walked all over, put her fingerprints on top of?"

Federici slumped.

"Did you tell her about the message on the mirror?"

"No."

"I didn't hear you, Steve."

Federici just glared at him.

Neuman felt in his pocket. "You got a tape recorder?"

"A deck, yeah."

"A deck? You mean like a deck of horse?"

"A *tape* deck."

"It plays one of these?" Neuman held out the cassette.

Federici laughed. "Jesus, Jake."

"Yeah, well. Play this, will you? It's from Dimanche's answering machine."

"What's going on, Jake? Did B.G. Harris kill Dimanche or what?"

"Just play it, Steve."

Federici plucked the cassette from Neuman's hand and slipped past him into the living room. He put the cassette in the tape deck, pressed buttons, threw switches, listened. "You've got the wrong tape, Jake."

"Who says?"

"This isn't from an answering machine. It has music on it."

"What kind of music?"

"Listen."

They listened.

Federici stopped the tape. "Did you say *The Last Waltz?*"

"Did I say *The Last Waltz* what?"

"Come on, Jake. You were asking me about *The Last Waltz.* How come?"

" 'Cause it was on the stereo at B.G. Harris's."

"Well, this song's from *The Last Waltz.*"

"What song?"

"This song." Federici started the tape again.

"I can't understand the words," Neuman said.

" 'Who Do You Love?' Ronnie Hawkins. He used to have a band called The Hawks that became The Band—the band called The Band."

"That's it?" Neuman said. "That's a short song."

"The tape ran out. Some machines only record about thirty seconds' worth of an incoming call."

"You're saying somebody called her and played the song over the phone?"

"That's what it sounds like. The quality's real bad. Listen. Here's something else."

They listened.

"Is that from *The Last Waltz* too?" Neuman said.

Federici shook his head. "Billy Ocean. 'Loverboy.' "

"That's somebody's name? Billy Ocean?"

"I don't think that's his real name—like Dimanche wasn't her real name."

They listened.

"I can't understand the words," Neuman said.

Federici translated: "It's a guy saying he can't stand the sight of a girl with somebody else, he wants to have her love all to himself."

"So the guy's, you know, jealous? Possessive?"

"What guy?"

Me. "The guy who called Dimanche, played the song over the phone."

"What're you saying, Jake?"

"Listen."

They listened.

"Pat Benatar," Federici said. " 'Love Is a Battlefield.' "

"How do you know all these songs, Steve? What do you, listen to the radio all the time?"

"While I'm running. I have a Walkman. Listen."

They listened.

"This sounds like a country song," Neuman said.

"It's whatshisname—" Federici snapped his fingers. "I can't think of it. The guy who used to be on *Maverick.*"

"Ed Bruce," Neuman said.

"How do you know that, Jake?"

Neuman shrugged. "He wrote the theme song. He also wrote 'Mammas Don't Let Your Babies Grow Up to Be Cowboys.' "

"How do you know *that?*"

"Remember Sam Branch?" Neuman said.

"I've heard of him. I didn't know him. He was before my time. He took a pension and a hike rather than sing about some brass, right?"

"I used to ride with him when we first started out," Neuman said. "He listened to country music all the time. What's the name of this song? 'If It Was Easy'?"

"Sounds like it, yeah. 'If it was easy, everyone would fall in love.' Listen."

They listened.

"Blues," Federici said.

"I can't understand the words," Neuman said.

"Wait, I've heard this song," Federici said. "It's— Oh, shit. What's his name? Johnson. Robert Johnson."

"I can't understand the words."

"He says if she gets unruly, if she doesn't want you, he'll get his thirty-two-twenty and cut her in two."

"This is a song?" Neuman said.

165

"Listen, Jake. Listen. He says she's got a thirty-eight Special. A thirty-eight Special, Jake. Dimanche had a thirty-eight Special in the play, it's what she was killed with."

"So was B.G. Harris," Neuman said. "Sort of."

"Meaning she killed herself."

"Is that it?"

That was it.

"Shit," Federici said.

"What?"

"I know where I heard that Robert Johnson song."

"Where?"

"Nell's. What's going on with Nell, Jake? Why were you at her loft? What's this about graffiti?"

"At that party you went to, Steve—were there drugs?"

"Yeah. Yeah, I suppose there were. You know, grass, coke."

"Was Nell doing any?"

"No. I mean, I don't know. Why?"

"How could you just stay there, Steve, when people were doing drugs? I mean, you're a cop, right?"

"Hey, Jake, you ever been at a party where people were drinking?"

"Drinking's not against the law."

"It was once. And drunk driving's against the law. Don't get moral on me, Jake. Face it, times change. People do drugs now, against the law or not, people who aren't criminals. You're an old-fashioned guy, Jake. You don't know what a tape deck is; you've never heard of Billy Ocean, Pat Benatar, *The Last Waltz*. You've heard of Ed Bruce—*Maverick*, for Christ's sake."

"Yeah, well." Neuman took the tape from the deck and put it in his pocket.

"You going to tell me what's with Nell, Jake, or not?"

"Where was Nell when Dimanche got killed, Steve?"

"You mean, does she have an alibi?"

"All right, yeah. Does she?"

"Come on, Jake. Why would she kill Dimanche?"

"Does she have an alibi?"

"I don't know, Jake, but I'll tell you this—she didn't kill her."

"Yeah, well. That's what I've been telling people about you and Nowhere Man."

166

"Good night, Jake."

"I'm sorry, Steve. I didn't mean that. I'm just tired. It's been a long day."

"You know what I think, Jake? I think you're having trouble at home, you're coming down hard on anybody you can find. You're having trouble at home, Jake, work it out, don't go walking the streets coming down on anybody you can find. I was right, you know? At first I thought, I got mixed up in this Nowhere Man thing, no sweat, Jake'll get me out, Jake's my partner, even if he's still retired, he's my partner for right now, he'll get me out. The other guys, McIver, they'll treat me like ratshit, but Jake's a guy who stands by his partner. Look how he stood by Bobby, even after Bobby was dead; when a lot of guys would've pissed on Bobby's grave, Jake was still standing by him. Then I thought, no—no, wait a minute, Jake's not going to get me out, he's not going to stand by me, he's going to cover his ass 'cause he's afraid people're going to start talking, going to start saying, 'Work with Neuman, you turn into a killer.' Get the fuck out of here, Jake. Get off the street. Go home. Go home and feel sorry for yourself. You're not a cop anymore, Jake; you're a . . ."

But Neuman was gone.

Federici went into the kitchen. The popcorn was cold; the butter had melted and congealed.

18

"This is rather like an Agatha Christie." Charly Johnstone lighted a new Sherman's from an old. "The principals gather in the drawing room to await the arrival of Hercule Maigret, who stuns them, and the reader, with an account of the labyrinthine path his ingenious mind has negotiated, and unmasks the murderer. So often—too often—it has to do with clocks: people turning back the hands of clocks so that entire households, villages, *nations,* are deluded into thinking it's eleven when it's actually high noon, during which counterfeit hour the, uh, perpetrator struck. Did one of you turn back the clocks at the Kean? To what end I can't imagine. And who's to play Hercule? I *know* what his surname is, Jay. Don't look at me like that."

Jay Dillen adjusted the roll in the cuffs of his bush jacket. "Look. Charly, Kevin, Marty—we've got a problem, people. Dimanche is dead and we're suspects. You've all talked to this cop, Neuman, right? He's a smart guy, but he doesn't know shit —or not yet, anyway. These things take time—weeks, months; it's not like in the movies or on TV. Neuman's got time; he can wait the killer out, wait for the pieces to fall into place, wait to find the pieces he's missing. While he's taking his time, we're all under the onus. *I* know I'm innocent, but I can feel people looking at me funnily—at the Vertical Club, at '21,' on the street—"

"I *thought* I was innocent," Martin Klein said. "Then I talked to the insurance adjuster, I found out I not only killed Di*manche,* I sank the *Titanic,* blew up the *Hindenberg* and fixed the 1919 World Series. Where's Amanda, Jay, speaking of suspects? Isn't she a suspect too? Supposed to be on the coast, making a deal for a Roeg film—you were trying to call her, for Christ's sake. Turns up without telling anybody—not even you, Jay—in plenty of time to've knocked off Di*manche.* And where're the Bee Gees? They go back to Australia?"

Dillen waited several beats, to make the point that he was the director and that it was his show. "The purpose of this little gathering is to make some informed guesses as to the identity of Dimanche's killer—guesses Neuman isn't prepared to make because he's not in the guessing business. I've left B.G. out of it because she's literally an innocent abroad; she doesn't know the town or anyone in it."

"And where's Viv Thib Wynd?" Charly said. "At church, probably, this lovely Sunday morning—Saint Bart's or some such Episcopal stronghold—settling up her tab with the Lord. You really ought to've invited *her,* Jay; think of the classy names she could add to our list. And what a list it will be, for as Leftenant Neuman put it in his inimitable argot, a woman like Dimanche, good-looking, smart, successful, rich—mustn't there have been a lot of people who wanted to pop her?"

Dillen screwed his Omega around to see the time. "I've also invited Terry Niles to stop by—"

"Wonderful." Klein looked up at the ceiling of Dillen's apartment—and past it, at Yahweh. "And tomorrow the whole town'll get to read about us sitting around fingering people."

"—because I'd like him to do a piece on how the show's going to go on, on how theater people cope with adversity—"

"The sort of piece a press agent might dream up," Charly said. "Did anyone think to consult with the press agent about this here endeavor?"

"—the sort of piece that, in the process, can put our alibis on record—something, again, that Neuman's not about to do. I've also asked Niles because six months or so ago he did an interview with Dimanche—"

169

"Prior to which he'd never to my knowledge set foot in a legitimate theater, being more the sort—"

"—just after we announced the casting."

"—who frequents theaters like the Pussycat."

"Perhaps he can shed some light on the one area that's still in shadow—namely, who is this man Dimanche had been seeing? Was he the man who struck her—"

"Smacked her the fuck around," Klein said.

"—and if so, might he also have killed her? Kevin, you say you have *no* idea who this fellow was. How is that possible?"

Last just shrugged, the possibility written in the red that rimmed his eyes, the eyes of a solipsist whose only curiosity is in how to get as quickly as possible from low to high.

"Where *is* Amanda, Jay?" Charly blew a smoke ring, and sighted through it at Dillen.

"Out at the Sagaponack house. Previews resume tomorrow. She needs a quiet place to work on her lines."

"The reason I ask is not so much to know the answer—'the Sagaponack house'; it sounds so . . . genteel—as to call attention to the credibility—the logic, even—of Kevin's not knowing anything at all about Dimanche's, uh, affair with this mysterious stranger. After all, we who know you so well, who have been by your side for nearly every waking minute, it seems, during the gestation of the living, breathing organism called *Dying Is Easy*—Leftenant Neuman was right; it *does* strain one's credulity, if one has one—we knew nothing, know nothing, about the, uh, well, working girl you've been having on the side. Nor, one supposes, did Amanda. Does she now, and is that why she's repaired to the . . . Sagaponack house?

"Do you know what I was reminded of, Jay, when I got out of the taxi a few moments ago and saw you nibbling on her neck right there in the lobby? You asked us for ten, Jay; I was here at the stroke of ten, and faced with the necessity of taking a turn around the block so that I wouldn't . . . em*bar*rass you? Is that the word I'm looking for? I was reminded of the scene in *Tootsie,* a film that I recall you excoriating because you felt it portrayed the soap opera director with such broad, unflattering strokes—the scene in which Tootsie spies that very director nibbling backstage on the neck of the actress with whom she shares a dressing room, a scene that seemed to me back then and seems to me now to earn high marks for verisimilitude."

"What working girl?" Klein said.

Dillen's face was bright red. "I don't know what you're talking about, Charly." He laughed. "But then, that's not unusual."

"What working girl?"

Another laugh, more affected. "Look, we've all got secrets, right? Everyone's got secrets. Times like this, the secrets look, well, darker than they really are. Everything we do, everything we have done, starts looking more suspicious. It probably looked suspicious that I bought a lottery ticket, looked like I was hoping for a big score so I could skip town or something. I lost, Marty. I didn't have one single number right. You were probably right—it's a way of giving hope to the hopeless. Never again. Not even for a dollar."

"What working girl, Jay?"

"I mean, just for example, Charly, speaking of those who've been by our sides during the gestation of a living, breathing organism, who would've thought that you were a suspect by virtue of your sexual preference?"

"Nice, Jay." Charly pushed a cloud of smoke away from her face. "Very nice."

"Your what?" Klein said.

Last snorted, but not at events, at something his own mind offered up.

Dillen got up to answer the intercom buzzer.

"Give her my love, you son-of-a-bitch," Charly said.

"Give who your love?" Klein said. *"What* sexual preference?"

Charly cupped a breast in her hand. "Suck my left, Martin."

"What *work*ing girl?"

She turned her back on him, looking out the window at Queens, dim and undifferentiated in the lingering morning haze.

"You know what working girl?" Klein said to Last. "You know what sexual preference?" But Last was asleep, or so it seemed.

Borne by the supersonic elevator, Terry Niles, inevitably bow-tied, inevitably bald, was at the door in a matter of seconds, then in the living room of the foyerless apartment.

"Everybody knows everybody, I think," Dillen said.

"I met you all when I interviewed Dimanche," Niles said.

Dillen guided him to the room's throne, a hypermodern chair of leather and chrome. "That's what we wanted to talk to you about, Terry. Charly here, and Marty, and Kevin especially, and I—we were all close to Dimanche, and yet we have no idea who this fellow is she's supposed to've been seeing a lot of lately. It seems a strong possibility—to me, anyway—that he, well, you know—"

"Killed her?" Niles said.

"Yes."

Niles sat and crossed his legs. "Anybody have a cigarette?"

"Kevin, give Terry a butt, will you?" Dillen said, slipping into what he thought was journalese. ". . . Kevin?"

Last opened his eyes. "He plays music."

They waited, but that was it.

"Who, Kevin?" Dillen was the only one standing, and looked uncomfortable about it.

"The asshole who was fucking Dimanche."

"He's a musician?"

Last snickered. "Who isn't?"

Martin Klein leaned forward in his chair. "Hey, Kev. You're the one who said he plays music, so don't make a quiz show out of it all of a sudden. He play music or doesn't he play music?"

Last took a pack of Rothman's from his Members Only jacket and tossed it in a low arc to Niles, who caught it as if they'd rehearsed for weeks. "He liked to call her up and play music over the phone."

Dillen moved closer to him. "She told you that, Kevin, and she didn't tell you his name?"

"I listened."

"You listened?"

"Yep."

"You mean, on another extension or something? Eavesdropped?"

"I listened to the tape."

"What tape, Kevin?"

"The answering machine tape."

"Kevin, tell us what you're talking about. Don't make us drag it out of you."

Last kicked out a lizard boot at something only he saw. "He fucking called her up when she was fucking out and fucking played fucking music over the fucking phone onto the fucking answering machine tape. You dig?"

"And you listened to the tape?"

"Fucking right."

Niles leaned between them. "What kind of music, Kevin?"

Last shrugged, as if music wasn't music unless it was his music.

"You have a light?" Niles said.

Last handed him a Cricket lighter and when he'd lighted up and handed back the cigarettes and the lighter, Niles said, "I wonder what kind of music because the cops haven't been able to make anything out of the message on Dimanche's mirror—words to a punk rock song, they look like."

Dillen laughed nervously. "Hey, Terry, I know you're a good reporter, but how do you know about the message? We all know, but the cops asked us to keep quiet about it."

"A source," Niles said. "Not that it matters—now."

"Hey, Terry. Of course it matters. We're onto something here."

Niles sat back again and crossed his legs. "I guess you folks haven't heard. Of course you haven't. It hasn't been made public yet. It will be this afternoon, according to my source."

"What will?" Klein said. *"You* going to start doing it now—playing cutesie with us with stuff you know that we don't know?"

"Can I trust you to keep it quiet?"

"Hey, Terry. Of course." Dillen looked a model of probity.

"B.G. Harris killed Dimanche."

The only sound was the sound of Sunday traffic, lazy and intermittent.

"That was my first mistake," Klein said. "Backing a play by a woman writer."

Last put a Rothman's in his mouth, but didn't light it.

Charly kept her back to the rest of them, but her shoulders were tense with anticipation.

Dillen lifted his hands and let them drop. "B.G. confessed, Terry, or what?"

"She left a note," Niles said. "A suicide note."

173

"Women," Klein said. "They can't just kill themselves; they have to leave notes explaining why."

"The cops've kept it quiet while trying to find her next of kin. It was pretty ugly, according to my source; she shot herself in the head with the same thirty-eight Special she used to kill Juliet. Speaking of music, the record on her turntable was *The Last Waltz*—not exactly a punk standard."

"*Ju*liet?" Klein said. "Who's Juliet?"

Niles cupped his hand under his cigarette, as if the ash were about to fall, then looked up and smiled. "That was Dimanche's real name—Juliet Marko. I find myself thinking of her as Juliet lately; I've been thinking about doing a column about how her dying made the stage name seem . . . not extravagant, exactly, but . . . I don't know. Anyway, if the reason you asked me here was for some insight into who killed her, well, as I said, I've got more than insight." He took out a notebook. "As long as I'm here, what can you tell me about B.G. Harris? Frankly, I thought that's why you'd invited me. I thought you'd heard and that you wanted to, well, disassociate yourselves from—"

"Come on, Charly, hey. I'm sorry." Dillen followed after Charly, who'd bolted out of her chair and was rummaging in the closet for her coat.

"Get away from me, you son-of-a-bitch."

Dillen took a step back, hands up defensively. "Say, you and B.G. weren't . . . ? Were you?"

Charly slammed the door behind her, creating a windstorm in the foyerless apartment.

"You got a lot of women working on your paper?" Klein said to Niles. "If you don't, you're lucky. Those old-time sailors were right. It's bad luck to have them around."

Niles took out a pen. "Can I quote you?"

"Quote me? No, you can't quote me. You want to quote me, quote me as saying the death of B.G. Harris was a great loss to the new American theater. She was a pioneer, a breaker of new ground in the tradition of David Mamet, Sam Shepard and whatshername—the broad who wrote the play about the girl who's going to commit suicide. She really killed herself? B.G? Jesus."

*　　　　*　　　　*

174

"Mr. Niles?" Jessica took her hat off and spun it on a finger.

"Yes?"

"I announced you before, remember? You went up to Dillen, thirty-six B. I knew who you were, anyway. I've seen your picture on the delivery trucks. It's pretty hard not to, uh . . ." She ran a hand over her hair.

Niles smiled. "If as many people read the paper as read the sides of the trucks . . ."

Jessica ducked her head. "I just wondered . . ."

"An autograph?" Niles reached for his notebook. "Sure."

She laughed. "No. No autograph—and no offense. I just wondered if you'd found out anything more about Nowhere Man."

"Anything more than what?"

"Than what you've written in the paper. Again, no offense, but I don't think you know anything about running. Am I right?"

"Absolutely right. I've heard rumors that some people do it, but the only time I do is to catch something I can sit down in —and preferably have a drink. Or after pretty girls."

"Just listen to what I figure. It'll just take a minute. That newsstand guy you wrote about? You didn't ask him, but I did, whether he was sweating when he got there—Nowhere Man, not the newsstand guy. The newsstand guy says he wasn't, so he hadn't run very far. That means he lived somewhere in the Village, in a doorman building, so he didn't need a front door key, and he either left his apartment door unlocked or he stashed that key—under the hallway doormat, maybe. There can't be more than fifteen or twenty buildings with doormen in the Village, and most of them're on Fifth Avenue. I've already checked about ten of them."

Niles laughed. "You? Why?"

"And you know what's weird? You know how you wrote about how nobody'd talked to the newsstand guy—no cops, I mean—or to anybody else who might've seen a jogger at that hour on that day? Well, no cops'd talked to the doormen I talked to, either. It's like somewhere, deep down, they don't really want to know."

Niles put a hand up on the wall behind her. "You know what a friend of mine who's a cop says? He says cops walk such a narrow line between the law and lawlessness that anytime they get a case there's a moment when they suspect themselves. Not literally, of course, but it's the reason it takes them a while to get their asses in gear."

"Jake Neuman, right?" Jessica said. "He's your friend, isn't he?"

"What makes you say that?"

"That's the way he talks. He has a poet's soul."

Niles laughed. "I'll tell Jake you said that. How do you know him?"

"He was around here, talking to Dillen—and Amanda Becker."

Niles nodded. "You wouldn't have a cigarette, would you? No, of course not. You're a runner. What did you say your name was?"

"Jessica."

"Jessica what?"

"Frank. But I don't want my name in the paper."

He smiled. "Saying you're conducting an independent search for Nowhere Man?"

She patted the pocket of her uniform tunic. "Would you be interested in seeing this?"

"I don't know. Would I?"

"You probably don't know anything about doormen, either, which is understandable. I figure Nowhere Man's doorman doesn't know Nowhere Man went out for a run because he was goofing off or sleeping or in the john or doing shit work, and he still doesn't know he went out because it might not even have been the regular doorman, it might've been the relief guy. So this list is just a start."

Niles was standing straight now, his hands in his pockets. "A list of men who live in doorman buildings between Eighth and Fourteenth and between Fifth and the river and've been missing since last Tuesday?"

"I told you, I've only done ten buildings. The ones on Fifth Avenue, starting at One Fifth, up to Fifty-one. And I couldn't really say *missing;* I just said who hadn't been around for a while. I told them I was a private investigator, working on a divorce case. Doormen get a certain amount like that; no one even asked for ID."

"Why're you doing this? You think you know the guy?"

She shook her head. "Let's just say I did something I'm not particularly proud of. I thought if I did a good deed I might . . . I don't know . . . sleep better."

"And you've got how many names?"

"Nine. But . . ."

"But what?"

"I'm a member of the Road Runners Club. They have a computerized membership list—and a list of everybody who's run in the last several marathons. A friend of mine works there, I asked her to run my names through the computer, and one of them rang a bell. Do you want to hear it?"

"Do you want to tell me?"

"I don't know. I guess I feel a little like Neuman—if he *was* the cop you quoted to me. I'm afraid that naming the name will make it so, will make Nowhere Man somebody."

"You want to just show me your list and point to the name? That way, you won't be naming him, exactly."

Jessica put her hand in her pocket and came out with a piece of paper folded over and over to the size of a quarter. "It has a star next to it."

Niles hefted it, then put it in the change pocket of his suit coat. "Have you tried calling this guy's number?"

"It's unlisted."

"Okay, well, I can probably get it. If it turns out he's alive and kicking, and if I follow up by asking around at other doorman buildings in that neighborhood, any chance your friend will run the names I come up with through the Road Runners computer?"

"Sure."

"You feel any better, now that you've done your good deed?"

"No."

Niles laughed. "When do you get off work?"

"I'm working a double today. The day guy's brother's getting married."

"Maybe you'd like to have a drink sometime." Niles took out his notebook and wrote his phone numbers. "We can talk about something else. We can talk about the weather."

Jessica shivered, although it was clement. "I'm not ready for winter. I was sure I was going to win the lottery, that I could kiss this place goodbye. I had two numbers, though—2 and 5. Anyone win? You're a newspaper guy; you must've heard by now."

"It's funny you should mention that, Jessica."

"Oh, you won—right?"

Niles tore off the piece of paper and handed it to her. "Call me sometime."

She folded the paper over and over, to the size of a quarter. "Maybe. Okay. Maybe."

"The fuck's he going?"

"Relax, Jerry. We got the skinhead in sight."

"Look at the meter, Artie, and tell me to relax. The guy takes taxis all over town."

"Whattaya expect? The skinhead's on a expense account. Anyway, Jer, what's a few bucks for a cab matter? Couple a days, we're gonna collect sixty million dollars, Jer. The fuck difference is a couple a bucks for a cab gonna matter?"

"Yeah, well. What if somebody else had the number?"

"First off, Jerry, keep it down. You think this cabbie wouldn't be happy to drive into a lamppost, knock us the fuck out, roll us for our Lotto ticket, collect the whole sixty mil for hisself? Look, he's a I-ranian, looks like, like the newsstand guy. Second off, I already *tol*ja, so somebody else has the same number, so what? It's thirty mil for him, thirty mil for us, fifteen for you, fifteen for me. *Two* other guys have the same number, it's twenty for both a them, twenty for us, ten for me, ten for you, nice even numbers, Jer, not like when it was seventeen, three thirty-three, three thirty-three for both a them, seventeen, three thirty-three, three thirty-three for us; eight, six sixty-six, six sixty-six for you, eight, six sixty-six, six sixty-six for me. I'm telling you, I got a pornographic memory for this stuff. Look, he's stopping."

"The fuck are we?"

"The Village, man. You don't know the Village? You should get out a the house more."

"I know the Village. I just mean what street, like?"

"Hey, cabbie! What street is this?"

"This is Bonk Street."

"It's Bonk Street, Jerry. There—you happy?"

"Bonk Street? I never heard a Bonk Street."

"*Bank* Street, you scumbag. Here. Abdul. Keep the change, man. Get a blanket for your camel or something."

"That's a *twenty,* Artie. You gave him a *twenty?*"

"Fuck do I care, man? Couple a days, I'll be wiping my ass with twenties. The fuck did Niles go?"

"Up there. The red house with the striped shutters."

"Those're awnings, scumbag. Not shutters."

"Holy shit. He *lives* there. No wonder he takes taxis all over."

"He don't live there, Jerry."

"He has a key. He opened the door with it."

"The skinhead don't live there."

"Yeah? Well, who does?"

"Don't you watch the news, Jer? You gotta watch the news more, man, 'cause you're a ignorant scumbag. You watched the news instead a wrestling, you'd know who lives there."

"Yeah? Well, who lives there?"

"Nobody."

"Fuck're you talking about? He has a *key.*"

"You watched the news instead a wrestling, you'd know who *used* a live there."

"Who?"

"Dimanche, scumbag. That's who."

19

If the sun were the size of the globe in the lobby of the Daily News Building and the earth, comparatively, were the size of a walnut and located at the main entrance to Grand Central Terminal, would mail order Christmas catalogues still arrive in September?

It was September, wasn't it? It must be: They were still playing baseball. Weren't they? Neuman couldn't remember the last time he'd paid attention to the baseball scores, unless it was when the Dodgers kayoed Doctor K, which had been about a hundred years ago. Hadn't it? Fourteen years married, thirty-three years a cop, fifty-four years old and a hundred years behind on the ball scores. Or was he now a hundred and fifty-four years old? He felt a hundred and fifty-four; he felt a hundred and sixty.

He drank some more Teacher's from the bottle and opened the Spiegel Christmas catalogue to a page someone had dog-eared. Maria? A burglar? The Ghost of Castle Neuman? It was a page of the lingerie section, headed *How to Make Up for Last Year's Blender.* How to make up for this year's vibrator—for not getting this year's vibrator—that was the question. Or was the question how to make up for the necessity, this year, *for* a vibrator? Had he given Maria a blender last Christmas? No—

he'd given her . . . socks. No—she gave him socks, argyle socks, like Nell Ward's sweater. Where were those socks? If he found them, he'd throw them away.

Cozy cotton flannel gown: demure Cuddleskin gown from Lynne Greene for Lady Lynne will make you feel so pampered, all over. Provocative, that comma. If you were pampered, all over, how demure were you? Not very, that's how demure.

Pretty Wonder Maid panties. Après-party sculptured wedge slippers. Après what party? For those who were pampered, all over, wasn't the après-party the party?

Satin teddy—a sensuous sleep piece, silk charmeuse nightshirt isn't just for sleeping. For what, then? Getting pampered, all over? Vibrating?

Elongated camisole and tap pants—our little necessities are becoming lacier. Berlei fuels the trend with their new underwire bra and brief set. All-over sheerness in a supportive nylon stretch lace looks terrific under revealing holiday fashions. Berlei fuels the trend with *its* new underwire bra. Come on, Spiegel. Get grammatical. Were holiday fashions revealing? Fourth of July fashions maybe, but Christmas fashions? What did he know?

More Teacher's.

A hat. He'd given Maria a hat last Christmas. A balaclava, actually—a revealing Christmas balaclava; it revealed her nose and mouth and a little of her forehead and cheeks. She'd been very grateful for it in February. . . . No, he'd given her the balaclava the Christmas before last.

Racer back body briefer. He could use a body briefer, with or without a racer back.

Calvin Klein's cute cotton rib knit thermal top and pants: a far cry from traditional long underwear. What was so bad about traditional long underwear? He wore traditional long underwear—gray, though somewhere he had a red pair. It made him feel toasty, all over—and even, sometimes, cute. Where was that red long underwear? In a drawer somewhere with his argyle socks, probably. He'd track them down with his questing eyes.

Shortie pajamas—especially enticing with bared shoulders and intricate lace at the neck. Lace-edged tap pants are high cut to show off a lot more leg. A lot more leg than what? Than tap pants cut low? Than tap pants without lace? Than longie pajamas? A lot more leg than arm? Come on, Spiegel—be specific.

"Jacob?"

Maybe he had given Maria a blender last Christmas. They had a blender; he used it in the summertime to make banana daiquiris, dressed in his revealing Fourth of July fashions—an undershirt and Bermuda shorts. *Was* Bimini in Bermuda? If not, were there Bimini shorts? If so, he ought to get a pair. If he weren't retired, he'd tell Klinger or Easterly he had to go to Bimini and back, for some shorts. They'd say, *Sure, Jake. Here's twenty-five large. Get yourself a key of blow while you're down there—for Maria for Christmas—to make up for last year's blender.* He'd go to Bimini, get some shorts, and never come back; he'd live off the twenty-five large, since he didn't do blow. Maybe he should do some. Maybe he was—how had Nell Ward put it?—missing an opportunity. An opportunity to do some with her. Was he retired?

"Jacob, the doorbell is ringing. Are you sober enough to answer?"

Sober enough? He was too sober. That's why he wasn't answering. He knew the doorbell was ringing, but he wasn't going to answer it until he got a lot less sober. It might be somebody who wanted to tell him something he didn't want to know. Something else he didn't want to know.

More Teacher's.

Maria made a noise in her throat and went through the living room into the foyer. She was wearing a flannel nightshirt. Did it make her feel pampered, all over?

Sheets. That was it. Flannel sheets. Last Christmas, he'd given Maria flannel sheets. He'd given himself flannel sheets too, he supposed, since the sheets were king-size and they had a king-size bed that they slept in together—or had, before Maria decided she'd rather sleep with a vibrator.

Maybe the blender had a vibrator attachment. Then he wouldn't have to make up for it. A blender with a vibrator attachment—now that would be a money-maker. Women wouldn't have to be embarrassed about going into a store and asking for a vibrator, asking and thereby announcing that their husbands didn't make them feel pampered, all over. They could walk right up to the counter and ask for a blender with all the optional attachments and if the salesperson thought they wanted it to masturbate rather than to make banana daiquiris—well, even if the sun were the size of the globe in the lobby of the Daily News Building and the earth, comparatively, were the size of a walnut and located at the main entrance to Grand Central Terminal, the walnut would still have its share of people with dirty minds. Wouldn't it?

"Hello, Lieutenant. Uh, Jake."

There were four of Federici, each dressed differently—one in a royal blue Adidas warmup jacket and designer jeans, one in a suit that was too big, one in a maroon-and-white-striped rugby shirt and baggy chinos, one in a tuxedo. How did Federici do that?

"Sorry to come by so late, Jake, but we didn't want to talk about this on the phone. Anyway, your phone's not answering. It's out of order or something."

"No está roto. Algún borracho lo descolgo." Maria said it rapid-fire as she walked between them through the living room. Her slippers slapped against her heels as she went up the stairs.

Neuman giggled. "She said it's not out of order. She said some drunk took it off the hook." How did he know that? He didn't know any Spanish. Maybe it wasn't Scotch he was drinking; maybe it was tequila. "Hell of a note, hunh, drunks coming into your house, taking your phone off the hook?" He screwed his face up, trying to focus. They weren't all Federici; they were all different: Federici, in the Adidas warmup jacket; whatshisname—the cop from the Sixth Squad—Winger, in the big suit; Matt McGovern, in the rugby shirt; in the tuxedo, Nell Ward.

He took a drink, then held out the bottle. "Anybody wanna belt? You prolly shun't, Matty. I hear you got sumpin wrong with your gut."

"It's good to see you, Loo," McGovern said.

"Look . . ." Nell Ward was standing right in front of his chair, so close he could kiss her, kick her, shoot her, if he was carrying a gun, which he would be if he wasn't retired. Was he retired? ". . . I don't want to stand around while you guys go through this gavotte where you all defer to Neuman because he's the last of the great gangbusters. I want you to tell him what we came to tell him. If you don't, I will."

"Wha' you wan' for Chrishmish?" Neuman said. "You wan' some Pampers?" He laughed.

"Shit. He's drunk. Let's go."

"Jake." Federici put his hands on Nell's arms to move her away. "Jake, don't talk, just listen. We know why you're upset. Nell told us what, you know, went down. Don't worry, we won't say anything, in case Maria's . . . you know." He cupped his ear, miming an eavesdropper. "Can you just listen, Jake? Can you?"

Nell stalked to a corner. "Just tell him, for God's sake. Why do you need his permission? You're all such children."

"Hey, wait a minute, sister." Winger swelled up, but somehow looked even smaller.

"Nell didn't kill Dimanche, Jake," Federici said. "If it comes to it, she's got an alibi. B.G. Harris didn't kill her, either—that's what you think and that's what we think. Dimanche was killed in her dressing room backstage at the Kean last Tuesday. To get backstage you have to go through the stage door—"

"Steve, I've heard this. If the sun was as big as the globe in the Daily News Building and the earth was as big as a walnut at the entrance to Grand Central, are there still going to be cops who waste good shoe leather, their time and the taxpayers' money running down amateur crackpot theories?" He must be too sober, to have said all that without a slur.

Federici took a breath, then went on: "We don't think anybody got past the stage doorman. We think that when they broke the rehearsal Dimanche called this guy, this guy she'd been seeing, the guy who nobody knows who he is, because she was upset at how Dillen and Klein and the rest of them were treating her. We think she either asked him to come by the theater or he offered to come by, meaning he lives or works close by because the break was going to be a short one, that she told him not to come to the stage door, she'd let him in the lobby door, that she took him to her dressing room, where he killed her with a thirty-eight Special with a silencer. He left the way he came in, through the orchestra to the lobby and out the front doors, which have panic locks.

"So Dimanche's killer is someone she knew, someone she was expecting, someone she'd invited, someone she told to come in the front way because she didn't want anyone to see him. It was

184

an opportunity killing, Jake. He was probably planning to kill her sometime—he had the gun—but knowing that he got backstage without being seen and would most likely get out again if he was careful, knowing there were a lot of people in the theater and therefore a lot of suspects, he took his best shot then rather than whenever."

Nicely said, for a crackpot amateur theory, for a guy who never spoke. Neuman wondered if Nell Ward had fallen in love with Federici for knowing about panic locks; and if she had, how did she feel about Federici's wearing Sergio Valente jeans —not exactly blue jeans—and a Casio digital—not a Rolex— and not using a Macintosh computer? Maybe he did use a Macintosh computer; he had a tape deck. "Isn't there a box office in the lobby?" He was altogether sober. Maybe someone was watering the Teacher's: Maria? The maid? They didn't have a maid.

"Yes, and it was open. But when it's slow the guy sits at a table that's below the height of the window, watching the tube. His alibi's that he was watching *General Hospital,* that there were no customers during that half hour, that he didn't see anybody come or go."

Neuman looked at Nell. "And what's your alibi? Your solid alibi?"

Nell lifted her chin and looked right back at him. "I was in bed with a man."

"Oh, yeah—a matinee? Who was the lucky guy?"

Federici got between them. "Jake, listen to the rest of it, will you?"

Neuman hefted himself up to see Nell. "What's the monkey suit for?"

"I went to a party," Nell said.

"With a man you didn't go to bed with? Or're you going to bed with him when you get back?"

Nell just shook her head. "Jesus."

"Who's we?" Neuman said. "You said all this is what we think. Who's we? You and Nell? So what do you think, Matty? And you, Winger—what do you think?"

Winger took a step forward, but Federici cut him off, taking a newspaper from the hip pocket of his jeans and slapping it open. "This is tomorrow's *Dispatch,* Jake—"

"Don't tell me any ball scores, will you? I can't stand it when you tell me the ball scores."

"Just . . . listen. It's a Terry Niles piece about Klinger's news conference. Klinger had a news conference saying B.G. killed Dimanche, then herself. It's got B.G.'s note, it's got *The Last Waltz,* which Klinger gave the press. And it's got something Klinger didn't give the press, which is a source in the M.E.'s office saying they found a hundred milligrams of Valium in B.G.'s blood, which the source says if it didn't kill her, at least it meant she was as good as dead when she was shot. You listening, Jake?"

Easterly had said they weren't going to give the press B.G. until Sunday. The *Dispatch* was a morning paper, which meant it must be late Sunday night or early Monday morning. In that case, where had he been since leaving Federici's Saturday night? In some bar? Some bars? He remembered a diner down by the Hudson, but he'd had coffee there. Hadn't he? He remembered getting in his car and looking out across the river at the Maxwell House coffee factory in Hoboken and thinking about Mira Esterowitz, the girl he'd gone with a hundred years ago who lived right across from the Maxwell House coffee factory, 1004 Hudson Street, thinking about their joke, about her saying, *You want to come in for a cup of coffee?* and his saying, *Let's just get some cups, walk over to the Maxwell House coffee factory, ask them to fill them up,* thinking about her name being Mira and his wife, whom he married, saying *mira* a lot, because she was Hispanic. He did know some Spanish; he knew *mira.* He remembered driving uptown but not driving across town, driving over the Queensboro Bridge, but not driving on Queens Boulevard, but being on it, far past his turnoff, out by the Van Wyck.

Kennedy Airport. That was it. He'd been at Kennedy Airport, not at it but on the shoulder of a road somewhere on its perimeter, watching planes take off and land, watching people standing alongside other cars parked on the shoulder pretending they were that guy, whatever he was called, on an aircraft carrier, directing planes on landings and takeoffs, a fat baton in each hand. While he'd watched, he'd drunk Teacher's out of a bag, which had made the people pretending to be the guy on the aircraft carrier seem very funny indeed. Where had he got the Teacher's? How had he got home? When had he come home? He didn't remember. He must not be altogether sober. "I'm listening."

"Good. Niles also has something about the message on Dimanche's mirror—'There's a needle in your arm and it makes you breathless'?"

"Yeah?"

"Yeah. He says he got it from 'a source close to the investigation.' He also has something about the music on the tape from Dimanche's answering machine. Same source. Have you talked to Niles, Jake? About the tape? I haven't talked to Niles. I didn't tell him anything about that tape. The only people who know about the tape're the five of us. I told Matty and Nell and Winger here 'cause we were going to come and see you."

Neuman laughed. "Which is like saying the only reason the ship's sinking is 'cause it has holes in the bottom. Hey, nothing personal, Matty, but it's not like you're real good at keeping a secret. I wanted to see something about myself on the late news"—like my wife uses a vibrator—"I'd tell it to you, tell you it was a secret. Or don't you do your drinking with reporters anymore?"

McGovern patted his stomach. "I'm on sick leave, Loo. I got something wrong with my gut. So no booze for me. I still hang around with the guys, yeah, I still hear stuff, but I didn't hear about the tape."

"What about the Valium? You hear about the Valium?"

McGovern shook his head.

"Jake, go easy on him," Federici said. "How could he hear? You and I were the only ones who knew about the tape; you and Easterly were the only ones who knew about the Valium."

"Fireman knew."

"What fireman? Oh—Jim Fireman. Matty doesn't drink with Jim Fireman, do you, Matty?"

McGovern shook his head.

"What about the message on Dimanche's mirror, Matty? You hear about the message on Dimanche's mirror?"

McGovern shook his head, then nodded. "I mean, yeah, I heard about that. I heard about it from Steve. Matter of fact, I had a drink with Terry right after I heard about it. I mean, no booze for me, Loo; I was drinking milk. But I shot the bull with Terry. But I didn't say anything about the message on Dimanche's mirror. Honest."

"Jake?" Federici was beside Neuman's chair, hunkered down. "The M.E. hasn't done an autopsy on B.G. yet. A bunch of Haitians cut each other up with machetes Friday night; they've got stiffs lined up around the block down at Bellevue."

"I heard about that, yeah," Neuman said.

"Listen to Winger, Jake. Winger, tell him what you told us."

Winger told him, his hands in the pockets of his big suit. "I tried to tell you this the other day, Lieutenant, but you weren't in a mood to listen, I guess. I can understand why, Lieutenant, hearing your partner here was looking at a murder rap. Couple of weeks ago, Lieutenant, we got a call from this Dimanche woman, saying she'd been mugged right outside her house just before dark, Lieutenant, by a Hispanic perp, late teens, early twenties, five six to five eight, one three oh to one four oh, blue jeans, black jacket, blue-and-white felony shoes, Lieutenant, took her purse with a few hundred bills, popped her in the eye, knocked her down. It smelled bad, Lieutenant. She's got a chauffeur, he drops her off in front of her house, it's two steps from the gutter to the gate, six steps up to the front door, Lieutenant, he waits, the chauffeur, till she's inside the door before he drives off, there're kids hanging around a lot trying to get autographs. So what happened—was the chauffeur looking the other way or what, Lieutenant? This Dimanche woman, she said, yeah, she got inside the house, the chauffeur drove off, then she came back outside, went down the steps, Lieutenant, 'cause she thought she'd dropped something out of her purse, a script she had to study that night 'cause she had to learn her lines for the play she was in, she thought maybe it landed on the steps or on the sidewalk. I said, wouldn't a script make a lot of noise, didn't she notice she dropped it when she dropped it, Lieutenant? She said, oh, yeah, it wasn't a script, it was a letter she meant to mail and forgot, she looked in her purse so she could put it out where she'd remember in the morning, it wasn't there, she thought maybe it landed on the steps or on the sidewalk, Lieutenant—"

"Winger?"

"Yeah, Lieutenant?"

"I got an idea. My idea is don't tell me what you told them.

188

Tell me a much shorter version of what you told them. You know what I'm saying?"

Winger buried his hands deeper in his pockets. "Yeah, sure, Lieutenant. Sorry, Lieutenant. Shorter? I guess shorter would be we talked to this Dimanche woman's neighbors, Lieutenant, they didn't see any mugger. But one of them, this kid who lives across the street, Lieutenant, he's about twelve, thirteen, he had the hots for this Dimanche woman, liked to look out his window at her, see if he could catch her, you know, getting undressed or whatever, he saw this guy, Lieutenant, leaving the house just a little after the limo left, after this Dimanche woman went inside, a little before the first white-top responded to the report of the mugging. He got a pretty good look at him, Lieutenant, he's a pretty good witness, the kid, even though he's about twelve, thirteen—"

"Winger?"

"Yeah, Lieutenant?"

"Shorter."

"Right, Lieutenant. I guess shorter, Lieutenant, would be the guy was Terry Niles, Lieutenant."

"How'd a twelve-, thirteen-year-old kid know that?"

"He's a smart kid, Lieutenant. Plays with computers and all that, when he's not playing with himself"—Winger laughed, but no one else did, so he turned it into a cough—"reads the papers, Lieutenant, said he'd seen Niles's mug on his column, on the delivery trucks."

"It fits, Jake," Federici said. "You see how it fits? Dimanche calls this guy, this guy she's been seeing, the guy who nobody knows who he is, asks him to come by the theater or he offers to come by, meaning he lives or works close by. The *Dispatch* is three blocks from the Kean, Jake. She lets him in through the lobby door, takes him backstage to her dressing room, he knows nobody's seen him, he pops her, leaves the way he came in. He wants it to look like somebody else popped her, he figures B.G.'s a good stooge, she doesn't know a lot of people in town, she's having trouble fitting into the Broadway scene, she's a little flaky, nobody's going to miss her too much, nobody's going to ask a lot of questions. He goes around to her place, thinking he'll pop her with the thirty-eight Special he popped Dimanche with, she's already dead or dying, loaded with Valium, he pops

189

her anyway, just to make sure, writes a note confessing to popping Dimanche, we buy it, the cops, case closed.

"But he's also a smart-ass, Niles, a hotshot reporter, a guy who never takes the official version of anything for an answer. He can't just write a piece saying what Klinger said, he's got to write a piece making the cops look bad, asking questions: If B.G. killed Dimanche, what about the message on Dimanche's mirror? If B.G. killed Dimanche, what about the music on the tape on Dimanche's answering machine? If B.G. killed herself with a thirty-eight Special, what about the Valium? I mean, it's perfect, Jake: Niles pops Dimanche, he rigs a suicide to make it look like B.G. did it, then he opens a can of worms, stirs them up by asking questions about the police investigation."

Neuman looked down at the bottle of Teacher's, which he held in his lap like an infant. He found the top on the table next to him, screwed it on, and put the bottle on the table. "And you're saying—what?—Niles beat her up a couple of weeks ago, then together they cooked up the mugging story to cover it up?"

Federici shrugged. "Why not? She wouldn't want the publicity of being beat up by a boyfriend, he wouldn't want the publicity of being the boyfriend who beat her up."

"Yeah, well. First of all, Niles and Dimanche—they're from different worlds."

Nell Ward moved closer. "Terry did an interview with Dimanche about six months ago. That's how he met her."

"Yeah? So?"

"When she died, he wrote a column about fame, about famous people, about how the public thinks they know all about their private lives, about whom they date, whom they sleep with, whom they love."

"Yeah? So?"

"I told you the story he told me—about whoever it was saying that in every love affair the new lover has to figuratively kill his new lover's old lovers—and Terry's thinking because Dimanche's new lover couldn't do that—because she was famous—he killed her literally."

"Yeah? So?"

"I think he was annoyed, frustrated, angry that Dimanche, for whatever reason, kept their relationship a secret, that she never wrote a song about him."

190

Neuman glared. "What're you, joking around here? This isn't the schoolyard, girlie; this is the pits, the gutter, the bottom of the barrel."

She met his look. "I'm not joking around."

"Yeah, well. People get annoyed, frustrated, angry all the time, Miss Ward, and most of them, ninety-nine percent of them—maybe it's more, maybe it's less; what do I know?—don't go around popping the people they're annoyed, frustrated, angry at, then popping somebody else to make it look like they're the one who was annoyed, frustrated, angry. You know what I'm saying?"

Winger took a turn. "The kid on Bank Street, Lieutenant, he doesn't just *think* it was Niles he saw leaving this Dimanche woman's house; he's *sure* it was Niles. Reason he's sure, Lieutenant, is he saw Niles at this Dimanche woman's house a lot the last couple of months."

"Yeah, well. If I were Niles's lawyer, and the only witness—the only witness—who could connect Niles to Dimanche was a twelve-, thirteen-year-old kid who had the hots for Dimanche, liked to peep at her out his window, I'd be thinking about whether I needed a haircut or not, whether I should get a new suit, so when I stood out on the courthouse steps after I got an acquittal—forget about an acquittal; there wouldn't even be an indictment—I'd look good for the TV cameras, case my mother was watching, or my girlfriend." Or my wife.

Winger flipped his hands without taking them out of his pockets. "How many tall, good-looking bald guys with bow ties are there, Lieutenant?"

"You tell me, Winger. You go out and count how many tall, good-looking bald guys with bow ties there are and if there's only one and if it's Niles, you come back and tell me. And be ready to tell Easterly and Klinger and borough D's and the chief of D's and the chief and the commissioner and maybe even the mayor and the governor and the president."

"Lieutenant Neuman." Nell Ward again. "The graffito on my wall? Terry saw it. He asked me about it. He was intrigued by it. He thought it was . . . 'unexpectedly poetic,' was the way he put it."

"Saw it when? You told me he was an old lover, you told me the graffiti was painted a couple of weeks ago. Now you're

191

telling me he still comes around?" And what about The Band and Neil Young and Neil Diamond and Van Morrison and Doctor John and Muddy Waters and Paul Butterfield? And Dylan and the men who wore blue jeans and Rolex watches and used Macintosh computers? And the Marines? Did they still come around too?

"He came around, since the graffito was painted, to borrow some records—"

"Records, Jake." Federici was standing now. How had he stayed squatting for so long? He should be a catcher. "He borrowed some records."

"I have some old records," Nell went on. "Blues records. They're collectors' items. You can't find them in a store—or not very easily. One of them was a Robert Johnson with the song that's on Dimanche's tape—'32-20.'"

"They're collectors' items and you just let Niles borrow them, just 'cause he was an old lover?"

Nell Ward smiled a sad, sad smile. "He taped them, Lieutenant, at my place. You're right—I wouldn't let him borrow them."

Neuman turned sideways and crossed his legs and waved a hand and shook his head. "I don't believe it. It's too fucking careless. You don't go to someone's house to tape the song you're going to play on someone's answering machine that the cops are going to find when that someone gets killed, when *you* kill her. It's too fucking careless."

"I didn't hear what Terry was taping," Nell said. "I was working on a Steenbeck—an editing table—in the next room. Terry said he wanted to tape some blues; he'd enjoyed hearing them when we were together; he missed hearing them. I said go ahead, that I had work to do. He didn't stay long—an hour, maybe. When he left, he asked me about the graffito."

"The graffiti he was going to write on someone's mirror that the cops were going to find when that someone got killed, when *he* killed her." Neuman turned the other way and crossed his other leg and waved his other hand and shook his head. "I don't believe it. It's too fucking careless." He turned back toward Federici. "Niles wrote a piece that the M.E. found Valium in B.G. when they hadn't even cut her up yet. Why?"

Federici held out the paper. "You want to read it?"

"No, I don't want to read it. I want to know why he wrote it."

"Maybe somebody told him they were going to cut her up, he wrote it even though it hadn't happened. They do that sometimes, newspaper guys. I remember one of them told me once he used to cover space shots, he'd write a piece about the blast-off hours before it happened, describing what it sounded like, about all the flames and smoke and everything, 'cause of his deadline. Sometimes, the blast-off was canceled on account of the weather or something, he had to call his office at the last minute, have them stop the presses or whatever they do."

"Only Niles didn't have them stop the presses, which is too fucking careless. Have you talked to McIver about any of this? Or Easterly or Klinger?"

"Jake, I'm a suspect in a murder. I'm not supposed to be snooping around somebody else's case. I'm only telling you 'cause we're, you know, friends, like."

Neuman turned the other way. "I don't like it. It's too fucking careless."

"Okay, Jake." Federici again. "Here's the last thing. The list? Bobby's list?"

"Bobby's dead, Steve."

"Tell him, Mac."

McGovern gave Winger a look, as if to say, *This is how you do it.* "Steve said he already told you, Loo, when you went by his place, that I told Terry about Bobby's list. I told him not to write anything, he said he wouldn't. But he asked to see it, the list, he wanted to see whose names were on it, I couldn't remember all the names. I didn't see any reason why not, he wasn't going to write anything about it. Steve was out on a squeal, I knew the list was in his desk, I took Niles up to the squad, I let him look at it."

"When was this, Matty?" Neuman said.

"About six months ago, Loo."

"Around the time Miss Ward here thinks Niles met Dimanche?"

"Yeah, Loo. Oh, yeah, there's one other thing, Loo. I know you know Terry a little bit, but since you don't smoke—I quit, Loo, on account of my gut—maybe you don't know how he's always bumming smokes. Always. Never has his own. Uh, Nell, here, said the same thing. We were talking about it on the way out here."

Neuman sat forward, eyes wide. "Jesus Christ, Matty, and he's out walking the streets? A guy who always bums smokes? What're we just sitting here for? We should get on the horn to Special Services, get snipers out to his house, make sure he doesn't do it again."

McGovern shuffled in place. "All I meant, Loo, was Steve told me they found these cigarettes in Dimanche's dressing room, some with her lipstick on them, some without. I just thought . . ."

Neuman looked at Federici. "I suppose you're going to tell me in the piece Niles wrote in that paper you're holding, along with something about the message on Dimanche's mirror and something about the music on the tape from Dimanche's answering machine and something about the hundred milligrams of Valium in B.G.'s blood, there's something about Dimanche being on Bobby's list."

Federici nodded.

20

"Larry Adler, Jeff Bridges, Mel Brooks, Johnny Carson, Gary Carter, Jimmy Carter, Joan Collins, Phil Collins, Jimmy Connors, Jeff Daniels, Phil Donahue, Michael Douglas, Linda Evans, Sally Fields—close enough; everyone thinks that's her name—Gerry Ford, John Forsythe, John Glenn, Gary Hart, David Hartman, Helen Hayes, Joseph Heller, Keith Jackson, Michael Jackson, Jim Jensen, Ted Kennedy, Larry King, Steven King—with a *v*, but no matter—Ed Koch, Ed McMahon, Jim McMahon, Eddie Murphy, Paul Newman, Jack Nicholson, Tom O'Neill—they're not going to get that one; they're not going to know I mean Tip—Richard Nixon, William Perry, Ronald *and* Nancy Reagan, Burt Reynolds, Pete Rose, Jonathan Schwartz, Sam Shepard, George Shultz, Sue Simmons, John Simon, Neil Simon, David Steinberg, Howard Stern, Elizabeth Taylor, Dave Winfield, Burt Young. . . . Not bad. Not great, but not bad. I need a Fonda."

Charly Johnstone extricated a Manhattan phone book from under the alp of papers on her desk and paged through it. "Fonda, Fonda, Fonda. Angie Fonda, Fonda Boutique, C. Fonda, Fonda Cup and Container Group, Fonda La Paloma Mexican restaurant, N. Fonda, R. Fonda, V. H. Fonda. Shit. Or a Tina Turner. Turner, Turner, Turner. T. Turner, T. Turner,

195

T. Turner, T. F. Turner, Theodore Turner. Shit. What was Lady Di's maiden name? Diana something. Diana . . . Diana . . . Diana. Shit. Willie Nelson. Nelson, Nelson, Nelson. Eureka. A Willie Nelson. *Two* Willie Nelsons. *Three* Willie Nelsons. Too late to call them. Call them in the morning. So much to do, so little time. A brilliant idea, though, brilliant.

"You must stop talking to yourself, Charly.

"It's the marijuana. I'm one toke over the line. Whatever happened to those lads—Brewer and . . .? Oh, hell.

"Brain damage. Alzheimer's. Neurasthenia.

"What a nice word. Nyoor-as-*thee*nia. We don't have words like that anymore.

"We don't have anything like we used to have. Anymore. Quoth the raven: anymore. Hark—speaking of ravens, speaking of larks.

"What, Charly?

"What, indeed? Or rather, who? It's four in the bloody morning. Who—who *else*—could be stomping around the theater at four in the bloody morning? The ghost of Edmund Kean, perhaps?

"Or of Dimanche.

"Don't talk like that. You're scaring the shit out of me.

"Shhh.

"He can't possibly hear me, love. Not with all the noise he's making.

" 'He'?"

"Well, it is a rather he-like thing to do, isn't it? Sneak into a darkened theater at four in the bloody morning. Most women —and you can take up the ramifications of it with your neighborhood feminist theoretician—most women don't do such things.

"You're in the darkened theater at four in the bloody morning.

"Working on the guest list for my brilliant conception, a party for the homonymous—wait till Bobby Zarem hears about it; he'll be green with envy—to be held at Elaine's. Not *the* Elaine's, of course, a luncheonette in Rego Park.

"It's a wonderful idea, Charly.

"Thank you.

"So who's that sneaking around the theater?

"I don't have the foggiest idea.

"Maybe it's Hercule Maigret, come to apprehend you for the murder of the lovely Dimanche.

"I didn't murder Dimanche.

"You loved her.

"That I did.

"Unrequitedly.

"I *loved* her, is the point. One doesn't murder the object of one's affections.

"Oh? Have you read any Greek tragedy lately?

"No. Have you?

"Well, maybe it's . . .

"Who?

"I don't know.

"Well, go *see*.

"What if . . . ?

"Oh, come on, Charly.

"Well, hush, then. Not a peep.

"You're the one who's talking.

"Shhh."

Charly turned off the light on her desk and tiptoed to the door. She opened it a crack and put her eye to it.

After a while, she closed it and stood with her back against the door.

"What?

"Interesting. Very interesting.

"What?

"Juliet. He called her Juliet.

"Who called who Juliet?

"Oh, be quiet, will you?"

"Excuse me."

"Sorry, I don't have any change."

Terry Niles pouted. "What a mistrustful world it's become. You can't even ask for directions anymore."

The man slowed down and smiled, a little contrite. "Directions I've got."

"Actually, I don't want directions. I wondered if I could talk to you for a minute."

The man accelerated. "Sorry, I'm in a hurry."

"You live at Forty-two Fifth, don't you? Sixth floor? The doorman pointed you out. Don't be angry at him; I was very persistent."

"If it's about the co-op, I don't intend to buy my apartment. Sorry."

"How about your neighbor? Mark Follett?"

"You'd have to ask him."

The light was against them but the traffic was scanty and they crossed Fifth Avenue and walked south along it. In the middle distance, the arch glowed golden in the morning light; above and far beyond it, the Trade Center towers looked like alien invaders, slightly confused. A stiff breeze made spinnakers of the coats of people walking toward them. Niles worried about his wig, but didn't reach for it. He put out his hand. "I'm Fred Adams. I'm with the, uh, government. Mister Follett's applied for a security clearance—"

"Mark?" The man laughed, ignoring the hand.

Niles took out a notebook. "Why does that amuse you, exactly?"

At Tenth Street, clotted with crosstown traffic, they waited for the light. When it changed, the man stayed put. "Just after I got out of college, Mr. Adams, someone who said he was from the Army came around and asked me questions about a former tennis teammate of mine. Actually, he hadn't even been a teammate: He'd been on the varsity when I was on the freshman team. We rarely practiced together and often had matches at different schools at the same time. I hardly knew him, but when this guy asked me to characterize my teammate, I didn't hesitate to say that I thought he was an arrogant, conceited son-of-a-bitch. I don't think I said son-of-a-bitch. He was up for some kind of job, I guess. I still occasionally wonder if he got it. Maybe they were looking for arrogant, conceited sons-of-bitches."

Niles reached inside his coat. "I can show you some identification."

"Show me a subpoena. Then maybe I'll tell you about Mark Follett, or anybody else." The man stepped off the curb.

And a litigious world, Niles thought as he turned back uptown. People watched too many television cop and lawyer shows; they knew exactly what their rights were. And a small

198

world: *He'd* been interviewed by an Army security investigator just after *he* got out of college too, concerning a *swimming* teammate of his; he didn't remember what he'd told him, but it was where he'd got the idea for his masquerade. He put a hand on his head from time to time as the following wind endangered his disguise. He hadn't wasted that much time, and he'd found out that 42 Fifth Avenue was going co-op, which meant he could put on another, so to speak, hat.

"Good morning, Heritage Management."

"Yes, my name is Adams. I represent Mister Mark Follett, who's a tenant in the building you manage at Forty-two Fifth. That is, I'm his banker. Would it be possible for me to obtain another copy of the red herring? I need it for my files."

"You'd have to talk to Mr. Greenstein, the agent for that building."

"All right. May I?"

"He'll be in after three."

"Could I leave my number, please?" Niles started to give the secretary the number off the pay phone, but it had been defaced, so he made up a number. "And could you do me one other favor? Could you check Mister Follett's file to see if that's the number you have for me on your records? It was recently changed."

The secretary asked him to wait a moment—which surprised him; he'd expected her to say he'd have to talk to the agent, or that there was no such thing as a file for Mr. Follett—and while he did he wondered if the phone number he'd made up from all but one of the digits of the winning Lotto numbers, 2, 5, 8, 9, 42, 44, had other implications. Maybe Mark Follett had picked the Lotto numbers from numbers in his life: he lived at 42 Fifth Avenue; 42 and 5 were two of the numbers. Maybe the other numbers—2, 8, 9, 44—had significance, as well.

"Mister Adams?"

"Yes?"

"The number you gave me is not the number in our records."

"Exactly. It's been changed. The number you have is . . . ?" She gave him the number and he wrote it down. "If you could please change that to the number I just gave you, I'd be most appreciative."

"Our records also show that Mister *Tim*berlake is Mister Follett's banker."

"Was. Or, that is, he's on sick leave. I'm handling his duties for a while."

"So you're with Stuyvesant Savings too?"

"Right."

"Eighty-six Eighth Avenue?"

"Right."

"One-double-oh-one-one."

"Precisely."

"All right, then. I'll change it."

"Thank you. Uh, have a nice day."

"You too. Oh, Mister Adams?"

"Yes?"

"As long as I have the file out, is Mister Follett's number still correct?" She read him a number with a 982 exchange and he wrote it down.

"Yes, that's correct."

"Goodbye."

"Goodbye."

Bingo. Nine-8-2 equaled 2, 8, 9. And the secretary had saved him the risky business of calling the phone company and impersonating a police officer to get Mark Follett's unlisted number.

That left 44. Maybe Follett was a Reggie Jackson fan. Had been a Reggie Jackson fan.

"Stuyvesant Savings. Bob Timberlake."

"Mister Timberlake, this is Fred Adams. Heritage Management."

"What can I do for you, sir? You sound like you're in a phone booth."

Niles laughed. "As a matter of fact, I am. I was just on my way to a meeting when I remembered some information I need from you. My secretary must've gotten on the phone with her boyfriend the minute I walked out, because it's been busy for twenty minutes. So I thought I'd call you myself."

"That's usually the best way. What can I do for you?"

"Mark Follett? A tenant at Forty-two Fifth?"

"Sure. I'm handling his mortgage."

"He is buying, then?"

"Last I talked to him. Al Greenstein knows all this."

"Right, that's the problem. Al had to go out of town and something came up with one of our other buildings. It seems we have two buildings with tenants named Mark Follett. Not that common a name, I would've thought, but . . . Your Mark Follett —what's his occupation?"

"He invents computers."

"Invents them."

"That's right."

"For whom?"

"As I understand it, for whoever needs one. He just sits at home and stares at the ceiling and . . . invents computers for clients."

"Un hunh. So he works at Forty-two Fifth, as well?"

"Yes, but he's not under a professional lease. I want to make that clear."

"I understand, Bob. So the nine-eight-two number, that's his work number, as well?"

"That's it."

"That should take care of it, Bob. Thanks much. Oh. One more thing. Just to be sure we keep these two Mark Folletts straight—what's your Mark Follett's birthday? Not likely they'd both have the same birthday."

"Hang on a sec. His file's right here. . . . March twenty-two, nineteen forty-three."

Bingo. He was forty-four years old. Two, 5, 8, 9, 42, 44 stood for a forty-four-year-old man who lived at 42 Fifth Avenue and had a 982 telephone exchange. "Bob, you've been a great help. We'll have to have lunch sometime."

"Anytime, Fred. You know, when you said you were from Heritage, I thought for a minute there might be a problem with Follett's mortgage. I'm glad to hear it's nothing like that."

"No problem at this end, Bob. Any problem at yours?"

"No problem in the mortgage department. Our problem with Follett is he doesn't like banks."

"Well, no offense, Bob, but who does?"

"But most people confronted with a fifteen-dollar-a-month fee on NOW accounts don't take their money out of the bank."

"Fifteen's a little steep, Bob."

"Maybe so, but he had twenty-two thou on deposit. He would've been exempt from the service charge."

"Took it to another bank, I guess, hunh?"

"Took it home and put it in a shoebox in his closet, to hear him tell it."

"Yeah? Well, it takes all kinds, Bob."

"Say hello to Al, will you, Fred?"

"You bet." A forty-four-year-old man who lived at 42 Fifth Avenue, had a 982 telephone exchange and twenty-two thousand dollars in a shoebox in his closet.

Niles started down Eleventh Street, thinking he'd go to a coffee shop and think of a way to get into Follett's building. He stopped, remembering something Jessica Frank the smart doorwoman had said about Nowhere Man: . . . *he lived somewhere in the Village, in a doorman building, so he didn't need a front door key, and he either left his apartment door unlocked or he stashed that key—under the hallway doormat, maybe.*

"Who you want?" The Hispanic doorman at 42 Fifth, whom he'd chatted with and who had pointed out Follett's neighbor, was on a break. A porter, a dour Middle European, a Czech or Hungarian, was relieving him.

"Mister Follett. Mark Follett. Six B. I'm Mister Timberlake, Stuyvesant Savings."

The porter opened the door. He didn't care. It wasn't his building.

Niles took the elevator to six and went the wrong way down the hall, then back the right way to B. Which had a doormat.

He rang the bell. No answer.

He knocked. No answer.

He moved the doormat with his foot. Nothing.

He moved it the other way. Nothing.

"Damn."

He looked down the hall, then stooped and turned the doormat over.

Bingo. The key was in a pocket cut with a razor or knife in the fabric of the mat.

Niles took it out and replaced the mat.

Uh oh. The door had a Fichet lock and two Segals. The key in his hand was for a Segal.

202

He tried it in the top Segal. It fit but didn't turn.

He tried it in the bottom Segal. It fit, turned once counter-clockwise and another quarter for the button lock. The door opened. The Fichet wasn't locked.

Niles went inside and closed the door and locked both Segals and the Fichet. "Hello, Nowhere Man."

"The fuck's he doing in there so long?"

"I gotta take a piss, Artie."

"He hangs around the building, he talks to the doorman, he walks a couple a blocks with the guy who came out a the building, he makes a couple a phone calls, he goes back to the building, he goes inside, he's in there for a hour. The fuck's he doing? The fuck's the skinhead wearing a rug?"

"Why don't you stay here, I'll find a luncheonette, take a piss, I'll come back?"

" 'Cause what if he leaves while you're gone, that's why. What am I, gonna draw a arrow on the telephone pole, that's the way I went?"

"What're we following him for, Artie? We been following him since yesterday. We didn't go to work last night, we been following him. We lost our jobs, prob'ly, on account a we been following him. What're we following him for, Artie?"

"We don't need those jobs, Jerry. We got the winning Lotto ticket. Only thing is, on account a you told Niles we *took* the ticket, on account a you also told him the number on the ticket, we got a little problem, which is we can't cash in the ticket long as Niles is walking around the street."

"He ain't walking around the street now. He's in the building over there."

Artie sighed. "I don't mean *walking*, I don't mean around the *street*. I mean *alive*. I mean as long as Niles is *alive* we can't cash in the ticket. So I'm gonna pop him."

"You were gonna pop him, why didn't you pop him last night? He was all alone, a couple a times, walking down the street."

"What're you, Jerry, saying I didn't see he was all alone a couple a times? I saw he was all alone a couple a times. I wanna know what he's up to, that's why I didn't pop him. The fuck's he up to? First he goes to that building up on the East Side; he comes out in a little while, he talks to the broad who's the doorman, she hands him a piece of paper or something, he puts it in his pocket; then he goes to Dimanche's house, stays a hour, comes out wearing a rug; he goes to a luncheonette, has breakfast, goes to his office, before he goes in his office he takes the rug off, puts it in his pocket; he's in there most a the day, he comes out, he goes to a building on Eighty-ninth Street, there's a tag on the door says he lives there, he stays there about five minutes, he comes out with the rug on, he goes to the Port of Authority Bus Terminal, he sits on a bench and reads magazines till three-thirty in the morning, he goes to that theater, the Kane—"

"The Kean."

"The governor a Jersey's Kean, but they don't say Kean, they say Kane. He goes in the stage door, he's got a key—what, has he got a key to every place in town?—he stays a half hour, he comes out, he comes downtown, he starts going in and out a apartment houses, talking to doormen; all night long, he talks to doormen; he talks to the doorman in that building there, he comes out, he goes down the street, around the corner, he has some breakfast again, he comes back, he hangs around the building, he walks a couple of blocks with the guy who came out a the building, he makes a couple a phone calls, he goes back to the building, he goes inside, he's in there a hour. The fuck's he up to? The fuck does he sleep? The fuck's he wearing a rug?"

"So what're we gonna do?"

"I just tolja—we're gonna follow him, that's what we're gonna do."

21

"I need some more," Nell Ward said.

The fat man said, "Some more what, babe?"

"Jumbo."

He laughed. "It fucking jolts you, doesn't it? Sorry, babe, I'm out. It's real popular."

"Get some more."

Another laugh, with no humor in it. "Hey, babe, you read the papers, you watch the tube? There's been stuff all over the papers, all over the tube, about jumbo. Over here you got everybody and his little sister wanting some, over here you got the narcs coming down hard on it. The word is out and the word is cool it."

Nell Ward's fingers fussed with the knot of her bow tie. She suffered them, as if they were someone else's. "Some coke, then. The regular stuff. Ten grams."

The fat man shook his head. "Won't do a thing for you, babe. After the jumbo."

"I'll base it."

"You base it, babe, you'll wind up at Bellevue with a tag on your toe."

She took a handful of his Dead Head T-shirt. "Now, mother-fucker."

205

He slapped her to the floor.

She came up with a gun in her hand.

"Hey, Nell—"

She shot him in his fat stomach. And again. And a third time.

22

This was what it was like, police work: slumping on the sprung seats of a worn-out car with grimy windows, a grimy dash, no door on the glove compartment, one sun visor, ripped floor mats, a handle to roll the window or one to open the door but never both, halves of sets of seat belts, the stink of blood and vomit and pizza and sweat; squashing old coffee containers with your feet every time you changed the way you were slumping; spilling coffee on yourself, on the seats, on the floor, because there was no place to put the container while you let the coffee cool off, which you hoped would make it taste better but it just tasted like cold burnt coffee; reading the paper all the way through, even the recipes you wouldn't make because you couldn't cook and the investment tips you wouldn't follow because you were broke and the advice to the lovelorn you wouldn't heed because you weren't in love, you were married, even Today's Chuckle *(Gravity isn't just a good idea; it's the law)* that you didn't chuckle at, you sneered, because you were a cop and therefore paranoid and read into the joke a disparagement of law and law enforcement in general and you in particular; talking about sports, which was a mistake because the guys you were waiting with knew either nothing about sports or everything; talking about money, which was a mistake because the guys you were waiting with always had more than you, even the third grades, or spent it like they did, or talked like they spent it like they did; talking about women, which was a mistake because it's always a mistake to talk about women, there's nothing to say, they just are, like mountains, like dog shit on the sidewalk, depending on your point of view; talking about the brass, about politicians, about D.A.s and judges and shysters; talking about the great busts you'd made and the great cops you'd worked with; talking about the greater busts you would've made but for the brass, the politicians, the D.A.s and judges and shysters, and the assholes you'd worked with; staring at the brownstones on the block of Eighty-ninth Street between West End and Riverside as if their stolid faces could tell you something about the people who lived in them; seeing those people as they came out to go jogging, to walk their dogs, to go to work, and not being able to tell a thing about them; having to piss and wishing you hadn't had all that coffee; getting more coffee and drinking it because it was something to do; playing with the hinged lid on the ashtray, which was a mistake because a cigar smoker'd been using the car and a wet butt popped out like a turd-in-the-box and you got crud under your fingernails when you tried to jam it back in and you could smell the crud when you picked your nose; trying not to look like you were picking your nose, trying not to notice that the guys you were waiting with were picking theirs.

The guys Neuman was waiting with . . . There were hundreds of guys who wore white pants, pastel jackets, rope-soled shoes with no socks, gold watches, and carried Bren 10's; guys with commendations coming out of their ears, minds like steel traps, more contacts than a Park Avenue madam, a sixth sense for danger, two-hundred-degree peripheral vision; guys with marksmanship medals, Ph.D.s in psychology, sociology and forensic medicine, fluent in ten or twelve languages; guys who could bench press their weight, run up the steps of the Empire State Building, swim the Hudson in the wintertime, drive like an Unser, kill with a fingertip. There were thousands of guys like that. Neuman waited with one guy on sick leave with something wrong with his gut, one who was a suspect in a murder case and kept his popcorn in the freezer, one who had a suit that was too big and said Lieutenant every other word. That was what it was like, police work.

Winger rested his chin on the back of the front seat. "I don't think Niles is coming out, Lieutenant. I think we should go up, Lieutenant."

"I don't want to go up, Winger. I want to see where he goes. We go up, he won't go anywhere. And he's got to come out, he's got to go to work."

"Maybe he's at work, Lieutenant."

"Did you call his office, Winger, when I asked you?"

"Yeah, sure, Lieutenant. He wasn't there, Lieutenant. But you know, Lieutenant, he could've been on his way in. We could've missed him, Lieutenant; he could've left before we got here and been on his way in. I say we go to his office, sweat him, Lieutenant."

"We've been here since four o'clock this morning, Winger. You think he left for work before four o'clock this morning, Winger? The *Dispatch* is a morning paper, Winger, his deadline's eight, nine o'clock at night. Why, Winger, would he leave for work before four o'clock in the morning? If the sun was as big as the globe in the lobby of the Daily News Building, Winger, and the earth was a walnut at the main entrance to Grand Central Terminal, why would he leave for work before four o'clock in the morning, Winger? If we go to his office, Winger, you know what'll happen, Winger? We'll get TV cameras stuck in our face, Winger, that's what'll happen, 'cause Niles had what they used to call a scoop, Winger. I don't know what they call it these days, Winger, but whatever they call it, Winger, there're going to be TV reporters, radio reporters, reporters from the other papers hanging around the *Dispatch* to ask Niles where he got whatever it is they call it these days, Winger. They see us, Winger, they see me, Winger, they're going to want to know what I have to say about Bobby's list, Winger, which I have nothing to say to them about, Winger. So, Winger, we're staying put, Winger."

Winger looked at Federici and McGovern to see if they agreed with him that Neuman was a candidate to maybe eat his gun. McGovern was doing the Word Jumble; Federici was rolling between his fingertips something he'd picked from his nose. Even a classy guy picked his nose, a guy who had a thing for punk rockers, modern dancers, painters, writers, filmmakers, a guy who sometimes wondered if they weren't doing something he ought to be doing, not that he was an artist or anything.

Winger opened the door, first rolling down the window and reaching for the outside handle because there was none inside. "Anybody want any coffee?"

Nobody said anything. Winger shrugged and got out. He walked to the corner, his sleeves and pant legs flapping.

"Jake?" Federici said. "I know we've been through this, but—"

"Steve, we've got nothing on Niles to take to the brass—"

"The autopsy—"

"Nothing."

"The music. The graffiti."

"Nothing."

"Dimanche's house—"

"Nothing."

"He knew her."

"You knew her."

Federici shut up.

They waited. All over town, judges were issuing bench warrants, district attorneys were handing out grand jury subpoenas as if they were massage parlor leaflets; there were sting operations, legitimate business fronts; there were strike forces with the FBI and the DEA and ATF—with the CIA, probably; there were paramilitary operations with command posts and walkie-talkies and Special Services teams with Ruger Mini-14's, Beretta 9's, twelve-gauge shotguns, helicopters, dogs, fleets of cars with superchargers and roll bars, phone hookups to headquarters and City Hall—to the White House, probably; operations in which everybody had a number and nobody moved without his number being called—called by the chief of patrol or the chief of D's or the chief or the commissioner or the mayor—called by the president, maybe. But Neuman was sitting in a grimy, smelly car with a guy on sick leave with something wrong with his gut, a suspect in a murder case who kept his popcorn in the freezer, and a guy with a suit that was too big; with no go-ahead, no backup, nobody who knew what they were doing or even where they were; without an idea what the fuck they were doing there or why, for that was what it was like, police work.

Winger came back with four containers of coffee. They drank it, spilling some on themselves, on the seats, on the floor, then shoved the containers under the seats and squashed them and clamped their thighs together and wished they hadn't had all that coffee, because that was what it was like, police work.

"You know something, Loo?" McGovern said.

"What, Mac?"

"Terry doesn't always go in to his office."

"He'll go in today. He had a scoop or whatever they call it these days."

"What I mean, Loo, is he doesn't have to go *in* to write his stuff. Sometimes he writes at home, files his stuff over the phone. He's got one of those computers you can send stuff over the phone with, Loo."

Neuman rested his forehead on the steering wheel. Waiting for someone to leave his apartment and go to work, then finding out he might not have to leave his apartment to do his work, which, since you hadn't seen him go in his apartment, might mean he wasn't in his apartment, which you hadn't determined except by calling his apartment and getting his answering machine, which didn't tell you anything because the answering machine could be on even if he was at home—that was what it was like, police work.

"I should've said something sooner, Loo. Sorry."

Neuman sat back. "Steve, in the play Dimanche was supposed to be in, *Dying Is Easy,* who kills her? I mean, who plays the character who kills the character Dimanche was supposed to play? I think I said that right."

Federici shook his head. "Why?"

"I don't know why. But if I asked, I must want to know." Neuman turned on the AM-FM radio. It worked with the ignition off. You sat for hours in a grimy, smelly car, drinking coffee, reading the paper, picking your nose, bullshitting, wishing the radio worked with the ignition off so you could hear a ball game if they played in the daytime anymore, which they didn't, except on weekends; or music, which you didn't like, except some Sinatra, but the stations that played Sinatra also played Johnny Mathis, who you didn't like; or a call-in show—

211

Bob Grant or somebody like that practically sliding out of his chair with contempt for his listeners, provoking them to call up, then hanging up on them because they forgot to turn their radio down, or Imus even, or whatshisname—Howard Stern. Even Bernard Meltzer. But not Dr. Ruth. At Dr. Ruth you drew the line; Dr. Ruth would say, *Vat's rrrrrong vit your vife hafing a fibrrrrrator?* You sat for hours like that, then found out the radio did work with the ignition off. That was what it was like, police work.

There was news on and Neuman reached to tune to music, but the announcer was saying, *"There is one very unhappy individual somewhere out there today,"* and Neuman waited to see if the announcer was talking about him.

"The good news is, New York State Lottery officials have confirmed that there was a winning ticket sold for last weekend's sixty-million-dollar Lotto jackpot. The bad news—and it's very, very bad news—is that at the same time, the officials announced at an Albany news conference that the drawing has been declared invalid because one of the forty-eight numbered balls got stuck on its way into the mixing chamber from which the six winning numbers were picked at random. The person or persons holding the winning ticket still hasn't come forward, which has Lottery officials somewhat puzzled. Since the televised drawing Saturday night, they've been besieged by hundreds of self-proclaimed winners, all of them bogus. . . .

"Police Department officials refused to comment this morning on a report in the New York Dispatch *linking the recent murder of pop star Dimanche with a series of murders committed more than two years ago by Detective Sergeant Robert—"*

Neuman switched the radio off.

23

"Fuck're you talking about?"

" 'Snafu Voids Lotto Drawing,' that's what."

"Lemme see that. 'History's biggest-ever lottery drawing was declared null and void today by state officials, who said thousands of entrants were inadvertently deprived of a chance to win sixty million dollars in Saturday's Lotto Forty-eight contest because one of the numbered balls got stuck on its way to the chamber from which the winning numbers were selected.' I don't believe it."

"Believe it, Artie."

" 'The mishap meant that forty-seven balls, instead of forty-eight, were in contention to be among the six numbered balls removed at random from the chamber, the officials said.' So what? I mean, it's breaks of the game.

" 'It was not immediately clear how many dreams would be shattered by the decision, which followed a day-long scrutiny of videotapes of the drawing. The officials said it appeared from computerized records of Lotto Forty-eight ticket sales that only one ticket picking the six winning numbers—2, 5, 8, 9, 42, 44—had been sold. The holder or holders of the ticket, which was apparently purchased in Manhattan, had not claimed the prize *by the time officials announced the decision to nullify the drawing.'* Fucking-A right, we didn't claim the prize. We got a year to claim the prize. It says so on our ticket."

"It's not our ticket, Art."

" 'It is not unusual for apparent Lotto winners to wait a few days before coming forward, the officials said. Often the ticket holders consult with lawyers, accountants, family and friends before exposing themselves to the blizzard of media attention that surrounds any big lottery jackpot.' Right. That's right. We had a consult with our lawyer, our accountant. That's why we didn't turn in the ticket."

"We didn't turn it in, Artie, on account a we stole it."

" 'The officials said even had the winner claimed the prize, they would have had no choice but to void the outcome. "Any Lotto drawing, like any horse race or prizefight or sporting event conducted under the laws of New York State, must be scrutinized for its fairness before it is declared valid," said Richard Rubin, a spokesman for the New York State Lottery. "A videotape analysis of the drawing begun immediately after it was conducted determined that one of the numbered balls failed to reach the mixing chamber, depriving perhaps thousands of ticket holders of a fair chance at the prize." ' Well, fuck 'em. Fuck the thousands a ticket holders, 'cause they still picked six numbers and we had 'em. All six a them: 2, 5, 8, 9, 42, 44."

"We didn't have 'em, Artie. Nowhere Man had 'em. This is his revenge."

"Fuck're you talking about, Jerry? Revenge for what?"

"For us killing him."

"Get a hold a yourself, Jer. We didn't kill him. We just took his ticket, that's all."

"We shouldn't a. I tolja we shouldn't a."

"You told me. You told me. Lemme read the rest a this. . . .*'According to the officials, the videotape analysis revealed that ball number 6 failed to reach the mixing chamber from which the balls were selected, becoming wedged in the chamber's loading tube.'* So the fuck what? So they didn't pick ball number 6? They picked balls number 2, 5, 8, 9, 42, 44, and we had 'em."

"They might a picked ball number 6, Artie. Don't you see?"

"What I see, Jer, is we should a done what I tolja we should

214

a done, which is fix the balls. I tolja, somebody makes the balls, somebody puts 'em in the jars, there's a way to fix 'em so they're too heavy to fly up when they open the little trapdoor or too big to fit through it, like, all but the ones we bet on, the ones we get the guy who makes 'em or the guy who puts 'em in the jars to make sure they're, you know, not like the other balls. That's what we should a done."

"What we should a done, Artie, is go to work like always. Now we got to kiss Leon's ass to get our jobs back."

"Will you shut up a minute, Jerry, and let me think? Can't you see I'm thinking?"

"You're a thinker, Artie. Like Jackie Sharps."

"Jackie Sharps, Jackie Sharps."

"Who's doing points in Rahway."

". . . I got it."

"That's what Jackie said. 'I got it.' Now he's doing points in Rahway."

"No, I got it, Jer. Really. I don't know why I didn't see it till now. It's beautiful."

"See what?"

"Niles."

"What about him?"

"Don't you see, Jer?"

"See what?"

"He must a killed Dimanche."

"Niles?"

"Don't you see?"

"No. No, I don't see."

"He went to her house, right?"

"So?"

"He had a key."

"So?"

"He's been sneaking around wearing a rug."

"So?"

"So he must a killed her."

"So?"

"So he comes out a that building 'cross the street, we slide up to him, tell him we know he killed her, it's gonna cost him to keep us from going to the cops, telling them he's got a key to her house, telling them the crazy stuff he's been doing, sneak-

215

ing around wearing a rug. Fuck can he do to us now, right? I mean, okay, so he knew we took Nowhere Man's ticket—on account of *you* told him, Jerry. We tried to cash it in, he could a told the cops, but the fuck can he do now they annulled the lottery 'cept pay us to keep quiet? Okay, so it won't be sixty million, but it'll be something. The skinhead makes a nice bundle, prob'ly, taking taxis everywhere and everything, it'll be a nice piece of change, Jerry, no more parking cars for us. It's beautiful, babe. I mean, he can't holler cop, can he? He's already a crook himself, a murderer."

"Artie?"

"What?"

"You're full a shit."

"Where you going?"

"To see Leon. Kiss his ass. Get my job back. I got a eat. I got a pay the rent."

"Hey, Jerry."

"Maybe you can win some books, Artie."

"Fuck're you talking about, books?"

"Read the part about the books. You're doing points in Rahway, you'll have a lot a time to read."

"Fuck're you talking about, Jerry?"

"Read the part about the books."

"Jerry, I get real tired a hearing you saying the same thing over and over. Real tired."

"Read the part about the books." Jerry walked away.

Artie watched him go, then read:

Lottery officials said there would be some small recompense for some of those who bought tickets for the $60 million jackpot, believed to be the largest in North American lottery history. Contestants will be able to mail in their tickets to the Lottery's Great Book Giveaway.

Under the program, 8,000 prizes of $25 each are awarded to those who mail four losing Instant Lottery tickets along with the name and address of a local bookstore. The awards are made in the form of a two-party check made out to the winner and the bookstore. The officials said that because of the unprecedented cancellation of the Lotto 48 drawing, every ticket purchased would be considered the equivalent of four Instant Lottery tickets in the Giveaway. They noted that a contestant's entry must still be picked at random from among all those submitted.

The Giveaway program, launched in 1985, was designed to encourage state residents to read and buy more books.

"Books," Artie said.

24

"Hi."

"Hi."

"Remember me?"

"Sure do. Lieutenant Neuman, right? And this is Steve Federici. Jessica Frank. Pleased to meet you."

Federici shook her hand warily. "How'd you know that?"

"Your picture's been all over town, Steve. They haven't done you justice, though—I probably shouldn't use an expression like that, should I? You ought to have a professional do some glossies; you're much better-looking in real life." Jessica took her uniform hat off and shook her hair loose. "I have a confession to make. I guess I should tell you too, Lieutenant. Did you get a phone call a few days ago, Steve? A sort of crackpot phone call from a woman who said she thought she knew who Nowhere Man was, except she didn't really, just where he might've lived?"

Federici laughed. "You?"

She blushed.

"That was her?" Neuman said. "That was you? That was your crackpot theory that he lived downtown, between Eighth and Fourteenth, between Fifth and the river, he ran downtown, stopped to buy a Lotto ticket, if he was out running without any keys and since nobody's reported him missing, he lived in a doorman building, which there aren't all that many of in that general area, maybe fifteen or twenty, most of them on Fifth, the rest're mostly brownstones?"

Jessica laughed. "Must not be such a crackpot theory; everybody's kind of singing along with it."

"Oh, yeah? Who's everybody?"

She shuffled her feet. "Did you come to see Jay Dillen?"

"Who's everybody?"

"He's not in. He's at the theater. Tonight's the first preview with Amanda in it. You probably know that."

"Who's everybody?"

She looked at Federici. "Does he always do this? Keep asking the same question over and over until he wears you down?"

Federici smiled. "Always. Who's everybody?"

She flicked some dust from the crown of her hat. "I told you, Lieutenant, there's not a lot to do working a door. What did you call it—'superficial torpor, interrupted by periods of wakefulness'?"

Neuman and Federici looked at each other; then over at the car, where McGovern and Winger waited; then at each other. They laughed.

"I wish you guys would tell me what's going on," Jessica said. "I know I'm only a civilian, but—"

"So there's not much to do when you're working a door," Neuman said. "So you—what?—dreamed up this crackpot theory, you've been trying it out on people? You tried it out on Steve, without telling him who you were, he tried it out on me, without knowing I kind of knew you. Who else did you try it out on?"

"You promise you won't tell him I told you?"

"Nope."

"What I mean is, there's no reason to tell him I told you; you can just tell him you figured it out for yourselves. I mean, it's not that crackpot a theory." She waved a hand, as if to erase what she'd said. "I take that back. You probably wouldn't have figured it out. I doubt if he would've, either; he didn't even think to ask the newsstand guy if he was sweating when he got there—Nowhere Man, not the newsstand guy."

"Niles," Neuman and Federici said together.

219

"Don't tell him I told you, okay? I mean, what's the point?"

"When was this?" Neuman said.

"Yesterday morning. I was working a double—the day guy's brother was getting married—so I was on when Niles came by to see Dillen."

"And he asked you what was your theory about who Nowhere Man was?"

She sniffed. "He didn't ask me, no. I told him."

"Told him what, exactly?" Neuman said.

Federici took a step that put him on Jessica's side of the discussion. "Jake, she just said what's the point. What *is* the point?"

"I don't know yet. I'm waiting for her to tell me what she told him."

Federici smiled at Jessica and shrugged. She smiled back.

"I told him," Jessica said, "that if Nowhere Man wasn't sweating when he got to the newsstand—"

"Okay," Neuman said. "We know about that and we haven't got all day."

Jessica pouted.

Federici put a hand on her shoulder.

Neuman rolled his eyes. You spent all day in a grimy, smelly car with a guy on sick leave with something wrong with his gut, a guy who was a suspect in a murder case and kept his popcorn in the freezer, a guy in a suit that was too big and said Lieutenant every other word, drinking coffee, reading the paper, picking your nose, bullshitting, wishing the radio worked with the ignition off, finding out it did; you finally admitted you'd struck out, so you went somewhere else, there was a good-looking girl you'd tried to do a favor for by warning that slime-bucket Dillen not to fuck around with her future, she fell for your partner, who wasn't really your partner because you were retired, and was the guy who was the suspect in the murder case and kept his popcorn in the freezer, and he fell for her. That was what it was like, police work.

Jessica went on: "I told Niles I thought Nowhere Man lived in a building with a doorman between Eighth Street and Fourteenth Street and between Fifth Avenue and the river. They *are* mostly brownstones; there can't be more than fifteen or twenty buildings with doormen, and most of them're on Fifth.

I told him I'd already checked about ten of them."

Neuman stared. "You? Why?"

"Niles asked me that. I told him I'd done something I wasn't particularly proud of. I think you know what it is, Lieutenant, and I'd appreciate it, if you have to tell Steve, tell him later, after you leave. I told Niles I thought if I did a good deed I might sleep better."

Neuman sighed. "A good deed would've been to tell the cops what you thought. They have special numbers for citizens with information on crimes. Everything's kept confidential and all that."

Jessica stamped her foot. "Crackpot numbers. I bet that's what you call them around the old station house. You know what, Lieutenant? Nobody'd talked to the doormen I talked to. No cops. It's like somewhere, deep down, they don't really want to know. I told Niles that and he quoted a cop to me—I think it was you—a cop who once said the line cops walk between the law and lawlessness is so narrow that anytime they get a case there's a moment when they suspect themselves. I said that sounded like the way you talk. I said you have a poet's soul. How about it? Did you once say that, Lieutenant Neuman?"

Neuman shook his head. "I don't think so. No. No, I didn't."

Federici patted Jessica's shoulder. "Go on, Jessica. What else did you tell Niles?"

She shrugged. "I told him what I told you on the phone, Steve —about doormen. I told him Nowhere Man's doorman probably didn't know Nowhere Man went out for a run because he was goofing off or sleeping or in the john or doing shit work, and he still doesn't know he went out because it might not even've been the regular doorman, it might've been the relief guy. I told him my list was just a start, that I'd only done ten buildings, the ones on Fifth Avenue, starting at One Fifth, up to Fifty-one. I told him I'm a member of the Road Runners Club. I told him the club has a computerized list of members and of everybody who's run in the last several marathons. I told him a friend of mine works there. I told him I asked her to run my names through the computer. I told him one of the names was on the list I got from talking to doormen. I told him the guy had an unlisted number; he said he could probably get it—through the paper, I guess. He said if it turned out not to be the guy, could

221

he check any more names he came up with against the Road Runners computer. I told him yes. He asked me to have a drink with him. He said we could talk about the weather. I told him I'm not ready for winter. I told him I was sure I was going to win the lottery, that I could kiss this place goodbye. I had two numbers—2 and 5, and I might've had 6, but 6 was the ball that got stuck. I asked him if anybody'd won. He said it was funny I should ask. I thought he meant he'd won, but I guess he was talking about their canceling the drawing because the 6 ball got stuck. He probably heard it around the paper or something." She shrugged again. "That's what I told him."

"What, Winger?" Neuman said.

Winger had crossed the street and stood a little way away, his hands in the pockets of his suit coat. When he lifted them, he looked like a nestling thinking about flying. "I called my squad, Lieutenant, just to check in, Lieutenant. I had to tell my lieutenant I was working on something with you. I didn't tell him what, Lieutenant. He said there's a rocket going around that Lieutenant Carrara, Narcotics, wants to talk to you. He's got something you'd want to know, Lieutenant."

Neuman nodded at Winger and waved him away. He turned back to Jessica. "Did you tell Niles the name?"

She shook her head. "I told him I felt a little like you—if you *were* the cop he quoted to me, which you say you weren't. I told him I was afraid that naming the name would make it so, would make Nowhere Man somebody. So I just gave him the list and told him the name had a star next to it."

"What was the name?"

She shook her head again, in refusal this time. "I still feel the same way. What if he's not the right guy?"

"Then he won't be the right guy."

"Well, what if he *is* the right guy?"

"Then he will be, and you'll've been a lucky beginner."

Jessica looked at Neuman for traces of sarcasm, but saw only respect. "Mark Follett, Forty-two Fifth Avenue."

Federici groaned.

"You *know* him?" Jessica said. "Oh, my God. I knew I didn't want to tell you. Now they'll definitely think you killed him. You do think it, don't you, Lieutenant Neuman? You think Steve killed him just because he knows him."

Neuman started to say that he didn't think anything, but Federici was talking, walking back and forth as if exhorting a crowd. "It can't be. It's not possible. Dimanche was killed between three and three-thirty on Tuesday afternoon, Nowhere Man was killed around five-thirty Tuesday morning—ten hours earlier, roughly."

"What're you talking about, Steve?"

"She can't've been with him if he was dead."

"Who, Steve?"

"Mark Follett."

"No. I mean, who's 'she'?"

"Why would she tell me that if it isn't possible?"

"Steve?"

Federici stopped. "Nell Ward knows Mark Follett. She told me he was the guy she was having a matinee with when Dimanche got killed. He's her alibi."

25

"Bob Drummond."

"Mr. Drummond, this is Fred Adams. I'm a free-lance writer doing a piece on some of the more interesting behind-the-scenes people in the business. I wonder if you have a minute to talk about Mark Follett. I understand he's done some work for you."

" 'Work' is an understatement. Mark designed a forty-five-megabyte hard drive that saved HyperTech's ass. And you're a little late, I'm afraid. *Popular Computing* did a big piece on Mark a couple of months ago."

"Right. I have it in front of me. But I want to do something about personalities, not technology. What can you tell me about Mark's, well, his private side?"

"Mark knows you're doing this?"

"And he gave me your number, which is unlisted—correct? *Popular* called Mark a recluse. Would you say that's accurate?"

"Not exactly. A classic loner, I'd call him. A high-tech cowboy —self-reliant, self-sufficient, self-confident."

"High-tech cowboy. I like that. Hobbies, pastimes?"

"His work is his hobby and his hobby is his work. Pastimes? Jogging. He doesn't call it jogging, he calls it running; he can go on for a long time about the distinction. He stayed at my place on one of his trips to Palo Alto and I never saw him watch television or read a book or a newspaper or a magazine—except a running magazine. That's not true, actually; he sometimes reads Latin. He taught himself; he said it helped him think, that it's a very orderly language. I wouldn't know."

"A dead language—interesting. I've seen the Latin books around his apartment and wondered about them, since he has so few other books. Has he ever been married?"

"Beats me. I doubt it. Won't he tell you?"

"Cowboys aren't very forthcoming, Mr. Drummond. That's why I'm talking to you. What about women friends?"

"If Mark caught every pass that was made at him, he'd be too sore to walk. Don't quote me on that. I nearly lost half my female staff when Mark finished his work here and went back to New York. You know, who you should really be talking to is Tony Cook. He was Mark's partner for a while, until Tony got seduced by the Apple mystique. He's down in Cupertino, if you need the number."

"Thanks. I already got it from Mark."

" 'Seduced'? How about jilted?"

"By?"

"By Mark. He wanted to go his own way, is the nice way to put it. The not-so-nice way is he couldn't stand sharing the credit any longer. But this is history. I don't want to talk about it."

"How about off the record?"

"No. What's the point? Mark got famous; I found my niche. Have you talked to Carrie?"

"Who?"

"His wife. His ex-wife."

"Ah—Carrie. This is a bad connection; I thought you said something else. I plan to talk to her. I have her number right here."

"People magazine's interested in Mark?"

"One way to look at it is we've done just about everybody else."

She laughed. "They call what you write puff pieces, don't they?"

"Some do, yes."

225

"I mean, you never write anything bad about anybody, do you?"

"Not unless being bad is part of their shtick."

She laughed again. "It's certainly not part of Mark's—not of the public Mark's, anyway."

"Do you want to talk about it?"

"No. Yes. I don't know. It's none of my business anymore."

"You don't have any kids?"

"I thought you said you'd talked to Mark."

"Which is like talking to a high-tech cowboy."

Another laugh. "No kids. I wanted them; he didn't."

"Because of his work?"

"That and the . . ."

"The what?"

"I feel funny saying this on the phone."

"Tell me off the record. Maybe we can find a way to say it on the record."

"Mark's a cocaine addict. How would you say that on the record?"

"Is that why you split up?"

"Off the record?"

"Sure."

"Yes. And no. Or partly, I guess. Mark screws every woman he sees, or he wants to; he thinks it's his birthright. You called him a high-tech cowboy; I used to call him the high-tech Warren Beatty."

"This is Deborah. Please leave a message and I'll call you back. You can talk as long as you want. Have a nice day."

"Hello, you have reached Bonnie's telephone answering machine. Bonnie isn't here right now, but I'll record anything you have to say to her and play it back when she returns. Are you ready? Here comes the beep."

"This is Katherine and I'm happy to say I'm out of town for two weeks. If you're a burglar, please don't take this machine, so I can hear who else called when I was away. If you're not a burglar, leave a message. Thanks. Goodbye."

*　　　*　　　*

226

"Yes, you have reached an answering machine, which means I'm not here or I don't want to talk to you. During the day, you can try me at work. If you don't know where I work, I probably don't want to talk to you. Ciao."

"The number you have reached is not in service or has been temporarily—"

"Hi. I'm out right now or I can't come to the phone. But I'll call you back. It would be extremely helpful if you would say the day and time you called. Thanks. This is Susan."

"Hello?"

"Hi. Is this Jane?"

"Who's this?"

"My name's Fred Adams. I'm a friend of Mark's."

"Mark?"

"Mark Follett."

"Mark Follett doesn't have any friends."

"He speaks highly of you."

"Oh?"

"I'm from out of town and in need of some company. He said I might enjoy having dinner with you."

"Mark's pimping now?"

"Look. I'm sorry. I guess I misunderstood. I didn't mean to embarrass you—or me."

"It's typical of Mark to make his friends embarrass themselves."

"This is Sandra—"

"This is Phyllis—"

"This is Margo—"

"This is Penny—"

"This is Hilary—"

"This is Mary—"

"This is Audrey—"

"This is Lynn—"

"This is Rose—"

"This is Nancy—"

"This is Nell Ward. Please leave a message and I'll get back to you."

"Nell. Terry. Meet me at the information booth at Grand Central at ten o'clock tonight—Monday. It's about Mark."

"City Desk. Cooper."

"Coop. Terry."

"Where the hell are you, Terry? You going to give me a column or what?"

"It's going to be something big, Coop, but it's not going to be ready for the One Star. Put some moonlight in the One so I'll have a big hole to fill for the Three."

"Moonlight? What moonlight?"

"Use one of my any-timers from the bank. For one edition, for Christ's sake."

"There're TV crews all over the building, Ter. They want to know where you got the stuff about Redfield's list. Aren't you going to follow that up?"

"I've got something better for you, Coop. I've got Nowhere Man."

"No shit? You have his killer?"

"I may have, but not before the Three."

"You're not going to tell me where you got the stuff about Redfield's list, are you, Terry?"

"If I tell you, you'll know. Better you can say you don't know. Oh, and Coop—tonight's the first night of previews for Amanda Becker in *Dying Is Easy*. You should send somebody over to cover it."

"I'm sending a photographer. It's a picture story."

"Send a reporter."

"You mind telling me why?"
"So you can thank me for telling you to."

The fuck is he doing in there? He's been in there all fucking afternoon.

I gotta piss. Shit, I gotta piss. I go piss, he'll leave. If fucking Jerry'd stayed here, I could go piss, he'd watch.

Jerry. Shit. I went to piss, he watched, Niles came out, he'd prob'ly slide up to him, tell him what we're doing, tell him we know he killed Dimanche, it's gonna cost him to keep us from going to the cops, telling them he's got a key to her house, telling them the crazy stuff he's been doing, sneaking around wearing a rug, way he told him everything else. The scumbag.

Shit, I gotta piss.

26

"I've been on Operation Karate Chop—who dreams up these names? Jake, Steve, Matty—what'd you say your name was? Singer?"

"Uh, no, Lieutenant. Winger, Lieutenant."

Nick Carrara stared. "You're a lieutenant?"

"No, Lieutenant. I'm a third grade, Lieutenant. Sorry, Lieutenant. I mean, I didn't mean to make it sound like I was a lieutenant, Lieutenant."

Carrara looked at Neuman, who just smiled and settled himself for the performance. He knew that Carrara always came to the point and that there was no interrupting him; an amateur opera tenor, he would sing till he was sung out.

"Anyway, like I said, Operation Karate Chop, we work out of the Seven on Pitt Street, which is what it is, a dump, was supposed to get every dealer off the streets from the Bowery to the river from Houston to Fourteenth, it worked, so to speak, they all moved indoors. Smack, mostly, two hundred thousand decks, Jake, can you imagine that, a lot of blow, some reefer, basically small-time, steerers, runners, pushers, dealers, the occasional supplier. Then it changed, Jake, crack, it's a new ball game, new dealers, new customers, you can't tell them from the civilians 'cause that's who they are, recreationals who used to buy at the office or from a friend, a lot of first-timers, a lot of kids. Dealers're back on the street, standing on corners making like they're cracking a whip, but a lot of it's indoors, crack houses, like opium dens in some old movie, apartments, lofts, abandoned buildings, garages, people go there for two, three days, spend all their bread, some of the women, Jake, Jesus, the things they do to keep on getting high, it turns you on, it gets you kinky, it makes me sick, Jake, just to think about it, the medicos're scared of it, the docs at the rehab centers, I've never seen that.

"DEA raided a crack factory in Harlem, nothing major, couple of pounds a day, which adds up to a net of about half a million, about what you and I make a day, right, Jake? They gave us a look at everything, one of the phone numbers they found was for a guy named Richie Gallman, Tiny they call him 'cause he's a big guy, we been watching him run a fair-sized off-the-street business down on Mulberry, a lot of artist types for a clientele, actors, dancers, some good-looking women, Steve, you should get that detail, you're not married or anything are you, I know you're going to beat this other rap, babe, don't worry about it, if Jake's with you, I'm with you.

"We stepped up the surveillance on Tiny's place figuring maybe he'd lost his source he'd switch to another, we'd get a make on another factory, my guy scoping the place this morning, which is one of Tiny's heavy office hours, he saw people coming, ringing the bell, getting no answer, going off, like maybe Tiny wasn't in, he knew he was in, the guy he relieved watched him go in last night, five, six o'clock, he had a couple of customers, his lights were on all night, which was usual, Tiny sleeps days, he didn't like the look of it, my guy, I mean Macy's doesn't close on Saturdays does it? To make a long story short, Jake, he got the super, went upstairs, went in, one dead Tiny, three forty-five slugs in his body, count 'em, three.

"It had to go down late last night, early this morning, it had to be one of the customers my guys saw go in, unless it was somebody climbed down the fire escape, forced the window, which it wasn't, there's soot on the fire escape, nobody's walked on it, the window was locked, it's got a gate on it, unless it was somebody in the building, which is doubtful, the tenants knew what Tiny did, they didn't like it, but they don't look like vigilantes, Butler's got the homicide, Jake, Paul Butler, you can check this out with him if you want to, there were three of them, customers, male, white, the usual bullshit, nothing to go on, the point, Jake, is I was looking through Tiny's phone book, I saw a name that rang a bell, I thought I better let you know, I know it's just a name in a phone book, maybe she knew him when he was straight, Tiny, maybe they went to high school together or something, but I know from the scuttlebutt she's been tagging around after you guys, making a movie or something, Nell Ward."

Winger said, "Jesus, Lieutenant."

Neuman said, "Nick, any of these customers, male, white, the usual bullshit, any of them five seven to five nine, thin, real thin, one-ten, one-twenty, wearing a suit, a tie, a sweater maybe, one of those floppy golf hats?"

"You been reading my mail, Jake?" Carrara said.

"Nick, there any missing pieces in the Department, lost, strayed, stolen, forty-fives, I mean, like Steve's? I don't mean off the top of your head, I mean you should tell Paul Butler to check it out, I got a feeling the piece that killed your friend Tiny's a piece that was lost, strayed or got stolen from somebody in the Department." He was talking like Carrara.

"You think she took my piece, don't you, Jake?" Federici said. "Nell, I mean, she's been in my car three, four times, you think she took my piece, killed Nowhere Man, took somebody else's, killed Tiny."

They were all talking like Carrara. "I think it, yeah. She's been hanging around a lot, guys relax around her, let down their guard." Let down their pants, or think about it.

A uniformed cop was at the door of Carrara's office. "There was a call for you, Lieutenant Neuman. She said she couldn't stay on the line, but a woman named Charly Johnstone wants you to call her at the Kean Theater, or come by if you're in the neighborhood."

Neuman nodded his thanks. "Nick, you just did me a favor, now I need another favor. I'm retired, or something, I'm driving around with a guy on sick leave with something wrong with his gut, a suspect in a murder case who keeps his popcorn in the freezer, and Winger here, who's investigating this Dimanche's mugging but not her murder. None of us has the credentials to go up in front of a judge and ask for a search warrant for Nell Ward's apartment, it's in a loft down in SoHo, I almost made it upstairs, but not quite, I'll give you the address, Nick—"

"Say no more, Jake," Carrara said.

"You'll have to figure out a grounds. I mean, something to do with your investigation."

"No problem, Jake."

"I also need a search warrant for an apartment at Forty-two Fifth Avenue occupied by someone named Mark Follett, maybe you could say he was in Tiny's phone book too, we'll have to worry about that later."

"No problem, Jake."

"Yeah, well. The problem might arise when somebody finds out I and Steve and Matty and Winger here went downtown and tossed these places before the warrants were issued, which is what we're going to do because I don't think we've got a lot of time to hang around waiting for the wheels to turn, so to speak."

"Just leave it to me, Jake, will you? Christ, you're retired, you forgot how things're done around here."

"Come to think of it, Steve, Matty, Winger, I think you should go downtown, do the tossing, split up the places however you want, I'll go over to the Kean and see what Miss Johnstone has to say. We had such good luck with it before, Steve, don't forget to play any answering machines you find, who knows what we might hear?"

"It's a small world, isn't it, Jake?" Carrara said.

Winger snapped his fingers. "That's what you meant, Lieutenant, isn't it, Lieutenant, when you said it's like the sun's as big as the globe in the lobby of the Daily News Building and the earth's like a walnut at the main entrance to Grand Central Terminal? Right, Lieutenant?"

27

In Grand Central Terminal, a score of nuns was bound for
Toronto. The 8:35 from Westport was twenty minutes late. A
feral man slept beneath the Off-Track Betting windows. The
Kodak panorama was of a rural autumn landscape. A beautiful
blond mother and her beautiful black-haired daughter, both
with punk haircuts, argued about the latter's smoking. Two
boys with White Plains High School jackets tossed a Frisbee. A
slim black boy listened to L. L. Cool J on a blaster. A janitor
followed a wide broom across the marble floor, making a mo-
raine of cigarette butts. A refugee from the sixties, ponytail,
bandanna headband, buckskin jacket, tie-dyed shirt, blue jeans
with embroidered patches, Frye boots, sang "Stairway to
Heaven," accompanying himself on an acoustic guitar with
peace signs on the sound box, a wilted daisy on the fingerboard.
A three-year-old spilled a bag of M & M's; they skittered on the
floor like insects; her father rolled his eyes and smiled.

"Hello, Nell."

"Terry? A wig?"

"Someone said naked is the best disguise, but unfortunately
naked attracts too much attention, even in a place like this."

"What *are* we doing here?"

"You don't know?"

"If I did why would I ask?"

"If you don't why would you come?"

She frowned. "I don't really want to play mind-fucking games, Terry. You asked me to meet you."

Niles prompted her. "To talk about Mark."

"Right. Who is Mark?"

"Mark Follett, Forty-two Fifth Avenue, forty-four years old, nine-eight-two telephone exchange."

Nell Ward shook her head. "Means nothing to me."

"You're in his phone book."

She made circles with a forefinger. "Whoopee."

"No one else knows, Nell. I haven't written anything."

"Not like you, Terry, to keep a secret. No one else knows what?"

"Is that what he did—violate some confidence?"

"Who?"

"Mark."

"Ah. Mark. Mark Follett, Forty-two Fifth Avenue, forty-four years old, nine-eight-two telephone exchange. Those could be lottery numbers."

"In fact, they were the winning lottery numbers, but a ball got stuck."

"What a pity."

"It's hard to imagine what your motive could've been—unless it was just simple jealousy. From his collection of phone numbers, you had a lot to be jealous about."

She came closer. "Terry?"

"Yes?"

"What're you talking about?"

He touched the knot of his bow tie. "Did you find the money? I couldn't."

"What're you talking about, Terry?"

"There was a key under the doormat. Do you know that? At first I thought you didn't, and that that was where you'd screwed up—by not taking it. Then I thought you did, and that you'd been smart not to take it, so that when someone finally came out of the woodwork and said he kept a key there—some of the other women must've known—it wouldn't raise more questions by being missing."

Nell laughed.

"If you did find the money, my advice is take it and run. That's why I suggested we meet here rather than Kennedy or La Guardia or Newark. Taking a train's a lot less conspicuous; you don't have to give a name, for one thing. You can be just about anywhere before anyone knows you're gone. There's a train in the morning for New Orleans that'd put you fairly close to Mexico. There's one in a few minutes to Canada, but I don't think you'd like Canada. Mounties and all. Or you can just go to Philadelphia or Washington or Baltimore and take a plane from there. Those trains leave from Penn Station—the New Orleans train may too; I'm not sure—but you can just hop in a cab. I wouldn't go back to your place. There is one other person who knows about Mark, and she's acquainted with Neuman; I don't know that she's talked to him, but I don't know that she hasn't."

Her eyes hadn't moved from his. "This is fascinating."

"I guess you could say I'm doing it for old time's sake. I always liked you, Nell. Killing him while he was out running was brilliant; the hat and the overcoat were a mistake. You should've dressed like a hooker or something, in the event you were seen, which you were. Was it coke? Had he reformed and was pressuring you to, too? Or did you just want his stash as well as his money?"

Nell looked down at the floor. The sixties throwback sang "Wooden Ships."

"What's in it for me?" Niles said. "Is that what you want to know? I don't want any of the money; however much it is, it can't be enough for you to live on all that long, so you'll need every penny. I will want to write about it; I figure it's worth a prize or two, maybe a book deal. This guy Lindsey from the *Times* struck gold with his falcon and his snowman, and I think this is better; sex and drugs is better than espionage, which is always a little tawdry. You'll stay in touch with me —we'll work some kind of mail or phone arrangement out— and I'll be able to write about how you got on with your life in some exotic foreign land. I won't say which, of course. But I'm going to need your motive, Nell. And it has to be a good one. Without a good motive, it's just another . . . hysterical woman."

She slapped him, knocking his wig awry.

236

The sixties vestige stopped in midphrase and murmured, "Far out."

Niles laughed. "Was it as simple as that? He called you a cunt?"

The fuck's the skinhead standing there talking to this broad this whole time? What is she, a dyke, dressed up like a guy? She looks like Jackie Sharps.

Jackie Sharps, Jackie Sharps, Jackie Sharps. I'm starting to do it.

Shit, I got to piss again.

Holy shit. She popped him. She knocked his rug off. I bet he gets her somewhere there ain't so many people, pops her back. The skinhead.

"You know who Burt Young is, don't you, Leftenant? Of course you do. But so many people've been saying, 'Who's Burt Young?' Poor man. His face is ever so famous, but his name just ain't. Is there another Jacob Neuman, Leftenant? I'd be delighted to invite him. And you too, of course. Since word got out, quite a few of these illustrious people are simply dying to meet their everyday homonymns. You don't know a Jane Fonda, do you? Or even a Peter? Or even a Henry. I'll stretch the rules and admit a dead man if I can just get a Fonda. . . .

"Dead. Dying. Funny how much a part of our quotidian vocabularies such morbid words are. 'I'll kill him'—or her: how often we say things like that. 'I'll wring his neck.' 'I'll slash my wrists.' " Charly Johnstone shivered and lighted a Sherman's with an Ohio Blue Tip. "I thought about it for a nonce or two —slashing my wrists. Not because I killed Dimanche, mind you. I didn't kill Dimanche, though I did love her, unrequitedly but deeply. I miss her, quite simply, miss the pleasant pain of loving her unrequitedly. The pain of missing her is only pain. You don't seem surprised to hear that I'm a practitioner of the love that dares not speak its name; I guess you've heard gossip, innuendo, slander. *Rumor volat,* the Romans used to say, and if they didn't know, who did?"

"Uh, Miss Johnstone—"

"Terry Niles," Charly said. "I called to tell you about Terry Niles. Terry Niles and Juliet Marko. I wonder if there's a Juliet

Marko—for the party. But of course no one would know who she is. You don't know, do you, Leftenant?"

"That was Dimanche's name," Neuman said. "Uh, Miss Johnstone—"

"Oh, of course you know. You're so observant. Those questing eyes. It was Sunday morning, Leftenant. We'd gathered at Jay Dillen's sterile flat to contemplate the, uh, severity of the situation. Jay, Marty Klein, Kevin Last and *moi*. It was rather like an Agatha Christie—the principals gathered in the drawing room to await the arrival of Hercule Maigret, who stuns them, and the reader, with stuff about clocks. Don't sigh like that, Leftenant. I'm getting to the point. It was Terry Niles, not Hercule, who arrived. He'd been invited by Jay Dillen to—how did he put it?—enter our alibis into the record. You, Leftenant, weren't interested in making public the reasons why none of us could've killed poor Dimanche, and we were encountering icy stares from the salespeople at Bergdorf, being told our regular table at Le Cirque just wasn't available; we couldn't get a taxi; we couldn't get arrested. Hah. Someone—someone other than each of us—had to bruit it about that we were innocent. Terry said—don't pace, Leftenant, please—Terry said the question of our guilt or innocence had been mooted by the suicide of B.G. Harris, who had gone to the trouble of writing a note—"

"Miss Johnstone, for Christ's sake."

Charly swelled up. "He called her Juliet."

"Who did?"

"Niles."

"Called Dimanche Juliet?"

"Yes."

Neuman slumped. "You better tell me the whole thing."

Charly beamed a victor's smile. "He said—this was in the nature of a revelation, you understand; the police were looking for poor dear B.G.'s next of kin before making the tragedy public—he said, and I believe I'm quoting him directly, or at any rate paraphrasing him accurately, 'B.G. shot herself in the head with the same thirty-eight Special she used to kill Juliet.' Martin—dear, dense Martin—said, 'Who's Juliet?' and Niles did that thing . . . Have you ever noticed how people do it, Leftenant? Surely you have, you and your questing eyes . . . He made a sudden move, sweeping his hand under his cigarette as

238

though the ash was about to plummet to the carpet—Is there a carpet? I don't remember. Or just fashionably bare floors? At any rate, he made what I believe the observers of human and animal behavior call a displacement action, one designed—half-unconsciously—to distract us from his unease . . . his unease at his slip of the tongue. I had my back to him, but when I heard the slip, I took a glance and saw his distress. He recovered rather nicely, said something about his having called her Juliet because he'd been contemplating doing a column about her death's having rendered the stage name—what did he say?—extravagant. Horse manure. Who calls people with nicknames or stage names by their real names, Leftenant?"

"I don't know. Their mothers."

Charly laughed. "And their lovers. With the lovers of famous individuals, it's a way of laying claim to a private patch of what is otherwise in the public domain. Did you read the piece Terry Niles wrote about Dimanche just after her death, Leftenant? An extraordinary document. I have it here." Charly rummaged among the papers on her desk. *" 'Fame is a kind of dying. . . . The famous have no apposites. . . . The famous are like sharks. . . . Their shadows fall full length even at noon. . . . It's as if their lives were those sashes that Boy and Girl Scouts wear, from which badges of both merit and demerit hang immutably. . . . Those sashes are encrusted with dates, places, people—with steps that though false are frozen forever, with lovers who though dismissed stay loved, with gestures that though contradictory are the arabesques of one long dance. And when they die, it isn't an end; it's another accretion. They die forever.'* Extraordinary. The words of a bitter man, a man who resented—that's the only word for it—loving a woman who though she may have loved him was also loved by a multitude that—"

"Yeah, well. We sort of already had an idea Niles and Dimanche were, you know, mixed up," Neuman said.

Charly cocked her head. "Really? Then this isn't a bolt from the blue?"

"Uh, not exactly. No."

She pouted. "How about the fact that he was here in the darkest hour before the dawn."

"Who?"

"Terry *Niles*. Honestly."

239

"When?"

"Today. It seems like centuries ago, but it was just today."

"Here. Here in the theater?"

"The Kean, yes. Where dying is easy."

"Who let him in?"

"Not I. And I was the only one here."

"Did you talk to him?"

"Of course not. I was scared to death."

"What did he do?"

"Can't say. I stayed in here, quiet as a mouse. A light was on, but he took no notice. Just the lamp on the desk; perhaps through the frosted-glass door it looked like a light that gets left on all night."

Neuman wagged a thumb toward the door. "What's happening out there now?"

"There?"

"On stage."

Charly looked at her watch. "The play is nearing its climax."

"Which is?"

"The murder of Di— Sorry. Of Amanda. Of Cass, that is—the protagonist, the actress who is about to make her debut in a Broadway play about the murder of an actress who is about to make her debut in a Broadway play, et cetera, et cetera, et cetera."

"The play ends with the murder of the protagonist?"

"It's a most unusual play. Poor B.G."

"She gets shot, right—with a thirty-eight Special."

"Indeed."

"Who shoots her?"

"Kevin Last. Buddy, to the audience."

"Where does he keep the gun when he's not acting?"

"Well, you see, it's a gun Buddy takes from Cass, who, in Dimanche's interpretation, carried it with her throughout the play. It was a sticking point between her and Jay. I would imagine that the fair Amanda's been directed to hew to the original business, which was that Buddy takes the gun from a chest of props in Cass's dressing room."

"Is the gun kept in a chest of props?"

"In a locker, yes."

240

"In Amanda's dressing room?"

"No. Right out— Oh, my God. You don't—"

"Is there someplace we can watch?" Neuman said.

Beneath his wig, Terry Niles's head was flooded with sweat. "No autopsy?"

Nell Ward smiled. "Not at the time you wrote there'd been one. The message on the mirror, the music on the answering machine—you wrote about too many things that only one person could've known, Terry. The killer."

Niles looked around. The sixties leftover played "Season of the Witch." "Did you tell anyone you were coming here?"

"When I got your message, Terry, it was clear to me that you were the only one who'd help me. You killed Dimanche because she wouldn't be open about your relationship, didn't you? You wanted to see yourself with your arm around her in *People* magazine. Men."

"You're quite the hypocrite, Nell."

"There's a difference. A big difference."

"Save your breath, Nell. We're birds of a feather—and we've got to figure out where to fly to."

"Fly? You were just talking about taking a train."

"There may not be time. How much money is there?"

"About twelve thousand."

"Twelve? I thought it was twenty-two."

"Thought it, why?"

"It's not at your place, I hope."

"It's in a camera case that I checked at La Guardia. I've been thinking ahead, Terry. We can get a Carey bus right across the street."

"Even better, we'll take the subway—the Flushing line to Roosevelt Avenue. There's a city bus that goes to La Guardia." Niles smiled. "We could go around the world."

"Not without a passport. Do you have yours with you?"

More sweat. "No."

Nell shook her head disapprovingly. "I'm not sure I should run with you, Terry. You've made an awful lot of mistakes. Are you one of those criminals who subconsciously wants to get caught?"

241

There. I was right. He's taking her somewhere there ain't so many people, he's gonna pop her back.

The fuck're they going? On the subway? The lowlife skinhead. Shit. The skinhead's got tokens. What is he, a fucking boy scout. Shit, there's a line. I don't have a token. Shit, I'm gonna lose him. Fuck it, I'll hop the turnstile. Oh, fuck. Oh, shit. A cop.

"Hey, officer, I can explain. Really, hey. I mean it."

Kevin Last twirled the gun like a cowboy. " 'Oh, Cass. You just don't get it, do you?' "

" 'I get it, Buddy,' " Amanda Becker said. She giggled. " 'I can't believe I'm going to say what I'm going to say.' "

" 'Please spare me'? "

She shook her head. " 'You'll never get away with it.' "

He brought the gun up. " 'We'll see, won't we?' "

Charly Johnstone rushed onstage. "Kevin, don't!"

A trouper might've improvised. Kevin, a tyro, pulled the trigger.

Charly, who had knocked Amanda sprawling, was hit in the stomach.

The audience stirred with dissatisfaction at the introduction, so late in the play, of a new character.

28

"Arthur Fenestra?"

"Who wants to know?"

Neuman read from the yellow sheet on a clipboard. "You work at the E-Z-Park Garage, on Crosby Street?"

"I use ta."

"You apprehended for theft of services by Transit Patrolman Leonard Jackson for allegedly hopping a turnstile at the Grand Central Terminal stop of the Lexington Avenue IRT?"

"I *told* him, I put a token in the turnstile, it got stuck or something, I heard my train coming, I was in a hurry, I hopped over."

"Transit Patrolman Jackson found a twenty-two-caliber Smith and Wesson revolver on your person, Artie."

"So?"

"You're not licensed to carry such a weapon."

"I had a license. I lost it."

"You ever drive into the city from Jersey, Artie, or Connecticut, see those signs they got up about New York State's one-year mandatory sentence for illegal possession of a firearm? No exceptions."

". . . I was following somebody. I was gonna make a citizen's arrest."

Neuman laughed. "Following a murder suspect, Transit Patrolman Jackson says you told him."

"Right."

"Named Terry Niles."

"Right again."

"What makes you think Niles is a murder suspect, Artie?"

"I figured it out."

"You're a smart guy, is that it?"

"Yeah."

"So who'd he murder, Artie?"

"Dimanche."

"Dimanche the singer?"

"You know another one?"

"And you're—what?—a fan?"

"Hunh? Yeah. No. I don't know. I like Patty Smyth."

Federici tapped Neuman on the shoulder and handed him the phone. "McIver."

Neuman took it and put his hand over the mouthpiece. "Yeah, well, I like Patti Page, Artie, and what I want you to think about while I'm talking on the phone here is, if the sun was as big as the globe in the Daily News lobby and the earth was the size of a walnut at the entrance to Grand Central Terminal, do you think there'd be more coincidences, or fewer, or just as many? Yeah, Tim."

"Charly Johnstone's going to make it, Jake."

"Hunh? She looked like she was going to be dead. But what do I know?"

"The slug's a thirty-eight. It's on its way to the lab right now."

"Yeah, well, it won't be from any piece we've seen before. Niles had to leave the thirty-eight he killed Dimanche with at B.G.'s, so he would've had to get another thirty-eight to plant in the theater to keep his string of thirty-eights going."

"Nick Carrara's looking for you, Jake."

"Did he say what about? I love Nick like a brother, but I hate to talk to him sometimes, I get superficial torpor."

McIver laughed. "I know what you mean, Jake. Yeah, he told me what it was about, it was about Paul Butler, who's investigating this guy Tiny Gallman's rub-out, Butler thinks the forty-five he was killed with might be one that's been reported missing from Crime Scene, guess who was in Crime Scene a couple of weeks ago talking to people about a movie she's making?"

"You're starting to talk like Nick, Tim. Yeah, well, I can guess who you mean. Is that it, Tim?"

"That's it, Jake."

Neuman hung up and walked back behind Artie. "So, Artie, what do you think, would there be more coincidences if the sun was as big as the globe in the Daily News lobby and the earth was the size of a walnut at the entrance to Grand Central Terminal, or would there be fewer? I'm talking about this Lotto ticket Transit Patrolman Jackson found on you, Artie, along with the twenty-two. I'm talking about you and a friend of yours being the guys who found Mark Follett's body—"

"The fuck's Mark Follett? I don't know no Mark Follett."

"Mark Follett who Terry Niles and some other people think just before he bought it he bought a Lotto ticket—"

". . . That's his name? That's Nowhere Man?"

"It's the winning ticket, Artie—2, 5, 8, 9, 42, 44—or it would've been if one of the balls didn't get stuck. Hell of a bad break, Artie. I'm surprised you didn't kill yourself or something. Unless you had another idea, Artie—which was what? You were going to blackmail Niles? It's kind of pathetic, Artie. You want to blackmail somebody, Artie, you blackmail rich people, not newspaper reporters. Okay, Niles writes a column, has his picture on the trucks, maybe he makes a hundred large a year, you probably make about twelve, right, plus tips, a hundred large sounds like a lot. . . .

"So what's the connection between you and Niles, Artie? He was writing stuff about Nowhere Man, asking questions, he put it together that you and this friend of yours took Nowhere Man's Lotto ticket, he was going to turn you in or— No, I get it, *he* was going to blackmail *you*. Is that it, Artie? He knew you had the ticket, when he found out it was the winning ticket he wanted a piece of the pie—before it turned out the pie was just a pie in your face, is that it? Come on, Artie, give it to me. I'm getting tired, I just watched somebody get shot up a little while ago, somebody somebody could argue if they felt like it wouldn't've got shot up if you'd hollered cop about Niles instead of following him around, I got things to do. You don't give it to me, Artie, you'll be meeting a few of my, uh, confreres, the ones we have to keep in the station house, they have a way of throwing people through plate-glass windows if we let them work in the streets. Don't give me that look like you know your rights, Artie, anybody lays a finger on you you'll go to the press, there'll be brutality charges, cover-ups, corruption, all that, you'll be a fucking hero, that's just in the movies, Artie, on TV, in real life we want information we get information. You ever see a cattle prod, Artie?" Why was he talking like this? He was retired. Wasn't he?

"Jerry told him."

Neuman looked at the clipboard. "Jerry Marder?"

"The scumbag."

"Told who?"

"Skinhead Niles."

"Told him what, Artie?"

"Told him we took Nowhere Man's ticket. Told him the fucking number, even. He wanted to meet with us, Niles, yeah. He wanted a piece of it, yeah."

"So you did what, Artie?"

"I followed him. We followed him. Then Jerry chickened out, the scumbag."

"Chickened out, why? 'Cause you were going to blow Niles away?"

". . . I want a lawyer."

"You followed Niles where, Artie?"

"All the fuck over town. He went to Dimanche's place. He had a key."

"How'd you know it was Dimanche's place?"

"I seen it on TV."

"Where else did he go?"

"Some theater. The Kane."

"Kean."

"Kean, Kane."

"Where else?"

"To some apartment house on Fifth Avenue."

"Number Forty-two?"

"Yeah. I think so. Yeah."

"Where else?"

"To Grand Central. He's wearing a rug all a time, you know, Niles."

246

"A wig, you mean?"

"A rug, yeah."

"What happened at Grand Central?"

"He met this broad—dressed up like a guy. She popped him."

"Popped him?"

"You know, hit him, like. Slapped him. Almost knocked his rug off a his fucking skin head."

"You ever see her before?"

"Who? The broad? Nah."

Neuman looked at the clipboard. "Lieutenant McIver says that just before you and Jerry Marder found Mark Follett's body you saw a woman, near the E-Z-Park Garage."

"A bag lady, yeah."

"The woman Niles met at Grand Central—was she that bag lady?"

"Hunh?"

"Was she?"

"Holy shit, I never thought a that. She could a been, yeah. She might a been. I mean, she's skinny, this broad. And young. But with a coat and all, one of them coats bag ladies wear even in the summertime, and a hat, yeah. Yeah, she could a been. The hat the broad at Grand Central was wearing, it was the kind a hat the bag lady was wearing, one of them golf hats, like. Yeah."

Neuman patted Artie's shoulder. "It's funny how you start remembering things, isn't it, Artie, when people start talking about cattle prods? So you followed Niles and the woman to the subway, you hopped the turnstile—what a stupid fucking thing to do, Artie, but nobody ever said you were in the wrong line of work parking cars, you ought to be doing brain surgery, did they?—you ran into Transit Patrolman Jackson, who found the heat you were carrying. Where were they going, Artie, Niles and the woman?"

Artie shook his head. "Fuck do I know?"

Neuman snapped a fingertip against Artie's earlobe.

"Ow!"

"Jesus, sorry, Artie. There was a bug or something on your collar—a mosquito. I was just trying to get it off. You know, people're getting scared, what happens if a mosquito that bit somebody who's got AIDS bites you, do you get AIDS? You're

247

not going to like doing points, Artie, speaking of AIDS. There're guys doing points who've got AIDS in triplicate, Artie. They got it from shooting horse, they got it from taking it up the ass, they got it from junkie whores. What if one of them decides he wants you for his girlfriend, Artie? If one of them decides he wants you for his girlfriend, Artie, you win the jackpot, you can skip the joint, and go straight to the cemetery." His repartee needed work, but what the hell, he was retired.

"They went down two flights a stairs," Artie said.

Neuman spread his hands. "What does that mean, Artie? They went down two flights of what stairs?"

"In the subway at Grand Central you go down one flight to get the Lex, you go down another flight to get the shuttle."

"Wrong, Artie. The shuttle's at the other end of the station on the same level as the turnstiles."

"Well, there's something down there. The train that goes to Shea."

"You a Mets fan, Artie?"

"Yeah. Kind a. You know. I like Hernandez."

"My wife likes him too. She thinks he's sexy. I don't know how I feel about him, after that cocaine stuff. I'm never comfortable with a guy who testifies under immunity. The Mets're playing at home tonight, aren't they? I don't know, I think so. It is still September, isn't it? It is still baseball season? I can't remember the last time I heard a score, unless it was when the Dodgers kayoed Doctor K, which was about a hundred years ago, wasn't it? Fourteen years married, thirty-three years a cop, fifty-four years old and a hundred years behind on the ball scores. I used to be a Mets fan myself, Artie, till about five seconds ago, when I found out you were, you fucking lowlife. Let's go to La Guardia, Steve. Matty, tell McIver he can have this lowlife back, tell Winger to get out to Roosevelt Avenue—make sure you say Avenue, not Island; he'll go to Roosevelt Island—check with the drivers on the bus line that goes to La Guardia—the Q-something-or-other, did they see a woman in guy's clothes, a guy with a bow tie and a toupee. They say no, it could mean they changed to the E at Roosevelt, took it to Union Turnpike, took the Q-whatever-it-is to Kennedy, tell him to go to Union Turnpike, ask the drivers there."

*   *   *

248

They took the FDR to the Triborough to the Grand Central. There was no traffic and they didn't have to use the whirligig light on the top of the car. The light didn't work anyway; that was what it was like, police work.

Federici drove. Neuman studied the map he'd found in the doorless glove compartment. It was a map of New York City, which surprised him; more often than not, what it was like, police work, was finding the map in the doorless glove compartment was of Philadelphia, or Wisconsin.

"Why the hell did Niles plant that live piece at the theater, Jake?" Federici said.

"Like you said, Steve, he's a smart-ass. He killed Dimanche, killed B.G. Harris to make it look like she killed Dimanche, he wanted Amanda Becker killed to make everybody say, 'What the fuck is going on here?'—to make us say it. He threw everything in the pot—Bobby's list; everything—and stirred the fuck out of it."

"I guess he's not just a smart-ass, Jake. I guess he's crazy. What about Nell? You think she's crazy too?"

"You know, Steve, you get a guy, a hard-core, he holds up a liquor store, somebody makes a move he doesn't like, he wastes him; or a guy does a B and E on an apartment he thinks is empty, it turns out there's some old lady home, he rapes her, he shoves a broomstick up inside her, he caves in her face with a hammer; or a guy stops somebody on a street late at night, asks for his wallet, the guy gives it to him, there's just a few bucks in it, he blows him away; or a guy's dealing drugs, somebody moves in on his turf or sells him some bad shit, he goes to the guy's house, kills the guy, his wife, his kids, his in-laws, his neighbors; or a guy's a professional wise guy, his *capo* says ice somebody, he ices him. . . . Or a guy like Bobby Redfield, he goes to Nam, it's war, it's hell, he comes back, the world's different, he doesn't fit in, women especially're different, they want more out of life, he thinks they're after what ought to be his, he starts popping them. Guys like that, you don't think they're crazy, you just think they're, I don't know, antisocial. The guy who shot Reagan, the guy who shot John Lennon, that Harris woman who shot the diet doc, them, you ask if they're crazy, you get testimony from shrinks, they cop to insanity pleas. A guy like Niles, a woman like Nell, it'll be the same with them. Their friends, their families, people they work with, they'll shake their heads and say, 'I just don't understand it.' The other guys, the guy in the liquor store, the guy does the B and E, the mugger, the dealer, the wise guy, the guys like Bobby, nobody says, 'I just don't understand it. They were so normal.' But what's normal? What's the difference between the other guys, the guy in the liquor store, the guy does the B and E, the mugger, the dealer, the wise guy, the guys like Bobby, and Niles and Nell? So I don't know what I think. What it's like, police work, is driving in worn-out cars, drinking burnt coffee, talking about sports, about money, about women, telling war stories, drinking more coffee, picking your nose—not thinking."

Federici laughed. "That's a dig at me, isn't it, Jake, 'cause I told you *Miami Vice* was pretty good sometimes, on what police work was like."

Neuman looked down at the map on his lap. He'd never realized how close to La Guardia Riker's Island was. He'd never known that Riker's Island was part of the Bronx. He had heard of North Brother Island and South Brother Island, but he'd never known where they were. He'd never known there were so many other islands: Big Tom, Cuban Ledge, Green Flats, Rat, Chimney Sweeps, High, the Blauzes, South Nonations, East Nonations (which was north of South Nonations), Middle Reef, Hog. When he got through with this case he wouldn't have to go to Bimini and back; he could go to Hog, or Rat. *Sure, Jake,* Easterly would say, *you did such a good job, you kept us informed at all times of what you were doing, running all over tout New York with a guy on sick leave with something wrong with his gut, a suspect in a murder case who keeps his popcorn in the freezer, a guy with a suit that's too big, here's a rowboat, Jake—it leaks and it's got no oars, but it's all we got—and a life preserver—no, we don't have one with no holes in it. Go to Rat, Jake, and don't come back.*

29

The only other passengers on the bus were a pair of young lovers. She had bobbed blond hair and perfect skin. He had combed his brown hair straight back when it was wet and now that it was dry it stuck up in spikes here and there; his face was dappled with acne. They were both in denim jackets and jeans; she wore a turquoise acrylic cardigan with imitation-pearl buttons, he an inside-out navy blue sweatshirt. She had white high-top Nike sneakers with a powder blue swoosh, he scuffed cowboy boots with pointed toes. She looked like a teenaged Jessica Lange, he like a teenaged Sam Shepard. He probably ached to suck the breasts that were palpably bare beneath her sweater, their nipples pimpling its soft fabric, but had to settle for nibbling at her neck. She sat primly, feigning interest in the view, which was only of the reflected interior of the bus, suffering his caresses, conscious that they weren't alone, of how Nell stared.

How Nell stared. She couldn't take her eyes off them any more than the boy could keep his hands off the girl. She wanted to be them, to feel flowing through her the same unadulterated sap. She wanted to know as little as they, to be as indifferent to as much, to have traveled such a short distance and left so few blazes on the trail.

251

And she wanted to warn them that just as the bus would come to its terminus, so this time of their lives would come to an end, not because it reached some benchmark but because even as they sat there they were being warped, corrupted, contaminated by the world around them—by the likes of her. She wanted to shake them, slap them, rail at them: *See this? See me? This is what it comes to. This is what you turn into. This is what you have to look forward to.*

The boy wouldn't listen. The boy would think she was crazy —would know she was crazy. He'd tell her to fuck off. *Fuck off —lady.* The girl would hear the ground bass of truth in her ululation.

"Nell?" Terry Niles reached for her, but she got away, going hand over hand up the aisle against the inertia of the bus. Niles crossed his legs and propped an elbow on the back of one hand and with the other hand veiled his face.

"Hi."

The girl looked at the boy, who nodded, then looked at the girl and rolled his eyes.

"Could I have a word with you?"

"Me?" The girl spread her fingers on her delectable chest.

"We can sit in the back."

"Hey, lady, what the fuck?"

"Bil*ly.*" The girl got out from under Billy's arm and stepped across his legs. When they had sat in the middle of the rear seat, she said, "Are you in trouble?"

Nell giggled. "Me?"

"That guy you're with"—she moved her eyes but not her head—"he looks *creepy.*"

"It's the toupee," Nell said. "He's much better-looking without it. . . . He won't be faithful to you. You must understand that *now.*"

The girl looked at her sideways. "You mean . . .?"

"Not Billy, not any man. You're too young to know what it's like for them. They don't have any will, any self-control; they're led around by their cocks and when they find a place to poke them, that's all they want to do. They won't want to know about your feelings, your moods, your thoughts, your desires. They just want to fuck, and when they find out you want more, they'll be gone."

The girl just stared.

"What's your name?"

"Tracy."

"I know it sounds trite, Tracy. It is trite. Because they're trite. They're walking clichés; their lives are one long beer commercial. Oh, sure, you'll find a few sensitive ones, ones who'll tell you—you'll never see it for yourself, but they'll tell you—that they're different, that they're in touch with the feminine side of themselves. It's a line; don't buy it. It's as much a line as their talk about how much money they make, how successful they are. They all want one thing and they want it with a minimum of discussion before, during and after."

Tracy fidgeted with the inseam of her jeans. "That's what my mom always says."

"Well, she's right. Just because she's your mom doesn't mean she's full of shit. Because she's your mom, she knows exactly what she's talking about. Trust her. Trust me. Trust any woman who tells you what I'm telling you and don't trust any woman who doesn't, because she's been brainwashed, been seduced by material things, usually—by a microwave oven or diamond ring."

"My father just got my mom a computerized stove. It talks."

Nell laughed. "So he doesn't have to. Why're you going to La Guardia? That is where you're going?"

Tracy nodded. "To watch the planes."

Nell snorted. "Come on, honey. He wants to get you in a dark place and pull your pants down, fuck you from behind standing up. He's got it all worked out. You can't do it at home, right? You both live with your parents, right? I bet he told you he wishes you wore skirts more often. Hah. There. You see?"

Tracy pouted. "He loves planes. He wants to be a pilot."

" 'He loves planes. He wants to be a pilot.' Come on, sweetie, of course he loves planes. Planes fly away; they take you a long way from where you are in a very short time."

"Where're *you* going?" Tracy said it to her lap, for Billy had turned in his seat.

"Me? I'm taking a trip."

"A vacation? That's super."

"No, not a vacation. I need to get away from New York for a while—for the rest of my life, maybe."

253

"Where's, you know, your suitcases and stuff?"

Nell smiled and patted her shoulder bag. "This is all I have. What I'm carrying and wearing."

"That's a great outfit," Tracy said. "Is your boyfriend going with you?"

"My boyfriend's dead."

"Oh . . . I'm sorry."

"I killed him, actually. I killed two people—two men. Don't be afraid; I'm not crazy. They were crazy—both of them. Mark, especially. Let me tell you what he did, and you tell me if you don't agree. We were together for six months. The first two were blissful—fucking, eating, going to the movies, laughing a lot. Then he started getting distant, started getting angry at little things. He blamed it on me, said I was complaining too much, that I wanted too much, that I wasn't satisfied with what we had, that I was making it sound like it was his fault that we didn't have more time together when it was both of us who mutually agreed on how much time that time would be. You don't understand me, do you? You're too young. I wish I could make you understand. I wish you weren't frightened of me. I did the right thing. Terry doesn't understand, either—my friend there—even though he killed someone too: a woman. Two women. His was an interesting situation, actually—the flip side of the usual one in which a woman is the moon of a man. He was seeing a famous woman, but no one knew about it—because, I guess, she decided that for once in her life she'd like a little privacy. Because she was a woman whose every fling is usually widely documented, it was as though the relationship didn't exist. She was a smart woman. I suspect she felt that they had a better chance to make it if they kept it to themselves; but he couldn't see it her way. He felt slighted by her because the rest of the world wasn't being allowed to see how desirable he was. Or something. I don't really understand it. He's a man, after all.

"I did the right thing, though. If we had more time, I could make you see that. But there's the airport. What's your address? I could write to you. Or you could come visit, once I get—"

Nell looked up at a commotion in the front of the bus. Billy

254

had Niles by the lapels and was shaking him. "Tell her, man. Tell your fucking old lady to fuck off."

Niles just sat and let himself be shaken. His toupee slipped down on his forehead.

Nell looked away, nauseated. When she got control of it, she smiled at Tracy. "Hey, listen—why don't you come along? I have a lot of money—or enough, anyway, for us to have a good time before we have to get serious about getting some more. I cut film; I can make money doing that anywhere where there's film production going on. I was a waitress, a thousand years ago; I could always do that again to make ends meet. I'm not proud. Hah. That's a funny thing for a fugitive to say, isn't it?"

Tracy pushed past her and ran down the aisle. She pulled Billy away. They got off at the next stop, short of the airport. Billy grabbed a handful of stones from a construction site and hurled them at the bus. They sounded like hard rain.

"Sugar?" Terry Niles set two coffee containers on the table. Nell Ward shook her head.

Niles sat and pushed one of the containers close to her. "I think Houston's a good choice. We can go any number of ways from there, and it shouldn't be hard for me to get a phony passport."

Nell put her arms across her stomach and gripped her elbows.

"That was a stupid thing to do, Nell." Niles sipped his coffee. "Fortunately, those kids're members of the postliterate generation. They'll just switch their minds, if you can call it that, to another channel. MTV, murderers—it makes no dent in their self-absorption."

"I'm not going with you, Terry."

Niles began to sweat again.

"The ticket's paid for. I'll give you some money. But I'm not going with you."

"Hey, you're not getting panicky, are you?"

She looked over his head at a clock. "Is that the right time?"

Niles reached across the table for her hand. "Nell." He sat back when she pulled away. "Okay, okay." He looked at his watch. "I wonder if . . . Excuse me, miss, do you have a radio back there?"

255

The counterwoman just shook her head.

"A radio for what?" Nell said. "They can't be looking for us yet."

Niles hesitated to tell her about Amanda Becker. Some perverse sense of sisterhood was liable to turn her against him, just when he needed her most. He wouldn't need her all that long—just until he had some credentials, until he had a little spending money. "If you're carrying a gun, you'll have to get rid of it before we go through the metal detectors, of course. I've already, uh, taken care of mine. Are you worried about the cocaine?"

Reflexively, her hand went to her bag.

Niles smiled. "You can hide it in your privates. Did you hear that joke? Queen Elizabeth and Princess Diana were out for a drive—"

"Terry!"

"Relax, Nell. Jesus."

"It's Neuman. I just saw Neuman go by the door."

Neuman saw her too, but kept on going. For one thing, he didn't have a gun; he was retired. Nor a badge. He did have a Detectives Endowment Association card and he hoped that a uniformed cop wouldn't think he was some car salesman with an honorary membership. If he could find a uniformed cop.

He couldn't find Federici, either—Federici, who also didn't have a gun, since he was a suspect in a murder case. That was what it was like, police work: You said, *You go that way. I'll go this way,* then you couldn't find each other.

He went to a courtesy phone on a wall and picked it up. It was dead.

He went into a pay phone and searched his pockets for a quarter. He didn't have one. He dialed the operator. Nothing happened. He saw Terry Niles come out of the coffee shop; Nell Ward was at a trash can by the door, emptying a tray—and something from her shoulder bag. She followed after Niles. Neither looked Neuman's way—the mark of a true amateur, who thinks that if he keeps his eyes to the ground no one will see him.

Neuman went to the trash can and put a hand in. He felt among the debris for a paper napkin, then used it to lift out the

gun—a .45, the .45 from Crime Scene, he was sure. He put it
in his right coat pocket and the napkin back in the trash can.

Federici saw Terry Niles and Nell Ward coming and ducked
into a newsstand. He picked up a copy of *Time*.

"See the sign, Jack?" the vendor said. "This ain't a library."

Federici reached for his badge, but he didn't have a badge; he
was a suspect in a murder case. He took a dollar from his jeans
and tossed it on the counter.

"Buck fifty, Jack."

Federici tossed the magazine on the counter and followed
after Niles and Nell.

"Hey, Jack, what're you doing?"

What, indeed?

Neuman found a Port Authority cop and showed him his
DEA card. "Emergency undercover"—whatever that was.
"Come with me."

"That card don't mean shit, bro," the cop said.

"I know," Neuman said, and went on by himself.

"I'm not going with you."

"You're going with me. It's going to take two of us to hijack
this plane."

"You're crazy."

Niles laughed.

"I threw the gun away."

"I have a gun."

"I thought you said—"

"It's a toy. A prop. From a play."

"A play?"

"It looks real. Don't worry."

"They won't let us take off."

"There's the gate. All we have to do is get on board. Then
we're in control."

"I'm not going with you."

Nell bolted.

"Nell!"

"Niles!"

Niles turned to face Neuman. He took his toupee off and

257

threw it aside. He reached inside his coat and took out the prop gun. He put the barrel in his mouth.

Neuman stopped and held his hands out. "I'm not armed, Terry."

Niles pointed the gun at Neuman.

Neuman drew the .45 and shot Niles in the chest.

30

Nell Ward ran.

Jet engines shrieked.

Lights so intense they had weight and density shone on her, deflecting her from . . .

From what? From getting from where she was, which was nowhere, to where she was going, which was east of nowhere.

Or was it south?

Something told her it was east, not that it mattered. Something inside her felt that east was a good way to go, not that it mattered.

A fence. Chain link. With barbed tape at the top.

The end.

No. No, wait. You see? This was meant to be, this flight, eastward or wherever, from nowhere to . . .

To what?

She slid under the fence where it had been ripped out of the ground to make an unauthorized entryway to the tarmac. Ripped by whom? By kids, probably, looking for a place to fuck. By boys.

Her Hunting World bag caught on the fence and she tugged and tugged but couldn't free it. She left it behind.

An incoming jet passed so close overhead that she fell to the ground. She thought she would drown in its noise.

She didn't drown. She rose up and ran.

There was a road to her right, to her left a field. No, not a field: water. She could swim for it, but somewhere along the way she'd neglected to learn to swim; when she might've learned, in school, it had been cool to cut gym.

Cool. She'd always been cool; she'd been cool before it was cool to be cool, and long after. Cool. Frigid.

I'm not frig*id, Mark.*

You never come.

You *come too fast.*

I've never had that problem with other women.

Meaning it's my *problem?*

He'd shrugged, meaning *Of course.* He was cool too.

Neuman ran for a stretch, then trotted, then scurried, then walked like Groucho Marx.

He saw her go under the fence, but by the time he got there he couldn't see her anymore. She was young and swift; he was old and slow.

An outgoing jet battered him with noise and he cringed.

He tried to crawl under the fence, but her bag hindered him and he had to free it before he could try again. That took a week.

He made it under the fence on his second try, getting dirt in his hair, his eyes, his nose, his mouth, down his neck and down his pants. Good thing he wasn't wearing his pastel linen jacket, white pants and white rope-soled shoes.

He looked around for Federici in the car. He didn't see him. That was what it was like, police work. You said, *I'll go after her. You follow me in the car,* and then you couldn't find each other. Federici had probably been having trouble getting the car onto the tarmac, since he didn't have a badge, since he was a suspect in a murder case and kept his popcorn in the freezer. Now that Neuman was off the tarmac, he'd probably get on. That was what it was like, life.

What did the people in the cars think about her? Did they think she was an eccentric jogger, dressed in a suit and tie and cap and saddle shoes? Did they think she'd run out of gas somewhere back along the road?

Once, in Miami to make a film about . . . something, she'd rented a car and driven down the Keys a way. On a straight stretch of road with nothing but saw grass and sky around her, she'd passed going the other way a barefoot bearded man in a tattered robe, carrying a wooden cross as big as he. Driving back much later that same day, she'd caught up to him and passed him again. All she'd thought was that it was a free country.

Did you see that person running along the road?
What about him?
I think it was a her.
What about her?
Do you think she needs help?
Why do you think that?
Because she's running along the road.
It's a free country.

Neuman thought about flagging down one of the oncoming cars, flashing his badge, standing on the running board as the driver made a U and pursued Nell along the verge. Except cars didn't have running boards anymore, and he didn't have a badge. And drivers didn't stop for anybody, under any circumstances.

He did have a gun. He wondered how many bullets were in the clip, but he couldn't slow down to check. Not that he was moving fast; he was moving like a man under water, under water in a bog, under water in a bog with shackles and chains on his ankles, under water in a bog with shackles and chains on his ankles and a yoke around his neck, dragging a wagon full of men: the commissioner, Klinger, Easterly, Federici, Terry Niles, The Band, Robbie Robertson, Neil Young, Neil Diamond, Van Morrison, Doctor John, Muddy Waters, Paul Butterfield, Dylan, men who wore blue jeans and Rolex watches and used Macintosh computers, and the Marines.

There was a spaceship waiting to take her away. A huge one, like the one in *Close Encounters*. It would take her far away, maybe even far enough.

261

No. It was a stadium, a ballpark. It wasn't going anywhere.

Still, it was a place to sit down, a place to stop running, a place to think.

Think about what?

All right, then. Don't think. Just sit.

Holy shit, she was going to Shea. Fourteen years married, thirty-three years a cop, fifty-four years old and a hundred years behind on the ball scores, and he was going to get to see a ball game.

It was kind of late for a ball game, wasn't it? Late in the year and late in the day. It was still September, wasn't it? It was still baseball season? He was sure it was, even though it had been a hundred years since the Dodgers kayoed Doctor K. But it *was* late in the day, late at night. It was after midnight, wasn't it? It was the next day, wasn't it? He was sure it was.

But the lights at Shea were on and there were cars in the lots and Neuman could see people in the corridors behind the stands and hear the public-address announcer.

That could mean only one thing. The Mets were locked in another of their epic extra-inning contests—a donnybrook, a free-for-all, a no-holds-barred, knock-down-drag-out slug fest. Unless it was a pitchers' battle. What did he know?

He might never know if he didn't get across the road. How had she gotten across the road? She was young and swift, that's how, and he was old and slow and moving like a man under water in a bog with shackles and chains on his ankles and a yoke around his neck, dragging a wagon full of Nell Ward's men.

"You can't go in, buddy."

"I'm, uh . . ."

"Oh. Sorry. Thought you were a guy."

"I'm picking up my son, officer."

"Your son?"

"Yes, he's here with his . . . his Cub Scout troop."

"Kind of late for them, isn't it?"

"Yes. That's why I've come to pick him up."

"How you going to find him?"

"The . . . scoutmaster told me where they're sitting."

"Kind of late for kids to be out. It's a school night."

"I know. That's exactly why I'm here."

"I'm not supposed to let anybody in, lady."

"Please. I'm afraid my son might be ill. He wasn't feeling well this afternoon and . . . It's just a feeling I have."

"I know what you mean. A maternal feeling, like."

"Exactly."

"Go ahead, lady. He stayed this long, he's not going to want to leave, though. Nothing-nothing, bottom of the sixteenth."

"I'll stay with him, then. As long as I know he's all right."

"The way it's going, you'll be here all night."

"I hope so. Thank you."

"Don't mention it, lady."

"Okay, buddy. Hold it right there."

"I'm a cop."

"No, I'm a cop. You're a gate-crasher." His name tag said *Graff*. At first, Neuman thought it said *Graft*, which would've been too ironic, unlike everything else. At first, he'd thought the cop was he, for he was short and squat and rumpled and cynical; thought that he wasn't under water in a bog, he was just dreaming.

Neuman took out his wallet and showed his Detectives Endowment Association card. He hoped the gun in his pocket didn't show.

"Never heard of it," Graff said, handing back the wallet.

Neuman nodded; he'd never heard of it, either, when he was in uniform. He handed the wallet back. "Read the name."

Graff did. "So?" He handed the wallet back.

"You never heard of Jake Neuman?"

"Nope."

"How 'bout Bobby Redfield?"

Graff cocked his head. "He's in the one-oh-seven, isn't he?"

"No. He's dead."

Graff nodded. "Un hunh. Well, I can't call him up and ask him if it's okay for you to go in, can I?" He laughed.

It was simple enough; he should just explain it. He didn't have anything else to do; he didn't have anyplace better to go. "I used to work out here."

Graff rocked on his toes. "It's a small world."

As small as a walnut. "The first year the Mets won the pennant. The series."

"Hunh."

"I got Tom Seaver's autograph."

"No shit."

"I was on the gate right behind home plate."

"Doing what? Taking tickets? Those guys make a lot of money on the side. I never would've thought it—letting people in who can't get a ticket, people with coolers, bags of beer and stuff."

"I was a cop."

"Bullshit."

"Is Phil Impelliteri still the commander around here?"

"No."

"How about . . . whatshisname . . ."

"He ain't here, either." Graff laughed.

". . . Ward? Sandy Ward? Sandy for Sanford? A big black guy? A sergeant?"

"Nope."

Neuman sighed. "Graff?"

"Yeah?"

"Lift 'em."

Graff stared at the gun. "The fuck?"

"Lift 'em, just lift 'em. Get 'em up and turn around."

"You are fucking crazy, man. You are fucking fucked. You're a dead man. You haven't got a chance in hell. The fuck do you want, anyway? You want the gate receipts? You worked out here, you should know they take the gate receipts out of here around the seventh inning. You want the Stevens receipts? Not a chance. They got guards all over the place. You're fucked, you're dead, you haven't got a chance. You hear me?" Graff looked over his shoulder, then turned all the way around.

Neuman was gone.

The grass was so beautiful. The lights shone so brightly. The uniforms were so white, the other team's the palest blue.

She couldn't remember the last time she'd been to a baseball game. She remembered the stadium—not one of these modern cantilevered stadiums that put you farther from the field the higher you went; an old-fashioned stadium that shared in its architectural details features of the best skyscrapers and bridges. Yankee Stadium?

Nell panicked. Her cocaine was in her bag. She couldn't go on like this without it.

She breathed more easily. She had a vial in her jacket pocket with a rock of crack. But she had no pipe, no lighter. She'd have to snort it.

She opened the vial and tapped the rock into her palm and used the vial to crumble it. She put a pinch at a time in her nostrils—one, two, three, four, five, six, seven, eight, nine, ten, eleven—

The rush jolted her backward in her seat and she dropped the vial and spilled some of the cocaine. She put her head between her knees to try and retrieve it and felt as if she were somersaulting out of the upper deck. She came slowly upright, and kept her eyes shut.

"You like baseball?" Neuman said.

She opened her eyes, but didn't look at him. "Hi."

"Hi."

"Now what?"

"Now we go back down, soon as I get my breath back."

"How'd you know to come *right* here? There're thousands of people here."

"It's where I would've come. That's what it's like, police work —you try and put yourself in the other guy's shoes."

"The bad guy?"

Neuman looked down at the field and tried to figure out what was going on. Players were running and the crowd was yelling, but none of what was happening made any sense. But he was a hundred years behind on the ball scores, wasn't he? Maybe they'd changed the rules since then.

"Do you ever think you'd like to be a bad guy?" Nell said. "Since you know so much about how their minds work."

"No. I don't have the nerves for it. I'm not smart enough, either. Some of them're the smartest people I've ever run into, bad guys."

"That doesn't include me, I guess."

Neuman shrugged. "You made some mistakes. You have some bad luck. If Follett'd had some ID on him, people wouldn't've been anywhere near as interested in him."

265

"Terry wouldn't've, you mean."

"Terry's dead, Nell. He pulled a gun on me and I shot him. His gun was a prop gun from Dimanche's play, the gun I shot him with was the gun you stole from Crime Scene. I pulled it out of a trash can back there in the airport."

She snorted. "Ironic."

"Yeah."

"Dying is easy."

"I never killed anybody before."

She put a hand over his. "I'm sorry, Jake." She took her hand away before he would have had to move his.

Whatever had happened on the field, it hadn't changed the score; it was still nothing-nothing, bottom of the seventeenth. "I don't know exactly what the procedure is here, since I'm still retired. I guess I am. I don't know. But just to be on the safe side, you have the right to remain silent. You have the right to a lawyer. Anything you say now—"

She put a finger on his lips. Turning away from the smell of her, sweet and at the same time stinking with fear, he saw the cops fanning through the stands, coming toward them.

Nell saw them too. "There's one thing I'm glad about, Jake."

"Yeah?"

"I'm glad we didn't make love. Not that I wouldn't've liked it; I think I would've liked it."

"Nell, shut up."

"I never liked it with Mark—and Mark was supposed to be such a wonderful lover. You didn't even have to ask him what a wonderful lover he was; he'd tell you."

"Don't, Nell. You'll maybe get a chance to cop to an insanity plea."

She looked offended. "I wasn't insane."

He shrugged. "Juiced, then. Wired."

"I'm wired now. I wasn't then. I was wired when I killed Tiny. Do you know about him?"

He nodded.

"He was an asshole."

"Yeah, well."

"Mark was an asshole too—the overeducated kind. He was a master of seduction, but he couldn't deliver. I never had an orgasm with him. That's why I killed him."

266

Neuman's head spun. That Duane Reade bag Maria had brought home the day Klinger and Easterly and Federici—and Nell—came to see him . . . she hadn't gotten a vibrator, she'd gotten a gun, gotten it at some black market gun shop that put its wares in Duane Reade bags. That afternoon at Nell's—if he hadn't seen the graffito, if he hadn't gone away, if he hadn't given her an orgasm, she'd've shot him.

"It takes . . . special handling for me to have an orgasm. It's not just a question of technique and foreplay; it's a question of state of mind. Mark was like every man I've ever known: He *was* a good lover, but it was all technique; there was no emotion, not even a thought about something like state of mind. State of crotch was the only thing he responded to; if he was hard, it must be time to make love; if he was soft, the lovemaking must be over."

Neuman didn't want to listen to this, and he tried to figure out what was happening on the field. What was happening was that Ray Knight was striking out.

"It's funny how my automatic thought was to run away with Terry. It's how I've defined myself—in terms of men: the men I was with or the men I wasn't with. God, the list of men I've been with. I've been like a Siamese twin—except that from time to time I've changed my sibling."

Neuman knew all about her siblings. He was dragging a wagonload of them around.

"Okay, wise guy, it's your turn to lift 'em."

"Hello, Graff," Neuman said.

"I said lift 'em. Get the hell out of here, lady."

"Graff, uh—"

Graff put the barrel of his revolver behind Neuman's ear. "Lift 'em."

Neuman lifted them.

"Scram, lady, I said. Get lost."

"Graff, she's a suspect in a murder case."

"Yeah, and I'm Bill Cosby."

Nell was walking down the stairs, away from the aisle that led to the exit. A wave that had started in right field reached them and when the fans stood with their arms upraised, Neuman lost sight of her.

When he found her again, she was at the railing.

267

"Graff, I'm getting up."

"Stay put, motherfucker, and give me that piece. Nice and slow."

"I'm getting up, Graff."

"Stay put."

"I'm getting up."

"Stay put."

Neuman got up and went down the steps two at a time.

But Nell had already jumped.

Neuman stopped short of the railing and shut his eyes, waiting for the sound of the bullet from Graff's gun, waiting for the crump when she hit the lower deck, whichever came first.

What he heard was the roar of the crowd. Len Dykstra had homered, ending the game.

31

"Jake, are you retired or what?" Klinger stood with his back to Neuman, looking out his window at his view of Chinatown.

"I don't know, Lou."

"Is there anybody who does? Anybody I could call or write or, you know, meet on a street corner or one of those palm-reading places or something?"

"I saw a headline in the paper—'Retired Cop Cracks Nowhere Man Case, Dimanche Murder.'"

"Is that supposed to be funny, Jake?"

"No."

"Good. 'Cause it's not funny."

"I said I didn't think it was, Lou."

"Inspector."

"Inspector. Unless I'm retired, in which case I can call you anything I want."

"That you think is funny, right, Jake?"

"Kind of, yeah."

"You mind telling me just what it is that makes you such a ballbreaker, Jake? What is it you're so pissed off about?"

"I'm pissed off about Bobby."

Klinger turned on him. *"Bob*by? Bobby's dead."

"We've been through this, Lou. He was executed to save the Department embarrassment."

"And when we went through it, Jake, what did we decide?"

"We didn't decide anything. I told you what I thought; you said I was wrong."

"And since I outrank you, Jake, that *makes* you wrong."

"Unless I'm retired."

Klinger turned back to the window. "Fuck you, Jake."

"I think I'd like to come back," Neuman said.

"Come back to what? Come back *from* what? The funny farm you've been plowing."

Neuman laughed.

"That you think is funny too, Jake?"

"It was, uh, nicely said."

"Too bad I didn't think of it at that news conference yesterday. Reporters were asking me what you'd been doing the past couple of years, I could've said you'd been plowing a funny farm. I thought you were moving to Texas, or something."

"We thought about it, but they have tornadoes there."

"We're supposed to have a hurricane. You hear it on the news?"

"I said I'd like to come back, Lou. I've only got one condition."

Klinger whirled around this time, pointing a finger like a weapon. *"You? You've* got a condition. Jake, you're lucky you're not looking at doing points for obstructing an investigation, at the very least. You do come back, you're looking at a departmental hearing, not to mention maybe a grand jury. So if that's your condition, the answer is shove it up your ass."

"A departmental hearing I expect, a grand jury I can take. My condition is I want an investigation into Bobby's execution."

"That's your word, Jake, not mine."

"I'll be happy to stop using it, Lou, if somebody can show me that it was the commander on the scene acting according to his best judgment, not according to what somebody downtown told him to do."

Klinger turned back to the window. "You know what Miles Easterly says?"

"I should be in the ballbreakers' hall of fame."

"That's exactly what he says."

Neuman got up. "So I'll hear from you, I guess."

"You got a boat, Jake?" Klinger said.

". . . Why?"

" 'Cause if you got a boat, I'd like to recommend that you go sailing during the hurricane. Then maybe I won't have to deal with you anymore."

"I've been thinking about getting a boat. One of those big fast ones—cigarette boats. They have these races I'd like to get in on—to Bimini and back."

"Go to Bimini, Jake, that sounds like a good idea, but don't come back."

Neuman laughed.

That you think is funny too, Jake? You know, the United Nations, the Common Market, all these things that're based on the idea that people think alike, act alike—how the fuck can they be expected to work when two people the same age, the same background, living in the same city, doing the same work, one of them thinks something's funny, the other one doesn't even know what the fuck he's laughing at?"

"I hear you're coming back, Ja— Lieutenant," Federici said.

"Yeah, well. I've still got some miles in me. May as well use it to catch some bad guys, instead of plowing the funny farm."

Federici laughed. "Thanks for everything, Jake."

"Yeah, well. I'm not sure what I did, exactly."

"You stuck by me. Just the way you stuck by Bobby."

"Bobby was a killer, Steve. I didn't see that till it was too late."

"Jessica says hello, Lieutenant."

"Who's Jessica? Oh, yeah—the doorperson."

"She just got a part in a play. Some off-off-Broadway thing, but she thinks it might move to off-Broadway."

"One step at a time, I guess, hunh, Steve?"

"Yeah. She asked me to ask you if you'd like to come and see it."

"You, uh—you know—involved with her, Steve?"

"We went out for dinner, yeah. We've got a lot in common. Hey, do you know we both picked ball number 6 in the lottery —the ball that got stuck?"

"Do yourself a favor, Steve—don't marry her based on that."

271

Federici laughed. "We've got more going than that, Jake. We're both runners; we're going to run in the marathon together."

"At the end of two hundred sixty miles I guess you'll really be involved with her. Tell her, uh, I appreciate the invite, but I'm kind of unenthusiastic about going to see a show right now. She's a smart woman; she can probably understand why. Tell her maybe when it moves to off-Broadway I'll come see it."

"Matty's coming back, Lieutenant. The doctor says his gut's better."

"Matty was a big help, for a fuck-up."

Federici laughed. "Winger said to tell you, Lieutenant, that he's been thinking a lot, Lieutenant, about it's being like the sun was the size of the globe in the Daily News Building, Lieutenant, and the earth being the size of a walnut at Grand Central Terminal, Lieutenant, and he's been thinking about calling his book 'The Size of a Walnut,' Lieutenant."

"What book?"

"He's writing a book, Lieutenant."

"Winger?"

"Yeah, Lieutenant."

"What about?"

"About what it's like, Lieutenant."

"Police work?"

"Yeah, Lieutenant."

"Stop it, will you. Call me Jake. Even if I come back, even if you're my partner, don't ever call me Lieutenant again. Understand?"

"Okay. Jake."

"Leftenant Neuman?"

"Miss Johnstone."

"It's terribly good of you to come and see me. I was very angry at you for running off and leaving me at the theater like that, bleeding to death and all. I understood the necessity from your point of view, of course, but there was something I wanted to tell you. Dying *isn't* easy; it's painful, extremely painful, and the worst of it is you don't see your life flashing before your eyes; what you see, almost in the form of a list—Things to Do Today—is all the things you haven't done: places you haven't been, conflicts you haven't resolved, commitments you might've made but neglected to, rejoinders you never delivered, and on and on. It makes a mockery, almost, this list, of what you've deluded yourself into thinking of as life lived to the utmost. I just wanted you to know that."

"Yeah, well. The doc says you shouldn't talk too much."

"Which, I've explained to him, is akin to saying the sun shouldn't shine, the rain shouldn't fall."

Neuman smiled and squeezed her hand. "I'll see you around, I guess."

"You're not leaving?"

"I guess I don't have a whole lot to say."

"There is something you came to say. I can see it in those questing eyes of yours."

Neuman waddled in place. "It was pretty stupid to run out on the stage like that when you knew that gun was the real thing, not to mentioned loaded. It was pretty brave too, since Last might've shot Amanda Becker."

Charly stretched her neck. "And has she thanked me, Amanda? She has not. The opening of *Dying Is Easy* has been postponed until the spring—there *is* such a thing as too much publicity—and Jay Dillen and Amanda Becker have flown the New York coop for the gilded cage that is Hollywood. Something about a Roeg film for Amanda and a rumor that those in a position to get such a thing done have been wondering if it wasn't time for another sequel to *The Exorcist*—though what they'll do about Linda Blair's rather extraordinary breasts I have no idea—and if Jay wasn't just the man to direct it, which, since he has absolutely no experience in the film medium, I would have to say qualifies him wholly. Did they say goodbye before they went from N.Y. to L.A., as they say in the trades? They did not. Not even a telegram, a bouquet a flowers, a box of candy. They just split, like the people totally without class and style that they are. They—"

"Uh, look, Miss Johnstone, I've got—"

"Charly, please, Leftenant."

"I've got to be going, uh, Charly, and, well, maybe we can have lunch sometime. You know, my treat this time."

"I'd love that, Leftenant. I'd absolutely love it."

"Jake, okay? Call me Jake."

"I'd love that too . . . Jake. You look so tired, Jake."

"Yeah, well. I sat on my duff for a while, I'm sort of out of shape. I'm not used to being rialtoed."

Charly laughed. "Who is?"

"Jacob?"

"Yeah, babe?"

"Are you watching the ball game?"

"I'm not really watching, no. I'm just kind of listening. My neck hurts like hell, I can't really hold my head up."

"We can talk another time, then."

"It'd be like me to say we should talk another time, Maria, to use what's going on as an excuse not to talk about stuff that needs to be talked about. I don't want to do that anymore."

She sat down. "All right."

"I want to go back to work, Maria."

"I thought you probably would. But I wonder: Are you doing it just because you killed a man?"

"You mean, to give it the stamp of approval, like? It was okay 'cause I'm a cop, I just happened to be retired at the moment?"

"Something like that."

"I don't think so, no."

"You are a very good policeman," Maria said.

"Yeah, well. Somebody's got to do it, it may as well be somebody who's good at it. I also want to, you know, see somebody."

"I am not sure what you mean."

"A therapist, like."

"Good."

"You don't believe me, do you? You'll believe it when you see it, won't you?"

"You do not like it when I tell you what you're thinking, Jacob. Do not tell me what I am thinking."

"Right. Well. Okay. What are you thinking?"

"I am thinking that it is good that you want to see a therapist. . . . And I am thinking that many things will be made good as a result."

Neuman sat up and rubbed his neck. "Maria?"

"Yes?"

But he didn't tell her that he'd kissed Nell Ward, that he'd been on the brink of her bed. He hadn't wanted to know about the commissioner, Klinger, Easterly, Federici, Terry Niles, The Band, Robbie Robertson, Neil Young, Neil Diamond, Van Morrison, Doctor John, Muddy Waters, Paul Butterfield, Dylan, men who wore blue jeans and Rolex watches and used Macintosh computers, and the Marines; there was no need to tell Maria about Nell. All he would be doing would be trying to show her that he was desirable—that he'd been desired by a woman—by a woman who had killed two men. "My neck really hurts. You got anything for it?"

"You mean like aspirin?"

"Yeah, I guess. Or some Ben-Gay or something. Or what's that stuff you got that time? Tiger Balm."

Maria giggled.

"Isn't that what it's called? It comes in, you know, those little jars."

"I was laughing because I thought of something that might make your neck feel better."

"Yeah, what?"

"My vibrator."

MYSTERIOUS PRESS—

**the exciting new crime imprint from
Arrow Books**

☐ A CAST OF KILLERS	Sidney Kirkpatrick	£2.95
☐ ROUGH CIDER	Peter Lovesey	£2.50
☐ WEXFORD: AN OMNIBUS	Ruth Rendell	£5.95
☐ WOLF TO THE SLAUGHTER	Ruth Rendell	£2.50
☐ KILL ZONE	Loren Estleman	£2.50
☐ MOONSPENDER	Jonathan Gash	£2.50
☐ HARE SITTING UP	Michael Innes	£2.50
☐ THE JUNKYARD DOG	Robert Campbell	£2.50
☐ THE COST OF SILENCE	Margaret Yorke	£2.50
☐ THE GONDOLA SCAM	Jonathan Gash	£2.50
☐ PEARLHANGER	Jonathan Gash	£2.50

ARROW BOOKS, BOOKSERVICE BY POST, PO BOX 29,
DOUGLAS, ISLE OF MAN, BRITISH ISLES

NAME ....

ADDRESS ....

....

....

Please enclose a cheque or postal order made out to Arrow Books Ltd.
for the amount due and allow the following for postage and packing.

U.K. CUSTOMERS: Please allow 22p per book to a maximum of
£3.00.

B.F.P.O. & EIRE: Please allow 22p per book to a maximum of £3.00.
OVERSEAS CUSTOMERS: Please allow 22p per book.

Whilst every effort is made to keep prices low it is sometimes necessary
to increase cover prices at short notice. Arrow Books reserve the right to
show new retail prices on covers which may differ from those
previously advertised in the text or elsewhere.